War King

War King

Hakon's Saga Book III

Eric Schumacher

To my family and friends, for your love, patience, and continued support.

Acknowledgements

This is the third book in the story of Hakon the Good, and there are many people to thank for its existence. I again want to thank Marg Gilks and Lori Weathers, whose keen eyes and attention to detail honed my thoughts and words into the story you are about to read. I am also indebted to Gordon Monks, chief marshal of "The Vikings" re-enactment group, and all of the early readers, who served as an invaluable source of insight and feedback during the final days of writing. I want to thank my graphic designer, David Brzozowski, whose masterful artistry helps my covers stand out in the crowd, and my publisher, Creativia, for taking a chance on not just one of my stories, but three. And last but certainly not least, I want to thank you, my readers, for nudging me, encouraging me, and patiently waiting for me to finish this novel. It is to you all, and to the countless others who have gladly accompanied me on this journey, that I owe a huge debt of gratitude.

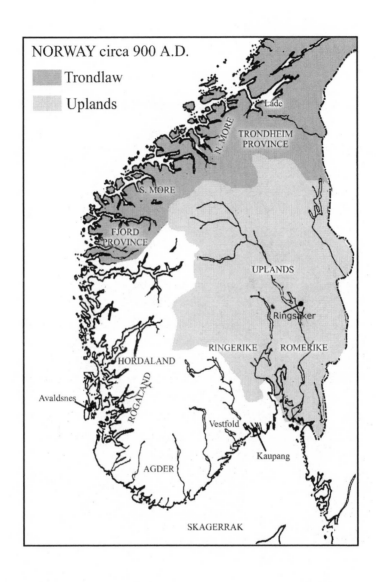

NORWAY circa 900 A.D.

Trondlaw

Uplands

Lade

N. MORE

TRONDHEIM
PROVINCE

S. MORE

FJORD
PROVINCE

UPLANDS

Ringsaker

RINGERIKE   ROMERIKE

HORDALAND

ROGALAND

Avaldsnes

Vestfold

Kaupang

AGDER

SKAGERRAK

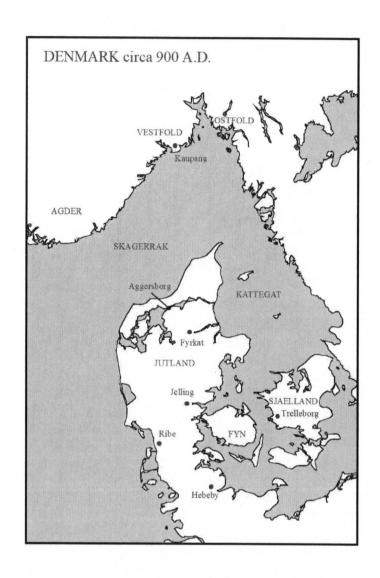

DENMARK circa 900 A.D.

OSTFOLD

VESTFOLD
Kaupang

AGDER

SKAGERRAK

Aggersborg

KATTEGAT

Fyrkat

JUTLAND

Jelling

SJAELLAND
Trelleborg

Ribe

FYN

Hebeby

Glossary

Aesir – One of the main tribes of deities venerated by the pre-Christian Norse. Old Norse: *Æsir*.

Balder – One of the Aesir gods. He is often associated with love, peace, justice, purity, and poetry. Old Norse: *Baldr*.

bonder – Free men (farmers, craftsmen, etc.) who enjoyed rights such as the use of weapons and the right to attend law-things. They constituted the middle class. Old Norse: *baendr*.

bragarfull – A ritual drinking cup or drinking horn upon which men swore oaths and made promises. Also known as the "promise cup" or "chieftain's cup."

burgh – A fortified settlement.

byrnie – A (usually short-sleeved) chain mail shirt that hung to the upper thigh. Old Norse: *brynja*.

Danevirke – A defensive earthwork "wall" that stretched across the southern neck of Jutland. The main portion is believed to have been built in three phases between AD 737 and 968 to protect the Danes from the Franks. Old Norse: *Danavirki*.

dragon – A larger class of Viking warship. Old Norse: *Dreki*.

Dubhlinn Norse – Northmen who live in Dublin.

Eastern Sea – Baltic Sea.

Frey – Brother to the goddess Freya. He is often associated with virility and prosperity, with sunshine and fair weather. Old Norse: *Freyr*.

Freya – Sister to god Frey. She is often associated with love, sex, beauty, fertility, gold, magic, war, and death. Old Norse: *Freyja*.

Frigga – She is the highest-ranking of the Aesir goddesses. She's the wife of Odin, the leader of the gods, and the mother of god, Baldur. She is often confused with Freya. Old Norse: *Frigg.*

fylke (pl. **fylker**) – Old Norse for "folkland," which has come to mean "county" in modern use.

fyrd – An Old English army made up of citizens of a shire that was mobilized for short periods of time; e.g., to defend against a particular threat.

glima – A form of Viking wrestling, which can also be used as self-defense. It is still practiced in Scandinavia today.

godi – A heathen priest or chieftain. Old Norse: *goði.*

greave – Armor worn on the shin (or forearm) to protect that part of the leg. These were most likely "splint greaves", i.e. strips of metal connected by leather straps.

hird – A personal retinue of armed companions who formed the nucleus of a household guard. Hird means "household." Old Norse *hirð.*

hirdman (pl. **hirdmen**) – A member or members of the hird. Old Norse: *hirðman.*

hlaut – The blood of sacrificed animals.

Hogmanay – The feast preceding the Yule, which has come to be associated with the last day of the year.

infirmarius – The monk or nun attending the sick in a monastery.

Irland – Ireland.

jarl – Old Norse for "earl."

jarldom – The area of land that a jarl ruled.

Karmoy (or Karmøy) – Karm Island. The island on which King Hakon's estate, Avaldsnes, is located. Old Norse: *Kǫrmt.*

Kattegat – The sea between the Northlands and the Danish lands.

kaupang – Old Norse for "marketplace." It is also the name of the main market town in Norway that existed around AD 800–950.

knarr – A type of merchant ship. Old Norse: *knǫrr.*

Midgard – The Norse name for Earth and the place inhabited by humans. Old Norse: *Miðgarðr.*

Night Mare – The Night Mare is an evil spirit that rides on people's chests while they sleep, bringing bad dreams. Old Norse: *Mara*.

Njord – A god associated with sea, seafaring, wind, fishing, wealth, and crop fertility. Old Norse: *Njörðr*.

Norns – The three female divine beings who influence the course of a man's destiny. Their names are Urd (Old Norse *Urðr*, "What Once Was"), Verdandi (Old Norse *Verðandi*, "What Is Coming into Being"), and Skuld (Old Norse *Skuld*, "What Shall Be").

Odal rights – The ownership rights of inheritable land held by a family or kinsmen.

Odin – Husband to Frigga. The god associated with healing, death, royalty, knowledge, battle, and sorcery. He oversees Valhall, the Hall of the Slain. Old Norse: *Óðinn*.

Orkneyjar – The Orkney Islands.

seax – A knife or short sword. Also known as scramaseax, or wounding knife.

seter – A simple wooden cottage in the mountains with a barn where farmers (bonders) brought their livestock (cattle, goats, and sheep) to be milked after a day of grazing in the mountain pastures.

Sjaelland – The largest Danish island.

sjaund – A ritual drinking feast held seven days after a death to celebrate the life of the person and to officially pass that person's inheritance on to his or her next of kin.

skald – A poet. Old Norse: *skald* or *skáld*.

shield wall – A shield wall was a "wall of shields" formed by warriors standing in formation shoulder to shoulder, holding their shields so that they abut or overlap. Old Norse: *skjaldborg*.

steer board – A rudder affixed to the right stern of a ship. The origin of the word "starboard." Old Norse: *stýri* (rudder) and *borð* (side of the ship).

skeid – A midsize class of Viking warship.

skol – A toast to others when drinking. Old Norse: *skál*.

Terce – A service forming part of the Divine Office of the Western Christian Church, traditionally held at the third hour of the day (i.e., 9 a.m.).

thane – A word used to describe a class of military retainer or warrior. Old Norse: *þegn*.

thing – The governing assembly of a Viking society or region, made up of the free people of the community and presided over by lawspeakers. Old Norse: *þing*.

Thor – A hammer-wielding god associated with thunder, lightning, storms, oak trees, strength, and the protection of mankind. Old Norse: *Þórr*.

thrall – A slave.

Valhall (also **Valhalla**) – The hall of the slain presided over by Odin. It is where brave warriors chosen by valkyries go when they die. Old Norse: *Valhöll*.

valkyrie – A female helping spirit of Odin that transports his favorite among those slain in battle to Valhall, where they will fight by his side during the battle at the end of time, Ragnarok. Old Norse: *valkyrja* (pl. *valkyrjur*).

wergeld – Also known as "man price," it was the value placed on every being and piece of property.

woolsark – A shirt or vest made of coarse wool.

Yngling – Refers to the Fairhair dynasty, who descended from the kings of Uplands, Norway, and who traces their lineage back to the god Frey.

Yule – A pagan midwinter festival lasting roughly twelve days. It later became associated with Christmas. Old Norse: *Jól*

Part I

The fire-spark, by the fiend of war
Fanned to a flame, soon spreads afar.
The Heimskringla

Prologue

Ostfold, Fall, AD 954

The old man was tied to a flame-blackened post. His matted gray beard rested on his chest and his legs were splayed out before his body. He leaned forward so that only his arms, which were pulled behind him and tied to the post at the wrists, held him upright. To Hakon, he looked as dead as the corpses lying around him.

"He lives," called Toralv, Hakon's champion, whose massive frame dwarfed the man he knelt beside as he felt his wizened neck for a pulse.

Hakon exhaled loudly with relief. This was the fourth razed settlement they had found along the Ostfold coast. A survivor had been left in each of the other villages in a similar manner, but this old bugger was the first they had discovered alive. Now, hopefully, they could learn more about the raiders who had lain waste to this stretch of coastline.

"He will wish he had died when he awakens to this," commented Ottar, who was the head of Hakon's hird, or household guard. And he was right, for there was nothing left in the seaside settlement save for smoke and ash and bloated corpses on which an army of flies feasted. Ottar was the nephew of Hakon's longtime friend Egil, who had held his same position before him. Ottar had joined Hakon's service when Hakon was but a whiskerless teen, and he not much older. Now, deep grooves lined the commander's hawk-like face and his forehead, high-lighting the keenness of the eyes that studied the destruction.

"Untie him," called Hakon to his champion as he ran a dirty hand through his sandy hair. "And give him some water."

Hakon need not have wasted his breath, for Toralv was already pulling his knife from its sheath. They had known each other so long, the one knew what the other would say long before he said it. Toralv cut the man's bindings and gently lay him on his back, cradling his old head in the crook of his muscled arm so that he could pour some water over the man's chafed lips.

"A silver coin says he dies before nightfall," wagered Bjarke, who rested his thick forearms on the head of his long axe. He was a thick man with a mane of wheat-colored hair that encircled his round head. Among Hakon's hird, only Toralv was taller.

"I'll take that wager," said the smaller man next to him. Garth was his name. He was a good man, but a better scout, whose red hair, big ears, and small, dark eyes often put Hakon in mind of a harvest mouse. And like a mouse, something on him was always moving. Busy fingers. A tapping foot. Active eyes. At the moment, it was his head, which swiveled on his neck as he took in the grisly scene around him. "This man is lucky. The birds have made a right feast of the others, but there's not a peck on him. Aye, I'll take that wager."

"Have some respect," growled Ottar, "and make yourselves useful. Bjarke, search inland for survivors. Garth," he called to the harvest mouse, "take some of the others and check the corpses and dwellings. See if there is anything here left to claim."

"Mayhap you will find the silver coin you will owe me," Bjarke quipped as he hefted his axe onto his shoulder and moved out. His friends, Bard and Asmund, went with him, looking like gods of war in their byrnies and helms, which gleamed in the pale autumn sunlight. They had also been with Hakon a long time, and had profited handsomely in his service. But they deserved it. They all did. Those in Hakon's hird were the finest of the fine when it came to warcraft, and to Hakon's mind, deserved every ounce of the riches they wore.

"You mean the one I will be adding to your lost wager?" Garth called after him.

Bjarke waved away the back talk with a grunt and wove through the wreckage in the direction of the tree line. Garth headed in the opposite direction, using his foot to poke at the corpses while batting at the angry flies that swarmed about him.

"Danes, do you think?" asked Ottar.

Hakon shrugged as his blue eyes swept over the smoke-shrouded bodies. "Danes. Swedes. Some bold sea king trying to make a reputation for himself. Only God knows. Hopefully now we shall find out," he said with a nod toward the unconscious old man.

"Whoever they are, they grow bolder," his nephew, Gudrod, said as he sleeved beads of sweat from his high forehead. Long ago, he'd been a thin man with wiry muscles and a shrewd face, but summers of wealth and peace had rounded his cheeks and softened his body. He wore a patch of cloth over his left eye to cover the wound he had received in a battle many summers before, so that it was with his right eye that he now appraised Hakon.

The renewed attacks could not have come at a worse time. For Gudrod's cousin, Trygvi, who ruled this area and who relished a good fight, had tired of the peace that had graced his realm these past summers and had just sailed west in search of adventure.

"Your cousin has picked a poor time to raid in the West," remarked Hakon, giving voice to his sour thoughts.

"Do you not find it strange that raiders should come now, after so many years of quiet? It is as if they knew Trygvi was gone," Gudrod said with a suggestive lift of his brow.

The thought jolted Hakon, for it suggested something larger than a series of random attacks was at play. "How long has Trygvi been gone?" Hakon asked.

"Not long, lord. Mayhap half a moon," Gudrod said, then swatted in annoyance at the flies attracted to his sweating face. "Damn flies."

Hakon grunted. "Long enough for word of his absence to spread."

"Aye," Gudrod confirmed. "Word often travels quicker than man."

"Lord!" called Garth, drawing Hakon's mind from Gudrod's troubling suggestion.

Hakon and Gudrod picked their way through the carnage and stopped by the hirdman, who was now kneeling beside a partially burned shield, running his finger over a painted black rune that stretched from the shield's top rim to its bottom. Garth's eyes shifted from Gudrod to Hakon, then back to Gudrod. "Have you ever seen the like?"

Gudrod scratched his beard. "No. Never," Gudrod said.

"Do you know anything of this rune? Or its design on a shield?" asked Hakon.

Gudrod shook his head. "It is the rune of the one-handed god, Tyr. But beyond that, I know not what it could mean. I will ask the traders in Kaupang. Mayhap they have seen the like before."

Gudrod ruled the only trading town in the North, Kaupang, which lay north and west of their current location. For the right price, a man could find all he needed in the town, including information.

"Do so," Hakon commanded.

The search revealed no more clues, so Hakon ordered his warriors to burn the villagers' bodies. Their bloated carcasses were filling the air with their stench and the birds were returning to the scene. He could not leave them for the animals and the maggots to devour.

The warriors dug a shallow ditch in the center of the settlement, which they then lined with logs. These they covered with fish oil before placing the bodies onto the wood. Hakon ran his eyes over the dead. There were eighteen in all. Most were old, though some infants also lay in the grave. All had been brutally killed. Butchered, then burned by the flames that engulfed the settlement's structures. The young and healthy had been captured and carried off to a grim future of thralldom. Though he had seen such atrocities too many times to count, he had never grown accustomed to the wickedness and injustice of it all. It was a cruel fate indeed for these villagers, and one they certainly did not deserve.

Eric Schumacher

Ottar touched a flaming brand to the oil-slick wood, which responded instantly to the heat. Fire snaked across the logs and the bodies while the warriors looked on silently. Grimly. Some clutched the amulets at their necks. Others spat in the turf to show their ire. Hakon said a silent prayer for their souls, then turned from the flames and stalked to his ship.

The old man's haunting scream shattered the still night. Hakon sat up with a start and grabbed his weapon, the hair on his arms standing up straight. That is, until he realized it was just the old man, at which point he cursed. Around him, his men grumbled. They had brought the man on board and wrapped him in furs to keep him warm, and these he now threw off as he peered about him with a face full of fear and confusion.

"Balls," Bjarke grumbled as he put his head back down.

Near him, Garth allowed a smile to stretch across his face. "I will collect my coin in the morning, Bjarke."

Hakon approached the old man. "Peace," he said. "You are among friends now."

"Who are you?" the man croaked. His lips had split, so that he spoke with a mumbling dullness devoid of enunciation.

Hakon offered him a skin full of ale. "I am King Hakon, and these are my men. We saw the smoke from your settlement and came to investigate. We found you there."

The man's fear evaporated, replaced instead by a mask of grief. "My settlement," he croaked, the ale in his hand forgotten. "It is gone."

Hakon kept his eyes on the man, knowing that many of the people in that settlement had been his friends and his kin. He could see that truth in the old man's eyes. "It is gone," he confirmed gently. "I am sorry."

The man drank then, and Hakon could see his hand shaking. When he finished his swig, he looked back at Hakon and narrowed his eyes under his gray brows. "They left me alive so that I might tell my rescuers what I saw."

"And what did you see?" Hakon asked.

7

He looked at the crew, then back at Hakon. It was clear in the way he swallowed and cast his eyes about that it troubled him to say it, but he knew he must. "They told me that their father is dead, and that they have returned to take back what was once his."

Hakon stared at the man for a long moment, trying to untangle the riddle of his answer. "Who has died?"

"Erik Bloodaxe."

Hakon did not try to hide his shock, nor did his men, who had heard the old man's words and sat up to hear more. "Bloodaxe? Dead?" Hakon muttered. "When? Where?"

The man nodded. "I know only that he is dead. Nothing more."

With effort, Hakon regained his wits and raised his hands for silence, for the old man's words had sparked disquiet among his crew. "What was the name of the man who told you this? Did he give his name?"

"Aye. He said his name was Gamle Eriksson, lord. That is who told me this news."

Hakon knew what this man's answer would be, but it still hit him like a punch to the gut. Long ago, Hakon had captured his half-brother, Erik Bloodaxe, who had then been king. At the time, his men had urged him to kill Erik and his family and end the feud that was sure to come. Hakon had not, instead driving them from the realm. Hakon had been tired of fighting, and tired of killing. He would not raise his sword to his kin. It was a mistake that Hakon long knew would return to haunt him.

And now, it seemed, that time had come.

Chapter 1

Avaldsnes, Rogaland, Spring, AD 957

Hakon woke with a start. He had been dreaming, and like so many of his dreams of late, it had turned against him. An attacker had come to his bedchamber, a bloody sword in hand, ready to strike. Hakon had scrambled in the darkness, tried to rise, but his feet tangled in the bedding, and the villain's sword came down.

Hakon's gaze shifted to the closed door, the very same one through which the attacker of his dream had just come. The light of the dying hearth fire in the great hall seeped beneath it and cast a soft glow over the oaken walls and the blade-sheath that leaned, point down, against the bedframe near Hakon's head.

Slowly, he slid from under the bearskin and sat on the edge of his bed. As he worked the stiffness from his muscles, he became aware of the sounds and smells of early morning: the faint scent of beeswax candles that had long since surrendered to the night air; the stale stench of the previous night's feast; the snores of his hirdmen in the great hall; the fragrance of his mistress Gyda, who lay curled under the bearskin beside him.

He pulled on his clothes, then crept from the room, past his slumbering warriors, and out into the receding darkness. The night sentries mumbled a greeting to their lord as Hakon passed through the north gate of the palisade surrounding his hall and worked his way down a well-worn path to one of two burial mounds that sat like warts on the top of the nearby hill. No one knew for sure who was buried in the mounds, though the skalds liked to say they covered the remains of the first owner of the estate — a king named Augvald — and his son.

Winter had not yet released its purchase on the land, and the frost-covered grass glistened and crunched as Hakon climbed the mound and sat on its crest. He gazed out at the waking world with eyes that watered from the air's chill. Below him, the waters of the bay quivered in the gentle breeze and lapped against the two warships tied to his dock. Beyond the bay, the Karmsund Strait stretched north and south toward the sea like a dark vein. And beyond the water, east, stretched the rolling hills and valleys and waterways of Rogaland, the fylke to which Hakon's estate at Avaldsnes belonged. It was only a fraction of the realm he controlled — a realm that now reached from the snow-mantled fylke of Halogaland far to the north, to the rocky tip of Agder in the south, to the forested border of the Uplands far to the east. All of it was under his control or the control of his oath-sworn jarls, and most of those were his kin.

He rewarded the jarls richly for their fealty and in exchange, they fought vigorously to keep peace in the realm. But peace was never constant so long as men sought fame and silver and land. It mattered not that Hakon had restored trust in the laws that his brother Erik had spurned or that, in recent years, he had built a system for coastal defenses to protect his people. Raiders still came to his shores. Men still stole and murdered each other. And feuds raged on. It was the way of things, he knew. Yet the strife left in its wake an older king with streaks of gray in his sandy hair, scars on his body, and lines of worry etched on his face.

Time brought with it more than just physical strife. It brought hard memories of people and places that cut just as deeply as any blade. Memories such as Hakon's childhood love, Aelfwin, who long ago had sacrificed herself for the sake of Hakon's army. Memories of his long dead foster-father, King Athelstan, who had raised him as a Christian in Engla-lond and was the first to plant the seeds of kingship and legacy in Hakon's youthful mind. Memories of his kinsman and counselor, Jarl Tore the Silent, with his damaged throat and his big heart that had just stopped beating in his chest not one moon before. A man whose life he would soon celebrate on the northern island of Frei. Memories of his half-brother Erik, with his wild orange curls and mighty axe and brood of sons — sons who even now terrorized the Northern seas, gaining wealth and power and men, and who would eventually bring their death to Hakon's realm in full force. Hakon wiped the sleep from his face with a calloused hand and the memories vanished.

A tempest was brewing. Hakon could feel it in his bones, and in his gut, and in the ravens that landed each morning for the past month on the burial mounds where he now sat. Ravens were the messengers of Odin, who brought the news of the world to the Alfather's ears. Though Hakon clung to a different faith, he had lived long enough to know that the earth held its own secrets and that something was amiss — something beyond his control. Something greater than winter's thaw and spring's bloom. The elders, who for decades had held the North in balance, were dying; the young and the brash were gaining strength. Old. Young. Order. Chaos. Like storm-driven currents, the opposing forces were colliding, and when they did, Hakon would have no choice but to face the tempest and resist.

"Sleep robs you too, boy?"

Hakon turned his gaze to the shadowed figure at the base of the burial mound. He wore a long cloak with a hood that concealed his face, though Hakon didn't need to see the man to know it was Egil Woolsark, who had once commanded the king's hird and now helped train the younger warriors in sword craft. He had been old long ago. Now he was ancient. Which was why he still called the middle-aged Hakon, "boy," a nickname he had used for Hakon since Hakon had been but a stripling.

"Aye, Egil. Sleep comes less easily to me these days."

Planting his walking stick in the earth one step at a time, the old man worked his way slowly up the slope of the mound. Hakon rose to offer him assistance, but Egil knocked his hand away. When he reached the crown of the mound, he sat with a grunt beside his lord and huffed. "That is not as easy as I remember it being."

Hakon laughed, but chose not to tease his aging friend. "How go the preparations?"

"From what I gather," Egil began as he rested his walking stick across his lap, "your ship will be ready to sail before the sun is directly overhead. The thralls and men have everything assembled. It needs only to be loaded."

Hakon nodded as his eyes moved to the dock and the warship they would be taking north, which was called *Dragon*. The mighty ship had once belonged to his renowned father, Harald Fairhair, and now was his. Once it was loaded, Hakon and half of his hird would sail to More to attend a feast celebrating the life of Jarl Tore. That thought weighed on Hakon like a wet cloak, for Tore had been more than the husband to Hakon's older sister; he had been an unfailing friend who had helped Hakon win the realm and keep the peace in the North. Now he was gone.

"It was no way for a man such as Jarl Tore to go," Egil grumbled, referring to the way the old warrior had died. According to the messenger who had delivered the news, Jarl Tore had been surveying some work on his estate and had simply fallen to the ground, dead. It was not a hero's death, to be sure, but at least it had been quick. "I hope that old One-Eye and his valkyrie see him for who he was and that he is feasting with his kin in Valhall right about now."

According to the Northern faith, the valkyrie chose the heroes worthy of fighting by Odin's side in the battle at the end of time, Ragnarok. Until then, they trained, fighting each day and feasting through the night in the hall of the slain, Valhall. "Death is a mystery, Egil. You may pray for Valhall. I will pray that Christ is in need of some good and valiant souls to take on the demons of this world."

Egil spat. "Curse your Christ."

Hakon smiled. Even in his mid-thirties, he loved ribbing his old friend, who had never adopted Hakon's faith. It was not a requirement for serving Hakon, though most of the men had allowed themselves to be baptized in the faith, if only for show and the shiny silver cross Hakon gave them to wear. If asked, most of his men would proclaim the name of Jesus, but when facing their enemies in the shield wall, it was to the old gods that men turned with their charms and mumbled supplications.

Down below them, the first of Hakon's thralls began to appear on the strand, carrying pots and barrels and coils of rope to the dock for the long journey north to Jarl Tore's estate. Hakon turned his eyes to the sky and marked the sliver of orange above the mountain range far to the east that men called the Keel. Like the sun, his men would be rising in the hall to tackle the tasks of the day.

"Have you spoken to Ottar?"

Egil nodded at the mention of his nephew. "Aye. He has agreed to stay, though he is about as happy as a coinless drunkard to be missing the action."

Hakon nodded. "I do not blame him. It is a hard thing, being left behind and missing something like this."

Egil grunted. "He will do what you ask, as he always has."

Hakon held his lips tight, for Egil spoke the truth and there was nothing more to add.

"Well," said Egil, pushing himself to his feet with a long moan and a popping of knee joints, "I will leave you to it, then." He retreated down the slope with all the grace he could muster for his age.

When Egil was gone, Hakon rose and made his way to the church that stood on the western side of the palisaded estate. The place had grown from a simple structure with a dirt floor and makeshift stone altar to the most conspicuous hall on the island, with a high-beamed ceiling, beautifully carved pews, and a raised altar behind which hung a magnificent rood carved from an old oak. It would never compare to the massive stone churches of Engla-lond where Hakon had been raised, but its rustic charm spoke to Hakon's soul just the same.

A single candle burned on the altar as Hakon entered, its glow dancing on the rood and the bent shoulders of Hakon's priest, Egbert, who knelt in prayer. Hakon crossed himself and knelt beside his friend. He closed his eyes and willed his ears to focus on Egbert's whispered words.

"Blessed is the man who has not followed the advice of the impious, and has not stood in the street among sinners, and has not sat in the company of complainers."

Hakon picked up the trail of it, then joined his priest in reciting Psalm 1 as Saint Benedict had commanded for the Prime service in his Rule.

"But his will is with the law of the Lord, and he will meditate on his law, day and night. And he will be like a tree that has been planted beside running waters, which will provide its fruit in its time, and its leaf will not fall away, and all things whatsoever that he does will prosper."

The words sprang from the recesses of Hakon's mind and flowed like water down a well-worn path until the prayer reached its conclusion and his voice faded into nothing, leaving only the images the words had conjured in their wake. Slowly, Hakon opened his eyes and glanced over at Egbert, whose gaze was on the rood. After a moment, the priest crossed himself and acknowledged his king with a nod.

"You leave again," he said by way of greeting.

Hakon's joints cracked as he rose. He was not yet old, but a life of battle and movement had already taken its toll. "Aye, Egbert," he confirmed as he wiped the floor dust from his trousers.

"I suppose a priest such as myself would not be welcome among Jarl Tore's people?" Egbert pushed himself to his feet and faced his king. Hakon marveled at how little the man's clean-shaven, freckled face and mop of orange hair had changed since they'd first met in the courts of Athelstan as young teenagers. Save for the slight creases at the corners of his hazel eyes, he did not look nearly as old as Hakon felt.

Hakon shook his head. "No. Jarl Tore worshipped the old gods, as do his people. Your presence would be an affront to them and a risk to you."

Eric Schumacher

Egbert's eyes betrayed his disappointment. Long ago, as an idealistic teenager, Hakon had clung to the dream of bringing the light of the Christian faith to his people, but that dream had died with the deaths of Egbert's brother monks early in Hakon's reign. Other missionaries had come over time, but they had had about as much success converting the Northerners as a spider has trying to move a boulder. Christianity had seeped up from the land of the Franks to the Danes, and even to the Swedes. But here, in Hakon's kingdom, the old gods clung stoutly to the minds of men.

"It is a shame that even now, after all this time, his people could not look past my faith. Jarl Tore was a good man, and I would have liked to pay my respects."

Hakon nodded into his gaze and patted his friend on the shoulder. "He was a good man," Hakon agreed. "I shall pass along your condolences."

"When will you return?"

Hakon scratched his beard, which, unlike most men, he wore short to keep it from getting in his way. "A moon from now. Mayhap sooner. While I am gone, I leave you in Ottar's care. Do as he says."

Egbert's right brow rose. "Do you expect trouble?"

"There is always trouble," Hakon answered with a smile. "That is why I forced you to train with weapons and shields, and why I expect you to stay alert and follow Ottar's commands."

Egbert had not wanted to learn the way of weapons, but Hakon had refused to acquiesce. Warriors had murdered Egbert's brethren and many of the missionaries who came to the North. Hakon would not have Egbert's blood on his hands too, so he had issued an ultimatum: learn to defend yourself or leave the North. Egbert had chosen to learn. He would never be a king's champion, but he could protect himself well enough if it came to a fight. Even so, it was a skill he did not like to own, which was why he now blushed under Hakon's gaze.

"I will follow Ottar's command, lord. And I shall pray for Jarl Tore's soul and for your safe return."

15

"Keep that between you and me. I doubt Tore's people would be comforted by your prayers." He winked at his friend and left the church.

"Father!"

Hakon jumped at the shrill voice of his daughter, Thora, then relaxed when he saw the smile on her young face. She was running toward him, her long tangles of blond hair shooting in all directions as her slender legs carried her toward her father. She was tall for a nine-year-old, and athletic, and when she smiled, as she did now, her blue eyes put Hakon in mind of a spring's crisp sky. Hakon smiled at that thought, and at her, and bent down on a knee to receive her.

But she did not hug him as she normally did. Rather, she grabbed his thick forearm and yanked. "Come!" she commanded.

"What is it?"

"Come see!" she urged with another yank on his arm and earnestness in her eyes. "I will show you."

He laughed and glanced back at Egbert, who leaned on the doorframe of the church, arms crossed, a grin creasing his freckled face.

Thora ran off and Hakon chased her. They skirted the inside of the palisade and nearly toppled two thralls who were carrying a barrel of fresh water between them.

"Where are you going?" Hakon called as they passed the door of the great hall where Hakon's woman, Gyda, stood.

"The sow is giving birth!"

Thora disappeared through the open door of the barn and stopped before a pen. Hakon came up beside her and gazed down through the gloom at the sow lying on her side in the straw. One of the thrall women — a woman named Siv — knelt by the sow's hind legs, humming quietly as she gently coaxed a tiny piglet out of the sow's womb. Another women knelt by her side, ready to rinse the blood and birth from its tiny body with a damp woolen rag. Two piglets already lay by the sow's front legs, sucking contentedly from their mother's teats.

"It is remarkable, watching these new lives come forth, eh?" Hakon commented above the din of lowing cows and grunting pigs that filled the barn. The animals were hungry and no doubt sensed the excitement of new life in the air.

"How many do you think she'll have?" Thora asked as the head of the newest life slipped from her mother's body.

Hakon shrugged his broad shoulders. "I can no more answer that than I can fly," he said. "That is for God to answer."

She huffed and rolled her eyes. He laughed.

"Come," he said. "Let us let the women do their work. Have you eaten?"

"No, but I want to stay," she said firmly. "I want to see how many piglets the sow has."

Hakon knew her well enough to know that when Thora made up her mind, it was a difficult thing to sway. So much like her mother, Frida, God rest her soul. And himself, he supposed. "Very well," he responded after a moment. "But come along in a bit. I do not want to leave without a farewell hug."

Hakon left the barn and joined Gyda at the main hall. She had not moved from her spot at the doorframe. "Your daughter keeps you busy," she said with a grin that pulled her round cheeks up and made small crescents of the blue eyes that shone under her brown tresses. Hakon couldn't help but notice how much she glowed this morning. It was the glow of pregnancy, and it brought a smile to Hakon's face.

Gyda was the daughter of a wealthy bonder named Arvid who lived across the Bokna Fjord on an island called Fogn, not far from where Hakon's own mother hailed. Gyda was Arvid's youngest child, whom Hakon had noticed two winters before at the annual law-thing. She was a striking beauty whose wit, laughter, and grace had finally broken through the icy layer of grief that had gripped Hakon's heart ever since the death of Thora's mother, Frida, six winters before. Sensing the attraction between his daughter and Hakon, Arvid quickly blessed the relationship, as much for his benefit as for theirs.

A summer later, Hakon brought Gyda to Avaldsnes to live, but not to marry. As a youth, Hakon had been forced into marrying the daughter of a king named Ivar, whom Hakon despised. Though the marriage never came to fruition, Hakon swore then that he would never bind himself in such a way again. He held to that promise with Frida, and now with Gyda. Whether Gyda liked the arrangement, Hakon knew not, for she never raised the issue again.

"Life keeps me busy," Hakon responded now as he grabbed her shoulders and kissed her forehead. "How is my boy?" Hakon rubbed the small mound of her stomach and smiled.

"So it is a boy now, is it? I thought you said you had no opinion on the matter. That you would put your faith in God." She winked at him.

He felt the heat rise in his cheeks with the reminder of his words. "I —"

"Hold your tongue, lest you say something to make matters worse."

He shut his lips and scratched stupidly at his beard. Gyda grabbed his calloused hand and leaned in close to his cheek. "Come. There is something I must show you before you leave me."

They stepped into the gloom of the main hall. Most of his men had left, leaving the place empty save for a few thralls who toiled in the cavernous space, cleaning the remnants of the previous night's feast from the floor rushes and eating boards. They glanced briefly at their lord and lady, then made a show of their labor as Gyda pulled Hakon to the bedchamber.

Dragon and her crew were ready to sail by midday, as Egil had predicted. The wind had picked up nicely and the sun's rays danced on the rolling surface of the bay. Overhead, gulls called as they hovered on the air currents and searched for a meal on the crowded dock below. Hakon could only pray that this fine weather would last. As bright and cheery as spring could be, it could also be a fickle lover and bring with it sudden storms strong enough to flood newly seeded fields and force ships aground. Which was why Hakon's men who called themselves Christians ignored their king's dour gaze and cheered as Egil brought forth the blood of sacrifices in a wooden bowl.

"Do my sermons have so little effect on them?" Egbert grumbled from the side of his mouth.

Hakon glanced at his friend, whose orange mop of hair danced in the wind like a strong hearth fire, then sighed. "Sometimes I think they do these things just to vex me."

Out on the dock, Egil splashed the blood onto the hull of *Dragon* so that it dripped down the strakes and into the sea. Hakon and Egbert crossed themselves.

"Go with God, my lord," Egbert said with a final pat on Hakon's shoulder.

"Be safe, Egbert," Hakon countered before he scanned the growing crowd. Seeing the man he sought, he yelled, "Ottar!"

Ottar broke off his conversation with Asmund, jogged across the dock to the beach, and nodded in greeting to his lord. Hakon put his arm over the man's shoulder and walked him away from the crowd. "Egil tells me that you are not happy to be left behind."

Ottar stopped and peered at him. "My uncle has a big mouth. I meant only —"

Hakon held up a hand to cut him short. "I know what you meant and why you said it. But I need you to remain here with my family," he nodded his chin toward Gyda, who stood nearby with her hands resting on Thora's shoulders. Both of them gazed out at the ship and the men saying their farewells to family and friends. Hakon turned his eyes back to his hirdman. "I understand your frustration at being left behind, but the task here is important, which is why I am entrusting it to you. I would leave it to Egil, but I fear he might keel over at any moment" — he smiled — "and I want to be near him if that happens."

Ottar grinned through his graying beard. "If that is your worry, then leave Toralv." Ottar jerked his thumb in the direction of the black-haired giant positioning a barrel on *Dragon's* deck. "Egil is my uncle, so I too should be there if death comes to find him."

"Nay. Toralv would just empty my stores of ale and food."

"You speak the truth," Ottar conceded. "Very well. I will do my best."

Hakon squeezed his hirdman's shoulder. "Thank you."

They walked back to the group and Hakon joined Thora and Gyda. He knelt before his daughter and tapped the tip of her nose with his finger. She smiled. "I have a gift for you," he said.

The girl's eyes lit up. "Truly?"

He reached into the pouch at his belt and extracted a dagger. "This," he said, holding the blade up before her, "belonged to your grandmother, whose name, as you know, was also Thora. See here?" He pulled the dagger from its sheath and pointed to the runic etching on its blade. "That says 'Thora.'" He handed the dagger to the girl, who took it reverently in her small hands. "It is yours now."

"It is beautiful," she said as she waved it in the sunlight.

"And it is dangerous, so be careful with it," he said as he took her hand and guided the blade back into its sheath. He then hugged her tightly. "Be good, Thora. Do as Gyda says. Understand?"

She nodded.

He rose and kissed Gyda's soft cheek. "I will miss you." He rubbed her extended belly gently. She smiled bravely at him despite the tears welling in her eyes. "Listen to Ottar."

With a firm nod, he turned to go. He had planned all he could and said all there was to say. It was time to pay his respects to an old friend.

Chapter 2

Frei Island, North More, Late Spring, AD 957

Frei was the name of the island. Hakon had seen it a handful of times on his journeys to Sigurd's estate in Lade. It was hard to miss its craggy peak, Freikollen, which towered over the rest of the island and its flat neighbors like a slumbering giant. But Hakon had never been here. For on the island, in the shadow of Freikollen, was Jarl Tore's private estate at Birkestrand, the place he came to escape the pressures of ruling and matters of state, and to which he invited very few people.

As *Dragon* pulled into the bay on the east side of the island, it was suddenly clear why Tore clung so jealously to its privacy. The place was serene and stunningly beautiful, with a bay lined by a sandy beach, near which several ships lay at anchor. A broad pasture dotted with grazing sheep and split by a glistening stream sloped gently upward to Jarl Tore's hall and its outlying buildings. Behind the hall stood a forest of birch that rolled toward the rocky top of Freikollen, where streams and waterfalls cascaded like glistening strands of silver hair.

Jarl Tore's final resting place was on a small rise just to the north of the bay. There, under a large howe marked by a giant stone and surrounded by a line of birch trees were buried the remains of Tore, his ship, and what household items he had taken with him to the afterlife. Hakon felt a pang of remorse at having missed the ceremony honoring his friend, but it simply hadn't been possible for him to be there. By the time the messenger had reached Avaldsnes, Jarl Tore had been dead for many days. Best to bury him while he still resembled the vital man he'd been in life.

A throng of people approached the beach as *Dragon* glided closer. Hakon studied the crowd and a smile stretched across his face, for in the group he saw his friend, Jarl Sigurd, and the auburn curls of Sigurd's tall daughter, Astrid, who long ago had shared Hakon's bed. The smile faded as Sigurd's priest, or godi, stepped from behind the jarl. His name was Drangi, and he was a dwarf-like man with a bone-ornamented beard of gray and shifting eyes that never seemed to focus on anyone or anything longer than an eye blink. In the North, dwarves were thought to possess magic, and mayhap it had been that magic that had earned him a spot as one of Sigurd's chief counselors. Hakon had never witnessed Drangi's magic, which made the dwarf nothing more than a meddler in Sigurd's affairs.

Dragon bit into the pebbled sand and Hakon leaped from the gunwale, landing with a splash in the ankle-deep water. Such a leap had been easy for him as a young man, but now it took every ounce of self-control not to grunt with the jarring impact of his grand arrival.

Sigurd stepped forward with his arms wide and a wry smile on his weather-etched face. His auburn mane and beard were now silver with age, which complemented the jarl's torc that wrapped his thick neck. His bearlike shoulders and chest had shifted some to his belly, but there was still much strength in the crushing hug with which he received his king. "Welcome to Birkestrand, my friend. You are well met. And you too, you old dog," he called up to Egil, who stood beside the mast, surveying the scene on the beach and probably wondering how he was going to disembark.

Egil's gaze settled on the jarl. "Old dog?" he snarled, then spat poignantly. "Did your father never teach you to respect your elders?"

His surliness drew a belly laugh from the ageing jarl, who smacked Hakon's shoulder playfully. "It is good to see that some things do not change, eh, my king?"

"I could say the same of you, Sigurd," Hakon said with a smile. "I just wish I could say the same for Jarl Tore and his lot."

"Aye. As do we all," Sigurd admitted as his smile evaporated. "Come."

Sigurd ushered Hakon to a young man with a high forehead and thick, wavy blond hair, which he wore short on the sides but long and braided down his back. Hakon had last seen the youth four winters before; then, he had been a scrawny teenager with long limbs and pimples. He was a teenager no longer. The pimples had given way to fair skin and a strong jaw, and his muscles bulged beneath his fine tunic. He was a handsome lad, there was no denying that.

"Sigge," Hakon said, addressing Sigurd's son, who was also named Hakon, by his pet name. He grabbed the young man's thick forearm in the warrior's greeting. "You have grown into a man."

The young man's cheeks reddened above his well-groomed beard. "It is good to see you again, my lord." He leaned in closer and whispered, "My friends call me Hakon now, lord."

Hakon smiled at the comment and whispered back, "Nevertheless, I shall still call you Sigge, at least until you have earned my name." He winked at the younger man.

Sigurd snorted. "A man? A man chases fame in the shield wall, not women in the mead hall."

"Father!" Sigge hissed.

Hakon laughed and patted Sigge's shoulder. "Worry not, lad. Your father is just jealous he is no longer able to keep up with the women in *his* hall." It was a comment Hakon would not have dared speak four winters ago, when Sigurd's wife, Bergliot, lay dying in her bed from a wasting disease. That death had weighed heavily on them all. Now, though, he felt safe in saying such things.

Sigurd rolled his eyes. Clearly, he had different thoughts on the matter, as did Drangi, who emitted a strange tutting noise and stroked his beard more fervently.

Hakon ignored the dwarf and moved on to the next person in line, Sigurd's daughter, Astrid. Strands of silver now lined the temples of her auburn curls, while age lines creased the corners of her pine-colored eyes, accentuating the smile that danced within them and putting Hakon in mind of the first time they'd met all those years ago, when he had wondered at that same bewitching look.

"That was a grand entry, King Hakon," she remarked as she dipped her head in greeting.

He blushed at her sarcasm, for he had done it as much to show the others his strength as to impress her. She, of course, had seen right through his performance and, in her usual direct manner, let him know her thoughts on the matter.

"It is good to see you again, Astrid. It has been a long time. How fares Fynr?" he asked, meaning her husband.

The humor slipped from her eyes. "Fynr is dead, Hakon. He died last summer in the Sami lands."

Hakon's cheeks felt as if they might ignite. " I am sorry, Astrid. I had not heard. Forgive me."

"You could not have known," she said.

"Now that you have saddened my daughter," Sigurd interjected to break up the sudden awkwardness, "let us find some of Tore's fine ale. I am sure you and your men could use some about now."

"Where is Tore's family?" asked Hakon.

Sigurd motioned with his chin to a gray-bearded warrior standing at the head of a small group of other graybeards. "That is the only family Jarl Tore has left. Alov died many winters ago, as you know," he said, speaking of Hakon's older sister, who had been Jarl Tore's wife. "And you know what happened to my wife." His wife Bergliot had been the daughter of Jarl Tore. "The rest of his kin are scattered through the Orkneyjar and Frankland."

Hakon approached the graybeard. The man bowed at Hakon, a movement that threw off his balance and forced him to take a step back to right himself. "My lord," he slurred.

They clutched forearms. "Tosti. It has been many winters," Hakon said to the leader of Jarl Tore's hird — or rather, the former leader, now that Tore was dead. "You look well." Which was a lie. Tosti looked like he'd been chewed up by the goddess of the underworld and shat out her rear end. He smelled like it, too.

Tosti squinted his bloodshot eyes and raised an unsteady finger. "Do not sweeten your words. I look drunk. I *am* drunk."

"You are drunk," Hakon agreed.

"It is custom to mourn your lord with ale. He was a great lord, and so we drink greatly, me and my men," he said, sweeping his arm back toward his retinue. A quick glance in their direction revealed the truth in Tosti's words. The men could barely stand.

"And so we shall drink with you, Tosti," said Hakon. "For Jarl Tore was indeed a great man, and great men should be celebrated."

"Come then!" Tosti shouted to the crowd. "Let us drink!" He waved his arm toward the hall on the hill and staggered in that direction. His men cheered and stumbled after him.

Hakon turned to Egil, who had made his way down the gangplank and was leaning on his walking stick, which was planted in the shingle. "Have the men make camp, Egil. Then come to the hall. There is ale to drink!" Hakon said this last bit loud enough for his entire crew to hear, and they roared their approval. He then fell into step behind Tosti and the rest of Tore's staggering hirdmen.

"Poor rudderless bastards," huffed Sigurd when he came up beside his king. "They'll be needing another lord to follow."

"Mayhap. Mayhap not," Hakon responded, feeling his own breath shorten at the steepness of the path. "Could be that some of those men just want a comfortable bed, a warm hall, and a plot of land to farm. God knows they deserve it after all the fighting they have done in their lives. No one would think the lesser of them."

Hakon watched Tore's hirdmen weave their way up the hill. Some walked with an arm over the shoulder of a comrade. Others sang a bawdy song. It was hard to imagine such men settling down, but it was possible they would. Mayhap at a certain age, men's thirst for the battle-fray was slaked. "I will put the question to them," Hakon said. "We shall see which way they lean."

"Just do it when they are right-minded," said Sigurd through his panting. "Ale-sodden words cannot be trusted."

The guests filled Tore's mead hall and fanned out to the tables and benches. The hall was comfortable, but not overly large, so the guests squeezed into spaces wherever they could. The latecomers climbed onto the platforms lining the walls, or else stood near the hall's doors. As the guests of honor, Tosti offered Hakon and Sigurd the head chairs at the far end of the hall, then took his own seat at the table just before them. Hakon thanked his host, but chose to stand, for he had been many days on a ship and needed to stretch his legs. He leaned his shoulder against a large column and gazed out at the raucous crowd.

"You look content."

Hakon turned to Astrid and smiled. He *was* content. Sigurd had arranged a competition for the following day, but had kept the details of it to himself. It mattered not — just the idea of sport thrilled the men and filled them with boasts and bluster and barks of laughter that echoed in the cavernous space. And all of it lay on Hakon like a soft cloak; the more so because he knew it was just the way Tore would have wanted it.

"I am. It is good to see the men reunited and to hear their banter. I have missed it." Long ago, when the realm was more fractious, the armies of the various jarls had assembled more often. Now, those times came less frequently, which, Hakon supposed, was a good thing. Even so, he had missed the drinking and boasting, and even the occasional fistfight. "The only thing missing is Jarl Tore himself," he said. "And Fynr, of course," he added hastily.

Astrid's husband had been a distant relative of Sigurd's and a chieftain in Halogaland, a rugged fylke that stretched from the Trondelag to the land of the Sami people five days' sail up the coast. Their wedding had been a political move on Sigurd's part, but the bond that tied them together quickly developed into something deeper, at least for Astrid. Hakon had only seen her with Fynr twice, and in both of those instances, they did not hide their affection for each other. It had pleased him greatly to see her happiness, for arranged marriages were not always so.

Hakon's clumsy mention of Fynr returned that sudden sadness to her eyes, and she cast her gaze about the room. "He would have liked this," she admitted.

"They both would have," Hakon said, his mind turning to Jarl Tore and his fondness for feasts and fine ale. "I hope you do not mind my asking, but how did Fynr die?"

She turned back to Hakon and studied his face with eyes that revealed both confusion and ire. "You would ask me that now?"

Hakon shrugged. "Is there ever a good time to ask such questions?"

Her hard gaze softened and she sighed. "No. I suppose not. He went to collect the tribute from the Sami tribes, as he did every summer. Only this last summer, rather than presenting my husband with pelts, the Sami came with spears and bows and knives, and they butchered my husband and his men."

"Were they avenged?"

"Aye. As soon as my father heard the news, he brought his army against the Sami and killed those responsible for Fynr's death. Though he never found the bodies of Fynr and his men."

Or he spared his daughter those details, thought Hakon grimly. "I am sorry for your loss, Astrid. Fynr was a good man."

It was the worst kind of loss Hakon could think of, not only because of the love they shared, or the loss of their two offspring, who had never lived to see their third winters, but also because her husband's property could now be claimed by Fynr's brother, Ulf. In short order, she could be husbandless, childless, and homeless, unless she decided to marry Ulf.

A tear escaped her eye and trickled down her angular cheek. She wiped it away with the sleeve of her dress. "Thank you, Hakon."

"What will you do now?"

She shrugged and shook her head, then wiped another tear away. "Forgive me." She smiled to hide her embarrassment. "I will keep living on our farm, at least until Ulf comes to claim it or, if I am lucky, to hand it to me."

"You will not marry him?"

Astrid kept her eyes on the hall. "No."

If Hakon could have wrapped her in his arms then and there, he would have, but men were watching, and the last thing she needed were for men to get the wrong thoughts in their heads. Sigurd, too, was watching from his seat at the high table. And so Hakon simply held up his cup to her and smiled. "To happier times, then. May they come quickly."

She clinked her cup against his and tilted it to her lips. "May they come quickly," she repeated into her ale.

"Enough!" Egil smashed the table with his fist. His voice cut through the conversations like a fine blade through flesh, killing them in mid-sentence. All eyes shifted to him as he grabbed his walking stick and pushed himself to his feet. He then pointed his stick at Hakon Sig-urdsson, who had been laughing at some joke. The laughter died on the younger man's lips. "I may be old, but my eyes still see and my ears, hear."

"Sit down, old man." Sigge called down the table, trying to dismiss him with the wave of his hand.

Up on the dais, Sigurd glowered but held his tongue, his eyes shifting from his son, who was obviously drunk, to Egil, who now leaned on his walking stick in the space that men had cleared for him. Hakon moved back to the dais and sidled into the seat beside Sigurd.

"You joke with your friends about my age," Egil spat, "and how my memory must be failing me. You have all but said to your friends that I have lied about my deeds."

"I was only having a little fun. I meant no harm," called Sigge.

"Well then, you failed in that, for harm they have." Egil jabbed his index finger at him. "You have trod on my honor, Sigge, and now I must regain it."

Sigge looked at his comrades in disbelief, then back at Egil. "And how do you propose to regain it? By fighting me?"

"Aye, lad. That is exactly what I propose."

Sigge's cheeks reddened. "I will not fight you, Egil Woolsark."

"Before this goes too far, tell us what words you spoke, Sigge," called Hakon to the young man. "If you can speak them to your friends and they were not harmful, then let us all hear them. Mayhap there is a joke in them that will amuse us all."

Sigurd's son looked to his comrades, who suddenly found more interest in their ale cups and food.

"Let us hear them, lad," called Hakon again.

"I said that Egil's mind must be failing him because the number of his exploits seems to grow every time we see him," Sigge said into the silence of the hall.

"What else, lad?" Egil called.

Sigge swallowed, suddenly looking far more sober than he had when the exchange began.

"I said that I was surprised that at his age he could still drink as much ale as he does without pissing himself."

The utter lack of respect in Sigge's words, especially for a fighter and warrior as renowned as Egil, sent a low rumble of chatter about the hall. It so stunned Hakon that, for a moment, he had no words for the young man. And so it was his father, Sigurd, who stepped into the word-fray.

"By the gods, but you are a fool, son. I should beat you myself for words like that, but I will leave that to Egil. Get your arse off your ale-bench. If you have not the guts to speak such words to Egil's face, then at least have the guts to face him in a fight."

Sigge cursed and walked around the eating board to stand before the gray-bearded Egil. He stood almost a head taller than his opponent — though at the moment, he stood with his shoulders slumped in shame at having to go through with the fight.

"Come on, lad. Don't look so for —"

Egil never finished his comment, for just then, young Sigurdsson swung for Egil's jaw with his right fist. The move took Hakon by surprise, but not Egil. The crafty old warrior must have known Sigurdsson would resort to trickery, for he took a quick step backward and let Sigurdsson's fist sail past his face. Before the young warrior could regain his balance, Egil swung his walking stick up and into Sigge's crotch. The stick was made of hard oak and polished to a dark sheen, and it connected with force. Sigge grunted and grabbed at his testicles, before collapsing to the rush-covered floor and curling into a ball.

Egil lowered his weapon and stepped back. He spat into the rushes near Sigge's head and turned his gaze to Sigurd. "He better learn some respect before someone slits his throat."

There was nothing Sigurd could say to that, for it was true. Still, the rebuke raised the color in his cheeks. Looking for a place to direct his wrath, he turned to the table where his son's comrades sat gaping at their leader. "You lads," he roared at them. "Get him out of here. I don't want to see any of you, or him, back in this hall tonight. You have stained this evening with your antics."

The men scurried to help their leader to his feet, but Sigge pushed them aside and scowled at Egil.

"Don't say a word," Jarl Sigurd called to his son, "or I'll beat you myself. Now leave this place and save your temper for the morrow's sport."

The young warriors scrambled from the hall under the malignant gazes of the other guests.

Sigurd sat back in his chair and cursed sourly at the retreating figure of his son. Below him, Egil was enjoying the back slaps of Hakon's crew, which brought a smile a Hakon's face. It had been many springs since Egil had dropped an opponent in a mead hall fight. He was proud of his old friend, and was thankful things had not turned more violent. Hakon called Egil's name and raised his cup to the old warrior. Egil returned the gesture with a toothless smile, then drank deeply of his ale.

Chapter 3

The competitions began early the following morning under gray clouds that hung thick and low, pregnant with moisture. The men gazed at the suspect clouds with bloodshot eyes and pounding heads, their bluster from the previous night forgotten now that rain threatened. More than a few commented on how much better they would be with a few more hours of sleep and some warm food in their bellies.

Sigurd ignored their gripes and organized the men into five groups according to their crews: Hakon and his crew, Sigurd and his crew, the crew of Halogalanders who had come with Astrid, Tosti and his warriors, and Sigge and his men. The chipper jarl then explained that each crew would pick among themselves to compete in a series of sports: spear toss, axe throw, stone toss, glima, long-distance running, obstacle course running, and tug-of-war. Sigurd, Astrid, and Egil would judge the matches.

"Your king," called Sigurd, "will not be spared. He, too, must compete." The men howled with newfound spirit at the news, and Hakon smiled at their delight.

The spear toss came first and was foremost a competition of accuracy, though strength would play a factor as the men moved progressively farther away from the targets. There were five targets, and all five men would toss their spears simultaneously. The warrior who missed the target, or whose spear didn't penetrate the target, would be disqualified. After each successful throw, the spearmen were to move back ten paces and throw again until only one competitor remained.

"No offense, Jarl Sigurd, but even blind, I could hit a target that close," boasted a man in Tosti's crew as he hefted his spear. This got a few "ayes" from the others, since the wooden targets stood only twenty paces distant.

"We shall see, Alf," responded Sigurd.

Hakon's crew had chosen Asmund for this, for though he did not have Toralv's strength, he was more accurate, even at greater distances. The men lined up and waited for Sigurd to drop his hand. As they waited, the crews yelled their encouragements, goaded the competition, or wagered hack silver on their choice for winner. When Sigurd dropped his arm, the men jogged to the throwing line and tossed. The spears struck with a staccato of cracks. Thralls retrieved the weapons and the men moved back ten paces. The onlookers shouted, and Sigurd gave the signal again. And again, the spears struck home.

Asmund called to Sigurd, "I was hitting targets like this when I was but a beardless bairn."

"You're still a beardless bairn," Alf quipped as he stroked his long, gray-streaked chin-braids.

"Yeah, well, I heard your mother had a beard, which disqualifies you from this discussion," Asmund countered, which got a few chuckles from the onlookers.

"Very well," Sigurd interjected before the jibes turned more serious. "Move back another twenty paces. Now then," he said when they reached their new spot, "let us see which of you is boasting after this round. Ready?" He raised his arm.

The men hefted their spears and squinted at the targets as the onlookers shouted their wagers, their jokes, and their comments. Sigurd lowered his arm, and the men tossed. All of the spears struck home, save for the spear from Sigge's hirdman. That spear glanced off the outer edge of the target and lodged in the soft turf. Moans and grumbles rippled through Sigge's crew, followed by the jingle of hack silver changing hands.

In the end, it came down to Asmund and Alf, as Hakon expected it would. The targets lay at eighty paces and looked like small coins in the distance. Asmund picked a blade of grass and tossed it in the air to gauge the wind, for at that distance, even the slightest breeze could shift the spear's trajectory. The men hefted their weapons and focused their eyes and minds on the targets. The crowd placed their final bets. Hakon looked on anxiously, for even though these were just games, winning came with bragging rights that would live on in the minds of everyone present, and such things were important for the reputation of the competitors, and that of their lords.

Sigurd dropped his arm, and the men threw. The spears climbed upward into the gray day, then arced down toward the targets. Almost in unison they struck, and for the briefest of moments, the competitors raised their arms at their feat. But then, Asmund's spear wobbled and came free. Tosti's men cheered as Hakon's men groaned.

The other competitions were equally competitive, each with their own memorable drama that the men would relive that night over their bruised bodies, bruised egos, and cups of ale. Hakon's man, Bjarke, won the axe throw, for few in the North were better with that weapon, while Hakon's massive champion, Toralv, won the stone toss, which, in truth, was more of a boulder than a stone. The running competitions went to two brothers in Sigge's hird, Arne and Rolf, whose names meant eagle and wolf respectively and who, all agreed, were aptly named. Sigurd's foul-mouthed warrior, Leif, won the glima match. He was not the largest man, but his combination of strength and quickness gave him the edge over Hakon's warrior, Bard.

By the time they got to the tug-of-war, it was late in the afternoon and the smell of pine smoke and boiled meat hung heavy in the air. The men were impatient to end the bouts and start the celebration, but not impatient enough to give up on the final competition. Boasts and jeers flew across the field, where Hakon's men gathered to take on Tosti's. Tired of being a spectator to the men's fun, Hakon joined his hird. They cheered their king as he dug his heels into the turf behind Asmund. At Sigurd's command, the rope went taut as the men yanked. Tosti's older men pulled with all their strength, but their age and lack of sleep proved no match for Hakon's warriors. The bout ended quickly, with Tosti and his men heaped in a mass of laughing bodies.

In the second bout, Sigge's half crew joined forces with the Halogalanders to take on Sigurd's hirdmen. Sigurd, too, joined the fun with a few boisterous boasts that had his men, and even his opponents, smiling.

"That man could joke his way out of a pit of snakes," said Toralv appreciatively.

"If only his words could pull a rope," added Garth, for Sigge's young men were quick and pulled Sigurd's men off balance as soon as Astrid's arm dropped to signal the bout's start. After giving some ground, Sigurd's men dug in and started to pull back. Now it was Sigge's crew and the Halogalanders who started to slide forward.

Near the back of the line, the leader of the Halogalanders began to snarl. His name was Hemming, and he had been oath-sworn to Fynr. "Not another ell, Halogalanders!" he called. And just like that, the men from the far north tightened their grip and dug in.

"On my call," Hemming shouted, "heave!"

And the Halogalanders heaved as one. There was a barely perceptible shift in Sigurd's line but enough to give their opponents hope.

"Heave!"

This time, Sigge's men redoubled their efforts. Sigurd's men dug in their heels. Their muscles strained and their faces flushed, but the combined force of their opponents' pull yanked them forward involuntarily.

"For Fynr! Heave!"

With a roar, the Halogalanders hauled back on the rope, and the front of Sigurd's line collapsed. All but Sigurd, that is, who somehow managed to maintain his footing, and thus his dignity, in the face of his men's defeat.

"Let us hope they've used all their energy on the Tronds," said Bjarke.

"Have heart," said Garth, who was tapping his hand on his thigh in anticipation. "No one can move Toralv." He patted the champion's shoulder. "He is a boulder among pebbles, eh Toralv? Besides, Sigurd's men have softened them for us, like mallets beating frozen cod. See how they lie there?"

Which was true. The crews lay on the ground, sucking air into their lungs. Some rolled tired shoulders. Others armed sweat from their faces despite the chill in the air. But then, there was no figuring the will of men. It was a formless energy that could far outweigh skill or cunning or strength when it welled up in someone, as it just had in Hemming's crew.

"You're a genuine word-weaver, Garth," Toralv joked. "Next you will be thinking you are some sort of skald."

"I could live with that," responded Garth. "Mayhap when the shield wall with you louts loses its luster, I will take my words to distant halls and collect my silver, with a fair lass to keep me warm. Does not sound half bad, really."

"You cannot sit still long enough to enjoy a lass on your lap," called Bjarke, which received some nods of agreement from the men and a glare from the leg-tapping Garth.

"Come, men," called Hakon with a grin. "Let us show these young ones how to pull."

Hakon's crew strutted over to the rope — now warm with the friction of men's hands — and took their places in line. They rolled their shoulders and jiggled their arms to loosen muscles, then lifted the rope and planted their feet on the trodden ground.

"We promise to go easy on you, my lord," called Hemming as he and his men took their positions.

Sigurd took his spot at the center of the rope and raised his arm. The air rang with jokes and wagers and shouts of encouragement. The men leaned back and pulled the rope taut.

Sigurd's arm fell and the fight was on. Instantly, Hakon could feel the muscles in his arms and shoulders and back tighten with the strain. He was vaguely aware of his men grunting, of voices urging each other to pull. Sweat began to bead on his forehead, then trickle down his temples. Across from them, Hemming called through gritted teeth for his team to heave, which suddenly gave Hakon an idea.

"On my word, pull!" Hakon yelled.

On the other end of the rope, Hemming barked. "Ready?"

And a split second before he could give his command, Hakon barked his order. As one, they yanked on the rope, pulling their opponents off balance.

"Again!" Hakon yelled, but before the word "pull" sprang forth, Hemming screamed, "Heave!" And with that yank, even Toralv gave a step.

"Toralv, you bastard," Hakon grunted as sweat dropped into his eye. "Backstep. Now!"

The giant had the rope wrapped around his waist and clutched in both hands. "We move as a line, or we don't move," Toralv grunted.

"You have the strength of ten men. Pull, you bastard!"

And with a growl, Toralv pulled and stepped.

"Again!" Hakon called, and again Toralv met Hakon's challenge. Sensing what was happening, Hakon's men yanked with Hakon's call, and their opponents gave.

"For Fynr!" Hemming called, and the rope burned in Hakon's hand as it slipped forward again.

Every muscle in Hakon's body screamed. His hands from gripping, his arms and shoulders and back from holding and pulling, his legs and ankles from planting and resisting. Sweat seeped into his eyes. The old wound in his thigh throbbed. How easy it would be to let the rope go and end the fight. After all, was it not just a game? But he was not about to give this victory to Sigurd's ill-mannered whelp, even with a fine man like Hemming pulling with him.

"Pull, you louts!" Hakon yelled. "You are the king's men! Oath-sworn! Pull! Don't let these lads beat you!" And the line moved another step in their direction.

"For Fynr!" Hemming yelled again, but his call failed to rally his men. Their will was weakening. Hakon could sense it and moved instantly to challenge it.

"Let us end this," Hakon panted. "On my word, Toralv." Hakon braced himself. "Pull!" he cried.

Hakon yanked with what strength he had left.

"Pull!" Hakon called again, and again the men yanked and the line gave.

"Hold, you bastards!" Hemming yelled, but it was too late. The front of their line was crumbling, their feet slipping in the turf. If not for the Halogalanders, the whole line would have collapsed already. Hakon found it hard not to admire their resolve. But resolve or no, they had to break, and Hakon was determined to do it.

"For Tore!" he called to his men.

And with a final heave, the Halogalanders collapsed and Hakon's men fell to their backs in victory.

"How are your hands?" asked Sigurd. He grunted as he sat, then handed Hakon a cup of ale.

They sat on the hill just below the hall, looking out over the Kvernesfjord. It was early evening and the sun had finally broken through the clouds in the West, its last rays painting the calm waters of the fjord a brilliant orange. In the distance lay the low islands and fingers of land that were More, their fields and trees radiant beneath the sun's glow.

Hakon took the cup gratefully in his left hand and examined his right. There was a painful red line where the rope had seared his skin. "It will be fine. I did not expect the Halogalanders, or your son and his crew, to have so much backbone. They put up a fight."

Sigurd pulled his face from his cup and sleeved some ale from his lips. "Hemming and his men are a tough lot. Sigge and his crew?" He shrugged at the mention of his son. "We shall see. As it stands, my son is better at causing trouble than he is at anything else."

A flock of squawking long-tailed ducks sailed southward across the fjord. Hakon watched them for a time as he considered his friend's words.

"Has your son ever fought in a shield wall?"

Sigurd snorted. "He raided the past few summers with a ship I gave him. From his tales, you would think he is the greatest warrior alive. A real Beowulf come back to life. Truth be told, I think the only time his crew was ever blooded was when he went north with me to seek Fynr's banesmen. And even then, they fought in the second row."

Hakon picked a blade of grass and tossed it down the slope. It floated for a time on the breeze before settling. "Your son will be blooded soon enough," Hakon said. "Erik's sons are out there, and one day soon, they will come for me."

For a long moment, Sigurd did not speak, though Hakon could sense the jarl's mind working out the implications of that statement. "We should have killed the louts..." Sigurd waved away his sentiment before Hakon could speak. "Forget it. We have spoken of this many times before. What is done is done. To other things, then. I want my son and his crew to go with you when you leave here. He can fight well enough, but he needs to learn warcraft."

The words took Hakon by surprise. He was about to sip his ale but now lowered his cup and glanced sidelong at his friend. Sigurd was staring earnestly back at him. Hakon could not hold the gaze, and so turned his eyes back to his cup and stared at the liquid swirling within it to give himself time to formulate a proper response. Finally, he sighed.

"Your son has already angered my men. It is possible that they will not welcome his presence in their midst."

"I know."

"You know as well as I that in the blood-fray, cohesion is essential. If I take him and there is animosity with my men, it will weaken the group, like a rusting link in a byrnie. He and his men will need to prove that they are capable. Not just to me, but to my men. You understand what that means?"

Sigurd scowled. "Of course I understand. I was not born this morning. My son needs to learn, even if that means he takes a well-deserved pummeling from time to time."

"You know too that I cannot guarantee his safety. Or the safety of his men. I have no power over God's will."

"Or the Norns," Sigurd responded, referring to the sisters who, in the Northern belief, wove and cut the threads of each man's life.

Hakon ignored his friend's counter. "I will think upon it," he said, though in truth, he knew he would take the lad. Sigurd had done much for Hakon over the years, and he owed him this. He just needed to think how best to present it to his men.

"Thank you, Hakon."

They sat in companionable silence for a time, each lost in his thoughts as the shadows darkened around them and the hum of the feast increased.

"I was sorry to hear about Fynr," Hakon said after a time. "He was a good man. I hope the Sami paid mightily for his death."

"It was a bad thing, his death," Sigurd agreed after sipping some ale. "It never should have happened. Fynr got greedy. Took more than his share, and then some. The Sami made him pay for it." Sigurd sighed deeply. "I trust you will not speak those words to my daughter. He was a good husband to Astrid, and I would like him to be remembered that way."

"I will hold my tongue, Sigurd." Hakon scratched at the lice in his beard. "What will she do now?"

The jarl shrugged. "We will need to see if Ulf comes to claim his brother's lands. If he does, then Astrid will come back to Lade to live with me. At least for a time. Or mayhap she will stay with him."

It was a hard thing, that. But there was not much any of them could do about it. Unless he chose to give them up, Ulf was entitled to the lands by law.

"Does Ulf have children?" asked Hakon.

"Aye," Sigurd responded. "Several."

Which made his decision all the easier. His children could take the lands. If he was smart, he would keep Astrid on to manage the property until his children were grown, but whether Astrid cared for that role was anyone's guess. The whole affair weighed heavily on Hakon's mood, so he forced his mind to a different topic.

"I have been thinking of Jarl Tore and his realm. We will need to find a successor."

"Aye. I have been thinking the same. My vote is for Tosti."

"And mine is for you," Hakon responded.

Sigurd's guffaw erupted like a sudden belch. "Me? Think you that I do not have enough headaches in my own fylke?"

"I am certain you have plenty. But you are also adept at handling your bickering nobles. Besides, you are Jarl Tore's son-in-law, are you not? That is as close as it gets when it comes to kin."

"And what if his brothers or nephews come back to claim his realm?"

Hakon had considered that. Tore had several brothers. One ruled in the Orkneyjar, and another in Iceland. A third had been given land in the Frankish kingdom. "Last I heard, they are well set in their own realms. But if they do decide to return, can you not call on more blades than Tosti?"

Sigurd frowned. "Think you that Tosti will accept it?"

Hakon shrugged. In truth, he knew not what Tosti would say.

"By the gods, but you like to complicate my life, Hakon."

Hakon smiled. "I am only returning the favor."

Sigurd laughed again. "I suppose that is true." He finished his ale and belched, leaving a sour stench hanging between them. "If I accept your offer, I would have Tosti act as my man here. He knows the people and is well respected."

"Provided he swears an oath to you, that is fine."

It was no small thing to pledge an oath. The giver must be willing to pledge their life to their lord, while the receiver would be bound to provide food and silver to those pledging their swords to him. While Tosti and his men had already earned much in their time with Tore, it did not lessen the burden on Sigurd.

"I will think upon your offer and consult with Drangi, just as you will think upon mine. In the meantime," he smacked Hakon's shoulder and rose with a grunt, "let us feast before the scoundrels drink all of the ale."

Chapter 4

Hakon woke early the following morning. His head and stomach ached from the previous night's feast. His mouth and tongue felt like he had swallowed mud. As he pushed himself up, he noticed the sleeping form next to him and cursed under his breath. He had not intended things to go as far as they had with the thrall woman, but as the evening wore on, his reasoning had faltered.

Slowly, he climbed from beneath the furs and fumbled for his trousers, which lay in a heap on the floor beside the bed where the girl — what was her name? — had relieved him of them. As he pulled on his shirt and boots, his mind replayed the previous evening, searching for words and actions that he might regret, for a king who drinks overmuch, even among friends, plays a risky game. Save for his attentions on the girl — attentions that would surely earn him Astrid's acrimony and the ribbing of his own men — he could think of nothing too embarrassing. His thoughts shifted then to Gyda, and he cursed again in his head.

Hakon slipped from the bedchamber — a room that had once belonged to his friend and to which he, as the guest of honor, was now entitled — and made his way across the hall, where the sleeping forms of Tosti and his men lay in snoring bundles. The stench of ale and sour cheese, body odor, and smoke lay over the room like fog on a riverbank. Hakon moved through it to the door, then out into the chill of the morning, where the sun's soft light was just starting to announce the new day.

"You are up early."

Hakon spun. Standing just outside one of the guest huts was Astrid, her auburn curls pulled back into a tight braid that snaked down her back. Beneath her cloak Hakon could see a rough tunic, leather breeks, and boots. In her hand was some bread, which she was packing into a knapsack.

"As are you," he countered when he had recovered from his surprise. His voice sounded rough and sluggish in his ears.

"I am going for a hike."

"Now?" he asked. "Is it not a bit early?"

"Now," she affirmed. "Before the world awakens. It is the best time." She wrapped a chunk of hard cheese into a cloth and shoved it into her sack. "Would you care to join me? Or are you too tired from your nocturnal adventures?"

Hakon felt the heat in his cheeks. "I feel fine," he responded lamely.

"I bet you do," she said with a smile.

He hesitated, not quite sure how to respond to that.

In the end, she rescued him from his discomfiture. "We will not be gone long. There is a place I used to visit when I was younger. It is beautiful there, and well worth the hike. I promise."

Astrid must have seen the curiosity in his face, for she smiled and urged him further. "Come. Grab your things. I will meet you where the trail enters the trees, just behind the hall."

She did not wait for his response, but brushed past Hakon and disappeared around the corner of the hall.

He stood there for a moment, weighing his duties against his absence. In the end, the promise of new adventure and time with Astrid won out, and Hakon scrambled back into the murk of the hall to collect his things: his seax, his spear, a piece of marginally soft bread, and a leather skin of water. Thus equipped, he jogged out the door.

Astrid sat at the trailhead and smiled when Hakon appeared. "I was just about to leave," she said as she stood and wiped the dirt from the rump of her trousers.

"I am glad you waited. Lead the way." He motioned for forward.

The amusement danced in her eyes, and for a moment Hakon was back on the beach where they had first met all of those winters ago, she with her smiling gaze and he with the fluttering butterflies in his stomach. She lingered. "I am glad you are coming."

"You have me curious. I must see this beautiful spot for myself," he said, deflecting her kind words to hide his embarrassment. In his belly, the butterflies took flight.

They set off into the birch trees on a meandering path, angling upward. It followed the stream that dissected Tore's property, though here, in the woods, the stream rushed more fervently and spat its contents onto the path, dampening the leaves that carpeted the trail so that they stuck to the soles of Hakon's boots as he walked. Astrid led, her lanky limbs graceful as they picked their way over exposed roots and water-slick stones. It was colder in the shadows of the woods. Though the exertion of the hike quickly warmed Hakon, the chill clouded before his face as he huffed up the trail, accompanied by birdsong and crickets and the rush of the water off to his right.

After a time the trail flattened and Astrid motioned for them to stop. She then held a finger to her lips for silence and pointed off to the right. There, through the trees, Hakon glimpsed a meadow in which three deer sipped at the stream, oblivious to the newcomers. Every so often, one of them would lift its head and gaze about, its rotating ears searching for foreign sounds. They had not yet detected Hakon and Astrid, upwind from the hikers as they were. Hakon glanced at Astrid, who smiled at him. He pointed to his spear and raised his eyebrow: *Should I?* She understood and shook her head. He nodded and frowned. Fresh venison would have been a welcome surprise in the mead hall, but this day, it was not to be. They moved on.

A little farther along, Astrid stopped again.

"Are we there?"

She turned and studied Hakon. "Almost. Are you tired? Should we stop for a break?" Her hair was moist at the temples and her cheeks rosy from the exercise.

"Tired? No," he said as he armed sweat from his brow and took a swig of water from his skin. He would never have admitted it if he was. "I was just wondering."

She sipped from her own water skin. "Just there is another path." She pointed up the trail about ten paces to a path that led off to the left. "We follow that for a ways, and then we'll be there."

"Lead on, then."

The new path cut across the hill they had been climbing so that now, through the trees to the east, they could see the glistening waters of the Kvernesfjord. To the right, west, the trees and rocks angled up sharply toward Friekollen. The path had not been used in some time, and the overgrowth forced Astrid and Hakon to step over or climb through shrubs and branches. It ended at a rocky promontory with a commanding view of the Kvernes and the islands that lay to the south of Frei.

"Is this the spot?" asked Hakon.

Astrid's eyebrows arched, though there was a gleam of humor in her eyes. "You wish for something more?"

Hakon laughed at her mock displeasure. "No. No. It is wondrous. Truly."

"I am glad you like it," she responded with a smile, then took a seat on a stone and unlaced the sack that held her bread and cheese. "This place always reminds me of my mother. She used to bring me here when we would visit Birkestrand, and tell me stories for hours. She was quite a storyteller, you know. Much like her father before he lost his voice to his wound."

Hakon could hear Jarl Tore's ragged voice in his head. "I never knew Tore before the wound but would have very much liked to hear his stories. If they were anything like your mother's, then they must have been entrancing." Hakon sat on the stone beside her and pulled the bread from his sack. In the dimness of the hall that morning, he had not noticed the teeth marks in it, but now he studied them solemnly.

Astrid glanced at the bread in Hakon's hand, then tore off a chunk of her own loaf and passed it to him. "Have some of mine," she offered. "And some cheese too."

He took the food gratefully and promptly bit into it. "Thank you," he said between chews, realizing for the first time just how hungry he was. "And thank you for sharing this with me." He swept of his arm toward the vista. "This spot reminds me very much of my stone at Avaldsnes, only higher."

She nodded. "It has been many summers since I sat on your stone at Avaldsnes. I should like to see it again someday."

"You are welcome any time, Astrid."

She smiled at him with reddened cheeks, then turned away. They stared for a time at the view before them, each lost in thought as they chewed on bits of bread and cheese to break their fast.

"How fares Thora?" asked Astrid. "She must be getting bigger."

"She is beautiful. Bright. Curious." He grinned. "Spoiled."

Astrid laughed. "That is because she rules your heart."

"You have the right of that."

A cloud passed over Astrid's face and Hakon fell silent. He looked down at the bread in his hand and searched for a new subject, for he knew her mind had turned to her dead children, and he did not want to wreck the moment; but it was too late for that.

"The gods have cursed me lately," she mumbled. "First my children. Then Fynr." Her voice trailed off.

"I am sorry, Astrid. I wish I could make it better for you somehow."

Astrid did not reply. It seemed her mind had wandered to some far off memory, and the silence stretched with it. As he waited, Hakon recalled his own memory of Astrid as a teenage girl and the time she had secretly prepared a bathhouse just for them. It was the first time Hakon had ever been with a woman. Every moment of that night was etched on Hakon's heart like the runes on the warriors' blades. How many times had he relived that evening in his mind? How many times had he yearned for that feeling again? The memory brought a sudden thought to Hakon.

"You could come with me to Avaldsnes," he offered quietly.

She turned her gaze on him and studied his face with sad eyes. "You are kind, but there is nothing for me there. You have a woman. You have your child."

"Better Ulf then?" Hakon regretted the words as soon as they slipped from his mouth.

Her eyes narrowed. "We should get back," she said icily and rose.

Hakon rose with her. "Please, Astrid. Stay. I spoke rashly."

She stopped and turned her malignant gaze on him.

"Please," he said again, softer now, his hands raised in surrender. "You have invited me to this place, and I have upset that peace with my careless words. I am sorry." His apology rolled from his mouth haltingly, like a cripple's staggered walk, for they were not words he was used to speaking.

Despite his awkwardness, the tears welled in her eyes and slipped down her cheeks. She wiped them away and returned to her seat. "There was a time when you were gentler in speech," she said as she sleeved another tear from her face and sniffled.

Hakon reclaimed his own perch. Her directness recalled so many conversations they had shared together as teenagers. How often had she asked questions no one dared ask, or spoken words that cut to the bone? It was part of what made her so unique, and so attractive. "I do not deny that, Astrid. I have commanded people too long. I am afraid my skill with delicacy has dulled a bit." His eyes scanned the rippling sea-lane far beneath them. "What I meant to say is that you are welcome at Avaldsnes, come what may. I understand if you do not accept the offer, but know that the offer stands and that are you always welcome."

Her silence stretched for so long that Hakon finally looked over at her to see whether she had heard his words. She, too, kept her eyes on the waterway below, though she gazed upon it with eyes filled, and cheeks glistening, with more tears. Hakon turned back to the water and left her to her sadness.

Finally, she whispered, "Thank you, Hakon."

Later, when they had returned, Hakon called Tosti and Sigurd to him. They met alone in the hall, which had been cleansed of the previous night's feast but not purged of the lingering odors. Hakon relaxed in the lord's seat at the head of the hall and gazed at the two men before him. Sigurd rested with his shoulder on one of the hall's columns, picking at his nails casually with his knife. Hakon held his tongue and sipped from his cup. It was a tactic he had learned from other leaders to make men feel uncomfortable, and it worked. Tosti's bloodshot eyes shifted uncertainly from Hakon to Sigurd as he waited for one of the men to speak.

"Well?" Tosti finally asked. "Are we just to stand here looking at each other? I beg your pardon, my lords, but I have other things to do."

Hakon sat upright, then rested his elbows on his knees and stared at Tosti. He kept his face expressionless as his eyes wandered over the warrior, as if trying to determine something. Tosti shifted his feet and glanced over at Sigurd, who had not lifted his head from his grooming.

Finally, Hakon spoke. "With Jarl Tore gone, we need to look to the welfare of his fylke. In particular, we need to find someone who can lead the people. Sigurd here," he motioned to his friend and counselor, "believes that person should be you."

Tosti nodded to Sigurd in thanks, though the uncertainty had not left his face, for it was clear he sensed that there was more in Hakon's words and he knew not what those words would hold for him.

"I have decided to give the jarldom of More to Sigurd instead."

Tosti's brows bent toward his old, broken nose. "May I ask why?"

"You may. The law demands that the jarldom should go to Tore's closest kin. One of his brothers. But those brothers are off seeking their own fame elsewhere and have not returned here for many winters. Is that not so?"

Tosti nodded at that.

"So, Sigurd is Tore's son-in-law and now the closest and most powerful kin Tore has in the area." Tosti opened his mouth to speak, but Hakon stayed him with a raised finger. "But Sigurd is not of this place and he has the Tronds to rule. Which brings me to you. I want you to rule in Sigurd's name here in More."

Hakon let the words settle on Tosti and work their way into his head.

Tosti responded by scratching his grizzled cheek. "So," he said after a time. "I am to be Sigurd's man?"

"Aye," said Hakon firmly. Sigurd peeked sidelong at Tosti.

"I do not wish to sound ungrateful, or to offend Jarl Sigurd," Tosti motioned to the jarl, "but why not just make me jarl and make me your man?"

"It is a fair question," Hakon answered as he glanced at the wily Sigurd, who had known this question would come and glanced at Hakon. Amusement danced in the old jarl's eyes, even if his face betrayed nothing. Hakon ignored him. "Here is why. Let us imagine that you were jarl and that war came suddenly to More. How many swords and spears could you muster?"

Tosti's brow furrowed again. It was unclear whether he perceived an insult in the question or he was just trying to calculate the answer to Hakon's question. Either way, Hakon answered for him.

"The answer is, not enough." Hakon continued before the older man could say anything. "With no legitimate claim, men might soon challenge you for Tore's seat. I am too far away to lend ready assistance. Sigurd is closer, but why should he fight for you if you are not his man? By giving Sigurd the jarldom — a man, I might add, who is kin to Tore and therefore has claim to Tore's seat — I seek to quell the fighting before it happens, make you the most powerful man in More, and give you Sigurd's army to call upon. In return, Sigurd and his men will back none of your rivals, should they come looking for support. You will live like a jarl in all but name."

Tosti scratched at his beard again. "And if I decline? What then?"

"Then you are on your own." Which was a gentle way of saying that Hakon would take the fylke for himself if he had to. Those were hard words, but Hakon needed to say them just as Tosti needed to hear them. Given its position along the northward sea-lane, it was too important an area to be ruled by a possible adversary. For the sake of the entire kingdom, Hakon needed a man in More he could trust.

Tosti nodded. "I will think upon it, and discuss it with my men, for this decision will affect them too."

"Do so quickly, Tosti," responded Hakon. "I must leave soon."

In the end, Tosti and his men chose the wiser path and bent their heads to Sigurd's knee. To celebrate the new bond, the warriors feasted yet again. Only this time, Hakon declared that the hall belonged to Tosti — a gift for his fealty to Sigurd. The men cheered Hakon's generosity and Tosti's luck, though luck had little to do with it. For his part, Tosti blushed and bowed deeply to Hakon in thanks.

"Come," Hakon called to the old warrior with laughter on his lips. "Sit beside me and gaze out at your new hall."

Tosti climbed onto the dais and sat to the right of Hakon in the seat of honor — a seat that Hakon had purposefully left empty. "You leave me without words," Tosti said into Hakon's ear so that only Hakon could hear it over the din.

Hakon clasped the old warrior's shoulder and raised his cup to him. "I wish you nothing but happy times in this hall, Tosti!"

Tosti said something in return, but Hakon did not hear it, for Sigurd, who sat on Hakon's left, had nudged him.

"There is one thing still undone, my lord." He gestured with his chin to his son, Sigge, who sat on the opposite side of the hall, laughing at some comment one of his own men had made.

"Did you ever think that I would refuse your request, Sigurd?"

Sigurd grinned through his beard. "The thought had crossed my mind."

"I will take your lad, though my words of caution remain. It might be best for you to reinforce my words with your own. Speak to him before you bring him to me."

"That I will do," Sigurd said. "Skol!"

"Skol!" Hakon toasted to seal the deal, and drank so deeply from his cup that he belched.

Hakon and his men departed two days later under a sheet of solid gray clouds. It was morning and the wind blew southward. Howled, really. It had picked up the previous night and now churned the fjord into a frenzy of whitecaps and salty spray, bringing with it an annoying drizzle that fell sideways across the landscape and soaked the clothes and hair of the men who had gathered on the beach to say their farewells.

"Like getting pissed on by the gods," Egil grumbled before barking a command at young Sigge and his men, who had been tasked with loading *Dragon* and struggled under the weight of a water barrel they were hoisting onto the deck. "Use your damn muscles! You there," he shouted at Sigge, who was coiling rope near the foredeck. "Drop the damn rope and help your men!"

Sigge hastened to the aid of his friends, and hauled the barrel over *Dragon*'s gunwale with a grunt. But in the midst of his hauling, he lost his grip on the barrel's rain-slickened handle and it dropped awkwardly to the deck. Thankfully, the lid was sealed tightly enough to stay on, despite the fall.

"Careful, you lout!" Egil roared.

"Egil's enjoying this as much as Sigge is hating it," remarked Hakon as he watched the exchange from the beach.

Beside him, Sigurd smiled at the comment. "My son has much work to do to get on Egil's good side."

"Good side? Think you that Egil has a good side?" Hakon said through his own smile. "If that is what your son seeks, then he may as well give up and go home."

Sigurd barked a laugh and patted Hakon on his shoulder. "Ah, Hakon. It has been good to see you these past few days, my friend."

Hakon turned and clasped his friend's forearm. "And you, Sigurd."

Sigurd grew suddenly serious and pulled Hakon in closer. "Drangi tells me that there is strife awaiting you. Much strife." His eyes searched Hakon's face for a reaction. "Fare safely."

Hakon scowled. He did not appreciate such portents of danger before setting sail. "Tell that dwarf to keep his lips tight. God alone controls my fate." Hakon softened his tone, for he did not wish to leave his friend with a rebuke. "Worry not, Sigurd. I will be back as soon as I am able. In the meantime, keep your eye on More."

Hakon sensed movement to his right and turned to see Astrid, who had stopped a few feet away. Hakon went to her and reached out his hand. She took it in her own and peered out from beneath the sodden hood of her cloak.

"I hope your affairs get settled to your liking," he said formally, lamely.

She smiled sadly and nodded. "As do I."

"My offer stands, Astrid. You need only ask."

The pain in her eyes clutched Hakon's throat, forcing him to swallow in order to breathe. She squeezed his hand, but spoke no words.

"I shall see you again soon, I hope," he said, then turned away and gazed through foggy eyes at *Dragon*.

There was so much of him that wanted to stay, and yet he knew he must go, for he sensed in his gut that a storm of steel was coming, and there was much to be done before it arrived.

Chapter 5

A storm hit four days south of Frei. Only this storm brought no rain, or lightning, or thunder. Nor did it bring shields, or swords, or spears. It brought a biting wind that howled northward over the water and whipped the seas into a rolling frenzy that bent *Dragon*'s strakes and crashed relentlessly against her hull. The ship would rise precariously on the swells, then plunge into the frothing sea troughs. With each dip, cold, gray ocean washed over the gunwales and across her deck, filling her holds and dousing the warriors struggling at the oars. Two of Sigge's men worked fruitlessly belowdecks, bailing water that would just as quickly wash back into the holds.

"We need shelter," called Toralv above the wind. He stood at the steer board, struggling to keep the ship's prow heading into the swells.

Hakon pointed to the high-cliffed promontory that towered over the sea in the near distance. "We head for the bay at Stad," he yelled back, meaning the bay on the opposite side of the mighty headland.

Though their destination was not far from their current position, it took them most of the afternoon to round the headland and enter the protection of the bay's high cliffs. As soon as they did, the scream of the wind softened to a whistle and the seas flattened beneath *Dragon*'s hull. The sodden crew slumped at their oars, exhausted from their efforts but relieved to be safe.

"This is Eldgrim's land, is it not?" Seawater dripped from Toralv's hair and clothes as he gazed about.

"Aye," responded Hakon as he brushed his sopping hair from his eyes and scanned the rugged cliffs that rose on either side of the bay. Eldgrim had been a warrior in Tore's hird, whom Tore had rewarded with this land for his service. Hakon remembered the warrior from a battle long ago, and from some legal trouble with his son some summers back. Hakon had banished the son for murdering a neighbor, a verdict Eldgrim had protested. The memory made Hakon wonder if time had softened Eldgrim's ill feelings about that event, or if they would find a sour welcome at the warrior's hall.

A broad beach lay deep within the bay. As *Dragon* drew near it, a line of warriors — mayhap a dozen in all — hastily formed to greet them. They were a disheveled, poorly armored lot who shifted nervously as Hakon climbed to the high prow.

"I come seeking Eldgrim, and shelter," he called to the group.

"And who are you?" asked a man from the center of the line. Of the group, he was the best armored and their obvious leader.

"I am your king," called Hakon, making sure to project the annoyance in his voice. He was tired and wet and cold, and in no mood to prove his identity. "Who are you?"

"King Hakon?"

"Is there another king you serve?"

The man turned to a younger warrior, who raced back toward a large hall that lay inland from the beach. "I am Knut," the man called back to Hakon. "I am the leader of Eldgrim's hird."

"You will not be the leader much longer if you do not let us land our ship and warm ourselves."

"Very well," Knut said after a long pause. "Land your ship and come ashore, King Hakon. I shall take you to Eldgrim."

"How very kind of him," hissed Asmund, whose lips were blue from the cold.

"I will land my axe in his skull," grumbled Bjarke. "Who does he think he is?"

Hakon waved them silent and ordered the crew to remove *Dragon*'s prow beast, lest they upset the land spirits. The men rowed *Dragon* forward until its keel slid across the pebbled beach and came to a halt some twenty paces from the greeting party. Hakon instructed Sigge and his men to make camp and to move the stores to land. He then gathered Egil and Toralv to him and disembarked.

Knut met them on the beach. He was a grizzled man not much younger than Hakon, with a vicious scar that disfigured his cheek and pulled the corner of his left eye down toward his scruffy beard. He was lucky to have survived such a blow. The warrior nodded to the king and his men, then escorted them to the door of the hall, where Eldgrim met them.

Despite his graying hair, Eldgrim was thick in his chest and gut, and not yet hunched in his shoulders. His arms looked strong enough to squash a man's skull in his grip. His eyes regarded Hakon and his men dourly. "It has been many moons since last we saw each other, my king." Eldgrim extended his thick arm, exposing the wicked scar he had received in the sea battle against Thorgil and Ragnvald nearly two decades before, when Eldgrim had fought in Tore's hird to help Hakon seal his rule of the North.

Hakon enveloped the scarred forearm in his tight grip. "Since we fed Thorgil and his army to the crabs."

A snarl-like grin appeared in Eldgrim's beard — a bushy affair streaked with orange strands — then just as quickly vanished. "What brings you to Shadow Haven?" It was a fitting name, thought Hakon, for a hall that stood in the shadow of cliffs and rarely felt the sun's warmth upon its thatch. "Has my son done something again?"

The suddenness of the question, and the bitterness in Eldgrim's tone, set Hakon on guard. "I have no word of your son. We seek only a place to escape the winds and the high seas," Hakon explained, and gestured to his wet clothes. "We were at Jarl Tore's estate and were making our way home when the winds picked up."

Eldgrim cast his eyes to the sky as if he could see the howling wind, then turned his hard gaze on Hakon. "I have not forgiven you for banishing my son, King Hakon. Nevertheless, I was Tore's man, and he was oath-sworn to you. And so for that reason, I invite you inside to eat and warm yourself by my hearth. Your men," he gestured toward the beach, "can make camp on my shores. Knut, see that we lend them the assistance they need."

Hakon nodded his thanks and followed the old warrior into his hall, which was musty and dark. Mayhap once it had been filled with light and the bluster of young warriors and young life, but that life was gone. Now, cobwebs dangled from the smoke-darkened beams over Hakon's head, wiggling in the drafts that snuck through the aging thatch. Flames sputtered in the few metal sconces set about the interior, casting a muted glow on the old beams and the furs that carpeted the wall platforms. Dry rushes crunched underfoot as they followed their host to the center of the hall where a small hearth fire crackled.

Eldgrim clapped his hands and from the dark corner of the hall, a thrall woman appeared. She was young and clearly nervous. "Hilde, fetch my guests some of my best ale and some of the stew you have been warming. Quickly now."

"We will not trouble you for long, Eldgrim," Hakon said as he sat near the hearth and held his cold hands to the flame. Toralv and Egil found stools and sat down beside him.

Eldgrim pulled up a stool and sat across the fire from Hakon, whose sodden clothes had already started to steam with the warmth. "As you can see," he said, sweeping his thick arms around him, "we get very few visitors, but it should suit your needs for now." He leaned forward then, right arm on his knee. "You say you came from Tore's? I did not see you there."

Hakon looked at his men, then back at his host. "We came late to his estate. I would have liked to pay my respects when they buried him, but it was not possible to get there in time. I heard his funeral was a ceremony to befit a king, and I am sorry I missed it."

Hilde arrived then with the ale and offered a cup to her master. His face stiffened. "Woman! It is our guests you should be serving first, not me." He nearly backhanded the cup from her hand before catching himself and relaxing. She moved quickly from Eldgrim and proffered a cup to Hakon, who took it with a nod of thanks.

"You must excuse my thrall. She is yet young."

"I take no offense," said Hakon as he wiped the rim of the cup with his fingers to remove the dust that was lingering there. "Anyway, I would have liked to have been there. Jarl Tore was a great man and deserved every ounce of praise and celebration."

Eldgrim took his cup from Hilde and held it up. "To the memory of Tore. May he be celebrating with his shield-brothers in Valhall as we speak. Skol."

Hakon ignored the reference to the hero's heaven of the Northmen and took a sip of his ale, which was strong but sour. He swallowed it with effort.

"Good, eh?" asked Eldgrim, meaning the ale.

Toralv grunted and raised his cup. Egil acted as if he had not heard, leaving Hakon to answer for them all. "It is strong." Which was true, and about the only honest answer Hakon could give.

Eldgrim was about to respond when the door to Shadow Haven burst open and a young warrior stormed in with Knut by his side. They strode to the fire and bowed to their lord. The younger man's cheeks were ruddy and wind-chapped, his dark hair tangled. His watering eyes darted from Eldgrim to his guests. It was clear he had never met his king, though he did have the good sense to recognize the stature of the guests by their clothing, and so nodded his greeting to them before turning back to his lord.

"Begging your pardon, Lord Eldgrim. Another ship is coming into the bay."

Eldgrim's right brow cocked. "A warship?"

"Aye."

Eldgrim turned to Hakon. "Were you expecting anyone?" Suspicion laced Eldgrim's words, but Hakon ignored it. The older man was right to be cautious. Hakon would do the same.

Eldgrim's eyes moved back to his warrior. "It is a strange wind indeed that brings two warships in one day to our shores. Knut," he said to the leader of his retinue, "go see what this ship wants, but leave the scouts on the bluffs in place. Let us make sure there are no others."

"Toralv, go with Knut," ordered Hakon. "If there is foul play, let us add our muscle to the shield wall. Get the men into their byrnies." Hakon knew his champion, and knew well that things had been a little quiet for him lately.

As if in answer to that thought, Toralv set his ale aside and unfurled his huge frame from his seat. "Gladly," he quipped as he joined Eldgrim's men and left the hall.

Egil made to rise too, but Hakon stayed him with a hand. "Not you. I want you here with me."

Egil reclaimed his seat with a muffled curse. He might have been old, but he still relished the thrill of fighting, and preferred it far more to meaningless banter by a hearth fire.

"You mentioned your son. Have you not heard from him, Eldgrim?"

Hakon had exiled the young troublemaker, Olaf Eldgrimsson, from the North five summers before for the murder of another man. His exile had caused quite a stir in these parts, and had angered Eldgrim mightily. The mention of him now stopped Eldgrim in mid guzzle.

"I heard he joined your brother, Erik." Eldgrim grinned as he let the words settle on Hakon. "That was several summers ago, before Erik fell."

The news did not come as a surprise. Many disenfranchised young men had done the same, seeking fame in the ranks of exiled lords like Erik, where many of their friends and relations also fought. It was a story he had heard many times before, and so he kept his expression even as Eldgrim relayed the news to him.

The old lord shrugged. "I know not where he is now, or if he yet lives."

"Do you think he could be fighting with Erik's sons now?"

The older man looked from Hakon to Egil, then back again, his eyes narrowing beneath his unruly brows. "And if he is?"

"Erik's sons have designs on my realm and are even now plying the waters of the Vik and the Eastern Sea, gaining fame and gathering men to them. If your son fights with them, that could complicate loyalties," responded Hakon, keeping his tone mild. "I do not like complication where loyalties are concerned."

Eldgrim's face soured at the implied threat. He had not the men to defend himself against the king, and Hakon knew it. Still, Hakon had little intention of fighting the man. He merely wanted Eldgrim to know that he was watching.

Hakon guzzled the remainder of his ale with effort, banged the cup on the nearby eating board, then rose to his feet. "Come. Let us turn our attention to other things. There is a ship approaching. Let us see what they want."

The three men exited the dark hall and strode toward the beach, where Hakon's men had armored themselves and stood in a rough shield wall alongside Eldgrim's men. The wall blocked Hakon's view, though he could see the ship's sweeping prow above their heads. Hakon pushed his way through the warriors and stopped cold. For there, coming toward them, was his own ship, *Sea Snake*.

Toralv glanced at his king. "Egbert stands in the prow."

Hakon could just make out the shock of red hair. His presence here twisted Hakon's stomach, for it could only mean ill tidings.

"Who is Egbert?" Eldgrim asked.

Hakon did not answer, but instead waited for *Sea Snake* to land and for the priest to leap to the shore. "What news?" he asked Egbert before the priest had even reached him.

Egbert dripped seawater from head to toe, and his skin bore the pale hue of seasickness. He smiled weakly and lifted his arms wide. "By the holy grace of God. It is truly a miracle that we have found you." The silver cross that hung from his neck glinted in the pale afternoon light.

"A Christian priest?" Eldgrim blustered. "What is this?"

"What news?" Hakon asked again, louder this time. He was in no mood to hear of miracles or placate men who had no space in their small thoughts for other deities.

Egbert's arms dropped to his side, and his face turned serious. His eyes scanned the expectant faces in the shield wall. It was clear he did not want to speak his words before so many.

Hakon cared little for such formalities — the men would know soon enough. "Out with it, Egbert," he barked a bit too angrily.

"The news is dire, my lord. Erik's sons are on the move. Their army came from the land of the Danes and attacked the Vik." The helmsman of *Sea Snake*, Eskil, and some of the crew came up from the ship to join Egbert as he delivered his message. "By the time we heard of it," Egbert continued, "the army was heading west around Agder."

Hakon cursed. He had suspected that something like this might happen. He had felt it in his gut. And now it had come to pass, and he was powerless to do much about it. From Agder, Erik's son could reach Avaldsnes in two days' sail on a good wind, which meant they were probably already there. It would take Hakon a hard five or six days more just to reach Avaldsnes, longer if the northward wind persisted. By the time he reached Avaldsnes, there might be nothing to return to.

"You are well met, lord," called Eskil. He was a tall, thin man who had spent much of his life at sea, and it showed in the deep creases of his leathery skin.

"How large is the army, Eskil?"

The lines of Eskil's face seemed to deepen. "We have heard varying reports, lord. Anywhere from ten to fifteen ships."

Which was not a massive fleet, but it was large enough to ravage the area. And Avaldsnes. "What of Gyda and Thora?"

Eskil shook his head and the deep lines on his face deepened even more. "I know not, lord. Ottar sent us to find you as soon as we heard the news. He wished me to bring Egbert. I did not ask why."

"Did he alert the other lords in the area?" This question came from Egil.

"Aye. He sent men to alert them, and to ask them to send warriors to protect Avaldsnes."

"Do the locals head to Avaldsnes?" Hakon asked with alarm. It took time to gather an army, and the possibility of them arriving at Avaldsnes after Erik's sons was high. They would be butchered if they came upon the camped army of Erik's sons one ship at a time.

"The men of Karmoy are to come to Avaldsnes at all haste," Eskil interjected quickly. "Those from other areas are to evade Erik's sons at all cost and to gather at Hollkoppevik, north of the Karmsund Strait."

Hakon breathed a little easier. Hollkoppevik was a wise choice, for the inlet lay far off the coast in a cluster of rocky islands. Unless you hailed from Rogaland or southern Hordaland, you probably had no idea it even existed. Which meant the men could gather in safety, if they could get away from their homes before Erik's ships found them.

"Ottar is staying at Avaldsnes," Eskil continued solemnly. "He will hold it as long as he can."

Hakon grimaced, for the news was both welcome and bitter. Ottar had always been a clever man and a brave one. Now those two attributes would pit him against Erik's sons and their vastly superior numbers in order to give Hakon enough time to gather his own army. The king's eyes moved to Egil, for Ottar was Egil's nephew, and his loss at the hands of Erik's sons — men Egil had told Hakon to kill after Erik's defeat winters ago — would cut Egil deeply. The old man's eyes bored into Hakon. He then turned without a word, hobbled his way through the crowd, and disappeared.

Hakon felt the pain of Egil's silent rebuke, but there was no time to dwell on it. He turned back to his host. "What say you, Eldgrim? We sail south as soon as we can. We could use you and your men in this fight."

Eldgrim scratched at the gray hair hiding his jowls. "As you can see, my lord, I am no longer the warrior I once was. Winters ago, you could count on me to bring a warship to Tore's service filled with spear-warriors. Now, save for a few younger sons in my hird, my warriors are aging, as am I."

Hakon sensed the man was building a case to decline, and pressed him. "That may be true. But I also know your abilities, and those of your men, which is why I ask."

Eldgrim's gray brows slanted down toward his nose, and for a long moment he remained silent. "I was no friend of Erik's, which is why I threw my lot in with Tore. But now both men are dead. I have no quarrel with Erik's sons. And if my son fights alongside them, I would not wish to see him across the field from me."

"That sounds like a no to me," Toralv grumbled.

"It is a no," Eldgrim agreed icily.

The champion snorted. "You will be wishing it was an aye, lord, if Erik's sons win the day and come looking for their father's enemies."

Hakon, too, was displeased. "Forget him, Toralv. Eldgrim has his reasons, and he is his own man. As for us," Hakon raised his voice so his crew could hear, "wind or no wind, we leave on the morrow, at first light, for Hollkoppevik. Make camp here tonight and get your rest. We will need it for the journey south." Hakon then turned back to his host. "If you change your mind, you and your men are welcome on my ship."

Eldgrim sneered. "I will not be changing my mind. Erik was a bastard, but you banished my son, and now the Norns have tangled our threads and forced me to make a decision. I will come see you off in the morning."

Hakon struggled to keep his emotions in check. "Do not bother."

Eldgrim nodded curtly to his king. "As you wish." He then departed with his men.

"I do not trust that man," said Eskil when Eldgrim was out of earshot.

"Nor do I," responded Toralv. "Mayhap we should burn him in his hall tonight before we end up facing *him* in a shield wall." Several of Hakon's men grunted in agreement.

"We will do nothing of the sort," Hakon said with finality. "He has given us safe harbor and a beach on which to camp. Post guards tonight. If there is any sign of trouble, we will retaliate."

Toralv nodded, while Egbert crossed himself.

As the men saw to their tasks, Hakon remained in his spot, chewing on the dismal realities and questions and worries that accosted his mind as if they were a piece of gristly meat. Hakon was glad of only one thing: the wait was over. Erik's sons had finally come. On the morrow, Hakon and his men would sail for home, and for battle.

Chapter 6

Six days after leaving Stad on their southward journey, the low, dark islands of Hollkoppevik came into view on the horizon. They were nothing more than a group of jagged, sea-battered skerries painted white with bird shit, but they brought a smile to Hakon's face nevertheless.

It had been a mentally and physically difficult journey south. The strong southerly that had forced them to seek shelter at Shadow Haven continued for half the voyage. Though they were able to navigate the network of channels that defined the western coast of the North, it did little to protect them from the swells or the wind that hammered their hulls. It often felt as if the men pulled at the oars only to ensure they did not glide backward in the water. At night, they lay at anchor in whatever bay they could find to get out of the howling gales and preserve what little progress they had made during the day. They could light no fires, nor could they converse much in the maelstrom. Not that they had the energy to, or the desire. After a day at the oars, most of the men ate what stockfish they could stomach, then covered themselves as best they could to rest.

Hakon sensed there was something more, though it remained unspoken — a heaviness that weighed on their spirits. If they felt anything like Hakon felt, then they too would be feeling that aching eagerness to reach their loved ones and that nagging feeling that the weather, or mayhap something greater, was working against them.

He spoke of it to no one, for they, like him, would never admit to it; like them, he bore the ache in silence and prayed for the weather and their luck to turn.

Three days into their southward journey, they awoke to a wind that had finally shifted in their favor. With a cheer, the crews hoisted their sails, thanking the gods for the sudden reprieve. Like the wind, the mood on board suddenly changed, and so it was with renewed energy and lighter spirits that they fared down the channels for three more days and out into the open sea where the low islands of Hollkoppevik lay in the distance.

Now, *Dragon* and *Sea Snake* approached Hollkoppevik from the northeast. As they drew closer, Hakon ordered the sails furled, for the currents swirled heavily here and were too much for the helmsmen alone. Oars were the only way to counter that force and keep their ships from slamming against the skerries.

"There!" called Toralv from the prow as he pointed to the channel that would take them into the bay they sought. The channel was little more than a tear in the landscape only slightly wider than twice the breadth of *Dragon*'s hull. Eskil, who now helmed Hakon's ship, pulled hard on the steer board to align her with the swells that shot the channel. Behind them, *Sea Snake* followed *Dragon*'s lead.

A swell built under *Dragon*, carrying her swiftly toward the gap in the rocks. Hakon gripped the gunwale, for there was no coming about and no room for error.

"More to port!" Toralv called from the prow, gesturing frantically with his arms to the left.

"Oars in!" Eskil called as he made a slight adjustment on the steer board.

"More to port!" Toralv called again as the rocks grew before him.

Hakon held his breath, expecting at any moment to hear the crunch of wood against rock. But Eskil knew his craft and had judged the ocean correctly. At the last minute, a swell bounced off the island wall and rolled back at *Dragon*, shifting her slightly so that her prow dove into the rocky channel. Jagged slabs littered with mussels and seaweed sped by the ship's wooden hull. The gray ocean careened off of them and shot upward to either side, splashing the deck and dousing the men who held tight to the ship. And then they were through, and the ship slowed. But the danger was not yet over, for the swells continued to push them forward. If *Dragon* did not turn, she would slam against the small bay's far wall.

Eskil pushed hard on the steer board to turn *Dragon* southwest, away from the swells. "Port side! Oars down!" he called.

Those on the right side of the ship slid their oars into the sea and held mightily to their sweeps. Slowly, the warship responded and came about. As it did, the other ships came into view, and their crews cheered.

"God is good," said Egbert as they gazed upon the ships. He stood by Hakon's side with a wide grin on his face and his cross in his hand.

Hakon did not share Egbert's joy. Instead, he cursed softly as he looked at Toralv. The champion was looking back at his king, his face a mask of concern.

"What is it?" Egbert asked.

"It is not enough," grumbled Egil as he came to stand beside his king and the priest. He kept his voice low so the rest of the crew did not overhear.

"Not enough?" The priest looked from the old warrior to his king.

Hakon kept his eyes on the ships, tallying the numbers in his head. In all, there were eight ships, none of them large, which meant that if he were lucky, mayhap two hundred or so men had answered his call. And few would be hardened warriors like those in his own hird.

"There are not enough ships, which means there are not enough men," Hakon explained quietly to Egbert as *Dragon* glided forward and *Sea Snake* slid into the bay behind her.

"Surely more will come," Egbert said with alarm in his voice.

Hakon looked at him. "Keep your voice low," Hakon warned, then turned back to the scene before him. "When will they come, Egbert? In two days' time? Three? We cannot wait that long."

The joy that had graced Egbert's face moments before evaporated. "God will help us," he said.

Hakon grinned sardonically. Years ago, he would have believed those words without question. But he had seen enough in his life now to know that prayers often went unanswered. Still, it could not hurt to call upon God for help. "If you have some prayers to aid us, Egbert, now is the time to use them."

Three more ships arrived that night, but by then, it was clear to all that they could be sailing into poor odds. They'd originally planned to attack Avaldsnes head on from the Karmsund Strait, but now their numbers and their lack of information about the enemy force required a more deceptive strategy.

That night, Hakon called a meeting on his deck. The chieftains listened intently to their king's new plan, which he laid out in detail. He did not mince words or attempt to paint a favorable picture of what lay before them all. Rather, he stated the facts as much as they were known, and made it clear that they would be fighting for their homes.

"Return to your ships," he concluded with no ceremony, "and get some rest. We leave with the first gray of morning. Give your men a measure of ale tonight, but make sure they don't drink overmuch. The morrow will be a taxing day, and they will need their energy."

The chieftains returned to their ships to prepare for the coming day. Hakon surveyed his own crew, most of whom rested against the gunwales or their sea chests, working the rust from their byrnies or sharpening the blades of their various weapons. In the aft deck, Egbert's huddled form whispered prayers to Christ.

"What is *he* doing?" Sigge grumbled.

"Praying to his Christ God," answered Toralv as he ran his thumb along the edge of his axe.

Sigge scowled. "I would never —"

"Careful," Toralv warned with the lift of an eyebrow. "That is the king's priest, and we are the king's men. Any ill words you speak against the priest, you speak against us all."

Sigge glanced over at Hakon, who was sharpening his seax beside the praying Egbert, then back at Egbert. "I am just wondering why the king would allow such things. That is all. Seems to me we would all be better off praying to the true gods of battle."

"Says the boy who has never stood in the shield wall with this crew and his king," chided Bjarke. "Pray as you will, Sigge. No one is stopping you. But do so with this knowledge: we were winning battles before you were even born, lad. And with the Christian God at our backs, no less." This received a few "ayes" from the others.

Sigge frowned, but wisely let the matter drop and turned his attention back to his sword.

The moon was just beginning to sink in the western sky when the crews hauled in their anchors and rowed through the eastern channel. There was just enough light to see the dark swell of waves and the white spray of seawater as the ocean crashed against the skerry walls. At the end of the channel, the whitecaps frothed on the open sea. *Dragon* raced toward them, dipping and climbing on the swells until she poked her prow into the open ocean. Free of the danger, Eskil let the current and waves pull *Dragon*'s prow east, toward Karmoy, then called for the sail. The rest of the fleet followed.

They were headed for a deep bay on Karmoy's west coast called Vigsnes. At the bayhead sat a small fishing village, and from there it was an easy jog east to Avaldsnes. If the wind held, the ships would arrive before the moon disappeared on the horizon. It was what they needed. There was still a chance that enemy scouts might spot them, but Hakon doubted Erik's sons had been that cautious. And even if they had, it would take a few hours to alert the army and assemble it for battle on the western shore. By that time, Hakon and his men would be ashore and ready.

Darkness faded to a dull gray morning that revealed the waterway. It cut into Karmoy like a sword wound, digging deep into the countryside with jagged lines and rough islands painted white like bones from bird droppings. With the wind blustering in the bay, the fleet's crews furled the sails and took to their oars to better control their approach. The water here was shallow and filled with submerged rocks, so the ships sailed in single file with *Dragon* in the lead, accompanied by crying gulls awakened from their slumber by the intruders. In the prow, keen-eyed Bard guided the ship through the lurking dangers with hand signals. As he scanned the waters, Hakon studied the shoreline for enemy scouts. He saw none, but that didn't mean they were not there.

They reached the fishing village at the bayhead and back-rowed to a halt. The village was little more than a few small, dilapidated dwellings nestled beside several old boats upon which fishing nets lay. Save for a barking dog and some clucking chickens, the village was quiet.

"Get the men into their battle gear," Hakon whispered to Toralv.

Toralv nodded and moved among the men, passing along the order. Quietly, the warriors fished into their sea chests and shrugged into their byrnies. Several made last-minute inspections of their weapons. Hakon cinched his belt over his mail and looked over at the other crews to make sure they were doing the same. Satisfied, he motioned the ships forward.

The ships scraped onto the rocky shore just as a villager emerged from his hut. He spotted *Dragon* and, with a startled shout, retreated into the darkness of his dwelling and slammed the door.

"Bard!" called Hakon. "Tell the villagers who we are and why we have come. Swiftly. Before they sound the alarm."

Bard called to several men and the group poured over the gunwales in a flash of metal and shields, sprinting toward the huts.

"Egil!" Hakon called at the aging warrior as the other ships landed. "We are setting a fast pace. Take Sigge and his men and come as fast as you can behind us."

"The boy can go with you," he growled loud enough for Sigge to hear. "I can fend for myself."

Hakon crossed the deck to his friend, trying but failing to restrain his agitation. "It is not you I am worried about," Hakon whispered sharply. "I need someone to keep an eye on the young bucks. I do not want them racing to the battleground. And when we get there, I do not want them running around like headless chickens in their eagerness. Keep them together."

Egil grunted his understanding and hobbled off to organize Sigge and his men.

"You men will go with Egil," Hakon called over the old warrior's head to them.

"No!" Sigge called back. "You heard him. He can fend for himself. We march with you, King Hakon."

The entire crew stopped and glared at the youth.

"Do as your king asks, boy, or this crew and I will see you are fed to the crabs. Do you hear?"

Sigge and his followers marked the faces of the other warriors, and wisely nodded their understanding. But that did not stop the crew from tossing curses in Sigge's direction or sharing their own hard thoughts on the matter.

"Speak like that again to your king and you'll find yourself without a tongue," growled Bjarke.

"That would be an improvement," chuckled Asmund as he leaped over the gunwale.

"His lady friends will not think so," added Toralv, and the crew erupted in laughter.

Hakon left the men to their taunts and turned to the aft deck. "Egbert," he called to his priest.

"Lord?" Egbert acknowledged as he rose from his final prayers.

"Stay close to me. I will need you before the fight."

Egbert's eyes went wide. "Need me for what, exactly?"

"You shall see. Come."

With the village secure, the army set off down a track that stretched due east to Avaldsnes. In the far distance, the rising sun had not yet appeared above the Keel, though its soft glow illuminated the sky and the grassy fields through which they now marched. To the untrained eye, they strode in a giant clump of armed men. In reality, they marched in groups according to their allegiances. Silent. Grim. Determined. At their head walked Hakon and his household warriors, save for Egil, who brought up the rear with the disgruntled Sigge and his embarrassed crew. Hakon marched in plain sight. He did not try to mask the sounds of his army's approach. If the army of Erik's sons was as large as the reports suggested, then it would be camped in the meadows to the west of Hakon's estate. Hakon wanted that army to see him coming. He wanted it away from Avaldsnes, and away from the uneven ground that surrounded his estate.

"There." Toralv pointed with his axe.

Hakon stopped and peered ahead. Though his sight was not as sharp as his champion's, it was not difficult to spot the colored standards waving among the trees or the mass of tents that littered his land. Near the tents, dark shadows scurried like chased rats.

"They see us," Toralv said.

Hakon scanned the landscape. Where they stood was as flat as an eating board. About one hundred paces ahead, a cluster of pines bordered each side of the field through which the road passed, forming a natural alleyway about three hundred paces wide. Hakon pointed at it. "That is where we fight."

Hakon's army advanced and assembled between the pines, spreading out across the field so that the flanks reached to the trees on either side. Hakon turned back to the enemy camp, where a dark line of men now advanced. It was then that Hakon's heart began to thunder. He had fought in battles beyond count, and his body's reaction to an imminent fight never varied. This was the moment that tested a man's mettle. When the action had not yet started, and a man's nerves teetered. When reason told a man to run, and courage told him to fight. No amount of experience could ever quell the rising thrill and overwhelming dread of looming battle. One could only harness it and use it, and so Hakon breathed deeply of the morning air and welcomed the rush of battle blood to his veins.

"Their shields, lord," remarked Toralv.

Hakon focused his gaze, but at this distance, he could not distinguish what it was that Toralv saw.

"The mark of Tyr," Toralv added. "It is the shield we saw at Strommen in the Ostfold."

It came as little surprise. In fact, it only confirmed what they already knew — that Erik's sons were at Strommen and other sites besides. Hakon put the thought aside and called, "Egbert. Garth. To me!"

The priest and the warrior trotted to their king. Hakon spoke to them quietly, ignoring the apprehension in Egbert's eyes as he laid out his idea to them. The men nodded their understanding, bowed to their king, then retreated to the back of the shield wall.

Across the field, the sons of Erik and their vast army drew closer. They clearly outnumbered Hakon's men, though by just how much was still unclear. Hakon crossed himself, cast his eyes to the sky for a brief prayer, and for the briefest of moments wondered whether God concerned Himself with skirmishes like this or whether the pagan supplications mumbled by his warriors drowned out his own prayers.

"About two to one, I'd guess," stated Toralv, interrupting Hakon's thoughts.

"Even odds, then," quipped Bjarke, who stood nearby with a mild grin on his face.

Hakon smiled through his beard. Behind them, several of the other men chuckled as well, which was good — they would need their spirits this day.

"Come," Hakon said to Toralv. "Let us meet our foe and get the measure of them."

Toralv hefted his axe and followed his king. Neither man spoke, though each studied the advancing line closely. Like Hakon's army, they were broken into loose groups, each with a chieftain who marched at its head. Two banners flapped over the center group. One displayed the mark of Tyr on a light blue field; the other, a black axe on a red field. The mark of Bloodaxe.

The leader of the middle group raised his left hand and the army halted. Hakon and Toralv stopped and waited.

"Do you think Avaldsnes has already fallen?" asked Toralv suddenly.

It was a question Hakon had been considering for some time, but now he was more certain of the answer.

"If Avaldsnes was theirs, they would be standing on its walls, not marching out here in the open. No, Avaldsnes yet stands."

The leader of each group — four men in all — stepped from the enemy lines and strode toward Hakon and his champion. Hakon's mind tried and failed to reconcile the image of the boys who had left the North so long ago with the warriors who now approached him. They were men now. Gods of war in their glinting chain mail and leather breeks. None wore helmets yet, affording Hakon time to take in their features as they came closer.

The oldest, Gamle, walked a pace ahead of the others. He had become a bear of a man, his confident bearing so much like his father's. Unlike Erik, he had hair the color of chestnut, which was pulled back from his square face into a long braid. Above a well-groomed beard that hung to his chest, light, alert eyes regarded Hakon.

To his left strode a thinner, shorter man with raven-black hair and ice-blue eyes that darted left and right. Guthorm. The last time Hakon had seen him, his mother had been clutching his shoulders to keep him from protecting his brother Gamle from Toralv. To Gamle's right walked a scowling, heavyset man with ruddy cheeks and hair as red as his father's. His nose had been broken at some point and sat bulbous and bent in the middle of his round face. And to his right walked another man, this one also red-haired, but with a pale, freckled face and round, watchful eyes that put Hakon in mind of Egbert. Of the four, he seemed to be the only one scanning the enemy lines.

Erik's brood came to a halt ten paces from Hakon and eyed their uncle malignantly. The heavy man spat into the grass. Hakon ignored the gesture. "I am glad you have come, Uncle," called Gamle, though there was no welcome in his face.

"Long ago," Hakon said to them, "your father took the High Seat of this realm after murdering those of his brothers that he could. Ragnvald. Bjorn. Olav. Sigfrid. Did your father ever speak their names to you?"

Erik's brood stood mute.

"I thought not," said Hakon. "But you should know that after I defeated your father, my counselors begged me to kill him as he had killed his brothers. I refused. They urged me also to kill your mother and the lot of you. I refused again. Do you wish to know why? Because I wanted the kin killing to end." Hakon raked his eyes across the faces of his nephews. Judging from their dour expressions, none seemed to care much for his words. Hakon plowed ahead anyway. "My counselors knew you would come again. That Erik would poison your thoughts with words of hatred, despite having been given the chance at making a new life and a new kingdom elsewhere. In my heart, I knew too that you would come, but every day, I hoped you would not. Not because I feared you, but because I did not want to kill you."

Gamle snorted. "Fine words, Uncle. But it does not change what happened. You took what was our father's, and we have come to take it back. You also took something from me." He lifted his gnarled right hand. "I have dreamed of repaying you both since that foul day."

On the morning of Erik's departure from the North, Hakon had secured Erik's oath never to return by threatening to kill Gamle one stab at a time. Erik had capitulated after the first stab, which had ruined Gamle's hand.

"I should have taken both of your hands when I had the chance," Toralv called.

Gamle turned to the giant. "Today you shall have the chance, Toralv."

Hakon interrupted them, drawing the conversation back to his nephews. "So tell me, Gamle, should you be lucky enough to take back what you believe to be yours, who among you will rule? You are but seeds from your father's kin-killing loins. If I had to guess, I would say the lot of you will be fighting each other before my corpse has grown cold. Either that, or the Danes to whom you whore yourselves will take it from you as soon as you have done the dirty work of killing me."

"Enough of this banter, brother," the black-haired Guthorm cut in. "It is a waste of time."

Hakon turned his sharp gaze on the man. "Guthorm, is it?"

The man nodded.

"Tell me. Is the mind behind those blue eyes as short on intelligence as it is on patience? Will you not give your brother enough time to count my men, just as my champion counts yours?"

Gamle chortled and Guthorm flushed. Hakon made a mental note of the exchange as his eyes shifted to the handsome redhead.

"You must be Ragnfred?" Hakon asked the man.

"That is Ragnfred," the young man said, indicating the thicker fellow with the broken nose. "I am Harald."

Hakon shrugged, feigning indifference. "It will not matter to the worms."

The thickset Ragnfred spat toward Hakon again. "I will paint the grass red with your blood, Uncle."

Hakon turned his gaze on him. "I see you have inherited your father's temper, Ragnfred. Have you also inherited his battle prowess? Come, Toralv. We have heard enough. If these men fight like they speak, we have nothing to fear." Hakon turned his back on his nephews.

A rough sack landed with a thud in the grass beside Hakon and rolled to a stop near his feet. Hakon glanced back at Gamle, who had thrown it. "A gift for you, Uncle," called Gamle. "Go ahead. Open it."

Hakon motioned to Toralv, who picked up the sack and peered inside. His face contorted, as much from the stench as from the sight of whatever lay within it. Slowly, he reached into the sack and withdrew its contents. Hakon's heart froze, then sank, for staring at him through its sightless eyes was the head of Ottar.

Hakon swallowed his fury and stared back at his nephews. They must have seen the ire burning in his gaze, for they laughed then, purposefully adding fuel to Hakon's growing rage.

Hakon pointed his finger at Gamle. "As God is my witness, you shall pay in blood today for the death of this man."

Gamle's face hardened at Hakon's oath. "I wish I could tell you he died honorably," Gamle growled, "but alas, I cannot. He was just protecting your stupid bitch." He waved his arm over his head, and from the lines came two figures. Hakon squinted to see who these new people were that approached so awkwardly.

"No," Toralv whispered under his breath, and that one word was enough to stop the blood in Hakon's veins.

The two figures that neared were a warrior and a woman. Their awkwardness was due to the woman's clumsiness, for she was bound by rope at the wrists and ankles. A third rope ran from her neck to her master's hands. The woman's face was a mask of bruises and clotted blood, and she walked with a slight limp, but even so, there was no mistaking her. Gyda. The sight of her battered body brought on a wave of molten ire, guilt, and pity that threatened to drown Hakon with its force. For a long moment, he could do nothing but stare through eyes clouded with tears.

"I commend you on your taste in women," said Gamle, pulling Hakon from his shock. "I regret her mistreatment, but it could not be helped. Had she not fought us as we took our turns with her, we would have had no need for such violence." The brothers laughed at Gamle's words, but there was no mirth in Gamle's eyes. Only icy fury and hatred. "You see, Uncle, words are for prickless fools who have nothing to bring to the table." Gamle walked over to his warrior and grabbed the guiding rope from his hands. He then yanked it so hard that Gyda fell to her knees at Gamle's side. He stroked her hair delicately. "Would you like her back, Uncle?"

There was dried blood on her dress and legs, and the sight of it pierced Hakon's soul. Oh, how he wanted her back and yet, he knew it was not to be; that he would witness her death this day. "At what cost, nephew?"

"Simple. Take your army and leave, and I will let her go free."

"Do not do it!" Gyda slurred at Hakon. "Do not give these —"

Gamle's backhanded blow knocked Gyda to the ground before she could finish. Hakon made a move to save her, but the brothers drew their weapons and leveled them at their uncle. Gamle pulled the stunned woman to her feet again. She staggered to keep from falling.

"She has spirit, I'll grant her that!" he said with an edge of annoyance in his tone. "Now then. Shall we find out what she is worth to you, Uncle?"

Hakon knew he could never make such a deal, and that knowledge clawed at him. If he did not save her, what then? Would they keep her for themselves? Would they sell her into slavery? Would they kill her? And what of his unborn child? If it lived, what future would it have?

Hakon closed his eyes to calm himself. "Allow me to speak with my woman, Gamle?"

"As you wish," he said and stepped away, though he kept ahold of the neck line.

Hakon walked up to Gyda and lifted her downcast face. The visage that looked back at Hakon was both heartbreaking and horrifying. Her cheeks were swollen and purple, her eyes half shut from the beatings. Trickles of blood had coagulated at her left temple and on her lower lip. "There is no need for shame, Gyda," Hakon whispered, his eyes fixed on hers. "It is not your fault."

She nodded slightly. "I sought only to save Siv." A missing tooth and swollen lips slurred her words as a tear trickled from her eye and slid past her broken nose.

Hakon hardened his heart to her pain. "I know," he said, though he did not, for just how his thrall was involved in this affair was a mystery.

"Kill me," she whispered.

The words struck Hakon like a slap. "I cannot," he responded weakly, though he knew in his heart that he could not give her back to Gamle. She knew it too.

"Please. Do not let them take me. Do not let them take your son." Her whisper was desperate, yet resolute. Her tears came steadier. "Please."

He stared into her battered face and placed his left hand on her right shoulder, then bent his forehead to hers. "I am sorry," he whispered as their skin touched.

"Enough of this," Gamle grumbled.

Gyda did not waver. "Do it," she commanded and lifted her chin.

Quick as an adder, Hakon dropped his hand to his seax and pulled the blade free.

Gamle shouted and yanked on the neck line, but it was too late. Hakon's blade had found its mark and slashed across Gyda's throat. She fell backward with the force of Gamle's pull and landed in a heap on the grass. Dark blood rushed from her wound and pooled on the ground beside her.

"I am so sorry," Hakon whispered as the life slipped from her body and the tears welled in his eyes.

Gamle hastened to Gyda and knelt by her. Hakon stepped back from the shocked brothers, who stared at their uncle in disbelief. From Hakon's sorrow a dark fury rose, and he swept his gore-slickened blade at his nephews. "There will be no bargains with you. Ever." His voice came as a hiss through his clenched teeth.

Gamle stared at his uncle for a long moment. Hakon wanted to believe he was reassessing the man before him, seeing him perchance with new eyes that foretold a future of strife; that Hakon would not so easily give Erik's sons what they sought, especially now. In the end, though, Gamle chose to accept that challenge, for he nodded and rose to his feet as if coming to some sort of internal decision. "Very well, Uncle. It shall be blood, then. Come, brothers," he said and walked away, leaving Gyda where she lay.

Hakon waited for the brothers to retreat, then knelt by Gyda and closed her unseeing eyes with his hands. He signed the cross over her body in the small hope that the gesture would hasten her soul to Heaven. Carefully, he picked her up and walked back to Toralv, who eyed his king with an unreadable expression. "Bring Ottar's head with us," Hakon snarled as he lumbered past his champion and back to his army.

"What happened?" It was Egil who asked the question. The old man had just arrived with Sigge's men and was sweating from exertion, but alert and ready just the same. Around him, others looked on, but none had the courage to speak up, for most had seen Hakon kill his woman and feared the stony expression on their king's face.

"I will explain later," responded Hakon bitterly. He nodded to his champion. "Show him, Toralv."

The champion withdrew the sack's contents and showed it to Egil. The old warrior stared at the decapitated head of his nephew, and as he did, his face transformed from recognition to anger and then to sadness. Behind him, some of the other men looked away, unable to gaze on the foul remains of their comrade.

"I am sorry, Egil," Hakon offered, though his apology sounded more like a curse, for he could not keep the rage from dripping off his words.

Egil tore his eyes from Ottar's head and fastened them on Gyda's corpse. "The bastards will pay for this," he growled. He then took Ottar's hair from Toralv's hands and held the head high for Hakon's hirdmen to see. "See what they have done to Ottar?" he yelled. "See what they have done to Gyda? See what they will do to us if we do not fight like giants today?" He hobbled a few paces down the line of warriors. "They will pay for what they have done! They will pay in blood!"

The warriors cheered Egil, and as they did, Hakon handed Gyda's body to Sigge. "Take her to the rear, Sigge."

The young lord accepted the burden from his king without a word and retreated through the lines.

"They will pay!" roared Egil again.

"They will pay!" echoed Hakon as he raised his seax in the air, and others took up the cheer. "They will pay! They will pay!" The chant rippled down the army's lines, amplified by a thunder of blades on shield rims that stoked the beat of Hakon's own heart, calling him forward to the clash of steel. Hakon took up a position in the middle of the line and ran his eyes along the enemy force. His nephews would pay this day for their greed and their misguided thirst for vengeance. They would pay for Ottar and Gyda and for their invasion. He would send them whimpering like whipped hounds back to their ships and their Danish masters.

Hakon slipped his helmet onto his head, his hands shaking with battle lust, and adjusted it so that the nose plate sat comfortably against his skin. He then grabbed Toralv's thick arm. "I have a plan, Toralv. Listen carefully."

Toralv moved his ear closer to his king's mouth so that he could hear Hakon over the rising din. The big man nodded his understanding when Hakon finished his thoughts. "It might work," he offered, "if the gods are with us."

"It must work," Hakon said firmly, for the lots were cast and it was too late to back out now. The warriors were shouting for blood, and the blades would soon sing. His plan had to work.

Chapter 7

The battle began like so many others.

First, there was movement as the leaders organized their men and built the line according to strength and experience and weaponry. Stronger, more skilled, and better armored warriors took up positions in the front rank, guarded on either side by the men they trusted most to keep them alive. The less experienced and poorly geared warriors took up positions in the second rank. Too old now for the shield wall, Egil stood fifty paces behind the lines with Sigge's small troop. As the most experienced man on the field, it would be up to him to reinforce ranks with Sigge and his men if certain areas faltered.

Once positioned, spiritual and practical preparation came next. Men tightened loose straps and tested the sharpness of blades as they mumbled final prayers to whatever god would listen. In Hakon's army, that included their king's Christ God now. He had not failed them yet.

Hakon inhaled, then exhaled deeply to steel the nerves that churned his guts and gripped his heart. As a young man, he had struggled to control his nerves. Now he welcomed them, and used them to fuel the battle frenzy that would sustain him when the shields crashed and the blades sang. He tightened the grip on his seax and waved it over his head. "Forward!" he yelled. "For Ottar! For Gyda!"

His army took its first step toward battle, and their chant reached a new level of fervor as men dug within themselves for the courage to face the blades of their enemy. Across from them, the enemy line did the same, their shouts and yells and shield-pounding adding to the chaos of the morning.

Hakon studied the lines advancing across from him. The Tyr warriors came on smartly in the army's center, their shields tight and their footsteps aligned. Farther out on the flanks, a few undisciplined gaps opened. It was as Hakon had expected.

Hakon turned his head to Toralv and yelled, "Now!"

Toralv and twenty handpicked men stopped their approach and let the army advance past them. Once in the rear, they moved to the right, then worked their way to the front ranks again, directly across from Guthorm's men. It was there that discipline was weakest. With luck, the might of Toralv and his troops would break them quickly and shatter the resolve of the army.

At one hundred paces distant, the arrows began to fly. Though bowmen weren't numerous, especially in Hakon's army, there were enough to harass the men on both sides. Hakon waited for the arrows to begin their downward flight before calling the warning and dropping to a knee. His men followed his example. At the same time, the second row stepped forward and raised their shields above the first, forming a ceiling that the arrows pelted with their deadly staccato.

Hakon waited a few heartbeats, then rose. "Forward!"

On the second volley, an arrow thunked into Hakon's shield, its head poking through the wood, a reminder of how close death was to him and to them all. As if to echo that thought, somewhere along the line a man hollered in pain. Hakon rose and cut the shaft away with his seax.

The spears followed the arrows. Near Gamle, a helmeted warrior broke from the ranks and launched his spear. The shaft arced through the sky and landed with a dull thud several paces in front of Hakon. Hakon's man Asmund had seen the spearman make his move and timed his own throw moments after the enemy cast his shaft. Asmund's spear took the enemy warrior in the upper chest just as he turned and reclaimed his place in the front line. The man dropped and a cheer rippled down Hakon's line.

Up and down the ranks, the shield beating gave way to the cries of men, though it was no longer possible to discern cries of pain from the curses cast at the enemy. In moments, the shield walls would meet, and then chaos would reign. A cold calm washed over Hakon as he sought his first victim. Gamle was off to Hakon's left, so Hakon settled on a young man whose tawny hair shot from under his dented helmet like straw. Hakon thought he recognized him but did not have the time to try to place him in his memory, for the enemy was coming fast.

The shield walls met and the air thundered with the clash of wood and metal and shouts. The young man slammed into Hakon, momentarily lifting him from his feet. Behind Hakon, a spearman thrust his weapon at Hakon's assailant and the man ceased pushing. Hakon's feet found purchase, and he put his shoulder into his shield, stabbing with his seax through the momentary gaps that opened in the wall. His blade scraped something but came away bloodless.

An axe blade hooked the top rim of Hakon's shield. Instinctively, he ducked as the axe pulled and an enemy blade stabbed, poking the air where Hakon's face should have been. Hakon saw an exposed leg before him and jabbed his blade into it. The leg belonged to the shield partner of Hakon's assailant, and it buckled, taking its owner down with it. Bjarke, who now stood to the right of Hakon, drove his axe into the man's head, splitting his helmet and his skull in an explosion of red and gray. Hakon's attacker jabbed with his sword at Bjarke, but Hakon had anticipated the move and sliced down, taking the man's hand off at the wrist. He screamed and fell away, and just as quickly another warrior took his place.

Once again, Hakon put his shoulder to his shield and heaved forward. The enemy line gave a little ground, and in that moment, Hakon glanced about. Gamle's standard still flew to the left of him, though it was clear from its position that Gamle and his army were forcing Hakon's line backward. Off to the right, things seemed to be holding.

"We've got to get to Gamle," Hakon yelled. "Bjarke. Asmund. Bard. To me. Second line! Fill the ranks! Ready? Heave!"

Hakon pushed with all his strength, ignoring the enemy spears that slid past his shield rim. From behind, the second row pressed forward to add muscle to the push. A spear caught one of Hakon's younger warriors in the neck. He fell at Hakon's feet with his hands clutching the wound, oblivious now to the men who stomped around him. Hakon sliced below his shield, catching an enemy warrior in the shin. The man grabbed instinctively at the wound and Hakon finished him with a stab to the chest.

"Now!"

Hakon and his chosen few fell away, leaving the fighting to those who had taken their place. Hakon moved to his left, toward Gamle. Here and there, he stabbed or hacked where he could lend support, though he kept from committing until he was equal to Gamle's position. Hakon could see his nephew in the fray, jabbing and slicing with his left hand. For someone not born to it, he was more skilled with his opposite hand than most men might ever be with their given limb. Hakon glanced to his right, toward Guthorm's banner. It still stood in the melee, though Guthorm's line was beginning to bend. Toralv was making headway. Hakon wondered briefly about Egbert and Garth, then turned back to face his nephew.

"Gamle!" he bellowed.

The man looked up for a split second to seek his uncle's face, and in that instant, a lucky blade sliced across his cheek. Gamle recoiled briefly, then retaliated with a furious counterattack that left his assailant in a headless heap at his feet.

Hakon's men saw their king coming and set their feet. The enemy, too, saw their prize and yelled their curses and their oaths to kill the king. Hakon pressed into the melee with his warriors by his side. They kept their shields as close as possible in the tumult and swung their blades with the precision of men born to the task.

"You're a dead man, Hakon!" Gamle hollered over the heads of his men. The blood ran thickly into his beard from the gash on his face.

Hakon pushed a man aside in his desperation to reach Gamle. "Come, Gamle, and die on my sword!" An enemy spearman thrust his weapon at Hakon. Hakon evaded the jab, then sliced his blade into the spearman's neck, opening a wide gash that sent the enemy warrior to his death. "It is time to end this!"

And then Gamle was there, before him. Hakon eyed his nephew carefully, trying to anticipate the man's first move. It came in a flash of wood and metal. In one motion, Gamle swung his shield up and jabbed at an angle with his blade toward Hakon's gut. Hakon sliced sideways with his own shield, blocking the blade, though in doing so exposed his left shoulder to Gamle's shield boss. Gamle drove it forward and knocked Hakon backward. There was no time to ponder his mistake, for Gamle came with another sword thrust, which Hakon just managed to thwart with his shield.

Gamle had now outpaced his hirdmen and had exposed himself to the blades of Hakon's army. He blocked a blow with his shield, then parried another with his sword, all while stepping back into line with his oath-sworn men.

To either side of them, Hakon's men engaged Gamle's warriors. Asmund took a man in the throat with his seax, while next to him Bard turned a warrior's spear aside and quicker than an eye blink, slashed his blade across the man's face, opening a second mouth where the nose had been. Hakon smashed a man aside with his shield and onto the blade of another of his hirdmen.

Bjarke slammed his axe into the shield of the man protecting Gamle's left. The blade went clear through the battered wood and took the man's arm off at the elbow. The man screamed and staggered but somehow kept his feet and came back at Bjarke with his blade swinging. Bjarke blocked it easily, then twisted his wrist and, with a backhanded motion, buried his axe edge in the man's chest, where it lodged.

Gamle emerged from behind his shield and jabbed at Bjarke's side before he could protect himself. The big man let go of his axe and twisted to avoid the thrust, but was a second too late. The blade burst the rings of Bjarke's byrnie and sliced across his belly. Bjarke staggered backward and fell at Hakon's feet. His hands lay across his stomach, trying without success to keep his intestines from spilling through his fingers. He looked at the wound and cursed, his eyes not quite comprehending what had happened or why. Hakon jabbed at an enemy warrior to back him away from his fallen friend, then knelt and yanked Bjarke's seax from its sheath. The big man gripped the blade in his bloody paw, then rolled onto his side like a giant ship and died.

Hakon's hirdmen sensed the loss of Bjarke and stepped backward again to tighten their ranks.

"I will gut you like your friend, Uncle!" Gamle snarled.

Hakon was about to reply when a sudden cheer rose over the field. The sound stopped the fighting just long enough for men to see that the left side of Gamle's line had bent back on itself, forming a right angle toward Avaldsnes. Hakon's army had swelled in that area, which could mean only one thing: Egbert and Garth and Toralv had succeeded in their tasks.

Hakon turned back to Gamle, a vicious grin on his face. "It is you who shall die today, nephew!"

Gamle spat his anger but did not let it control his wits. "Back!" he ordered, knowing that if he pressed forward now with his left side collapsing, he would risk being flanked and overrun. "Retreat!"

A horn blasted and those of Gamle's men who could stepped back in line and locked shields. Step by step, they retreated from the fight with impressive order. A few foolish men tried to break their lines and died for their folly. Hakon and his hird had not the energy to pursue them. The battle was over, and so too was their passion for it. With hands on hips and gasps for breath, they watched as the enemy receded across the battleground and disappeared into the far tree line.

Off to the right, Guthorm's men were not so lucky. Egbert and Garth had reached the men at Avaldsnes, and those men were thirsty for vengeance. They had streamed into the fighting, forcing Guthorm's men to step backward to keep from being flanked. That is, until the horn for retreat sounded. Those lucky enough to escape ran from the field. Others bravely fought on, until all that remained of them were a handful of wounded Tyr warriors who could barely stand.

Hakon scanned the rest of the field. The dead lay in heaps, gawking at the sky or the gore-slickened earth with eyes that no longer saw. Beside them moaned the wounded. The youngsters among them cried or called pathetically for help. A few enemy warriors dragged themselves from the field until they were caught and killed for their gear. Already, the hum of flies was thick in Hakon's ears. Long ago, Hakon had vomited at such sights and sounds. Now, he just breathed deeply to control the ebb of battle-thrill that coursed through his body as he picked his way through the carnage.

Nearby, Asmund and Bard knelt by Bjarke's body. Asmund wept like a child, his shoulders heaving with his tears as Bard looked on helplessly. A stone's throw away lay the corpse of the first man to attack Hakon. In the heat of battle Hakon thought he had recognized the man, and now he knew why. It was Eldgrim's son, Olaf, who lay with his eyes open and his skin gray from loss of blood. Hakon sighed heavily, glad now that the lord of Shadow Haven had not come to this fight to see his son die.

Hakon made his way to Toralv, who stood with Sigge and Garth. At their feet, Guthorm's icy, lifeless eyes stared at the sky. He had a spear hole in his chest, though someone had already reclaimed the spear. Above him, Hakon's men were grinning, though Hakon found nothing amusing in their visage, for dark blood caked their faces, their arms, and their armor. Sigge, it seemed, had been blooded.

"You were supposed to stay with Egil," Hakon admonished Sigurd's son.

"I did," came his indignant retort. "It was Egil who sent me here when he saw Guthorm's lines faltering."

Hakon looked at Garth. "Where is Egbert?"

Garth's smile had already vanished at Hakon's tone. He nodded with his chin toward the priest, who was moving through the bodies, offering assistance where he could.

Hakon turned back to Garth. "If you had come any later, I would not be here to give you thanks."

Toralv frowned. "That is fine thanks you give to men who saved your skin, my lord."

Hakon was tired and drained and in no mood for graciousness, for though the day had gone their way, they had still lost much at the hands of Erik's brood. And so he gave Toralv little more than a smoldering glance before turning back to Garth. "Is Avaldsnes safe?"

Garth was scratching at his beard. "Aye, lord. We left a garrison there to protect it. It is fire damaged, but standing."

"That is good news, at least. So what, then, happened to Ottar and Gyda, if Avaldsnes is yet standing?"

At this question, another man stepped forward. It was Harald, one of the more senior members of Hakon's hird who had stayed with Ottar in Avaldsnes. Long ago, Hakon had offered Harald his life in exchange for helping him find the Dane, Ragnvald. That boy had grown into a handsome man with keen blue eyes, fair skin now covered in the gore of battle, and white-blond hair that he wore in a long braid down his back. "I can tell you what happened, lord," he began. "When the sons of Erik came, they did so in the early morning. We sounded the alarm, but all was chaos. Ottar exited the gates to assess the situation and get the sentries and thralls and grazing animals inside. This he did, even as the ships landed. But then Siv — the thrall — emerged from the west woods. She had been letting the pigs graze there. Gyda ran from the gates to try to save her, and Ottar followed to protect her."

Hakon could picture the scene in his mind. It was not unlike his woman to try to protect her thralls, especially his daughter's favorite.

"Arrows cut Ottar down before we could reach them," Harald continued, his head bowed. "And Gyda and Siv were taken. By then, the enemy had swarmed the hillside, so we retreated and barricaded ourselves in Avaldsnes to save it from capture."

"What of Thora?"

Harald brightened. "She is hale, lord."

Hakon absorbed the news with equal parts relief and sorrow. Thora yet lived, thank God. But Ottar, Gyda, Bjarke, and so many others were gone. He had lost many warriors, and many friends, in his twenty-plus winters as king, but he could not remember a day as dark as this. Not since the loss of his childhood friend, Aelfwin, who had been sacrificed on the eve of his battle with Erik, had Hakon felt so much pain in his soul. That pain coursed through his veins now like molten metal in the forge, made hotter still by the fact that Hakon could have killed Erik's whelps when they were young, and had not. He looked around for somewhere to direct his anger, but there was nothing save the sorry expressions of his men and the sickening aftermath of the battlefield. Hakon walked a short distance away, his fists clenched at his sides and a scream of wrath poised on his lips.

"Hakon!" Egil's voice cut through Hakon's dark thoughts. "Where is your mind, boy? Now is not the time to tarry. We must ensure that Gamle leaves these shores."

The grizzled old bastard was right, of course. Hakon turned his eyes to the sky, then gestured angrily at Guthorm's corpse. "Take Guthorm's body and come with me."

"And what of those men?" asked Egil, his seax pointed at Guthorm's surviving Tyr warriors.

"Bind them. Then bring them to me."

In the end, there was no need to drive Gamle and his brothers from Avaldsnes. They left of their own accord. Hakon watched their ships row across the bay beneath his estate. There were no longer enough men to man all of the ships, so Gamle left several on the shore. Behind them, Hakon had Guthorm's body hung high from a tree limb so the departing army could see it.

"Gamle!" roared Hakon, hoping his voice would carry across the water. "Witness the fate of your brother! It is the fate that awaits you all!"

"Every man dies, Uncle," came Gamle's response. "And only the Norns know when! Today was Guthorm's turn. Soon may be your time!"

"Sail home to your masters, Gamle. Next time, I will be waiting for you."

"I look forward to it!" Gamle's voice drifted to him, then faded.

Hakon watched the ships until they were gone, his heart thumping in his chest and his fists clenching and unclenching by his sides.

"Bastards," Toralv spat when the last ship had vanished from sight.

Hakon kept his gaze on the spot where they had disappeared. "Erik's sons took much that is dear to me, and they will take more before they are through. Even if I live to see them all dead, that knowledge eats at me, Toralv. Like a sickness, it fills my thoughts with darkness."

Toralv finally sighed. "The Danes have wanted our land for as long as men can remember. Now they have Erik's sons to do their bidding. So let that darkness move you to action. Once we have honored our dead, you need to look to the future and how best to protect your realm. Not just here, but everywhere, for no place is safe with those bastards on the prowl."

Hakon grunted. "I will know better how to protect the realm once I better understand the threat. Fetch the prisoners, Toralv. I would have a word with them."

As Toralv moved off to do his lord's bidding, Hakon hiked to the high walls of Avaldsnes to survey the damage Gamle and his brothers had wrought. Fire had charred the wood in many places where his nephews' men had tried to burn their way in, and the north and south gates had been cracked by battering rams. Here and there along the walls lay piles of enemy corpses and the broken remains of makeshift ladders. The estate's interior had fared better, but had not completely avoided the ravages of battle. Burnt thatch scarred several rooftops, while arrow shafts poked from the wooden planks of walls. These things could be easily fixed, but they indicated a new truth that was harder to accept. Toralv had spoken it already, but Hakon heard it now echoing in his head. No place was safe.

"Father!" came a shrill cry from the main hall.

Hakon turned to the sound and smiled at the sight of his daughter, who was running across the lane toward him. He bent down to receive her in his embrace.

"Father. You are back."

He smiled at her. "Aye. I have returned."

Suddenly, her bright expression turned cloudy. "Those men took Siv and Gyda, Father. Why?"

He stood and took her hand, and together they walked back toward the hall. "Because those men are bad men," he said, trying to keep it simple for her young mind.

"Will they come back?"

"Who? The men?"

"No," she said as the shadows of the eaves enveloped her. "Gyda and Siv. Will they return?"

Hakon knelt before her and looked into her expectant blue eyes. "No," he said. "They will not."

Her face crumpled and Hakon's heart broke yet again that day. He pulled her close and wrapped his sobbing daughter in his arms. When the sobbing abated somewhat, Thora rested her head on Hakon's armored shoulder. "Why will those bad men not give us back Gyda and Siv?" she asked.

Hakon could think of no response that would ease her pain, so he just stroked her hair and hugged her tighter.

Later that evening, as the funeral pyres burned the dead and took their souls to the heavens, Hakon had the prisoners lined against the high walls of Avaldsnes. Most were injured in some fashion, but all could stand. As Hakon strode down their line, they stood straighter, for they would not give the Northern king the satisfaction of seeing their fatigue.

"Tell me what I need to know and you shall die a good death with your swords in hand," Hakon began. "Tell me not, and I will sell you all as thralls."

A middle-aged man spat in Hakon's direction. "That is no bargain, Northman."

Hakon strode past the man, then suddenly turned and backhanded the man's temple with his ringed fist. The man had no time to evade the blow, and dropped unconscious at Hakon's feet. Hakon pulled out his sword, Quern-biter, and placed it against the belly of another prisoner. "You are a Dane?"

The man showed no fear, just contempt. "We are Fyrkat Danes."

"That means nothing to me." Hakon tried another tack. "I noticed the mark of Tyr on your shields. What is that? Is it a Danish symbol?"

"It is the mark of Bloodaxe's kin, whom we serve with the blessing of the Danish King Harald and his father, Gorm." He lifted his chin proudly. "It is also the mark of our favored god, Tyr, who grants us victory in battle."

Suddenly it all made sense. A one-handed god. A one-handed chieftain. Clever. "Well, Fyrkat Dane," Hakon said. "It appears that both failed you this day."

That produced some laughter from those of Hakon's men who had been listening.

"Laugh all you want, Northmen," the man said. "But know this. I am but one warrior. Where I fall, ten more sword-Danes will soon come, and with one purpose in mind: to win for our king even more land and wealth. We," he swept his arm toward his shield-brothers, "are merely the spear's tip, and this defeat but a drop of water in a weak ebb. The flood tide is coming, Northmen, and it will wash you from Midgard for good. Knowing that, we will go to our death grateful to Tyr for the honor of leading the way."

It was hard not to respect the man's courage. "You have told me what I need to know, Dane, and for that, I am grateful." Hakon turned to Toralv. "Kill them."

Hakon stalked away and climbed the burial mound on the hill that overlooked the bay. He needed to be alone to think, and to stew. He sat gingerly, feeling the bruises and the pain in his joints now that the thrill in his body had retreated. Below him, the funeral pyres crackled and spat their flames into the darkening air, washing the mourners and waters of the bay in wavering hues of orange and red and yellow. Somewhere in the conflagration, Bjarke's body burned; Hakon said a silent prayer for his soul. On the morrow, they would give Gyda and

Ottar the burials they deserved, and then they would sail to save the realm.

Part II

A ransom of the ruddy gold,
Which Hakon to his war-men bold
Gave with free hand, who in his feud
Against the arrow-storm had stood.
The Heimskringla

Chapter 8

Frosta, Trondelag, Summer, AD 957

The field at Frosta bustled with life. Tents crowded the finger of land that poked into the Trondheimsfjord, their canvas walls and banners flapping in the midsummer breeze. Around the tents, children ran while their parents cooked, toiled, hawked wares, or shared news from their various districts. The smell of smoked meat and fish hung thickly in the air. East of the tents, a group of boys and young men played a game of stickball known as knattleiker, while the young women looked on, whispering, pointing, and cheering.

Hakon surveyed the scene with satisfaction. This gathering was a supra-thing, or law assembly for the far northern fylke of the realm. This particular supra-thing was known as the Frosta Thing on account of the Frosta-field on which it took place. Hakon's brother, Erik, had made a mockery of the law assemblies during his short reign, but Hakon had worked hard to reinvigorate them, for he had learned the value of laws and legal judgments as a means for keeping chaos at bay.

But the assemblies were more than that. In a land divided by mountains, valleys, fjords, and snow, they were the people's chance to reconnect, to share news, to purchase goods, and to bond. And this summer, it was Hakon's chance to raise an army and build his defenses against his brother's sons, which was why Hakon had traveled from one supra-thing to the next since the battle at Avaldsnes giving speeches about the dangers that were not coming, but upon them already.

Sigurd greeted the arrival of Hakon's ship wearing his jarl's torc and a fine cloak of reindeer skin clasped at the shoulder by a brooch of polished silver. Silver armbands adorned his thick wrists. He wore his graying hair loose so that it danced about his head in the breeze as he waited for Hakon's ship to land. To Sigurd's left stood Astrid in a long green dress, her hair cascading in loose ringlets down her back like an auburn waterfall. It made Hakon glad that he'd bedecked himself in his own finery: a new ivory-white tunic, soft leather breeks, two golden wristbands, and a thick silver necklace he had just polished that morning.

Sigurd and Hakon embraced like brothers as soon as Hakon's feet touched the shore.

"By the gods, it is good to see you hale," Sigurd said through his smile. "If the skalds' stories are true, the battle at Avaldsnes was a bitter one. The skalds are calling it the Battle of Blood Heights."

Hakon snorted. "Heights? We fought on a plain. At least they got the bitter bit right, though."

Sigurd's smile faded. "We heard of Ottar. And Gyda. I am sorry for their losses." He patted Hakon's shoulder paternally. "I trust Thora is hale?"

The mention of his daughter brightened Hakon's spirits somewhat. "Thora is hale, as you can see." He turned and pointed to the little head that was peeking over the gunwale of *Dragon* at the mass of activity onshore. This was her first law-assembly and she was obviously impressed, if not slightly nervous. Beside her stood her caretaker, a stout thrall woman named Unn who had been a friend of Siv's.

Hakon moved to Astrid, who tucked an errant curl behind her ear and bowed. "King Hakon."

He smiled warmly at her. "I did not expect to see you here, Astrid."

"I did not expect to be here," Astrid countered with a forced smile.

Hakon understood instantly what that meant, and his manner sobered.

"Astrid is staying with us for a time," Sigurd explained, though he need not have.

Behind Hakon, his crew was coming ashore. As with his trip to Tore's funeral, Hakon had left half of his men at Avaldsnes, this time under the care of Garth and Harald. Egbert had also stayed behind, for the priest was not welcome in these parts.

"My son looks well," Sigurd observed, and chuckled. It was true. Since the battle, Sigge's air of confidence had climbed even further, drawing many of the younger men and women to him. Like flies to shit, Toralv liked to say.

Hakon glanced at the young man and shrugged. "He *is* well."

Sigurd smacked Hakon's shoulder and went to his son.

Hakon turned back to Astrid. "I am sorry, Astrid," he offered.

She nodded and looked at her feet. "We both knew it could happen, and so it did."

"So it did," Hakon acknowledged. "But that doesn't make it any easier to accept."

She smirked. "You have the right of that." She then peered past Hakon and bent down. "You must be Thora."

Hakon turned and smiled down at his daughter. "This is Astrid, the daughter of Jarl Sigurd. Can you say hello?"

Her blue eyes studied the woman in front of her from beneath her blond bangs. "Hello," she finally said.

"It is a long journey from your home to here," Astrid said. "You must be tired of dried fish and smelly men." Astrid scrunched her face as if she had smelled something foul, which made Thora giggle. Astrid reached out a hand to her. "Come. Let us find some food for you."

Thora took the woman's hand in her own. Hakon smiled. He had debated bringing his daughter on this trip after all she'd been through, but those misgivings fled from him as he fell into step behind Astrid and Thora. Unn followed close behind.

Astrid led them through the maze of tents that dotted Frosta-field. As they walked, people stopped their pursuits and either bowed to their king or called out friendly greetings, for Hakon had been to the

Trondelag many times and most of the people were at least familiar with him. Several were friends, and these Hakon greeted with clasped wrists and hugs.

Eventually, they reached Sigurd's large tent and the eating boards he had placed before it. Several men sat at the boards drinking cups of ale and laughing over some story or joke that had just been told. They stopped their laughter and gazed at Hakon through bleary eyes as Astrid and the king approached.

"Come greet your king," Astrid commanded gently. "Then leave us in peace."

The men stumbled to do their lady's bidding, then staggered off to find more ale.

"The new breed," Astrid huffed as the men disappeared around the corner of Sigurd's tent. She took a seat on a bench and beckoned Thora and Hakon to sit. "Ragna," Astrid called to a portly woman stirring a cauldron nearby. "Fetch us some ale. And some bread and butter. And bring some fresh water for the girl. You there," Astrid called to Unn, "Help her."

"Her name is Unn," said Thora boldly.

"Pardon?" asked Astrid as the woman waddled off.

"Her name is Unn," Thora repeated, holding Astrid's gaze. "She is my caretaker. I wanted you to know her name."

"Thank you for telling me. It is good to know who you address," Astrid conceded, then turned her smiling eyes to Hakon. "She does not lack for confidence."

Hakon smiled. "You are right in that."

"That is good," Astrid said as she looked back at Hakon's daughter. "Do not lose that trait, Thora. You will need it in this world."

The thralls returned moments later with two full cups of ale, some water, and a warm loaf of flat bread, all of which they placed before Astrid and her guests. When they had gone, Hakon raised his cup to Astrid. "It is good to see you again, though I wish it were under different circumstances. Skol."

Astrid's cheeks flushed. "Skol. And skol to you too, Thora. It is a gift to finally meet you."

Thora clinked her cup against Astrid's, then smiled at her father for being included.

"So what will you do now?" Hakon asked after he drank from his cup.

"I shall live in Lade for a time, I suppose," she responded as she tore a chunk of bread from the loaf and popped it into her mouth.

"My offer still stands," he said, speaking cryptically to avoid Thora's questions. He need not have, for the bread had captured Thora's attention and she tore at it contentedly.

Astrid smiled and gazed into her cup. "Thank you. I will think on it."

"Beating us to the ale, are you?" Sigurd's voice boomed across the boards. "Come, men. Drink your fill before your king takes it all! Ragna! Ale for the men!"

Hakon smiled at Astrid, then rose to meet his men, who moved into the space like a flood tide enveloping a beach. With a panicked look on her face, the thrall woman Ragna waddled off again to find ale for the warriors. Unn scrambled to help her. They returned with as many cups as they could carry, which was not many, and placed them before the men.

"Bard. Asmund," called Hakon. "Bring the barrel! These thirsty louts will grow angry waiting for the poor women to serve everyone."

Bard and Asmund moved off, then returned with the ale barrel between them. The men cheered their comrades and the arrival of the ale. Astrid remained by Hakon's side, watching as the men eased into their cups with a slight grin on her face.

After a time, Sigurd rose from his bench and held up his hand for peace. As the voices died down, he spoke. "Word of the battle of Avaldsnes has reached us here, but Hakon has reminded me that hearsay is never quite as accurate as a story told from the mouth of an eye witness. Perchance you, Guthorm Sindri," Sigurd said to Hakon's skald, "have woven a fine tale for us to hear?"

The eyes of the warriors turned to the skald, whose black hair was streaked with silver and whose byname Sindri meant spark-sprayer. It was a fitting name, for his words tended to mesmerize his audiences, much like the flames of a hearth fire. "I have indeed created a tale," answered the man. "But with your pardon, lord; I have been many days aship and need more ale to loosen my tongue. Grant me some moments to slake my thirst, and I will gladly give you your tale."

Hakon smiled at his skald's composure. He was not the biggest of men and did not fight in the shield wall with the rest. Nor did he claim to be a warrior of any prowess. His gift was his word-craft, and his purpose was to spread word of Hakon's fame. In this, he had done well enough over the past few winters to earn a place at Hakon's table.

Sigurd took no offense from the man's request and, indeed, laughed. "Well then, we will just have to wait for our skald to drink his fill," Sigurd called to the gathering. "I hope the wait is worth it, skald."

Guthorm Sindri nodded his thanks to Sigurd, and turned to the ale cup that Ragna placed before him. He downed its contents and called for another. The men turned back to their conversations, and Hakon leaned over to Thora.

"It is time for you to leave, Thora."

The corners of her mouth drooped. "But I wish to stay, Father."

"I know. But I fear this tale is not for young ears."

Astrid stood then and looked at Thora. "I have an idea. How would you like to stay with me in my tent? I can show you some of my new combs and mayhap brush those tangles from your sea-blown hair."

Thora's eyes grew wide. She looked at her father for approval. "Would that be alright, Father?"

"Of course."

"Come, then," Astrid said. The grin on her face matched Thora's own. "But first, tell Unn we will need her help gathering your things."

Thora scrambled from the bench and ran over to Unn to tell her of the new plan.

"Astrid is good with children," Hakon remarked as the trio disappeared into the tent-maze.

"Aye," Sigurd responded with a tinge of sadness in his voice. "She would have made a good mother to my grandchildren."

"Indeed," Hakon said, then switched the subject before Sigurd's spirits sank too low. "I will need your help on the morrow, Sigurd."

"How is that?"

"I need men. Warriors."

He grunted dismissively.

"The Danes are coming, Sigurd, and this time, I fear the Danish King Harald has ambitions that surpass his father's."

Sigurd glanced at Hakon and raised a questioning brow.

Hakon told him of the Dane's words at Avaldsnes. "They come for us with my father's grandsons to lead them. They will not stop this time, Sigurd. I feel it in here," Hakon said, pounding his chest.

Sigurd nodded. "And you wish to bring this request to the people?"

"Yes, but with your blessing."

"What is in it for me?"

Hakon had expected this response, for rarely did Sigurd act without some means for him to profit. "Peace," Hakon said simply.

Sigurd grunted. "We have peace now."

"You may have peace now, but if you do not act, you may find yourself with a new king soon enough."

This got Sigurd's attention, and his gray brows bent over his eyes. "Those are dangerous words, Hakon."

"Yet they must be said. The battle at Avaldsnes was a bitter struggle, and I fear it is not the last fight with Erik's sons that we shall see."

Sigurd's frown deepened. "Very well. You have my blessing. On the morrow, bring this to the men when they are assembled."

"Thank you, Sigurd."

Hakon then called to Guthorm Sindri. The skald nodded and stepped onto his bench, and from there, he climbed onto the eating board. The men laughed as they grabbed their cups and trenchers to protect them from the man's footfalls. With practiced patience, the skald waited until their banter died and only the crackle of the nearby fire could be heard. Then he began.

"Off in the west rose Erik's brood,
A den of wolves, an honorless crew.
In spear-din and Hel's maw,
'Gainst axe head and foe's claw.
Paved fame with wound's hoe,
'Til Norns thread laid the sire low,
And from the swords and wound-sea,
Did the mighty brood flee.

"Now among their Danish kin,
Did brothers seek again the spear-din
And glory with seax and sword and axe,
With byrnie strong and shields on backs.
Sold their swords to the foul ring-giver,
For land and riches and halls by a river.
To the north, to the west, did they sail,
With battle-sweat wove a sorrowful tale.

"'Round Adger they came with revenge in their hearts,
Seeking Hakon, his men, and his hall for starts.
On whale-road to Karmoy and Avaldsnes they reached
With their dragon ships and sea-drenched beasts.
So to that sacred place did Hakon race;
With his oath-sworn he set a god-like pace.
To Hollkoppevik bade the doughty king meet,
The Horders and Rygers with their sea-steeds.

"The king's voice then woke the vengeful host
Who slept beside the wild sea-coast,
And bade the song of spear and sword
Over the battle plain be heard.
Where heroes' shields the loudest rang,
Where loudest was the sword-blade's clang,
By the sea-shore at Karmsund Sound,
Hakon felled Guthorm to the ground."

Hakon's men chuckled, for they knew well that it had been a spear that had laid the prince low. Toralv, who sat near his king, guffawed. "So now you killed Erik's son, eh, my lord?"

Hakon smiled as the men shushed the champion so the spark-sprayer could continue his tale.

> *"And Guthorm's brothers too, who know*
> *So skillfully to bend the bow,*
> *The conquering hand must also feel*
> *Of Hakon, god of the bright steel —*
> *The sun-god, whose bright rays, that dart*
> *Flame-like, are swords that pierce the heart.*

> *"Well I remember how the king,*
> *Hakon, the battle's life and spring,*
> *O'er the wide ocean cleared away*
> *Erik's brave sons.*
> *They durst not stay,*
> *But 'round their ships' sides hung their shields*
> *And fled across the blue sea-fields. "*

The men cheered and smacked the eating board with their fists as Sigurd rose and raised his cup, first to the skald and then to the king.

"It is a good story, skald. I wish I had been there to see those whoresons flee." Sigurd tossed Guthorm Sindri a chunk of hack silver to reward him for his poem. "Skol to you warriors and your fallen friends! May we remember them always, and may they be feasting now in Valhall beside the gods."

"Fight with us, and you will have your chance, Sigurd," Hakon said as Sigurd reclaimed his seat. "Erik's sons will return as soon as they have licked their wounds."

Sigurd grunted but held his tongue.

Slowly, the day succumbed to night but not to complete darkness, for it was summer in the far north and the sun did not rest. Rather, it dipped behind the tents and remained on the horizon, casting a golden glow over the southern sky that faded into a darker and deeper blue the farther north it reached. It was in that blue that a few stars twinkled down on the revelers.

Hakon could feel the fatigue seeping into his bones. His belly was now full of stew and bread, and his head was thick with ale and the slurring voices of the younger warriors whose appetites for women and drink had not yet been slaked. Sigurd had long since retired to his tent. There was a time when the jarl could outlast most men at the boards, but age had robbed him of that stamina. Now it was Sigurd's son who took on that distinction. He held court across the small clearing with a cup of ale in one hand and a young woman in the other. Hakon could not hear his words through the din, but whatever Sigge was saying had those around him rapt.

Hakon pushed himself to his feet and went in search of his tent, which his hird had erected down near the beach. Hakon nodded to the sentries, who grinned stupidly at their lord from beneath their helmets. Hakon looked from one man to the next, then stepped into the murk of his tent. He hesitated at the entrance to let his eyes adjust to the sudden darkness.

Even with a head full of ale, he sensed that something was amiss, though at first he couldn't place just what was wrong. It was only after his eyes adjusted that he saw a human form lying under his fur covers. The form rose on an elbow, and in the half light, he could see her naked shoulder and the curls of her hair. Astrid.

Even now, after all this time and at his age, his heart hammered in his chest at the sight of her. "Sneaking into a man's tent is dangerous," he said as he shed his cloak and pulled his tunic over his head.

"Then I suppose you will have to punish me for my wrongdoings," she responded, letting the furs slip below her breast.

He joined her under the furs where the light touch of her fingers raised bumps on his skin and brought a tingle to his loins. Their lips

met and their limbs entwined, and his manhood stiffened with anticipation and desire. Long ago, they lay together as teenagers, exploring life's carnal gifts with all of the awkwardness of youth. Now they
ventured more slowly, more deliberately, rediscovering each other's
bodies with patience and skill, until they could hold themselves back
no more and their passion, primal and ravenous, swept them away.
Time and discretion became irrelevant. All that mattered was their
touch, their movement, their breath, until their bodies stiffened with
pleasure and their moans erupted, and they collapsed, panting and
sweating, in each other's arms.

Neither spoke. Neither needed to. Their bodies had spoken for them.
Hakon's arm cradled Astrid's head with its tousled curls. Astrid's nails
toyed with the hair on Hakon's chest, her sweat-slickened body tight
against his. Happy exhaustion washed over Hakon, and he slipped into
the darkness of sleep.

Shouts in the camp woke them. It took Hakon a moment to clear
the fog from his brain and to register that the noise was real and not
something conjured in his dreams. Astrid had her shift on by the time
Hakon roused himself from the bedding. He stumbled in the darkness
for his clothes, unsure of what time it was or what was happening.

"What do you see?" he whispered to Astrid, who stood at the tent
flap, peering out into the darkness.

"A group of people. Coming this way. With torches."

Hakon cursed, wishing he had a weapon, but weapons were forbidden at things, so he grabbed Astrid's wrist instead and pulled her from
the tent flap. "Get behind me," he said as he pushed the flap open and
stepped out into the night.

Toward him marched a small group of men, their faces and forms
illuminated by the flames of their torches. Even in the half light, he
could see the anger etched on their faces. In their midst, held between
them, was a beaten Sigge and a young, disheveled blond girl who was
clearly not the same girl that had been seated beside him earlier in
the evening.

"Halt!" yelled one of the guards who stood outside Hakon's tent. The group stopped, their shouts and growls dying away at the warning and the sight of their king. Others had also come from their tents but held their distance as they watched the curious incident unfold.

Hakon focused on the men holding Sigge, both of whom belonged to Sigurd's hird. "What is the meaning of this? Why is he beaten? And who is she?"

One of the men bowed his head. He was older than the others. His name, if Hakon recalled correctly, was Alvart, and he had been with Sigurd's hird a long time. "My lord. We caught this man with my wife!"

"*With* your wife?"

"Aye. With. Sleeping with," he clarified, though it was clear it pained him to do so. Around them, the growing crowd murmured.

Hakon looked at the girl. "Are you his wife?"

The girl glanced at the older hirdman. "Aye." Her voice came to Hakon like a whisper.

Hakon skewered his namesake with his gaze. "Is this true, Sigge?"

Sigurd's son was dazed from his beating, and perhaps still drunk with ale. As a result, he could only nod stupidly. Hakon turned to one of his guards. "Fetch Sigurd!"

When the guard was gone, Hakon raked the girl with his eyes. Were it not for the pine needles in her disheveled hair and the plain underdress she wore, Hakon might have thought her beautiful. She, of course, could not hold the king's bitter gaze and so sought the ground with her eyes.

Hakon turned to the girl's husband. He was maybe twice the woman's age, with a thick black beard hiding his round chest. "Alvart, is it not?"

"Aye, lord."

Hakon turned to Astrid, who stood stock still, frowning. "You should go."

She nodded. "I shall check on your daughter." And with one final glare at her younger brother, she stalked off into the night.

Hakon turned back to the group, considering his options. He knew Alvart to be a stalwart warrior in Sigurd's hird, but mayhap his wife's infidelity spoke to a hidden weakness? Even if discovered, that weakness did not give Sigge the right to sleep with the woman, nor her the right to stray, which, if she were found guilty, would bring death to her and dishonor to her family. And even if Alvart were found innocent, men would wonder and they would talk and Alvart's honor would suffer. On top of it all, Alvart had upset the thing's peace by attacking Sigge. Provoked or not, it was a serious offense. Whatever way Hakon considered it, the incident did not bode well for any of them.

Sigurd arrived just then and took in the scene. His eyes first registered Hakon standing before the entrance of his tent, but they quickly moved to Alvart, then to Alvart's wife, and then, finally, to his son. The old jarl approached his son and lifted his head by his hair. "You fool!" he spat. "I warned you to keep away from her. Alvart even gave you another chance on my accord. And what do you do?" He swiped impotently at the air. "I should gut you both!" he cursed, meaning his son and the girl.

"And you?" he rounded on Alvart. "Did you do this to my son?"

"But lord —"

"Save your breath for the council," Sigurd growled. "You know the rules."

"Sigurd speaks true," Hakon said. "This is a matter for the thing. We shall deal with it in the morning, when our heads are clear of ale and sleep no longer clouds our judgment. Take Sigge to my ship and keep him there. Alvart and his wife shall sleep in separate tents tonight, under watch. In the morning, we will present this to the council. Go now."

Sigurd and Hakon watched the crowd disperse until only the two of them remained. Sigurd faced away from Hakon, gazing into the sea of tents and the retreating figures. Hakon could sense the older man's fury, and so let him smolder until he was ready to speak. Finally, the jarl's shoulders sagged. "Sometimes I wonder if he was dropped on his head as a bairn," Sigurd said into the darkness.

In another circumstance, the comment might have brought a grin to Hakon's face, but in this instance, he knew it would irk Sigurd all the more. "He is yet young," Hakon offered delicately. "He thinks with his heart, not his head."

Sigurd rounded on his king. "If that boy lives to see another winter..." He let his words trail off, for such words were bad luck, and no matter how angry he was, it was folly to utter them. Sigurd sighed audibly. "I can no longer protect him from himself."

"No, you cannot," Hakon agreed. "Get some rest, Sigurd. The morrow will be a long day."

Sigurd grunted and stalked off into the night.

Chapter 9

The men assembled in the Frosta-field for the thing. Before them loomed the Speaking Stone, an ancient monolith said to have been lodged in the ground by the hand of giants in the time before man. Beneath that stone stood their king, a man whose reputation was now as large as any giant who had once walked the earth and who deserved the quiet respect they now afforded him as they gathered.

Hakon gazed out over the crowd, which stood in nine groups representing the nine areas of the Trondelag. It had been eight, but the death of Tore and the appointment of Tosti to his place now made it nine. Long ago, as a young teenager, Hakon had spoken on this very spot to win the Tronds' support in his fight against Erik. The following summer, he had gathered the Tronds again at Frosta to seek their support against the Danes. Subsequent summers had brought him back to this place, though save for the first two and now this summer, it was hard to think of another as dire.

When the field was sufficiently crowded, Hakon held up his hands to capture the attention of those gathered. Their conversations died as their eyes turned to their king. Hakon did not waste his breath on pleasantries, for he had already spoken his greetings to many the day before. "Friends. Comrades. I bring you dark tidings from the realm. The sons of Erik Bloodaxe have returned to the North." The dull rumble of voices that prompted sounded like distant thunder to Hakon's ears. He let the men curse and mutter a few moments before proceeding. "Some of you have heard of their attacks in the Vik and on my own estate at Avaldsnes. You may also know that they come with the support of the Danes, who supply them with warriors and ships. Let me speak plainly. These are not beardless whelps seeking adventure. The Danes who fill their ranks are all seasoned warriors. Spear-Danes. Sword-Danes. Warriors of Erik who now serve his sons." Hakon raised his voice to smother the rumbles. "This threat is real, and cannot be ignored."

"These attacks are well to the south of us. How does this involve us?" called a fellow in one of the front ranks of the assembly. He was a middle-aged man who Hakon knew to be a smith.

How typically provincial his response was. The North had never been a united land. Even now, with a strong king and jarls who served him, men sought to protect only what they could see and what they knew. Matters across the mountains or many days' sail to the south were beyond their concern.

Hakon leveled his gaze at the man. "When you and I were young, the Danes tried to take our land but they failed. Now the threat has come again, with leaders and warriors who have been tempered by battles in Engla-lond and elsewhere." Hakon let his words settle on the man, though he spoke loud enough for the crowd to hear. "The Danish kings have given them even more men, and now they come for me. And if I fall, then they will seek out my jarls," Hakon swept his hand toward Sigurd, "and any man who opposes their rule."

Hakon searched the Tronds' faces. The emotions displayed were as numerous as the faces looking back at him. Excitement, concern, anger, defiance. The only consensus seemed to be among the elders, who, to a man, frowned. Many had fought with Hakon against Erik, and most had not agreed when Hakon had spared Erik's life and the lives of his family. Now they were witnessing the ramifications of that mistake and it was sitting with them like the stench of rotten meat.

"I do not plan to wait for them to come," Hakon continued, unde-terred. "In early fall, I will attack the land of the Danes and end this threat before it comes to find us. If you join me, we will break the backs of those who threaten us, and you will return with as much Danish plunder as you can carry!"

The younger men cheered. They needed no more coaxing than that. The elders continued to frown, their age and experience keeping their emotions in check, for they knew that plunder did not come without sacrifice.

"Since the last full moon, I have traveled far to bring word of this threat to the land. Right now, the war arrow is on the move. From the fjords to the Vik, warriors are heeding its call and preparing themselves. I urge you to join them!"

A cheer rose from some of the adventure-hungry young men, but it was quickly punctured by an elder. "What of the harvest?" the graybeard called.

"If you decide to fight, then each lord must bring the men that the law prescribes. The rest of you must determine what is best for your homes and for the winter. If that means leaving some men to tend your farm, then so be it."

Sigurd stepped up then and raised his hands to quell the commotion Hakon's words had wrought. "The king has spoken. It is now for us to decide."

Hakon nodded his thanks to Sigurd, then waited patiently for the others to discuss his proposal. It started calmly enough but soon transformed into something more emotional and volatile. Sensing the agitation of his people, Sigurd stepped into the fray and slowly calmed the crowd. When the crowd had settled, Sigurd walked back to his king and explained the situation.

"The younger men want to go, but many are needed at home. Most of the older men and leaders do not think this is our fight. We will, therefore, put the matter to Drangi and have him consult the gods."

Hakon could feel his brows bend but knew well that it would be pointless to argue. Sigurd and his Tronds were devout followers of the gods, and Hakon had clashed mightily with them because of that over the years. He did not wish to do so now, so he held his tongue and nodded curtly at his friend. "I need an answer before I leave."

"And you shall have it," Sigurd promised.

The assembly disbanded. Those with cases to bring forth gathered their supporters and returned to the field and the Speaking Stone, where they awaited an audience with the king. When enough petitioners had gathered, Hakon motioned to a graybeard named Thorbjorn, who was the law-speaker in the Trondelag. He hobbled up to the Speaking Stone, and in a voice feeble with age, began to speak the Frosta Thing laws to the crowd.

"You will need to find a replacement for Thorbjorn," Hakon whispered to Sigurd as those at the back of the crowd pressed forward to hear the old man's words. "The man will be food for the worms before next spring."

"It is already in the works," countered Sigurd. "Thorbjorn has been teaching his son the laws. He knows his time is nigh."

When Thorbjorn concluded his recitation, the legal proceedings began. They ranged from minor theft to battery, from divorce to inheritance, and just about everything in between. In each case, both parties swore an oath to speak truthfully, then the plaintiff stated his grievance with the other party present. The defendant had a chance to state his or her side of the story. Each side could bring witnesses to support their claims, and often did. In some cases, the case was clear-cut and the penalty swift. In other cases, the matters were more complex and required much discussion to find suitable settlements.

As tedious as the proceedings were, Hakon forced himself to remain engaged. The things had existed for as long as anyone could remember; yet they had crumbled under Erik, who, through bribes and favoritism, had made a mockery of them. It had taken years for people to trust them again, and much of the reason for that was the priority Hakon had placed on their reestablishment. By showing people that each and every case was important to him as king, he instilled that sense of their importance in his people. Gradually it had worked, and now the law-things were stronger than ever. Which, of course, meant that there were more cases than ever, and why noon came and went and Hakon finally retired to a stool, his head aching with fatigue. The law-speaker and Jarl Sigurd sat to either side of him.

Hakon had a mind to halt the proceedings until the following day, and even rose from his stool to make his pronouncement, but when he saw the next petitioners, he reclaimed his seat and motioned the party forward.

"State your name and your grievance," croaked the ancient law-speaker.

"My name is Alvart Alvartsson, and I wish to bring my wife and her lover before you." Alvart motioned toward Sigurd's son and his blond lover. Behind Alvart stood three of his shield-brothers, who presumably had agreed to stand as witnesses.

Thorbjorn gazed at the group with his rheumy eyes. "Do you all swear to honor the law and speak the truth before the eyes of the gods?"

The three agreed.

"And do you understand that not speaking the truth shall render you open to the wrath of your gods?"

Again, they acknowledged that they understood.

"So be it," the law-speaker's feeble voice said. "We shall hear your case."

Hakon glanced over at Jarl Sigurd. His old friend mumbled a curse under his breath and looked at Hakon. "I cannot hear this case, my lord, and judge it impartially. Nor do I wish to know the outcome." And with a black, parting glance at his son, Sigurd walked away. Hakon did not blame his friend, nor did he try to dissuade him from leaving.

"What is the charge, Alvart Alvartsson?"

"Adultery."

Hakon's gaze shifted to Sigge and his lover. The girl could not look at the king or the law-speaker. Instead, her eyes sought her feet, just as they had done the night before. Sigurd's son, on the other hand, stood there with a bored expression on his bruised face, as if he were watching the conversation of two inconsequential strangers.

A sudden rage washed over Hakon then. Whether it was the embarrassment Sigge had caused his sister and father, or his indifference to it, Hakon knew not. All he knew was that the sight of the impassive Sigge enraged him to the point of fury. Were this not the thing with its rules against violence, Hakon would have slammed his fist into the fool's face and spat on his unconscious body.

"What say you, Hakon Sigurdsson?" asked the law-speaker.

"I have done no wrong," he said mildly. "Alvart may be a brave warrior in my father's shield wall, but in the bed, he is far from heroic. Though whether it was that or his heavy hand that caused his woman to stray is hard to say."

"You lying whoreson!" spat Alvart.

Most men would take offense at Alvart's words, but Sigge merely shrugged. "I did not make this problem, Alvart. A woman does not seek a lover if she is satisfied."

"Silence. Both of you." Hakon rose and approached the girl with the golden hair. "What is your name?"

She turned her blue eyes and her soft features to Hakon, and for a moment, her beauty took Hakon aback. But it did not change things. A wrong had been done, and no matter her attractiveness, she was at the center of it. "Turid," she said. "Turid Leifsdottir."

"And how long have you been married to Alvart, Turid Leifsdottir?" asked Hakon. In truth, he knew not where he was going with this questioning, only that he felt sorry for the lovely girl, who seemed caught between the affections of a privileged turd and a flawed warrior.

She paused to count the winters. "Six winters, lord."

"Does Hakon Sigurdsson speak truly? Has Alvart ever hit you in those six years?"

The girl looked sheepishly at Alvart, who seemed ready to leap from his own skin, then turned her eyes to Hakon Sigurdsson, who nodded at her reassuringly. Finally, she looked back at her king. "Aye, lord. Several times."

"I have never touched you, woman, and you know it!"

Hakon leveled his gaze on Alvart. Behind the warrior, his comrades shifted uneasily, and for good reason. In the North, it was considered beneath a man to strike a woman, and the mere act of doing so was cause for great shame. "Have you men seen this man strike his wife?"

"No, lord," they each admitted.

Hakon paced between the two parties as his mind raced. "You, Alvart, accuse your wife of adultery. Yet you, Turid, claim that your husband hit you. Do you also agree with Hakon Sigurdsson that Alvart is not satisfying you in bed?" Hakon stepped up to Turid and raised her chin with his finger, for she had begun to seek the ground again with her gaze. "There is no shame in admitting it."

She nodded quickly, then looked down again. Beside her, Sigge smiled triumphantly.

Hakon rounded on him. "Why are you smiling?"

The smile disappeared instantly.

"Tell me, please," Hakon hissed, "why you smile."

Sigurd's son gawked stupidly.

"Tell me!" Hakon roared. "Do you find this amusing?"

"No, lord," he stammered.

"You sleep with another man's wife and act as if it is of no consequence. Your lover commits adultery, which I need not tell you is a serious crime."

Hakon stepped away from them and took a deep breath to calm himself. "Law-speaker?" he asked. "What is the penalty for a wife who commits adultery?"

"Death, lord."

"And what of the man who disturbs the thing with violence?"

"Banishment from the next summer's thing."

"What about the man who strikes his wife?"

"She would be allowed to divorce him, lord, and reclaim her dowry, provided she has witnesses who can corroborate her claim."

"And what about the man who is unable to satisfy his wife in bed?"

"There is no penalty, lord, though again, the wife would be in her rights to divorce him, if she had witnesses."

"And would the penalty of death be applied to the wife who commits adultery because she is battered or neglected in bed?"

"No, lord. Though I would think it should not go unpunished."

Hakon nodded and turned back to the group before him. "Have you witnesses, Turid?"

"I am her witness," Sigge blurted.

Hakon's brow rose. "You saw Alvart strike Turid?"

"Aye. It —"

"You lie, Sigurdsson!" Alvart blurted and took a menacing step forward.

"Silence, Alvart!" Hakon shouted.

Sigge continued. "It happened several winters ago, during one of my father's feasts. I had left his hall to take a piss and saw them standing near the wall of my father's barn. Alvart was angry and struck her. He then went back inside the hall, and I went to help her. It is how we met."

"Lord. This man lies. You must believe me. I have never touched my wife!" Alvart pleaded.

Hakon stayed him with a hand and paced for a long moment. Finally, he turned back to the group, his face grave. A part of him had known it would come to this, but it was still not a verdict he wished to give. "I can see only one way to settle this matter, since one of you lies and we have no way of knowing which one. Tomorrow, we shall hold a holmgang. We will let God, and your swords, decide who speaks truly. If Alvart wins, then he will reclaim his honor and keep his wife. If he loses, then we must believe Hakon Sigurdsson's eyes did not deceive him that night beside Sigurd's barn."

Hakon scanned the group. Alvart had his arms crossed and was grinning. Turid's face blanched and her concerned eyes sought those of her lover. Sigge smiled at her, though his eyes told a different story.

"For disturbing the thing's peace," Hakon continued, looking at Alvart, "you shall be banished from all things for the full cycle of a year, including next summer's thing. That is, if you survive the duel."

He turned to Turid, whose sorry eyes could barely stay on her king. "And you. If your husband survives, we shall know he is innocent and you are guilty in this matter, and we shall re-try you as an adulteress."

Hakon reclaimed his seat, his head pounding furiously from weariness and hunger and the emotional storm that tore at him. "That is all." He waved the group away, wondering as he did so just how he would tell Sigurd and Astrid of the verdict.

In the end, he did not have to. Word of the ruling spread like fire across a dry field. Hakon braced himself for the tirade he felt sure would come, but it never materialized. Instead, Sigurd and Astrid welcomed him to the head table for supper and ushered him to the seat of honor. No sooner had he sat than he was handed a full cup of ale. Warriors from Hakon's and Sigurd's hirds already filled the other tables, as did Sigge and his followers, who sat nearby, looking none too distraught.

"My son seems satisfied with the outcome," Sigurd said before guzzling some ale.

Hakon glanced at the far table, then at his friend. "Are you?"

Sigurd wiped the residual liquid from his mustache. "I am angry, but my anger is directed at my son, not you. He is old enough to make his own decisions, as empty-headed as some of them may be."

Hakon regarded the far table and Sigurd's son in the midst of his comrades. He was laughing at some tale being told. "He seems to care about Turid, so mayhap to him, this trouble was worth it."

Astrid snorted. "He cares about many women. It is hard to fathom why Turid should stand out from the rest."

Hakon sipped his ale. "She is a pretty lass."

Astrid's eyes rolled. "So are the others."

The comment sparked an idea in Hakon's head. "Mayhap it is not the woman, then. Mayhap he seeks to build his reputation and has picked a fight?"

Sigurd frowned as he considered Hakon's words. "If that is true, then I wish he would have chosen another. Alvart has been with me for many winters. He is a friend and a good and faithful warrior. Whatever the result, I will grieve mightily." Sigurd took another guzzle of ale. As he did, Hakon stole a glance at Astrid. Her stony gaze was fixed on her brother.

"You are not so pleased with your brother's antics," Hakon said to her profile.

"He plays a risky game with our name and our family," Astrid said, which was true. If Sigge died, he would end Sigurd's bloodline, and do so as a philanderer.

"Then let us hope, for all of our sakes, that he prevails."

"Enough of this talk," interjected Sigurd bluntly. "It weighs on me and turns my stomach. Let us speak of happier things. Astrid has told me of your proposal, Hakon."

Hakon felt like a ship caught in a sudden squall, and it took him a moment of glancing at Sigurd, then at the smiling Astrid, to right his bearings. "What has she told you?" he asked hesitantly.

"That you wish for her to live with you, at Avaldsnes." Sigurd turned and grinned at Hakon.

"So you approve?"

Sigurd smacked Hakon on the back, splashing some of his ale onto the table as he did so. "Of course I approve! What father would not want his daughter to be happy?" He laughed and hoisted his cup.

Hakon toasted his friend and drank, then turned to the smiling Astrid. And in that moment, with the firelight highlighting the lines of her face and the deep creases at the corners of her eyes, his heart soared.

"You would not have said that winters ago, when I was to marry Groa."

Sigurd waved the comment aside. "Of course not! But that was then, and it was political. Times have changed." He placed on hand on each of their shoulders. "At least one of my children is capable of sound decisions! And who knows? Mayhap the gods will grant me a grand-child yet!"

"Father!" Astrid wailed.

Hakon smiled at his friend's comment, for it would not be a bad thing to have a child with Astrid. But the same thought turned his mind to the impending duel, and the peril in which he had placed his friend's child. And that thought, in turn, brought with it visions of Erik's sons, and Gyda, and the knife that had taken the life of his unborn child. He sat in silence for a time with those thoughts weighing on him. Astrid must have sensed his gloom, for she rose, kissed his head, and left him to his thoughts.

"What have you heard among your chieftains?" he finally asked Sigurd. "Think you that they will come to fight the Danes?"

Sigurd swirled his cup as he considered his king's words. "I think they will not want to risk their necks for the sake of other men. They will only do so if Drangi tells them it is wise."

Hakon was not surprised, for it was the way of things. Men saw only their own families, their own lands, their own harvest, and the will of their false gods in it all. Life was a struggle, and most did not have the luxury of looking beyond the next winter. "And you?" he asked Sigurd.

Sigurd guzzled the remainder of his ale and belched loudly. "I am older now, Hakon, and have won my fame. And I am no longer so eager for the blood fray. Nor have I much need for more riches. So unless you can convince me that there is good reason, I see no logic in poking the bee's nest." He raised a finger. "But, if I know my people, then I know there will be some young ones who *will* see a reason. Those that thirst for wealth and fame will join you, unless Drangi's advice is dire." He shrugged. "We will have to see."

"You sound as if you are satisfied with dying abed rather than protecting what is yours."

Sigurd glowered and raised a finger at his king. "Watch your words, my lord. I am no coward." He rose. "Now I must sleep. The morrow will be a bitter day, regardless of the outcome."

Sigurd disappeared into his tent, and Hakon glanced at Toralv, who sat to his right. The big man sleeved some grease from his beard and smiled. "Fine work, my lord. Nothing like calling your closest friend and ally a coward."

Hakon ignored him and took a swig from his cup to calm his rising anger. He had pushed as far as he could. The rest was in God's hands.

Chapter 10

A horn called the Tronds to the duel, which was to take place in a small space marked at the corners by hazel sticks. Ropes ran from stick to stick to mark the dueling area which, according to the law, was only five long paces by five long paces — not much room in which to maneuver. As a boy, Hakon had fought in several duels, and as he gazed at the men approaching the dueling ground from east and west, his mind flooded with the memory of his fear. Fear that had turned his stomach in knots and beaded the sweat on his brow. Fear that as a warrior, he was not supposed to show. He wondered if he had masked it as well as these men, for neither appeared the least bit apprehensive. Rather, both men smiled and joked with their comrades, paying their challenger little heed.

Both men were equally equipped, carrying a long sword in their hand, a seax at their waist, and a round shield. Both also wore a helmet and a byrnie that reached down to their knees. They were wealthy men and could afford such finery. Not all men were so lucky.

As the men entered the dueling ground, their friends and comrades called encouragement, or else heaped insults on the other man. Those who had no stake in the fight called out their bets to anyone willing to put a wager on the duel. Even women and children joined the ruckus.

Hakon held up his hands for silence and the crowd's clamor settled to an occasional shout. Aided by his walking stick, Thorbjorn stepped into the field and began to recite the laws of the duel in his age-weakened voice.

"This duel is between Hakon Sigurdsson and Alvart Alvartsson, alone. May no other man intervene or assist either man." The law-speaker's ancient eyes moved from one combatant to the other. "Each man shall have two weapons and a shield. Nothing more. Once the fight has begun, if either man puts a foot outside the field, it will be considered retreat. If he puts both feet out, it will be considered flight. If he retreats, he can return if he so wishes, and the duel will resume. If he does not return, or if he flees, he loses the fight and forfeits all that he owns. If a contestant dies, all that he owns will go to the victor. Either man will have the right to buy himself out of the contest at any time, if he so chooses. The price is half that man's possessions to the victor. Are the rules understood?"

Both men nodded. The law-speaker exited the small field and took his place beside Hakon. To the other side of the king stood a silent Sigurd. The jarl had performed a sacrifice that morning with Drangi, but it had done little to alleviate the concern that danced in his eyes and pulled at his features. His friend's concern tore at Hakon's nerves, for it would be a hard thing indeed to know that his verdict had killed his friend's son. Such a death would strain their relationship; of that there was little doubt. But more so, it would cut Sigurd deeply, irrevocably, and that was a fate Hakon wished on neither of them, nor on Astrid.

Hakon took a deep breath. "Ready?" he asked his friend.

Sigurd could only nod.

Hakon raised his arm, and the combatants braced behind their shields. The shouting resumed.

"Now is your chance to buy your life, pup," shouted Alvart above the din. "I won't think any less of you."

"I will enjoy humping your wife tonight," Sigge responded, "as your lifeless eyes look on."

Alvart's face flushed. "You swine! I will kill you slowly for that re-mark."

Hakon dropped his hand, and Alvart leaped forward. For a man of his size, bedecked in a heavy byrnie as he was, he moved like a rabbit. His speed took Sigge by surprise and put him instantly on the defensive. Sigge dodged right, but Alvart cut off his escape by slamming his shield rim into the right side of Sigge's own shield. The move turned Sigge's shield, blocking his sword arm while exposing his left side. Quick as a blink, Alvart thrust with this sword at Sigge's stomach. The young man jerked right to avoid the thrust, but the sword ripped through the chain.

The crowd gave a collective gasp, but Sigge did not seem to notice. Rather, he shifted his weight right, rose on his toes to gain leverage, lifted his right arm above his shield rim, and thrust down with his blade. The move was awkward, but Sigge's sword somehow found its way to Alvart's neck.

Alvart jerked his head back as if stung, dragging his blade free as he did so. "That was a lucky poke, boy," he growled.

Sigge pointed at him with his blade. "Judging from the blood I see, that was more than a poke, old man."

Confusion registered on Alvart's face as his hand moved to his neck and felt under his thick beard. His hand came away soaked in crimson.

Alvart's confusion transformed to fury as he charged again. But Sigge was ready this time and sidestepped the larger man's attack, taking the brunt of Alvart's lateral sword-swing on his shield before dancing two paces away.

Alvart turned to attack again, but now the blood pouring from his neck was plain for all to see. It soaked the left side of his byrnie and his left arm besides. "I will kill you, Sigurdsson!" he roared and came again, but his legs would not obey. He staggered and nearly fell.

Sigge jumped right, spun, and hacked at the back of the stumbling man's neck. Alvart tried to protect himself but was far too off balance and weak to lift his shield. The blade bit into his spine and severed his head cleanly from his shoulders. Alvart's massive body collapsed with a dull thud at the foot of his comrades, while his bearded head rolled awkwardly into their midst.

Silence fell across the field. No one had expected the duel to end so quickly, least of all Alvart's comrades. Short moments before, the big man had been joking with them. Now his headless torso lay in a bloody pool before them. Stunned eyes shifted to Sigge, who was feeling for bodily damage inside his byrnie. His hand came away clean. Somehow Alvart's sword had missed Sigge's torso, but how was anyone's guess, for they had all seen the blade penetrate his armor. Sigge grinned stupidly at his luck.

"A sad display of swordsmanship, that," grumbled Egil, who stood behind Hakon, shaking his head.

"He underestimated Sigge," said Sigurd, whose voice sang with pride as he stepped into the ring to embrace his son.

Egil spat as he was wont to do when he disagreed with something.

Hakon crossed himself in thanks to God, then addressed the crowd. "The duel is over. According to the law, Hakon Sigurdsson now has the rights to all that Alvart Alvartsson owned, including his wife. This matter is settled."

Hakon walked over to Turid, who stood back from the crowd, looking uncertain. "Do you see now what your foolishness has wrought?" Hakon asked her.

Her eyes narrowed as she gazed up at her king. "I would not change what I have done, my lord," she said. "Alvart was a pig and deserved the death that came to him."

The sharp edge of her emotion surprised Hakon, but heartened him as well, for a false heart rarely felt such emotion. He nodded to her. "Then I am glad for you, Turid. For God has seen your plight and chosen justly." And with that, he walked away in search of Astrid and his daughter.

He found them playing on the beach. Astrid and Unn were chasing a shrieking Thora with wiggling fingers that threatened to catch and tickle her. Hakon stopped and watched for a time with a smile on his face, letting the pure innocence of their fun wash away the recent violence he had witnessed. Astrid caught sight of him then and stopped her pursuit.

"Come catch me!" Thora called to her.

"Run along," Astrid waved to her. "Unn will catch you."

At this, Unn growled playfully and ran for her. Thora yelped and bounded away.

"So?" Astrid asked as she neared Hakon. Her face was anxious.

"Your brother lives."

Astrid's shoulders slumped in her relief. "Thank the gods."

"Aye," offered Hakon graciously, for now was not the time to bicker about religion.

He sat in the sand and patted a spot next to him. Astrid gathered her overdress above her knees and joined him.

"My brother is a fool," she said, though there was more sadness in her voice than bitterness.

"His youth makes him foolish," Hakon said, "though he is no fool."

"You are kind, though not entirely accurate. He gives my father fits. I hope, now that he is master of his own fate, that his mind and behavior mature."

"I hope so too," Hakon admitted, then turned his attention to Thora, who was shrieking as she charged across the shingle with Unn not far behind. As she looked back at her pursuer, Thora stumbled on a clump of seaweed and fell hard to the sand. Unn caught her then and tickled her ribs so that her brewing tears turned quickly to laughter.

"Your daughter is quite a girl."

"How so?"

"Do I really need to tell you?"

Hakon smiled. "No," he said. "She is my heart."

"She is a king's daughter. Strong. Mature. Self-assured. You and Gyda have done well by her."

Hakon grabbed a handful of sand mindlessly and let it pour slowly through his calloused fingers. "The credit belongs to Gyda. I have often been gone."

Astrid must have sensed that the mention of Gyda brought with it a wave of melancholy, for she scooted closer to Hakon, tucked an arm through his, and rested her head on his shoulder. Hakon's stomach warmed with the embrace, and he leaned closer to her.

"There is much in her that is you," she said. "I can see it. It would have been there with or without you, or Gyda."

The words swelled Hakon's heart with pride, though he dared not admit it. "She is a good girl," he said. "And you are good with her. It makes me glad that you will live with us."

Astrid sat up and kissed Hakon on his hairy cheek, then laid her head on his shoulder again.

Down on the beach, Unn was doubled over, breathing hard through her grin as Thora ran circles around her, daring her to give chase. Overhead the sun shone, while out at sea, a small breeze rippled the fjord waters. The threat of Sigge's death had vanished with the sight of Thora and Astrid, and in its place there was only happiness, and relief, and this momentary peace.

Sigurd stood at the head table, and as he did, a hush settled on those who had gathered at the eating boards. "Today," he began, "has been a hard day. My emotions" — the jarl pounded his chest with his closed fist to emphasize his point — "are swirling like a northern wind. While I celebrate my son's victory" — Sigurd raised his cup in his son's direction, a gesture that earned Sigge the backslaps and cheers of his fellow warriors — "I also mourn the loss of my oath-sworn hirdman, Alvart." Sigurd nodded to the table where Alvart's closest friends sat quietly. They had left an empty spot at the table for their fallen comrade.

Hakon and Astrid watched Sigurd speak from the shadow of the trees. They had spent the afternoon rolling in the furs of Hakon's tent but had risen with the sounds of merriment carrying to them from Sigurd's feasting area. Now, rather than disturb Sigurd's heartfelt words, they waited for the jarl to speak his mind.

"So that you might appreciate the man whose life you took today," Sigurd called to his son, "I would like to say a few words on his behalf." Sigge's friends suddenly sensed the inappropriateness of their jocularity and turned their attention to the jarl.

"Before you were howling for your mother's milk, Sigge, Alvart was wading through the blood-fray with his shield and sword by my side. He came from nothing. His father was a bonder who lost his odal rights to King Harald and then his life to a harsh winter when Alvart was but a bairn. Alvart made his way to his uncle's hall, and there was raised with his cousins.

"He joined me when I sought men to end the scourge of Erik and fought by my side at Mollebakken, where two of King Hakon's brothers perished. He swore his oath to me after that battle, when Erik's fame was on the rise and mine was at its lowest. Yet, he never wavered in his fealty, nor doubted my battle luck. From that day to this, he fought with me and feasted with me, and I was proud to call him a friend. He was a man with his faults, but who among us is faultless? I will miss his courage, his loyalty, and his faith in me. He died with his sword in hand, and for that I am thankful, for he will need it in Valhall, where I am sure he now sits, surrounded by his friends and comrades." Sigurd raised his cup. "To Alvart!"

"To Alvart!" those gathered responded, and even Sigge raised his cup.

With his eulogy now ended, Sigurd reclaimed his seat and the feast resumed, albeit more cautiously. Sigurd had let his feelings on the matter show, and no one wanted to be the fool to laugh into the fog of reverence that hung over their lord.

Hakon and Astrid emerged from the shadows and sat to either side of the jarl. Astrid placed a comforting hand on her father's round shoulder, which Sigurd covered with his own paw.

"Well spoken," Hakon added simply as he took a seat to Sigurd's right.

"It was a bad business," Sigurd said as he tore a chunk of bread from a nearby loaf and dipped it into his bowl. "I am just glad it is behind us and I still have my son at the end of it."

Hakon poured some ale into his cup. "I, too, am glad of that, Sigurd." He wanted to say more but felt that silence was a better companion, so he held his tongue and left Sigurd to his thoughts.

They ate in silence for a time, watching the feast unfold about them as afternoon turned to dusk and then to night. More folk came and others left, their moving forms wavering in the heat from the crackling fire around which the eating boards had been arranged. Men and women mingled, their rolling conversations punctuated by the occasional shout or laugh or snap of wood in the flames. As evening settled in, Astrid rose from her seat and retired for the night.

"It is time," a voice croaked, and Hakon searched the darkness for its owner. His eyes finally spotted Drangi standing a short distance from the eating board, his head no taller than most men's waists.

Sigurd glanced at Hakon. "Come. Let us learn what the gods think of your plan."

Sigurd ignored Hakon's questioning look and pushed himself to his feet with a grunt. Hakon stood also and reluctantly followed the waddling godi through the darkness to his tent. It stood away from the others and was illuminated by flames that hissed in two metal sconces by the entrance flaps. He and Sigurd were not the only men to have been summoned. All of the Trondelag chieftains, including Tosti, stood near the entrance, the firelight dancing on their uneasy faces.

The dwarf wove his way through the group and entered the tent. "Come," he called over his shoulder.

Hakon entered first. The interior of the tent was spartan. Save for a bed of furs against one wall, some drying herbs hanging from the crossbeams overhead, and a three-legged stool standing beside the small fire that burned in the tent's center, the place was devoid of furnishings. Hakon found a seat on the fur rugs that covered the grass. With a prolonged groan, Sigurd sat beside his king. The others found their places in a circle around the fire and the stool where Drangi settled.

Without a word, the godi pulled a ladle from a pot that rested on a heating stone near the fire and spooned the contents into a wooden bowl. Drangi then dipped a short pine branch into the bowl and, with murmured, guttural incantations, flicked the branch at his guests so that the contents of the bowl splattered on their skin and clothes.

Hakon tensed, knowing instantly that the liquid was the blood of sacrifice. The men accepted the blood reverently, closing their eyes and lifting their faces as the dark liquid splattered their skin, their beards, and their tunics.

Hakon clutched the grip of his sword when Drangi turned to face him. "Do not," he said.

Drangi scowled, as did some of the others in the tent. It was no secret that Hakon was a Christian, but even after all this time, his religion chafed many. Hakon ignored them and focused on the godi, who shrugged off the slight and pulled a leather bag from his belt. This he opened with his stubby fingers and, while murmuring some unintelligible words that Hakon assumed were prayers, dumped the contents of the pouch onto the furs. The bones rattled as they scattered, and the gathered men leaned in to see what they could. Drangi remained on the stool with his eyes closed and his brows furrowed. Every so often, his body jerked as his lips jabbered their prayers and his fat hands circled over the bones. No one spoke. No one dared break the godi's trance. Suddenly the fire leaped and the men retreated in fear. Hakon grabbed the cross that hung from his neck and waited, decidedly more on edge now than he had been moments before.

Drangi opened his eyes and studied the runes. He grabbed a twig and sorted through them, mumbling as he did so. No one spoke.

The godi-dwarf toyed with a bone hanging in his gray beard as his eyes moved across the etched runes. "I see force, like flowing water," he finally said in his toad-like croak. "It couples closely with movement. And rebirth." He gently moved aside some runes with his stick to reveal a solitary rune beneath the others. For a long time, he stroked his beard as his eyes studied the pattern. "Beneath it all lies Tyr, the rune of the warrior."

Hakon's heart skipped. "The rune of Tyr?" he asked.

Drangi and the others looked at him, though it was Sigurd who spoke. "Does that mean something to you?"

"It is the mark of Erik's kin. His Danes wear it on their shields."

This caused a low hum of expletives from the gathered men. "That is a strange coincidence," offered Sigurd, scratching his beard.

"It is no coincidence," Drangi's voice rumbled. "It is the gods speaking to us. Warning us."

Sigurd frowned. "Warning us of what?"

Drangi could not hold Sigurd's hard gaze and shifted his eyes back to the runes. "The gods are not always so direct, lord."

"Then what do you think they tell us, Drangi?"

The godi blanched. "The runes say that war is coming," he said slowly, carefully. "It is inevitable. A force like the tide."

Like the tide. Had not the Danish prisoner said something similar? Hakon shuddered. He did not believe in the sorcery of godis, but he was finding it hard to dismiss Drangi's words.

"Is it coming here, this war?" asked Sigurd.

Drangi stroked his beard and peeked at Sigurd, then at the flames. "This war will not just come to certain lands and miss others. Every man will feel its force. Like flowing water."

Sigurd grunted and stared at the flames of the small fire. The men in the tent seemed to hold their breath as they watched their jarl. Then, finally, Sigurd sighed. It was a deep sigh that spoke of resignation and reluctant acceptance. He tore his eyes from the flames and looked around the tent. "So be it. If war is inevitable, then war it shall be."

The following morning, Sigurd ordered the men to gather again in the Frosta-fields.

"The gods have spoken," he bellowed to the crowd when they had assembled. "War is coming. If we act now, we will fight alongside Hakon and his army, as one, in strength!" He curled his paw into a fist and raised it for the men to see. "Act not, and we will find ourselves on an island, fighting alone. Those of you who are oath-sworn to me, it is time to tend to your families and your farms. Those of you who are free to decide, the decision rests with you. But know this — it will be as Hakon says. You will find no bigger adventure. And should we prevail, no greater treasure than battle fame and Danish silver!"

The roar of eager men rippled across the field, bringing a smile to Hakon's lips. Even the elders took up the cheer, now that the gods had spoken, for who were they to defy the gods?

"In half a moon's time, we gather at Lade. I hope to see many of you there."

When the assembly ended, Sigurd grabbed Hakon's arm and walked beside him back to the tents. "I have been thinking more about your offer to my daughter..." His voice trailed off.

"And?"

"Do you think it safe for her to return to Avaldsnes with you now? Or your daughter, for that matter?"

The same thought had been bouncing around Hakon's mind. On the one hand, he could easily envision another attack on Avaldsnes, but then, was anywhere truly safe? He shared this sentiment with Sigurd, who grunted.

"Some places are safer than others, I think."

Hakon stopped and faced his jarl. "Speak plainly, Sigurd. What is it you want?"

"The times are uncertain, Hakon. At the moment, all I know is that there is an army of Danes that seeks your death. I do not want to put my daughter in harm's way if it can be avoided."

"I understand, Sigurd. But you must trust me when I say that Avaldsnes is as safe as any place. Gamle and his brothers attacked it by surprise and failed to take it. We are even more prepared now, should he return."

Sigurd's blue eyes studied his face. Long ago, those eyes had sparkled like glacial pools, but age and pain and struggle had robbed them of their luster. Sigurd's gaze softened and he sighed grandly. "Keep her safe."

"With my life," Hakon promised as his mind turned again to Gamle and his Danes and the bitter fights yet to come.

Chapter 11

The rocky peak of Freikollen loomed large in Hakon's view, though it was the beacon fire dancing on its peak that had him worried, and wroth. Lighting the beacon was no small matter, for beacon fires alerted the entire area of possible enemies, called men to arms, sent civilians into hiding, and disrupted life greatly. For that reason, they were only to be lit when large, unknown forces appeared. His two ships were hardly a large force, and were certainly recognizable.

He glanced back at Astrid, who sat with Thora and Unn near the steer board, huddled under a blanket of wool to fend off the biting wind. Hakon had just promised to keep her safe, but if the beacon warned of a larger force, what then? Would he need to return her so soon to Lade? He cursed under this breath and looked back at the flame.

They had left Frosta two days after the final assembly, on the first fair wind. Rather than sail all the way to Avaldsnes in a single ship, Hakon agreed to sail to Frei Island with Tosti and his men first, and there await the Trond army. Once Sigurd came with his ships, they would head south together and stop at Avaldsnes, then make their way to the Vik and the army of his nephews. Presuming, of course, that Gamle and his brothers hadn't sailed north first. Hakon eyed the beacon flame warily.

Hakon's two ships turned into the calm waters of the Trondheim-sleia, the strait to the north of Frei, then angled south into Kvernesfjord. Save for the nagging worry of the beacon fires, the evening was calm and beautiful on the fjord. The sun had emerged from behind scattered clouds to hover low in the sky, casting a magical golden glow onto the waterway that led to Tosti's hall at Birkestrand.

The ships turned and glided into the small bay below the estate, where several ships and a small throng of warriors greeted them, further proof that something was amiss. A family of loons protested the new arrivals and flapped noisily as they sought a quieter spot.

"Luck is with us," Tosti's spearman, Alf, said when the ships had landed and he had greeted his chieftain and king in turn. There was a grin on his face, but trouble in his eyes. "We were about to send men in search of you."

"Why?" Tosti asked, his voice guarded.

Alf's face turned serious. "Gamle and his brothers are close, lord," he said. "We lit the beacon when this man brought the news to us. We hope others see it and come to our aid."

Hakon turned his eyes to the plainly dressed young man with braided hair the color of wheat. His thin face and keen brown eyes were vaguely familiar to Hakon. "What is your name?"

"Asrod, lord."

"You have news of Gamle and his army?"

The young man raised his chin with its mottled beard. "Aye, lord. Gamle's ships arrived three days ago. From beyond the western horizon."

"Where are they?" Hakon felt his body tense. He didn't want to hear the answer for fear it was dire, but he had to know.

"At Stad — or at least they were three days ago."

Hakon cursed and cast a glance at Astrid, who was helping Thora from the ship. "Come. We shall discuss this matter inside."

Hakon gathered with Tosti, Alf, Toralv, Egil, and Asrod around a growing hearth fire in the hall, where they awaited the food and ale Tosti had ordered his thralls to bring. Egil held his wrinkled hands to the flames to warm his old bones, and it was he who spoke first.

"Well? Shall we just stare at the fire, or shall we discuss Gamle and his army?"

Hakon grinned at the old man's impatience. "Egil speaks as if he has someplace better to be. Very well. Asrod, speak to us of what you know."

Asrod sat up straight on his stool and cast his eyes about, clearly uncomfortable in the presence of so many lords and famed warriors. He cleared this throat. "Gamle and his army came from the sea three days ago, in the early morning. As soon as we saw their masts, Eldgrim's scouts blew their warning horns and lit the beacon fires. But Eldgrim had little time to prepare his defenses. As they approached, he sent me and some of his younger warriors to a place where he keeps a small ship, with orders to head north to warn who I could."

"Eldgrim must hold you in high regard," Hakon said.

"My father is his helmsman. I know ships too."

"How many men, Asrod?" asked Tosti impatiently.

"We counted twenty ships, lord." Asrod delivered the news in a hushed tone, then turned his eyes to his hands, as if the news were his fault and he was guilty for it.

"Anywhere from seven hundred to a thousand men," Hakon said with a sigh. "And I doubt they have come to parlay." Hakon's mind flew forward to the battle he knew would come. He did not fear it. He wanted to fight. He yearned for it, in fact. He had just hoped it would be on his terms, not theirs. Now he feared it was too late for that. "So," he said after a time, "what say you men? Do we fight them here or head back to Lade where we know we have some support?"

This comment had the men looking at each other. Hakon knew what was passing unspoken between them. They had never heard their king consider backing away from a fight, no matter the odds, and from their sidelong glances, he could tell that the thought did not sit well with them now.

"We have faced bad odds before," he explained. "But never this poor. So as I see it, we can sail back to Lade, gather men from Sigurd, and fight Erik's sons on our terms. Or we can stay and fight them here. You men already know how poor those odds will be."

The men looked at each other again, then at the fire snapping before them. The thralls returned with cups of ale, which the men drank in silence as they considered their options.

Egil broke the uneasy hush. "As you know, I was in many battles with your father, Hakon, and he gave battle sometimes with many warriors by his side, sometimes with few; but he always gave battle, and he always came off with the victory. Never did I hear him ask counsel from his friends whether he should flee. So, you shall get no such counsel from me, boy. You should fight, as your father would have. And when you do, I shall fight beside you, come what may."

"You are just eager for the battle-death, old man," joked Toralv. This brought some chuckles, though most knew Toralv spoke truly. "Still, what you say sounds true to my ears. I, too, say we fight. If we prevail, we will send a mighty message to those bastards. Besides, I will not allow Gamle and his brothers to believe our army is just one old man with a cane." This received more chuckles, and even Egil cracked a grin.

"Our group is small, but we are here to help," said Asrod earnestly.

Their eyes turned to Tosti and his man, Alf. Tosti shrugged as if it made no difference to him. "Do not cast your eyes on me," he said. "I am oath-sworn to Sigurd, who is oath-sworn to King Hakon. So whatever you decide, lord, we shall do."

The loyalty and the courage of his men humbled him, but Hakon was not ready to throw away their lives so easily. At the very least, he needed to even the odds in numbers, or strategy, or both. "If we stay, there is no time to seek help from Lade. We will send out the war arrow and gather what men we can from nearby. I have heard that the men hereabouts are stout. We shall now test the truth of that — eh, Tosti?"

The chieftain grunted, though whether in affirmation or disagreement was hard to say.

"Sail tonight for your neighbors, Tosti, for you alone know who is most likely to heed our call. My hope is that they have seen the beacon flame and are already making plans. What forces they can gather shall return here by morning, two days hence. While we wait, we shall survey the island and choose the most favorable spot to fight, somewhere to help even the odds. Asrod," Hakon said to the sailor. "Sail south again and bid my nephews come to Frei. I will have them fight me before they do more scathe in the land. Leave as soon as you can." The young man nodded his understanding.

Hakon's thoughts then turned to Astrid and Thora, and the promise he had made to Sigurd. Then, just as quickly, his mind filled with the memory of Gyda. "Alf?"

"Aye, lord?"

"I want you to take Astrid and Thora to Lade by land. Will you do that?"

"Of course, lord."

"Go with Tosti tonight. He will let you off where you can make your way back to Lade. Take whatever supplies you need, and another man if you wish."

The spearman nodded curtly.

Hakon drained his cup and stood. "Let us be about it. We have little time."

"And here I thought I would die abed," Egil said as he pushed himself up with his walking stick.

Hakon glanced at his friend. Losing Egil would be like losing a part of himself. Just the thought of it filled Hakon with equal measures of dread and sadness. "Do not speak so, Egil. I need you by my side for a long time to come."

Egil snorted. "Those things are not for you to decide. The Norns will decide my fate, boy, and no other."

"Then let us pray the Norns are not ready to cut your life threads. You may be ugly and old, but I am not ready to be rid of you."

Hakon wandered to the place where he and Sigurd had sat not so long ago, on the hillside near the hall. From there he could survey the activity on the beach as Tosti called out commands and chose those who would help him seek out warriors among the islands and waterways that surrounded Frei. He could also see Astrid emerging from the crowd and heading in his direction. Even from a distance in the half-light of night, he knew she was angry. Egil saw her too and wisely left Hakon in peace.

"What is this I hear about you sending me away?" she asked between panting breaths when she reached him. Her hands were on her hips and her brows were drawn down toward her nose.

Hakon had expected her displeasure, but still found it hard to hold her gaze. "It cannot be helped. You are not safe here. Nor is Thora. I made a promise to your father to keep you safe, and I fear with Gamle's return that I can no longer keep it."

She straightened haughtily. "I am a jarl's daughter. I can defend myself better than most, and I do not plan to leave my man so easily. Let Gamle come."

"You are a jarl's daughter, Astrid, and so much more to me. Which is why I do not want to lose you."

"Why are you so sure you will lose me?"

"Because Gamle and his brothers sail here with twenty ships. We have but three, and only partial crews in each. No matter how valiantly we fight, the odds are poor at best. We will gain others, but how many and of what quality, only God knows."

The hostility in her face softened. "Is it really so bad?"

He nodded slowly and let his eyes wander to the ships. "Aye. I knew they would come again, but they surprised me in how fast they mustered an army." His mind suddenly turned to the Dane at Avaldsnes and the words he had spoken. *I am but one warrior. Where I fall, ten more sword-Danes will soon come, and with one purpose in mind: to win for our king even more land and wealth.* The words sent a shiver through Hakon as he thought back on them now.

Astrid remained silent as Hakon mused. He could sense her sadness but could do nothing to stop it, could say nothing to change it. "If you stay," he continued, "I will not be able to protect you." His mind flew again to the bruised and bloodied face of Gyda. "What they did to Gyda was unspeakable. I will not have the same done to you if, God forbid, something happens to me." He clutched the cross at his neck to ward off the evil spirits who might have heard his words.

She swiped at her cheek, and Hakon realized that she was wiping away a tear. He sighed deeply. "I will send for you when all of this is over, Astrid. For now, though, I need you, Thora, and Unn to go with Alf. He knows this land and will get you back to Lade safely. Please tell your father that he was right."

Hakon had spoken his piece. The silence stretched between them. When she finally responded, there was a quiet intensity in her voice that broke Hakon's heart. "I only just found you again, and now this. Do not die, Hakon. Do you understand me?"

He pulled her close to him and let her rest her head on his shoulder. "I do not plan on dying, Astrid. Not yet, anyhow. Come. Let us find Thora."

They walked down to the beach, where men milled about and Unn stood with her hand on Thora's shoulder. "Father!" Thora cried, and ran to Hakon. She wrapped her surprisingly strong arms around Hakon's waist. "That man tells me that I must go with him, but I do not want to. I want to stay with you."

Hakon returned the hug. "I know, Thora. And I want to stay with you, but it is not safe here."

"Why?" Tears welled in her blue eyes.

Hakon peeled her arms away and knelt so that his face was level with hers. The tears streamed from her eyes, and he wiped them away with his thumb. His heart broke for the second time that day, and for the second time, he could do nothing to stop it. "Do you remember the bad men that came to Avaldsnes?"

She nodded fervently.

"Well, they are on their way here. So it is here we must stop them before they do any more wrongs to this land and our people," he said, holding her eyes with his in the hope that it would help her understand. "Unn and Astrid will stay with you until I return for you."

"When is that?" she asked as she stifled a sob. He could see she was trying to be brave, but her emotions were overwhelming her.

"As soon as I can, Thora. Now please; time is short. Go." He stood and nodded to Unn, who took Thora away.

Astrid embraced Hakon then and, without a word, followed his daughter to the ship where Tosti and Alf waited. He committed their sight to his memory, praying as he did so that he might see them again.

Chapter 12

In the end, only seven ships arrived from the neighboring lands, bringing the total, with Hakon's ships, to nine. Nine ships against Gamle's
twenty. A few more men came with their rusted helmets and hand
axes and spears from the various homesteads that dotted the island,
but in the end, it was Gamle's army of a thousand against Hakon's
motley hundreds.

Hakon's army straddled the north side of a plain called Rastarkalv,
which was a morning's hike south from Birkestrand. The clouds hung
dark and ominous above the plain, remnants of the fierce storm that
had blown through the day before and turned the plain into a mire of
wet grass and muddy pools. To their left was the gray sea. To their
right, the ground sloped upward to a low ridge. On its southern end,
the ridge angled sharply down to the bay into which Gamle's ships
now sailed — ships filled with sword-Danes with blood and vengeance
on their minds. They crowded the decks, their spear tips and helmets
gleaming darkly, menacingly, beneath the dark sky. When the men in
those ships saw the army that faced them, their shouts of fury rumbled
like thunder across the plain.

Hakon gazed down his lines. To his right, Sigge and his crew, and
some of the recent arrivals, stretched to the low ridge. To Hakon's left
stood Tosti's men and more of the locals, their numbers reaching to
the sea. One of the younger recruits in that group vomited in the grass.
Others displayed the raw fear that haunted men before battle. Hakon

could hardly blame them, for it was a hard thing to know that the army coming for your blood doubled your own in numbers. He spat into the slick grass, trying to dispel a thought that nagged at his mind like an annoying fly. Why had he not fled? Why had he let an old man talk him into this folly? He should have trusted his own gut rather than the bold words of a man bent on dying in battle.

"Yell all you can, fools!" bellowed Toralv, tearing Hakon from his reverie. "You'll be wishing you had saved your breath after charging across this field."

Some of the men laughed at this, but not many. Down the line, another of the younger recruits vomited. No one teased him, for many of the men had done the same before their first battle. Some still did.

Hakon turned to Egil, who stood next to him draped in his armor and his signature wool shirt. Long ago, he had worn only the shirt in battle, but with age came wisdom, and now he wore both. "It is time. Do you have the standards we discussed?"

"Aye."

"And your men know their roles?"

"I have been doing this longer than you have been alive, boy," grumbled Egil.

Hakon smiled at Egil's sour rebuke. "Then good luck, my friend. I will see you when this is over."

Egil donned his helmet, patted his king's armored shoulder, and without a word, hobbled back to the handpicked group of men waiting behind the lines with the standards of the local chieftains who had recently arrived. Hakon put them from his mind and walked down the line of his army, adjusting their armor and telling jokes to distract the men from the enemy roars rending the air.

"I'm beginning to wonder about your choice of battles, lord," called Sigge, though the smile on his face told Hakon he meant no malice. "Will you have us fighting giants next?"

Some of Sigge's comrades chuckled, but not Hakon. The comment pricked him like the sharp nettle on a pine. "Is this not just another predicament to wiggle out of, Sigge? You of all people should feel at home here."

Sigge's comrades hooted at this, but the smile evaporated from Sigge's face.

"Enough of the jokes," Hakon called to Sigge's warriors. "Do not be foolish this day. Hold the line with every fiber in your body. If they retreat, do not pursue in haste. If they press, give ground slowly, but stay together. That is paramount. Do you hear my words?"

The young men acknowledged their king with nods of assent. He had spoken these words to them before, but he knew Sigge and his men were eager and, therefore likely to make mistakes. This was one mistake they could not make. Not today. If they broke ranks, they would not only expose Hakon's right flank, they would cut off Egil. Hakon turned back to Sigurd's son and stared straight into his handsome face. "I am counting on you, Sigge. You are in charge here. Do not let your hounds off their leash."

"I will not let you down, lord."

Hakon reclaimed his place at the center of the line and studied the force massing on the beach to the south of him. They had disembarked quickly and formed a protective line to give those at the oar benches time to gather their weapons and helmets and fall in with the others. As at Avaldsnes, two banners flapped at the center of the growing line, one displaying the mark of Tyr and the other the mark of Bloodaxe. The distance was too great to see their faces, though Hakon suspected that Gamle took the center with his hirdmen, while Harald and Ragnfred took the flanks. Between them stretched two lines of Fyrkat Danes and behind those, still more men, which Hakon surmised were men conscripted for support.

"Is that Eldgrim's standard?" Toralv pointed at the area where the reserve troops gathered.

Hakon followed Toralv's finger to the rear of the enemy line. There, among the men, Eldgrim's raven on a red field snapped in the breeze. Asrod and his small crew had not returned, and Hakon had feared that

Gamle had killed them. Now he suspected they had rejoined their lord to fight in Gamle's superior army. "Aye," Hakon spat.

"Why would he do that?" Toralv asked. "Did he not send Asrod here to warn us?"

"That was before Gamle met with Eldgrim," Hakon said. "It appears that Gamle has turned the weasel to his side."

"You did kill his son, lord," offered Asmund from the second rank.

"Keep your teeth tight, Asmund," Toralv warned.

"Here they come!" yelled Tosti.

The air reverberated with the pounding of two thousand feet marching forward, blades and axe handles smacking shield rims, and the calls of leaders to their grim-faced men. This day, there would be no prebattle parlay, nor mercy for the losers — just swinging blades and screams and death. Below the din, Hakon could hear men in his ranks praying, like the rustle of leaves in a violent storm — though to which god or gods they offered their prayers was impossible to say. Mayhap to all of them, or to any one that would listen. Hakon kissed the cross at his neck, then pulled his seax from its sheath. He had planned to say something rousing to his army before the battle, but the time for that had passed.

The Danes reached the middle of the field and splashed into the pools of mud. Their feet sank to their shins in the muck. It was then that the yells and taunts began from Hakon's men. The fury and fear in their voices sent the birds in nearby trees to the skies.

Gamle raised his sword at the center of the line. Archers in the rear ranks lifted their bows to the sky. Seconds later, the wicked streaks of arrow shafts filled the gray morning. They fell onto Hakon's men like rain from the clouds above. Most slammed harmlessly into upturned shields. Others went long. A few found their mark. Hakon gritted his teeth at the cries of pain. When the hail of metal stopped, Hakon ventured a glance down his line and caught sight of a warrior who lay dead in the mud. It was one of the vomiters from earlier. *Poor child never even had a chance to swing his sword at the Danes.*

A roar rose again as Gamle and his men came on. Another volley of arrows arced over their heads as they splashed through the mud, and again the arrows pattered like rain onto shields and helmets and bodies and turf.

A third volley hit before Hakon gave his signal. He had not the men to spare and so waited until the enemy was thirty paces distant before calling on his archers. These he had positioned on the rise to the right, and with the wave of his standard, they let loose. The enemy had not expected the arrows from their flank; when they moved their shields left to protect themselves, Hakon's spearmen heaved their weapons, catching Gamle's men in a cross fire of missiles.

"Come on," Hakon urged under his breath.

Gamle unwittingly obeyed. Erik's oldest son shouted his fury and burst into an awkward sprint over the slick ground and sucking mud. His men followed, trying to keep their balance as arrows hit them from their left and spears from their front. Several men lost their footing and were trampled by others now senseless with battle-fury. Hakon surveyed the scene with satisfaction, for it had the intended effect. Gamle's organized charge was now a disorganized mess of men and shields struggling through mud to get to their prey.

"Shield wall!" Hakon yelled. And as one, his army hefted their shields.

"Ready with the nets!" he shouted again, and several men at the back of the lines dropped to their knees and reached for the fishing lines at their feet. Before them, the enemy rushed forward. Twenty paces distant. Fifteen. Ten.

"Now!" hollered Hakon and behind him, the men yanked at their lines.

Hakon had dug fish netting into the mud along the front of his army. The hapless enemy, who moments before had been splashing toward their prey, suddenly tripped as the buried lines coiled with their feet. They struggled to stay upright as their momentum carried them forward into the blades of Hakon's men. Spear points impaled some. Swords hacked others before they could rise. Behind them, the second rank faltered.

"Keep moving!" hollered Gamle, who stood off to Hakon's right. He had seen his army lose its momentum and could not afford to have his attack stall.

His men responded with a roar and pushed onward, over their comrades' fallen bodies and into the press of shields and spears and sword blades of Hakon's men.

"Kill them!" Hakon shouted above the din.

Hakon's men had the advantage of height, for they stood on a small dike, but the Danes had the advantage of numbers. For every Dane Hakon killed, another stepped up to take his place with no less fury or determination. Hakon kept his shield low, stabbing and slashing at any opportunity he saw. A blade slid past his thigh. Another glanced off his left greave. To his right, Toralv drove his shield boss into his assailant's face, knocking the hapless man from his feet and driving him backward into two charging Fyrkat Danes. To Hakon's left, Asmund had crippled a man with a spear thrust to the shoulder. At the same moment, Hakon hacked through the arm of the Dane slashing his blade at Toralv's left side.

Hakon's body did his will as if guided by a force greater than he. Here, he parried a blow. There, he ducked and countered with a jab that burst through his assailant's byrnie in a splash of crimson. An axe blade glanced off his helm, its blade stopping before it reached his shoulder by the upward thrust of his shield. He smashed his shield boss into the axe man's face, then chopped his seax into his neck.

"Shield wall!" Hakon screamed as he stepped back and regained the shields of Toralv and Asmund, then ventured a quick glance to left and right.

Tosti seemed to be holding firm on the left, though on the right, the line was bending. Gamle had shifted his attack so that his reserve troops now drove into Sigge's line. It was what Hakon had expected him to do. Thankfully, Sigge's banner still stood, but there was no telling how long that would last.

"Now!" Hakon bellowed to his standard-bearer, and his boar flag waved again.

He had no time to see the results. In his mind he envisioned Egil and his chosen men setting off just beyond the ridgeline to his right with their banners raised high and visible to the armies on the field. Even as Hakon parried a strike, he could hear Egil's horns sounding and the din of their blades echoing off their shield rims. The rocky crevices of Freikollen amplified their noise and made it sound as if the force moving to flank Gamle's army was as large as the one he now faced.

From the rear of Gamle's army, a horn blew and the assault stopped. The man attacking Hakon ventured a glance about and died on Hakon's seax for his carelessness. Men in the rear ranks shouted and pointed at the banners of the new force that had just appeared high to their left, and at that moment, the tide of the battle shifted.

In ones and twos, and then in groups, those in the rear ranks of Gamle's army peeled away and scrambled across the muddy field to reach the beach. They could not let this new force flank them and attack them from behind or scuttle their ships. Off to the left, Gamle bellowed for his army to fight on, but his men understood the risk and wanted little part in it. In short order, most of the army dissolved into a mass of retreating men.

Now was the time for Hakon to take advantage of the momentum. With a wave of his standard, his archers let loose, picking off men as they made for the ships. Hakon's army moved forward as one, their pursuit of the enemy across the field rapid, but orderly. That is, until Sigge's men broke ranks and surged ahead. They had passed the fishing nets and were in the open field, and knew that if they used their speed, they could reach the retreating warriors.

"No!" shouted Hakon, though he might as well have been screaming underwater for all the good it did.

Through the field Sigge and his men ran with hoots of battle joy on their lips, quickly reaching Gamle's force in their eagerness to kill more Danes. Gamle, too, saw the folly in young Sigge's move and rallied his men. They turned and with surprising alacrity, came together as one so that Sigge now found himself charging headlong into a tight shield wall of seasoned men. Still some fifty paces distant, Hakon could not reach Sigge in time to defend him, or lend muscle to his foolish charge. All he could do was watch as Sigge's warriors smashed into Gamle's shields and died viciously for their mistake.

Hakon called for his horn to sound the charge, then rushed forward as fast as his legs would carry him. At that moment, all sense of battle order broke. Men pressed forward across the field. Some headed for the fight between Sigge and Gamle. Others ran for the beach and the Danes trying to get their ships into the sea.

Something flashed from the corner of Hakon's eye, and he turned to see Egil and his knot of warriors rushing down the hill to aid Sigge. They too had seen his folly and had abandoned their standards and their ruse. They charged together with the limping Egil at their head.

Understanding dawned on Gamle, and he roared his fury. Hakon could see him behind his hirdmen, waving his sword to rally his warriors. Those on the beach turned to survey the battlefield. The more experienced among them ran forward to rejoin their comrades. Those less committed to the fight kept pushing their ships into the bay.

At that moment, Egil crashed into the fray and disappeared into the press of warriors. Hakon could hear his breath in his ears as he rushed to reach them. In his peripheral vision he saw Toralv's massive frame. Others splashed behind him. His hird. His oath-sworn.

And then they were there. Hakon ducked the wild swing of an enemy warrior and stabbed his seax into the man's gut. Toralv took the head off another man who was too slow to defend himself from this new attack. Asmund slung his spear into a warrior's chest. Bard ducked a swing, then thrust his blade under his enemy's shield and into the man's thigh.

"Shield wall!" yelled Gamle, and those of his hirdmen close enough to obey backed into a defensive line.

"Back!" hollered Hakon as he pulled away from the fight. "Now! All of you!"

Slowly, his men backed away and locked shields. The two lines faced each other, red-faced and sweating despite the chill. Behind Gamle's line, more men were running from the beach to his aid. With his own men now scattered on the beach and here, Hakon knew he had to end Gamle quickly or all was lost.

"Come, Uncle!" Gamle called when he saw who had come against him.

Asmund responded to Gamle's taunt with the spear he had retrieved from his enemy's chest. The weapon sliced though the air for Gamle, who shifted his body at the last instant and let the spear sail past him and into the stomach of the man behind him. As the man fell, Hakon shouted for his men to attack.

The king ran straight for his nephew. So vicious was the clash of their shields that both men faltered. Hakon regained his footing before his nephew and jabbed his blade at Gamle's face. Gamle knocked the blade upward with his shield rim and stepped back to regain his balance. It was as Hakon moved in for the second blow that Egil charged forward.

"Egil, no!" Hakon shouted, but it was too late, for the old hirdman had already moved past him, his sword held high. He angled his swipe for Gamle's neck, but Gamle lifted his shield to thwart the blow. As he did, the wily Egil planted his feet and shifted his strike downward. Gamle realized his mistake and corrected his shield, but not before Egil's sword had ripped into Gamle's hip. At the same moment, Gamle's blade connected with Egil's helmet. It was a solid blow that knocked the old man viciously to the turf.

"Protect the prince!" yelled one of Gamle's hirdmen.

Gamle stumbled backward with his shield hand clutching his side. Hakon moved in to finish him, but two hirdmen stepped into his path. He stabbed one in the foot as he smashed his shield into the other. The man was big and held his ground, retaliating with an axe swing that would have taken Hakon's head, had he not ducked. Hakon roared and rushed forward at the axe man blocking his path. He lifted his blade and shield high, and as his enemy rose to meet him; at the last instant,

Hakon dropped to his knee and cut clean through the man's left leg. The warrior hollered and fell to the mud and Hakon moved on, not bothering to finish him.

Gamle was jogging for the beach with his arms draped over two of his hirdmen. Those who had been running to his aid were now retreating again. Hakon saw too that some of the ships had already cast off, while pockets of other men fought on against Tosti and the other chieftains on the beach.

Hakon turned back to the fight on the field just as the last of Gamle's men fell. "To me!" he called as he dislodged a spear that was stuck in the turf near his feet. Hakon's remaining hirdmen gathered by his side. Asmund had a wound on the wrist of his sword arm, while blood dripped from Toralv's sliced lip. Nearly half of his hirdmen remained, though battered and physically drained. Hakon hefted his newfound spear. "Gamle is there," he pointed at the wounded warlord being helped from the field. "A sack of silver to the man who stops him before he reaches his ship!" He handed the spear to Asmund, who smiled wolfishly.

The men took off across the field, though the going was slower than Hakon had hoped. Footfalls had churned the field into a quagmire that sucked at their boots. Several of the younger, faster warriors slipped and fell in their haste to earn the prize.

For a moment it appeared as if Hakon and his men might catch Gamle, but as soon as Gamle's men reached the shingle, they hefted their lord between them and ran, maintaining their distance. Realizing there was not time to push their own ship into the surf, nor warriors to man it, they rushed past the pocket of men still fighting on the strand and out into the surf toward a ship that was pulling away. By the time Hakon and his men reached the water, several of Gamle's warriors had climbed aboard and turned back with arms outstretched to help their lord.

Asmund did not hesitate. He rushed forward and cast his spear with all his might. It arced out over the water and slammed into Gamle's back just as his men hoisted him onto the gunwale. The spear pinned

Gamle momentarily against the ship's hull, until his body weight pulled the spear clear of the wet wood, and he splashed into the water and sank.

Without their leader, the enemy lost their taste for battle. Some retreated to the nearest ship and climbed aboard. Others tried but drowned in the water. Hakon's men did not pursue them. The fight had sapped their energy, and all they could do was watch as the army rowed away.

When he had regained his breath, Hakon scanned the ships for his other nephews but could not see them. He then turned his attention to his own men. More than half lay dead or dying, their moans and cries raising the hair on Hakon's arms. The enemy had suffered equally, if not worse, and would find no mercy from Hakon's men.

"Where is Tosti" Hakon asked one of his warriors.

"He has been wounded, lord," said the man as he pointed down the beach toward a group of warriors.

Hakon's heart sank at the words. "Take me to him."

The man nodded and walked Hakon over to the press of men, who made way for their king. Lying on the ground in their midst was Tosti. A puncture wound in his belly leaked dark blood onto the sand. Death was hovering nearby. Hakon could see it in the older man's eyes, and in the pallor of his skin. Hakon knelt by Tosti's side and grabbed his cold hand. Tosti rolled his head and focused his distant eyes on Hakon's face. He smiled faintly.

"You fought well today, my friend," Hakon whispered to him. "I will see that your name lives on."

Tosti moved his mouth to say something, but nothing came out. Instead he squeezed Hakon's hand and smiled weakly, then released it.

"Rest now," Hakon said as he patted his chieftain's shoulder. "You have earned it."

Hakon rose and left Tosti to his comrades who knew him best. This was their moment to say farewell, and Hakon wished not to rob them of that. He made his way back to the place where Egil had fallen. He had not had time to think of his friend during the fight, but now, as he neared the spot, Egil's condition loomed heavily in Hakon's mind.

Corpses carpeted the place where Egil had fallen. It was a fitting spot for a warrior of Egil's renown. There was a vicious gash in the left side of Egil's scalp where Gamle's blade had split his helmet. The wound had bled so much that the entire side of Egil's face was caked in blood. Hakon rolled the old man onto his back and listened carefully for any breath coming from the old man's mouth, but there was nothing.

Egil was gone.

Tears welled in Hakon's eyes as he sat in the mud and stared at the man who had been more father to Hakon than his true father. The man who had never faltered in his loyalty, despite Hakon's many faults and failures; the one who had warned him vehemently that Erik's sons would come for revenge, and had died for Hakon's unwillingness to heed that warning.

"He's with your father now."

Hakon digested Toralv's words. "I hope that is true, for it is where he belongs."

The big man knelt by Egil and closed the dead man's eyes, then sighed heavily. "He had a long life and a lucky one, and a good death too."

Hakon heard the truth in his friend's words and nodded, but it did not quell the grief or the guilt he felt. Egil had died defending his king from the very threat he had warned his charge against so long ago, and that dark thought lay on Hakon like a stone. Hakon looked at the bodies of his other hirdmen who lay dead around them. They had all died because of him. Hakon had yearned for an end to the kin killing, and in the end it had only led to more death. He gazed out at the withdrawing enemy ships as a storm of emotion raged within him: sorrow, guilt, joy, relief. But most of all, a black fury that forced his hands into white-knuckled fists.

It was time to take the fight to his nephews and end their scourge once and for all.

Chapter 13

The clouds hung low and dark over Rastarkalv, as if the very heavens mourned for Egil, Tosti, and the others. A chill wind swept up the gentle rise from the sea, carrying with it a light drizzle and the smell of salt, neither of which did much to mask the stench of death still hanging over the grisly remains of the battle.

It had been seven days since that fight, and still the birds fought over the feculence that littered the field. Hakon's surviving warriors had burned their own dead on pyres several days before, the remains of which still smoked on the beach to the south. The enemy dead had also been burned, though with far less ceremony and only after they had been stripped of their wealth and weapons.

Hakon had erected a mighty pyre for Egil, upon which he had placed the warrior, his namesake wool shirt, and all of his earthly possessions: his battered shield, his swords, his armor, his cracked helmet, and the silver he had carried on his body. His ashes had been placed in an urn, which in turn had been laid within one of the enemy ships. The death-ship now sat in its shallow grave, the dragonhead removed from the prow and placed on the deck for fear it would frighten the gods on arrival in the afterlife. Cooking utensils had also been laid within, along with barrels of mead and wine, and victuals of all sorts to fortify Egil on his journey.

"The men sacrificed animals. Why do the gods then piss on this day?" Hakon muttered to Toralv as he peered through the drizzle at the

152

funeral scene. They had spoken their sorrow at Egil's graveside, and now sat on the hilltop where Egil had carried the standards into battle.

Hakon had been in a somber mood since the battle's end, and seeing the death-ship only aggravated his mental state. It did not help that his head was still thick with the effects of the previous night's sjaund, where long into the night the men had shared the ritual cup to celebrate the fallen and to discuss the transfer of property and wealth to next of kin. And where Hakon, deep into his cups, had vowed to repay the sons of Erik tenfold for the lives they had taken at Rastarkalv.

"Mayhap these are tears of joy shed for Egil's arrival in Valhall," remarked Toralv, who sat on the ground beside his king, his back resting against one of the three memorial stones Hakon had had erected to commemorate Egil, Tosti, and the others who had died on the field.

"Mayhap," Hakon mumbled, unconvinced.

"You have honored him, lord," said Toralv as he watched warriors lay three sacrificed pigs in the ship with Egil's ashes. "There can be no doubt of that. The men know you are opposed to the sacrifice and will thank you for that small kindness."

"I do not want their thanks. I would much prefer to have Egil and Tosti among the living. I should have listened to my gut, Toralv. That battle was not a wise fight, and many good men paid the price for our recklessness."

"We are not here to stay the hands of the gods with our actions," countered Toralv calmly. "We are here to live fully and boldly in their eyes. Egil did just that, eh? I can almost hear his sour voice in my head, asking us why we mourn." There was a sad grin on his face as he wiped a trickle of rain from his nose. "And he would be right in that. We have avenged his death by killing Gamle. Few warriors are so lucky."

"As God as my witness, Toralv, I will kill them all."

"*We* shall kill them all," Toralv corrected.

Hakon nodded. "Aye. We shall kill them all."

For their mistakes in battle, Sigge and his surviving crew of ten had been given the task of digging Egil's burial grave. The tired, mud-slimed men now began to fill it in under the dour gazes of Hakon's other men. Shovelful by shovelful, the ship vanished. Hakon said a silent prayer for Egil's soul as the mud slowly enveloped Egil's urn. Then, with a final nod at the grave, he left Toralv on the hillside and walked the long path back to Birkestrand alone, lost in his dark thoughts and his grief as the rain fell down around him.

Sigurd arrived three days after Egil's burial, on the afternoon of the tenth day since the battle. Though he arrived sooner than expected, and with more men than expected, it did little to lift Hakon's spirits, which had sunken into a dark abyss of swirling anger, impatience, and sorrow. Despite the feast that Hakon had ordered, and the presence of the celebratory Tronds, Hakon could not pull himself from the mire of his emotions. Sigurd had sensed it immediately, and called on Guthorm Sindri for a tale, but the words, which commemorated the recent battle, rang false to Hakon's ears.

> *"Scared by the sharp sword's singing sound,*
> *Brandished in air, the foe gave ground.*
> *The boldest warrior cannot stand*
> *Before King Hakon's conquering hand;*
> *And the king's banner ever dies*
> *Where the spear-forests thickest rise.*
> *Altho' the king had gained of old*
> *Enough of Freyja's tears of gold,*
> *He spared himself no more than tho'*
> *He'd had no well-filled purse to show."*

"Enough!" Hakon yelled, smashing his fist on the eating board to punctuate his point and spilling his ale cup in the process. "I will hear no more!"

Jarl Sigurd waved the skald back to his seat. "Go back to your conversations," he called to the Trond chieftains gathered in Tosti's hall. The men stole concerned glances at their king, then slowly drifted back to their chatter and their ale and their food.

Sigurd turned to his king as he settled himself back into his seat. "You forget yourself," he said.

"I do not need to hear the story of my battle exploits," Hakon hissed. "Especially when so many good men have died and are forgotten in the telling. What I need is speed so that we can avenge the loss of our men quickly."

"We just arrived," Sigurd protested. "On the morrow, we shall restock our supplies and prepare our ships. If the weather is fair the following day, we shall leave. The men are anxious for this adventure too, Hakon, but haste is no way to venture into enemy territory."

"They sail *not* into enemy territory, Sigurd." Hakon was struggling to control his voice. "They sail for Avaldsnes, and then the Vik. There is plenty of time to plan and to rest as we move. But the longer we take to reach the land of the Danes, the longer we give my nephews to prepare and the more bitter the fight will be. We must minimize our times of comfort and move at all haste."

Sigurd grunted. "Very well. If the weather is willing, we will leave on the morrow and gain a day. Does that suit you better?"

Hakon drained his cup and stood, and his eyes fell on Sigge, who sat among his fellow Trond lords, laughing over his cup and acting as if he had no cares in the world. The sight of it sickened Hakon.

Sigurd grabbed Hakon's wrist before he could leave. "Are you not forgetting something?"

"What is it, Sigurd?" Hakon growled as he yanked his wrist free of Sigurd's grasp. "I am in no mood for riddles."

Sigurd's own eyes narrowed. "Are you not curious about Astrid or your daughter?"

The question hit Hakon like a fist to the stomach. His dark mood and impatience had clouded his thinking, and that realization angered him all the more. Still, he could find no apology to offer Sigurd.

Sigurd snorted at Hakon's silence. "If you are curious, they are hale, and arrived in Lade in good order, thanks to the guidance of Alf and the favor of the gods. Your daughter wished me to give this to you." He reached into the pouch on his belt and withdrew the knife Hakon had given to Thora when he had left Avaldsnes. Hakon took it from Sigurd. "She wanted you to have it to keep you safe." Sigurd turned back to his meal and said no more.

Hakon cursed under his breath and stormed from the hall, needing a quieter place to cool his temper and ease his mind. He found a spot on the grassy slope that looked out over the beach and the army camped there. Voices and laughter carried up to him from the myriad fires dotting the bay. Near the fires, nineteen ships rested at anchor. He wondered briefly how many of those ships would return, and whether his would be among them. He spun the knife in his hand as he contemplated that thought.

"You normally do not see that, this time of year."

The voice startled Hakon, and he turned to see Toralv lumbering down the hill toward him. The champion carried an ale cup in each hand, though his eyes were focused on the northern sky. Hakon followed his gaze, where greens and violets and blues tumbled and danced. Toralv folded his long frame to the ground and offered a cup to Hakon. The king refused it.

"The more for me, then," Toralv said and, with three large gulps, drained one of the cups.

Hakon sighed and recalled a scene from long ago. "The first time I saw those lights was the winter after my return from Engla-lond. I was frightened by them." He grinned. "Egil scolded me for my fear."

Toralv smiled sadly. "I am going to miss that bastard."

"As am I, Toralv." Hakon kept his gaze on the dancing lights, lest Toralv see the tears welling in his eyes. After a time, he spoke the thought that had been rattling in his mind. "We are dying off, Toralv. One by one."

Toralv belched again. "Now there is a cheery thought."

Hakon grinned. "I did not ask you to join me. You did so at your own peril."

"Ha. So I did. But I did not come out here to speak of death."

"What, then?"

"I want to speak of Sigge."

Hakon's mind turned to the young lord and his crew, and to their laughter in the hall behind him.

"He and his men need to go, lord," Toralv said before Hakon could speak. "We cannot have him in our crew. I fear he will be killed before we ever reach the Danes."

Hakon glanced at Toralv. "Have you heard something?"

"Aye."

Hakon nodded, but did not press Toralv. In truth, he had seen it in the eyes of his men and had expected Toralv's response. "It will test Sigurd's loyalties, Toralv. This you know. He could easily turn and head for home. And without Sigurd, we are lost."

"I know. But what is worse to Sigurd? Sending his son away, or finding him murdered one morning?"

Hakon spun the knife in his hand as his mind sought an alternative but came up blank. "Very well. I shall speak with Jarl Sigurd on the morrow."

"Thank you, lord." Toralv finished the rest of his ale and rose to go.

"Toralv?" Hakon called.

"Aye, lord?"

"See that nothing happens to Sigge and his men this night."

"I will do my best, lord."

Chapter 14

Hakon rose early the following morning and ventured outside to check the weather. The summer sun was climbing to the southeast, revealing a pink- and blue-streaked sky partially veiled by thin wisps of cloud. A light breeze blew from the north.

Several thralls carried water buckets into the hall for the chieftains who would soon be rising. Others carried provisions, ropes, and barrels to the ships. The smell of baking bread carried on the air from the kitchen. Hakon moved to the nearest sentry and ordered him to blow his horn. It was time to wake the men and prepare to leave.

As the men rolled from their furs, Hakon went in search of Sigurd. He found him in one of the guest huts, rinsing his face in a water bucket. Sigurd blew his nose into the water and then turned his attention to Hakon, who stood in the doorway, waiting.

"I hope this morning finds you in a better mood," said Sigurd by way of greeting.

"We must talk," responded Hakon.

Sigurd's face soured. He fetched a comb from his belt pouch and began stroking the knots and straw and lice from his beard. "What is it now?"

Lying in the furs was one of the thrall women. Hakon ran his eyes over her, then turned his gaze back to Sigurd. "Privately, Sigurd."

Sigurd glanced at Hakon and sighed. "Lead the way, my king."

Hakon walked around the main hall and up the hill to the trailhead where not so long ago Astrid had waited for him before their hike. There, he stopped and waited for Sigurd to join him.

"What is it that requires such secrecy?" Sigurd huffed as he joined his king.

"We must speak of your son, Sigurd."

The older man's brow furrowed as he waited for Hakon to speak. Hakon did not try to weave a soft response. "The battle at Rastarkalv went poorly in part because of your son and his crew. They were ordered to stay in line and did not. Were it not for Egil, Sigge's recklessness could have cost us the battle. My crew no longer trusts him or his men. Some blame him for Egil's death. I fear they may turn that blame to vengeance."

Sigurd understood well the meaning in Hakon's words and cast his eyes to the ground. Uncertainty danced in his face when he lifted his gaze again. "How do you see it?"

"He is a fine warrior, Sigurd, but he is sometimes rash, as we both know. He did not obey my orders at Rastarkalv. I have punished him for it, but my punishment may not be enough. The men are angry."

Sigurd cursed and turned his gaze to the bay and to the army that assembled there. After a long moment, he sighed deeply. "By the gods, that boy...." He let his words trail off.

"You will need to speak with him, Sigurd. You can put him on another ship, but that may not spare him or his men. To truly guard him, you need to send him back to Lade."

Sigurd cursed again. "I will speak with him."

At midday, the ships rowed from the beach beneath Birkestrand, though two ships remained. The first belonged to Sigge and his crew, who had been ordered by Sigurd to return to Lade. They did not attempt to hide their ill feelings. Sigge glowered, while his comrades spat on the beach as the ships pulled away. Near them stood a small contingent of Tosti's older warriors. Hakon had left them to watch the hall and care for the wounded. He prayed no harm would come to them as the ships pulled from the bay and turned south into the Kvernesfjord.

The crews hoisted their sails to take advantage of the wind sweeping southward across the waterway. Just past Rastarkalv, Hakon cast his eye to the shore and gazed at the mound that covered Egil's remains. On the ridge above it stood the three stones, silent reminders of those who had perished on the field.

The ships followed the calm fjord as it flowed southwest, then took a hard right for the open sea. They reached the gray ocean by late afternoon, and there angled southwest, using the shoreline to guide them and the wind to push them over the gentle swells. It was a pleasant passage that required no rowing, so the men turned their attention to other pursuits. Some slept, others gambled. Still others sharpened their blades or repaired their armor. Few spoke.

For four days they sailed — four days marked by steady weather, a constantly rolling deck, and the incessant creak of the ship's strakes. The wind never shifted, affording the men the rare luxury of relaxation, if not some boredom. In all, though, it beat having to row or fight the sea or find a place to anchor each night.

On the evening of the fourth day, Stad's massive headland came into view. At the sight of the looming rock face, Hakon pulled the fleet together and gathered the chieftains onto *Dragon*'s deck.

"We sail for a hall at Stad," Hakon informed the men when they had assembled before him. "The hall sits in a broad bay on the south side of that headland. I will sail into the bay alone. The rest of you hold your position at the bay's mouth. If you hear three blasts of my horn, I will need your aid. Sigurd will lead you, should you be needed."

The men exchanged glances, and Sigurd spoke into their silence. "You heard your king. To your ships! It is getting late, and I, for one, would like to sleep under a roof tonight!"

As the ships pulled away, Hakon ordered his crew to armor themselves. They did so silently, for all knew too well the dangers that might be awaiting them in the dark bay.

Dragon slid into the shadow of the headland. If Eldgrim's men were there, there could be no doubt they would have seen his ship. Hakon's men sensed this too, and cast their eyes toward the cliff's tall heights, where sea birds circled and shadows played tricks on the eyes of men. At any moment, Hakon expected a horn to blow its warning or a beacon flame to ignite. But there was nothing. Only the crash of waves as sea met stone and the creak of strakes as *Dragon* glided ever closer to the entrance of the bay.

Once there, Hakon ordered the sail furled and the men to oars. "Remove the beast, Toralv," Hakon called to his champion, who was cinching the belt over his byrnie by the prow.

The champion did his lord's bidding as Eskil turned the ship toward the empty bay and the dark hall that sat inland from it. A small ship lay beached on the shore, which set Hakon's nerves on edge. He scanned the cliffs to left and right, looking for a glint of steel or a sudden movement, but his gaze met only rocks and shadow and shrubs. The crew sank lower behind the shields lining the gunwale.

In the end, an attack never came. *Dragon* slid forward on the rolling waves and met only silence as her hull crunched up onto the shingle. Hakon hefted his shield and called Toralv and those on the right side of the ship to arms. The left would remain in case they needed to make a hasty retreat.

"Which way?" asked Toralv as they knelt behind their shields on the beach.

Hakon pointed with his seax to Shadow Haven. "To the hall," he whispered.

They took off at a jog across the uneven sand with shields raised and weapons poised. As they neared the hall, a hound began to bark from within. The men crouched again behind their shields.

"Damn dog will wake the whole island," whispered Asmund.

Just then, the door of one of the outlying structures swung open. The men turned instinctively to the new threat, but it was only Eldgrim's thrall, Hilde, carrying a pail in her hands. At the sight of the men, she dropped her bucket and screamed, which echoed off the cliffs and sent birds squawking to the skies. Asmund sprang forward and tackled the woman before she could scream again. The hidden dog gnashed and growled.

A man exited the hall with a wooden spade in his hand. Judging from his dress and his thin build, he could only be another thrall. "Who —" The man started to say, but never finished his question. A hand axe lodged in his chest, and he dropped dead just outside the door.

Several of Hakon's men leaped the man's body and smashed into the hall with their shields ready. The dog barked furiously, yelped, then fell silent. Moments later, the men returned to the doorway; one called, "It is empty."

Asmund pulled Hilde to her feet. She gazed first at him, then at the approaching men. Even in the half-light, Hakon could see the terror in her eyes. "Please," she begged. "Do not harm me."

Hakon grabbed her by the arm and pulled her into the hall. She stumbled but managed to stay upright.

"Please," she cried as Hakon smashed her against one of the hall posts. She was trembling now.

"Where are the others?" he asked. "Where have they gone?"

"They left, lord. With the Danes."

"All of them?"

"Aye, lord. Eldgrim left only me and Bertram to mind the place." She was trying to control her sobs, and her words came in starts.

"Asmund. Search around the hall. Toralv. Take some men and check the beach and the cliffs."

Hakon turned back to Hilde. She was a thin girl in her late teens, with freckles that dotted her dirt-smudged nose and cheeks and chestnut hair that she wore in a long braid. Her name and manner of speech suggested she might have been a Frank before her capture.

"Whose ship is on the beach, girl?"

"That was Lord Eldgrim's. He left it here for us. To fish in the bay."

"When did Eldgrim leave?"

"Many days ago, lord. He took all of his men. He told us we were free, but we have no place to go."

Hakon lifted her chin so he could see her neck. Her thrall collar was gone, leaving in its place a still chafed but healing ring of skin. Hakon released his grip on the girl and stood back.

Just then, Asmund entered the hall. In one hand, he carried his spear and what looked like a bow. With the other, he dragged a boy by his motley clump of hair. The boy was still on his feet and fighting mightily to rid himself of Asmund's grip.

"Reinhard!" cried Hilde when she saw the boy.

Asmund marched over to Hakon and tossed the boy to the ground. He was a tall lad, with wiry limbs and a forest of brown curls on his head. Before the boy could stand, Asmund had his spear point at the boy's neck. "Try it, you little bastard, and I will skewer you." A trickle of blood dripped from the left side of Asmund's forehead as he spoke.

"What happened to you?" Hakon asked.

"This goat turd almost killed me with this toy bow of his." Asmund held the bow aloft and glanced at Hakon. In that instant, Reinhard knocked his spear aside and scrambled to his feet. Asmund tossed the bow and righted his spear but too late. The boy had produced a small knife from his belt and now faced Asmund, ready to strike. Asmund leveled his spear at the boy.

"If you wish to live, boy, then I suggest you drop the knife," said Hakon, who had drawn his own seax. The other men in the hall readied their weapons too.

"Do it, Reinhard," pleaded Hilde.

"They killed my father!" The blood rose in Reinhard's whiskerless cheeks as the tears welled in his brown eyes.

"Aye," said Hilde, more calmly now. "They did, and they will kill you too, if you do not obey them."

"What say you, lord?" asked Asmund. "Shall I skewer the little bastard?"

Mayhap it was the steel in his nerves or the fire in his emotions; whatever it was, Hakon liked the boy and did not want to see him hurt. "This is your last warning. You have my word as your king that we will not harm you or the girl if you put your blade aside."

Reinhard blinked. "My king?"

"Drop your blade," Hakon repeated, this time more calmly.

Reinhard blinked again, as if Hakon's words were chipping away at the fury that had possessed him and he was coming again into his own mind. The boy's eyes moved then from the blade in his hand to the armed men in the hall, and finally back to Hakon. He nodded and set the knife down. Asmund used his spear point to knock it away. It skidded across the floor and into the shadows.

With things more settled, Hakon turned back to Hilde and made a show of examining his seax. "You said there were no others. You lied."

Tears welled in Hilde's eyes again. "Forgive me, lord. Please. Reinhard is usually in the seter with the livestock. He is good with animals. There are no others. I promise you."

"I will take you at your word, Hilde. But if we find others..." He let the words hang in the air between them.

"Why did you kill my father?" This question came from the boy, who had regained his senses. His voice cracked with emotion as he asked it.

Hakon shrugged. "It was an accident. We are not in the business of killing defenseless thralls."

The boy raised his chin proudly. "He was no longer a thrall."

Hakon conceded the point with a nod. "No, he was not."

"You shall pay for his death," spat the boy.

"Reinhard!" Hilde pleaded.

"Mind your tongue, boy, before I cut it out of your head," added Asmund.

Hakon merely laughed. "I like your spirit, lad, but I would do as Asmund says." He turned back to Hilde. "My army is near and needs a place to camp. They shall stay here tonight, and you shall open your stores and this hall to them."

Hilde nodded her understanding.

Toralv returned then with his search party. They had found no others save for a few wandering goats, one of which was dead and draped over Bard's shoulders. Hakon nodded at Hilde. "I am glad you spoke the truth. For that, I will let you and Reinhard bury Reinhard's father. Asmund. Take some men and guard them."

That evening, the hall and the beach thrived with life. Though it was now nearly midnight judging from the position of the sun, the men could not resist the temptation of fresh ale and warm goat stew to supplement their diet. The prisoners buried their father down near the beach, then returned under guard to the hall, where Hakon had them seated and bound to separate posts near the head table. Hakon then explained their presence to his fellow warriors and forbade any man to harm the prisoners on pain of death, for though bound, they were still Hakon's guests at his feast.

"You have a strange way of treating your guests," Sigurd grunted between mouthfuls of stew, motioning to the prisoners with his spoon.

"I do not trust them, nor do I trust our men with them. So there they will sit until we leave on the morrow."

Sigurd drank deeply from his cup, then sleeved the ale-froth from his mustache. "So, will you tell me now why we are here?"

Hakon slurped from his spoon, relishing the rich, gamey flavor of the goat and its warmth in his belly. "Eldgrim is the name of the warrior who lives here. He was Jarl Tore's man. Long ago, I banished his son, who had murdered a neighbor unjustly. When Erik's sons attacked Avaldsnes, I was here and asked Eldgrim to join me. He refused. But he had no such quarrel joining Erik's sons when they attacked us at Rastarkalv."

Sigurd grunted. "So you have come for revenge."

Hakon nodded. "I have come for justice."

"And he is now gone. So what do you do?"

"I will ensure he has nothing to return to, though it sounds like he had no interest in returning anyway. If he sails with Erik's sons, mayhap I will meet him again and find the justice I seek. In the meantime," Hakon smiled, "I will eat his food and enjoy the warmth of his hall." He raised his cup. "Skol."

Sigurd returned the gesture. "Skol."

The warriors awoke the following morning to clear skies and a gentle wind. Hakon ordered the men to take what livestock, rations, and supplies they could find and to replenish their water and ale. As the men plundered the hall, the prisoners watched helplessly from their seats with eyes bleary from lack of sleep.

Hakon returned to Hilde and Reinhard when the army was ready to depart. By his side stood Asmund and Toralv. "We are leaving," Hakon announced. "As promised, you have not been harmed. I have placed your bow down on the beach, Reinhard, so that you can hunt once we are gone. If you try to retrieve it before we leave, you will be killed."

The color rushed to Reinhard's cheeks as he glared at Hakon. "You have killed my father. That is harm enough."

"I smell smoke," Hilde said.

"So you do," said Hakon. "I am burning Shadow Haven. I cannot leave it for Eldgrim." He raised his hands to halt their next questions. "I have released the remaining livestock from the barns."

Hakon motioned to Toralv, who moved to Hilde. Her eyes bored into Hakon as Toralv untied the ropes that bound her to the post. Once free, she worked her wrists to return the feeling to her hands.

"You will wait until we are gone. Then you will untie Reinhard," Hakon commanded her.

Hakon, Asmund, and Toralv left them and marched to the beach, where the army waited on their ships. Flames danced on the thatch of the various halls as ash swirled in the morning's breeze. In short minutes, those halls and all that was inside them would be engulfed and burn down to charred, smoldering frames.

As Hakon climbed aboard *Dragon* and motioned for the ships to pull away, Reinhard and Hilde rushed from the burning hall toward the beach. Hilde grabbed Reinhard's arm, but he yanked it free and retrieved his bow from the sand. The boy searched about him for a good arrow but found only broken shafts. Hakon smiled at his own foresight, for he had known Reinhard would try to use them.

"May God curse you, King Hakon!" Reinhard hollered, and the words echoed off the cliff walls, chasing Hakon and his ships back to the sea.

Chapter 15

Beacon flames and the doleful echo of warning horns greeted Hakon's ships as they rowed into the waterway that led to Kaupang, the only town in Hakon's kingdom. It was early evening, and on either shore, the sun's sinking rays shone on the spear points and helmets of watchful warriors. Hakon did not mind the unwelcome sights and sounds. In truth, he felt a heavy weight lifted from his spirits. Long ago, Hakon had given the town and the area around it to his nephew, Gudrod, to rule. As the town grew and trade flourished, so too did the need for its protection. It was good to see Gudrod's vigilance in this task, especially with Erik's sons so near at hand.

But there was another reason for the grin that now parted Hakon's sopping beard. As soon as the fleet hit the open seas south of Karmsund Strait, the blue skies turned as dark and gray as unpolished metal. Sheets of rain rolled in from the west, driven by a relentless wind that turned the rain sideways and pushed the waves against their hulls. For five days the rain came down, not strong enough to force the fleet to seek shelter, but potent enough to soak the men through and shorten their tempers as they struggled to round the south tip of Agder and reach Kaupang. Only that morning had the rain stopped, and as Hakon looked to the shores on the approach to the trading town, his vexation slipped away like the remaining raindrops on his cloak.

Eskil guided *Dragon* into the narrow waterway, and Hakon's good cheer turned to elation. For there, lined up on the beach, were more than a dozen warships.

"God be praised," said Egbert, who stood at Hakon's side. "That is a sight to behold."

Eskil steered *Dragon* up to the long dock, where a group of warriors waited. At their head stood a bull of a man with unruly brown hair that framed his wide face and cascaded onto his broad shoulders.

"We expected you days ago," called the man as he smiled through his wild beard. "What happened? Was Toralv navigating?"

The crew snickered as they hauled in their oars.

"That is some welcome, Trygvi," called Toralv from the bow.

The big man shrugged. "Welcomes are not my strength."

"The weather did not treat us with the respect we deserve," called Hakon as *Dragon* knocked against the dock's planking.

The man laughed. "You should have sacrificed the priest. That would have gotten Thor's attention."

Egbert frowned.

"You have us confused with another crew," Hakon said through his grin as he pointed in the general direction of the other ships, which were slipping into spots along the beach. "This crew only prays to the one true God."

The man rolled his eyes, then proffered his arm to Hakon. Hakon used the arm to hoist himself onto the dock, then embraced the man. "It is good to see your ugly face, Trygvi, which, by the way, looks not a day older than last we met."

"I have been off chasing wealth and fame and women in the West. It keeps me young. You should try it."

Trygvi was the son of Hakon's older half-brother Olav, a brash man who had died for underestimating Erik. Though Hakon had never met Olav, he heard tell that Trygvi had inherited Olav's brazenness. Were he not such a formidable fighter, his mouth and his recklessness would have long since been his bane.

"I would hear more of your exploits, nephew. But first, we must find your cousin. Where is he?"

"In the hall, counting his silver, no doubt." Trygvi pointed to the hall on the hill behind the town. "Come. I will take you there."

As Hakon's men disembarked, Trygvi guided Hakon through the wood-planked streets of Kaupang. The town bustled with life. Many winters before, the Danes had attacked Kaupang and burned it to the ground, but there were no signs of such struggle now. The streets teemed with people visiting stalls, bargaining, trading wares, and weighing coins and hack silver. An occasional shout and the rhythmic hammering of unseen blacksmiths punctuated the hum of conversation. As Hakon walked, he saw people of every color and heard the babble of languages too numerous to count. It was good to see and to hear, and to know that it all rested in the capable hands of Gudrod.

Hakon followed Trygvi up a path that wound from the western edge to Kapaung through a maze of defensive walls manned by armed warriors toward the massive hall on the hilltop.

At the doors to that hall, Gudrod met Hakon. He was dressed in a beautiful blue tunic with a gold-threaded hem, and leather pants that looked as soft as sealskin. An equally fine cloak draped his rotund shoulders, but did little to hide his girth. On the top of it all was Gudrod's smiling face and the finely combed strands of his gray-streaked blond hair.

His finery would make even the wealthiest king blush with jealousy, but it did not upset Hakon. Gudrod had earned every thread on his fat body. Gudrod's father, Bjorn, had once ruled Kaupang and its environs in King Harald's name — until Erik grew jealous of Bjorn's wealth and murdered him for it, forcing Gudrod to flee. After banishing Erik from the land, Hakon had given Kaupang and the Vestfold fylke back to Gudrod to rule in Hakon's name. Twice the Danes had come and burned the town, nearly killing Gudrod in the process, and twice Gudrod had rebuilt it from the ashes. After such trials, no man could deny him the wealth he rightly earned and openly displayed, so long as he continued to pay his portion to Hakon's coffers.

"Welcome, Uncle," Gudrod said with outstretched arms. His right eye shone with genuine cheer at the sight of his uncle.

"It is good to see you again, Gudrod." Hakon had come to Kaupang earlier that summer to implore him to raise men for his campaign against the Danes; as always, Gudrod had complied. "You have done well to gather so many men to the cause. You even brought Trygvi to join in our adventure," Hakon said, motioning to the larger man. "Though I doubt it took much asking to get him here — Trygvi itches for a good fight, eh, Trygvi?"

Trygvi smiled, managing to look pleased and wolfish at the same time.

Hakon backhanded Gudrod's belly. "I think both you and Kaupang have grown since last we met. You have been busy, eh?"

Gudrod laughed loudly through his graying beard and smacked his protruding girth. "Trade has been good for both of us."

"I do not think I have ever heard so many foreign voices," Hakon noted, turning his eyes again to the clutter of wattle and daub and thatch and wood that was the growing town.

"Aye, and it is a good thing, too," Gudrod concurred as he walked to the edge of the hill and looked out over his town. "They bring many wondrous things to trade. Gold. Spices. Salt. Slaves. Wine. All of which attracts even more traders to our shores — and puts more taxes in our coffers." He winked at Hakon with his good eye.

Hakon smiled back at him. "You have done well, Gudrod. I thank you for your efforts, and for hosting our army on the eve of our adventure."

"Of course! Why would I not? After all, you are king. Besides, armies drink ale and eat food and hump whores, and we profit from their commerce. Which reminds me, I have someone you must meet."

"Who?"

"A trader. With some information you might find interesting. Feast with me tonight, and I will bring him."

"That I shall do," said Hakon as he made for the path that led back down to the town.

"Bring Sigurd too," Gudrod called after him. "It will be like old times."

Hakon waved to his nephew and walked with Trygvi back to the ships. On his way down the hill, he stopped and let his eyes scan the beach. There were vessels of every size, warships all, stretching from the docks below the hall to a spot far to the south. "Thirty-three ships, Trygvi. From almost every fylke in the realm. Trondelag. More. Uplands. Rogaland. Agder. Vestfold. Ostfold. Even Hemming has come with his crew from Halogaland. All here to bring their wrath down on the Danes. It is impressive, is it not?"

"It is, lord," said Trygvi, who had stopped behind him. "With such a force and the favor of the gods, we just might end their scourge."

Hakon could feel his heart thunder a little harder in his chest. "Aye, Trygvi. We just might."

That evening, Hakon and Sigurd joined Gudrod and Trygvi for a lavish but intimate meal of duck, warm bread, soft cheese, and cabbage. There was also wine from Frankland and mead, which Gudrod's pretty thrall women served in silver cups. A small hearth fire cast its warmth on the diners and its glow on the shields and tapestries that hung from the high walls.

Gudrod lifted his silver cup toward Hakon, then Sigurd. "It is good to have you here, King Hakon and Jarl Sigurd. It has been too long. Skol!"

"Skol!" They responded in unison.

"Forgive me for not inviting more men," Gudrod said after a slurp of wine. "I thought it might be best to speak privately. It has been a long time since the four of us have sat together and spoken. I sense there are many tales to share and doing so in a large feast is difficult, eh?"

Trygvi guzzled his wine and belched. "That is my cousin. As shrewd as always."

"Tell me of your travels, Trygvi," said Hakon with his mouth full of duck. "I would hear of the many places you have been."

Trygvi sleeved some grease from his lips, then launched into a tale of his adventure to Irland, which sounded like a beautiful yet treacherous place. "There are a number of rival clans, each vying for the High Seat of the land and each willing to pay Vikings, who they call Ostmen, handsomely for their swords," Trygvi explained, waving his empty cup to emphasize his point. "The Gaels are wicked fighters, and they fight often. Alliances crumble regularly and friends turn to foes as naturally as day turns to night. Survival takes a good sword and a quick mind." Trygvi tapped his forehead with his cup.

"Then how did you survive, cousin?" asked Gudrod, earning him a sharp look from Trygvi and the appreciative laughter of the others.

"Oh, damn the lot of you," Trygvi said with a wave of his hand. His cup slipped from his grip and fell to the floor with a hollow clang and a splash of wine that brought on a fresh round of guffaws. "Thrall! More wine!" he roared.

Hakon turned to Gudrod when the men had regained their composure. "You said earlier that you have someone for me to meet?"

"Indeed!" He called to the guard at the door, "Fetch the trader!"

While the men waited, they talked of Erik's sons and the battles Hakon had fought, and of Egil and Ottar and Bjarke. The mood darkened at the mention of their deaths, though Gudrod was quick to point out that the warriors died as warriors should.

"That is well said," offered Hakon, though it still pained him mightily to hear their names and be reminded of their sacrifice. "I am glad for that, at least."

"And there is yet another thing we should celebrate," added Sigurd as his eyes moved about the men's faces. "Gamle is dead. That is one less snake we need to deal with."

"Aye," agreed Gudrod. "Though I hear Harald is the one to watch most closely."

This was the first Hakon had heard mention of Harald in this light and he pressed his nephew on it. "Why so?"

Just then, the door to the hall opened and in walked the guard. A tall, thin man trailed behind him. Even from a distance, the man smelled of pitch and salt and stale ale. The man had a thick beard that hung in braids to mid chest, and a shaved head as brown and weather-grooved as an old oak.

"Ah, Frode. Thank you for coming," said Gudrod. "Come. Sit." He gestured to the table.

The man's dark eyes surveyed the gathering. There was no fear there, only uncertainty, as if he was trying to divine the reason for his summons.

"We do not bite. Please," Gudrod urged again. "I will have my thralls bring food and drink."

The clap of Gudrod's meaty hands echoed through the hall. Moments later, a young woman rushed from the shadows with a trencher filled with food and a silver cup. These she placed on the eating board. Frode thanked Gudrod with a nod, then made his way to an empty chair, which creaked under his weight as he sat.

"Mead or wine?" asked Gudrod.

"Mead, lord."

The thrall girl poured a measure of the golden liquid into Frode's cup, then melted back into the darkness.

"You must be wondering why you are here. We have invited you because you have information that we need. Important information about the Danes."

Frode glanced at the other men, all of whom watched the trader closely.

"You are one of them. A Dane, I mean. Is that not so?"

"That is true," admitted Frode in a muffled voice. He gazed longingly at the duck leg in his trencher but did not dare eat it.

"Then you know of the projects your king is undertaking?"

"Projects, lord?" he asked cautiously.

"Aye. Those that you spoke of so enthusiastically last night over your ale cup. It seems you are rather amazed by some of your king's projects, hmm?" Gudrod sipped from his cup, eyeing his guest closely. "We shall hear of them too."

Frode stopped his eating, but before he could speak, Gudrod raised a finger in warning. "I have heard some of these tales already, so do not try to fool us. Speak openly and in detail, and we shall reward your loose tongue with silver."

Frode pushed his trencher away as if he had suddenly lost his appetite.

"Please," Gudrod gestured. "Proceed."

The trader drained the mead in his cup and looked at the lords. "There are many that Gorm and his son, Harald, have begun. In the south of Jutland, they reinforce the Danevirke. At Hedeby they are reinforcing the earthwork walls, which protect the western approaches to the town."

"It sounds as if they fear an attack from the Franks," offered Sigurd.

Frode shook his head. "I do not think the Franks will attack. The Danes have accepted the Christians in their realm and are building a church in Hedeby. There seems to be peace between the kings as a result. At least for now."

"That makes little sense then," said Sigurd.

"Are there other projects, Frode?" asked Hakon.

The men paused as the thrall women filled their cups.

"Aye," said Frode once the thralls were gone. "There are others. Ring forts, mainly. I have not seen all of them with my own eyes, but I have seen some and know of others."

"Ring forts?" asked Hakon. "Like those in Engla-lond that the Romans built and that Alfred turned into burghs?"

Frode shrugged. "I know nothing of those, having never been to Engla-lond."

A sudden thought occurred to Hakon, and he leaned across the eating board toward the trader. "Tell me, Frode: is one of these forts at Fyrkat?"

The man's eyes grew wider. "You know of it?"

Frode's response confirmed Hakon's fears. "I have some experience with the men from there. Are there other such forts?"

"Aye, lord. I have heard of at least five, where spear-Danes live and train night and day for battle. Rumor has it that they are the invention of Gorm's son, Harald, who uses the men and these forts to subdue and control more and more land."

"And now those men come here," added Hakon.

Frode scratched his head. "I did not say that. I know not what Harald plans to do with these men."

"But I do," said Hakon.

"Please explain," Sigurd prompted.

Hakon looked at the others, his stomach coiling as the pieces fell together in his mind. It was so simple, and yet he had not seen any of it until now. "King Gorm rules in Jutland, but he is old now and has given much of the control of his realm to his son, Harald. Harald has expanded his father's kingdom and now rules Jutland and the other Danish islands. To take these new lands, he needed men. Many men. And to control and protect them, he needs men in those locations."

"So he takes land and then builds a fort there," added Gudrod, who was always quick to catch the meaning of things.

"Aye. It was a tactic employed by the Romans and used also by Alfred to protect Engla-lond from the Danes and Northmen. And I assume," said Hakon as he turned his eyes back to Frode, "the forts are all close to waterways?"

"Aye, lord. And a road. Fyrkat is up a fjord that feeds into the Kattegat. Another lies on the Limfjord in northeast Jutland, at Agger. They are connected by a road that runs north to south. There is also Trelleborg on Sjaelland, which overlooks the trade route to Hedeby. I have heard of another on the eastern shore of Sjaelland, along the Oresund, though I know not its exact location."

Hakon looked at the others. "The Fyrkat Danes were with Erik's sons at Avaldsnes and Rastarkalv. I fear Harald Gormsson, now that he controls all of the Danes, is using his army to take what is ours. And he is using Erik's sons to bring this army against us. In fact, I am convinced of this."

"Which is why the Danes reinforce their center of wealth and the Danevirk in the south," added Gudrod.

"I do not follow," said Trygvi, who was scratching his hairy chin. "If they are using the armies to come north, why do they build in the south?"

"To protect their backs, Trygvi," Sigurd explained around a mouthful of bread. "They cannot leave their southern border or their largest trading center unprotected as they push east and north."

Hakon turned back to Frode. "Do you know where Erik's sons are?"

Frode drained his mead cup and wiped his mouth with his sleeve. "I think you know the answer to that question already."

"Fyrkat?" Hakon guessed.

"Aye, lord. Fyrkat. The king gave them lands there when they returned from Engla-lond."

Hakon looked at his jarls. "It is time to plan."

Gudrod turned to Frode. "I thank you for the information, Frode. You will be paid handsomely for it once the army returns."

Frode's expression soured. "Once the army returns? And until then?"

"Until then, your ship will be confiscated, and you and your crew will be my guests in Kaupang."

"I do not understand. Why are you doing this?"

Gudrod shrugged his meaty shoulders as if it were both trivial and obvious. "Because, Frode, you have loose lips, and we cannot have you speaking of this meeting while you drink ale in Hedeby. Besides, how else can I ensure you are telling the truth?"

When the planning came to an end, Hakon located the campfire around which some of his favored hirdmen sat. The men were laughing, but the laughter died on their lips when they saw their king coming.

"To what do we owe this honor, lord?" asked Asmund as Hakon stepped into the firelight.

"What Asmund means to say is, why are you out here in the cold when you could be sleeping in a warm bed with a young lass wrapped around you," said Toralv. "All you will find here are smelly men and bad jokes. The ale is decent though."

Hakon smiled at Toralv's words. "That may be, Toralv, but I have news to share and did not want to wait. We leave on the morrow," Hakon continued when he was sure he had his men's attention. "The weather permitting, of course." A hush fell over the men. "Ready your gear and do not drink much more than you already have. I need your heads clear for what is to come."

"And what is that?" asked Harald, who'd been whittling a stick.

"We go to pick a fight, Harald, and to avenge the deaths of our brothers."

Hakon studied the men's faces. To a man, they grinned, and Hakon knew what was on their minds — it was about time they took the fight to the Danes.

The only man not smiling was Egbert, who crossed himself instead.

Chapter 16

East Jutland Coast, Late Summer, AD 957

Hakon's ships attacked in the morning. Ahead of them lay a long stretch of Danish beach and a small cluster of huts. Behind the fleet rose the morning's sun, which illuminated the dwellings and partially blinded any on shore to the death that came toward them. The crew grunted at their oars, pulling with all their strength to maximize speed, and surprise. Hakon did not expect much resistance. This was not a well-guarded town or a rich church center. This place — whatever its name — was just a poor village that fate had placed close to Fyrkat. Nevertheless, Hakon did not wish to take a chance and so the crew pulled for speed.

"Oars up!" he roared as *Dragon* rode the white churn of surf into the shore.

As soon as her prow bit, Hakon and his men leaped from the gunwales with weapons and shields in hand and raced for the dwellings. Four other crews did the same, each with a yell in their throat and menace in their eyes. The remainder of the ships waited off shore.

The folk who lived in the village never had a chance. Some died in their sleep. Others woke long enough to see their death coming before the blade took their life.

"Spare the young and the animals!" Hakon called over the screams and mayhem. A chicken ran across Hakon's path, and he kicked it aside. It clucked in pain as its feathers flew.

"What should we do with the prisoners?" called Bard as he exited a house dragging a young boy.

"Put them in the pen with the pigs," ordered Hakon. "And guard them!"

Hakon rushed into a dwelling. A middle-aged man lay dead on the floor. His wife was splayed across the only table in the room, screaming as a warrior ravaged her from behind. In the corner, a little girl yelled for the warrior to stop hurting her mother, but he was oblivious to her pleas. Hakon grabbed the girl roughly and pulled her free of the dwelling. He could do nothing for the mother.

After depositing the girl in the pen, Hakon found Toralv and grabbed him by the arm. "Have the men search the dwellings for anything of value and pile it down near the beach. Go!"

The Northmen made short work of the dwellings and the people within them. Before the remainder of the ships landed, the houses were cleared and the inhabitants killed or captured. They did not burn the structures, for Hakon did not want other Danes to see the smoke. Not yet, anyway. He wanted to understand more about their surroundings before alerting nearby Danes of their presence.

Hakon studied the measly pickings they had collected. A silver bracelet. A few knives. An amber brooch. Two hand axes. Several shields. A dented helmet. Nothing more. These were simple farmers who lived off the land. They had no need for silver or implements of war. Hakon turned to the pen, where ten sobbing children huddled with the grunting pigs and bleating sheep. At least they had thralls and food.

The army quickly began the work of building a camp. Though he had purposefully not burned the dwellings, Hakon was certain that word of his army had already started to spread throughout the land. The Danes had sentries all along the coast, and a fleet as large as Hakon's would not go unnoticed. Should Danes come sooner than expected to drive them away, he wanted to be ready. And so his men felled trees and began the hard work of building a fence that could be used as a defensive perimeter. On the outside of this fence, others dug a shallow ditch in which they placed stakes whittled into deadly points. With the work under way, Hakon then saw to their next move. On some of the ships were horses, and these they brought ashore for their scouts. Mud flew from the horses' hooves as the scouts galloped off to locate targets that could swell their supplies and add to their paltry team of horses.

By noon, most of the scouts had returned to deliver their reports. They came to Hakon's tent, where the king sat in council with Sigurd, Trygvi, and Egbert around a small fire. It was as Hakon expected. Small farmsteads and fields dotted the countryside, though there was one larger hall not far to the south.

"How many men at this hall?" Hakon asked the scout who had discovered it.

"I counted roughly twenty, lord. Warriors and thralls both."

"Horses?" asked Sigurd.

"Several, lord."

Hakon contemplated the news. "Bring me one of the prisoners."

The scout returned shortly with the blond girl Hakon had taken from her dwelling. Hakon gazed up at the girl through the campfire smoke. She was mayhap a few winters older than his own daughter, Thora, and in fact resembled her a bit — a realization that unnerved Hakon. Her bloodshot eyes and her crestfallen manner spoke to the trauma of her day and the bleakness of her future, and he felt for her. Still, he could not let his feelings show to his men, and so he studied her stiffly.

"What is your name?" he asked coldly.

"Signe, lord," the girl said with a swallow of fear.

"There is a lord's hall to the south of here. Who is the lord of this hall, Signe? And how many warriors serve him?" He held up his finger to warn her. "You would do well to remember that I have the power to kill you or spare you, so speak truly."

Tears welled in her eyes at his harsh words. "His name is Halvar, lord," she said through her tears. "But I know not how many men he has." Her voice sounded desperate.

Hakon studied the girl for a long time. It had the intended effect. She shifted her weight nervously, and looked at her feet, but she shared no more.

"Very well," said Hakon as he stroked his short beard. "Do you know of the ring fort at Fyrkat?"

She stiffened. "Aye, lord."

Hakon glanced at his lords, then back at the girl. "Can you tell me of this place?"

Uncertainty clouded her face. "I have never been there, lord. I know only what I hear and that is that a great army lives there. I have not seen this place with my own eyes, but one of the men in our village helped build the fort."

Hakon sighed, knowing the man was dead and of no use. "Is this Lord Halvar connected to the warriors at Fyrkat? Do they serve him?"

The girl shrugged.

"This is useless. The girl knows nothing," Sigurd grumbled in frustration. "Let her be."

Hakon waved her away, but she pushed the scout's hand away before he could grab her. "What is to become of us, lord?"

"You are to be thralls, Signe," Hakon told her bluntly.

The girl's face dissolved into tears as the scout pulled her away.

"We have our next target," said Trygvi to no one in particular. "We should attack the lord's hall now."

"Agreed," said Hakon. "Gather the horses and twenty of your men, Trygvi. I shall do the same. Sigurd, I want your men to go out to the farmsteads. Take what food and goods and thralls you can find. Leave Hemming here to guard the camp."

Beside him, Egbert blanched, but wisely kept his lips tight.

Hakon and his small troop set out shortly thereafter, following the scout down a small track that skirted fields of sea grass and sand dunes.

The track eventually turned inland toward flat fields of grass dotted with birch trees. It was here that the scout left the path and continued southward along the dunes until they reached a thicker forest of birch under which the grass grew thick and green. He stopped about a hundred paces from the trees and waited for the others.

"We head into the trees, then angle west and follow the river, which will be on our left. Not far from where we enter, we will reach a meadow. That is where the hall sits."

"Lead on," Hakon ordered.

Once within the shade of the trees, the men spread out and slowed their horses to a walk. There were no paths here, so the men picked their way carefully through the shadows, keeping their eyes open for signs of trouble as they bent and leaned to dodge the low, white-barked branches. Off to their left, a river flowed lazily, its surface twinkling in the midday light.

As the trees thinned, the meadow and the hall came into view. Hakon called for a halt some fifty paces from the meadow and studied the scene before him. Men, women, and children streamed from the hall and the outlying structures, carrying buckets, sea chests, and other possessions to the water's edge, where a ship lay. A few women pulled goats with ropes. Some of the children carried chickens whose wings flapped in protest. A man stood near the ship in armor and helm, urging the people to hurry.

"They know of us," said Trygvi at Hakon's ear.

"Then let us give them a proper send-off." Hakon drew his sword, Quern-biter. His men followed his lead. "You take the hall. I will take the ship. And Trygvi, I want some of them alive."

Hakon tightened the grip on his sword and drove his heels into his steed's flanks. The horses raced forward, zigzagging through the forest as they approached the meadow. Ahead of them, the people heard the snapping of branches and thundering hooves and screamed in fear. Hakon cleared the last of the trees and sped into the meadow, his horse kicking up clumps of mud and grass as he dashed for his prey. Hakon's men charged beside him, filling the air with their battle cries, hungry for the slaughter and the booty that would soon be theirs.

"Protect Halvar!" called a burly man who stood near the lord. The man had drawn his sword and came forward with three others at his side.

Hakon pulled hard on the reins and dismounted, calling his hirdmen to him as they too leaped from their steeds. He yanked his shield from his back as his men gathered about him. "Capture the lord!" he yelled.

An arrow whipped past Hakon's face as he raced toward the lord's defenders. The burly man raised his sword to thwart Hakon's attack. As he did, Toralv swung his axe into the man's shoulder and dropped him. Hakon spun and hacked into the armored side of another man who was swinging at Bard. The man arched in pain, and Bard took his head from his shoulders. A man hollered in pain. Hakon turned in time to see the scout go down with a spear in his chest. Asmund skewered the scout's killer with such force, it lifted the man's feet from the ground.

Another arrow zipped past Hakon. He turned toward the new threat and located the archer. The man stood in the shadow of the hall, shooting his weapon as quickly as he could pull the arrows from his quiver. Hakon cursed at the man and rushed for him. The archer saw Hakon coming and clumsily nocked another arrow, pulled, and released. The arrow sailed past Hakon's shoulder. Seeing his peril, the man turned and tried to escape into the forest on the west side of the hall, but Hakon chased him down and sliced Quern-biter across the man's spine. He screamed and fell, and Hakon finished him.

Hakon turned back toward the meadow and the chaos. The women and children had dropped their goods and now ran for the safety of the trees, chased by the Northmen. Some of Halvar's warriors fought on, though most lay dead or wounded in the field. Chickens flapped noisily. Sheep bleated as they trotted helter-skelter from the fighting. Screams and curses echoed in the hall. Back at the ship, Halvar knelt at Toralv's feet. Hakon made his way to his champion's side.

"You are Halvar?" asked Hakon.

The kneeling man gazed up at Hakon. He was a portly man, with wide blue eyes that danced with fear and straight blond bangs that clung to his sweating forehead. "I am," he croaked.

"Why do you kneel, Halvar? I did not think Danes knelt to any man."

"Please," implored the lord. "I have silver. If you let me go, it is yours." Behind Hakon rose the cry of captured children and the scream of women. Halvar ventured a glance at the scene before turning his haunted gaze back to Hakon. "Please."

Hakon could feel the heat rising in his cheeks and his eyes narrowing. "Only a coward looks to his own safety before that of his women and children," he growled.

"Aye. Of course," blubbered Halvar with his hands raised to calm the warrior who stood before him. "My silver for the safety of all my people. Please."

Hakon had a mind to skewer him then and there, but the hard truth was, he needed Halvar alive; so he swallowed the bitterness of his wrath. "Show me this silver. If it is enough, I will consider your life and the life of your people."

The man's eyes narrowed. "Swear that you will let me live, and I will bring it to you."

Hakon scowled and raised his blade so that the point poked Halvar's neck. "You are in no position to bargain, Halvar. Get your silver."

Halvar rose and moved to the ship. He reached over the gunwale and lifted a small chest from the pile of possessions that had made it onboard. This he placed at Hakon's feet, opening the lid to reveal hundreds of silver coins. Halvar stepped back and gestured to the chest. "Take it."

Hakon did not move. Halvar's eyes shifted from Hakon to Toralv and back to Hakon.

"Bind his arms, Toralv."

Toralv moved to the ship and returned with a coil of rope. From this he sliced a smaller section and tied Halvar's arms behind his back. The Danish lord grunted in pain as Toralv tightened the binding.

"You will do something for me now, Halvar," said Hakon. "You will go to Fyrkat and tell the warriors there what you saw here."

The man nodded fervently. "Aye, lord."

"Tell the lord at Fyrkat that Hakon Haraldsson, king of the North-men, has arrived and wishes to repay them for the death they brought to my realm. Tell them also that I will ravage this land and its people until they come to fight me."

The man's eyes grew at the mention of Hakon and his intentions. "I will tell them, lord."

"Good. Now go." Hakon pointed west with his sword.

"What of my people?"

"Your people belong to me."

Halvar frowned but wisely kept his mouth shut. He turned and waddled westward toward the trees.

As he disappeared into their shade, Hakon called Garth and Harald to his side. He turned to the animated Garth, whose dark eyes moved right and left, then back to Hakon as he listened to his lord's instructions. "Follow him to Fyrkat, Garth, but do not let him see you. I want to know he made it. And I want to know every detail of that fort. Do not engage anyone. Do you understand?"

Garth nodded and took off after Halvar.

Hakon then turned his attention to Harald, who was wiping the blood off of his seax with his pant leg. He was not a born scout, but he was a Dane and knew these parts, which made him a better option for the mission Hakon had in mind. "I need you to head north, Harald. There is supposed to be a road that leads to a fort at a place called Agger. Take a horse and find it."

"And what then?"

"Watch it. If an army emerges, come find me. If there is no fort, or if no army appears, return in four days' time. Stay hidden."

"And if someone should find me?"

"Act like a Dane."

Harald smiled. "I am a Dane."

"Precisely. Now go!"

For two more days, Hakon and his army brought ruination to the Danes. Only now, the king wanted the presence of his army to be known, and to be felt. He wanted the Danes at Fyrkat to see the smoke and the destruction, and to wallow in their impotence until they could stand it no more. But just as importantly, he wanted to fulfill his promise to his men, and give them a taste of early victory. For a greater fight would soon be upon them that would take more than sword edges and spear points to prevail. It would take morale. And so he let his men carpet the fields with Danish blood, burn their halls and trample their crops, until Danish plunder filled his ships, and the sky above this bleak strip of Danish coastline rippled with the mournful cries of its people. It was brutal and it was vicious, but it was necessary to bolster the spirits of his men. At least that was what he told himself in the darkness of his tent each night as he prayed with Egbert for strength and for forgiveness.

Early on the morning of the third day in Jutland, Garth returned. He sat by the fire with a cup in his hands, mud-caked and red-eyed but otherwise hale. He was too tired to fidget and so just gazed at Hakon with eyes glossy from lack of sleep. Hakon gathered the jarls, Sigurd and Trygvi, and convened a small fireside council with a simple question. "Did Halvar make it to Fyrkat?"

"Aye, lord. The Danes met him at the fortress gates."

Hakon accepted the news with a nod. "Tell us then of Fyrkat, Garth. What have you learned?"

Garth set his cup aside and grabbed a long stick, then smoothed the ground with this hand. He drew a circle in the dirt and, to the east of it, a long semicircle from which two lines extended east. Farther to the west, on the opposite side of the first circle, he drew a number of small, scraggly circles. "This," he said, poking the large circle in the middle, "is Fyrkat. It is a circular earthwork structure that sits on a small hill, overlooking the head of the fjord here." He stabbed the semicircle. "And a small forest, here." He poked the small circles to the west. "A narrow road leads north from the northern entrance of Fyrkat and south from the southern entrance. There are several dwellings that sit on the shore of the fjord and six warships at the dock."

"How large is Fyrkat?" asked Sigurd.

Garth shrugged. "As far across as an arrow can fly, give or take."

Hakon stroked his beard. "And its defenses?"

"In truth, it is not what I expected."

"How so?"

"It is —" Garth paused to think of the word "— rudimentary. Still, it would take many men to attack it. First, warriors would need to charge up the hill while being fired upon from the walls of the fort, which look to be the height of four men. If our men manage to get to the base of the fort's walls, they would then need to attack up the sloping walls of Fyrkat to get to the men at the top. Or, they would need to get through the gates, which are thick-timbered and guarded from above by a bridge."

Hakon looked at Sigurd and Trygvi, both of whom were lost in thought as they studied Garth's diagram.

"That is not all," said Garth. "There are structures on the inside of the fort. Halls, it looks to be. Though how many is impossible to say from the outside."

"What of the fjord, Garth?" Hakon asked. "Is it guarded?"

"Aye, though not well." He took the stick and drew some lines out from the semicircle eastward. "There are guard towers on either side of the fjord, here and here. There are several men in each."

"And approaches to the fort?" asked Sigurd. "Is there a track or road from the fjord to the fort?"

"Aye, Jarl Sigurd. On the north coast, about fifty paces in from the fjord, is a track that intersects with the northward road, just at the base of the hill on which Fyrkat sits."

For a long moment, the men sat by the fire, staring at Garth's dirt sketch while weighing their options.

Hakon broke the silence. "My first hope was to ensure that Lord Halvar made it to Fyrkat and delivered his message. That has been done, and the Danes know now who faces them. I also hoped to learn of some weakness in the Fyrkat defenses, but I am thinking now that those weaknesses do not exist. Therefore, we will continue with the plan to draw them out against us."

"For how long?" Trygvi bluntly asked and forged ahead even after Hakon frowned. "We cannot do this forever. I say we attack the fort and be done with it or move on to better pickings."

"From the sounds of it, attacking the fort is folly," Sigurd grumbled.

"So instead we wait for the Danes to gather their entire force and come against us? How much bloodshed will that bring?" Trygvi countered with a scowl.

"I understand your concern, Trygvi, but wish to remind you of why we are here." Hakon looked at him square in the face and held his gaze. "We are here to fight. It is time to destroy the Danes or at least cripple them so badly that they will think twice before raiding our shores again. But we must fight with intelligence." He tapped his temple. "If Garth speaks truly, then attacking their fort is folly. So we must wait for them to come against us, and we must find a spot that is suitable for that battle. And when we are through with them," Hakon smiled faintly, "the door will be open for us to raid until the plunder threatens to sink our ships."

As if God had heard his very words, the sentries blew the warning horn. The lords stood abruptly and without further word, jogged to the gates.

Chapter 17

Hakon and his men hastened to the edge of the camp, where Harald sat astride his steed, shouting at the sentries who had leveled their spears at him.

"Lower your spears! I am King Hakon's man, you louts," he bellowed as he removed his hood. "Where is the king?"

"Let him through!" Hakon called to the sentries.

The guards opened the gate, and Harald dismounted. Sweat slickened his face and dampened his hair, and fresh mud caked his clothing. Froth bubbled at the corners of the horse's mouth. Hakon handed Harald his water skin, which he took gratefully.

"The army moves from the north, lord," he said after swallowing several mouthfuls and belching loudly. He showered his face with the water and wiped it away with his palm, leaving streaks of dirt on his cheeks. "They left last night, under cover of darkness."

"How many men?" asked Hakon.

"Mayhap three hundred men, give or take. A few horsemen, but most on foot."

"Headed to Fyrkat, you think?"

Harald nodded. "I know. I trailed them until early morning. They met a warrior bearing the Fyrkat shield on the road and followed him south. That is when I left them."

Hakon hooted and slapped Harald on the shoulder. "You have done well, Harald. Get some food and rest. We shall march soon."

By noon, the army had assembled and started to move. He left a rearguard of fifty men to watch the ships and the captured thralls, though he knew it was not enough, should things go wrong. Hakon sent Bard, Garth, and Harald out on horseback to scout ahead, and rode with Sigurd and Toralv by his side.

Though he did not say it, he felt strangely naked without Egil nearby. He had never fought a battle without the old warrior close, and Hakon found his absence both sharp and constant. It was not that Sigurd, Toralv and Trygvi weren't formidable warriors — they were. Egil had been the warrior whose mettle kept men in the shield wall when the gods felt unreachable and the battle, dire. Just who might fill that role now was hard to say, and that uncertainty clung to Hakon's thoughts like a wet tunic clings to the body.

"Think you that they may try to come down the fjord?" asked Sigurd as they passed the area that had belonged to Halvar. The sun had disappeared behind a veil of thin gray that muted the vibrancy of the summer landscape and added a crisp bite to the air.

Hakon studied the shadowed waterway through the trees. "I doubt they would split their forces, unless the intention of my nephews is to leave their allies stranded. Even so, I have Garth watching for ships. We will know if they come from that direction."

Sigurd nodded, satisfied, and turned his eyes back to the tree-dotted countryside that stretched ahead. "It is beautiful land, this. Fertile. Rolling. I am glad I came to see it."

Hakon smiled. "You are glad you came to plunder it, more like."

Sigurd barked a laugh. "Aye, that too. But in seriousness, a man could make a good living on the land in these parts."

"A rider is approaching," said Toralv, interrupting their pleasantries with a due-west stab of his finger. There, a single rider galloped down the face of the hill. The warriors at the front of Hakon's column drew their swords and waited.

"Hold!" Toralv thundered. "It is Bard."

The hirdman came at speed toward the column. "Lord!" Bard called as he reined in his steed and walked it through the press of men who parted to let him through.

Hakon moved to meet him. "What news?"

"The armies have met. They must have marched through the night and joined. They are moving toward us now."

Hakon nodded resolutely. It was as he had hoped. The Danes had left the safety of their forts and come for battle, and so, by the grace of God, Hakon would give them one.

"Lord?" said Sigurd with his eyebrow cocked.

Hakon looked at Bard. "You have seen the landscape, Bard. Where would you choose to fight?"

Bard did not hesitate. "You are gazing at it," he said as he pointed to the hill before them. It was a low, wide hill with a thick copse of trees standing on its crest. "The Danes are coming straight down the path that skirts the south side of that hill. They will march right into us."

Hakon nodded. "Very well. Forward, then."

They rode west and up into the trees at the top of the hill. On the far side, just within the tree line, they stopped and peered out over the landscape. Below them stretched a long, grassy slope that leveled off into a wide, flower-dotted field where several tall oaks stood like ancient sentinels. A dirt track bordered the south side of the field, beyond which a forest of birch trees stretched south to the fjord. Two arrow flights to the northwest was another, lower grass-covered hill.

Hakon's heart dropped. "Where are the Danes?" he asked.

"Some ways off yet," Bard responded.

Hakon nodded. "How far?"

"They will arrive by nightfall. Mayhap sooner."

"It is decided, then." Hakon turned to his lords. "Make camp. We shall meet them here, at this hill."

Hakon spent the late afternoon moving his army into position, arranging them so that they wrapped in a semicircle around the western side of the hill. This he did openly in the hope that the enemy scouts would see his movements and know what force they came against. He did, however, hold Sigurd's Tronds and Halogalanders back in the trees and away from the enemy's eyes. It could not hurt, he reasoned, to show less strength to the Danes than he actually had.

The enemy, however, did not come as he expected. They stayed away and camped to the west of Hakon's army. From the top of the hill, Hakon could see the sky brighten in the gathering evening where their myriad campfires burned. Below him, his warriors lit their own fires and settled in, seemingly unfazed by the Danes who camped so near. Their banter floated in the air like the bubbling of a stream.

A leaf crunched behind Hakon, and he turned to see Sigurd standing a few paces away, scanning the fading landscape with his eyes. "What are you thinking?" Hakon asked the old jarl.

"I am trying to put myself in their minds," Sigurd responded. "You?"

Hakon turned his eyes back to the distant skyline where the enemy camped. "I, too, am trying to divine their thoughts."

"And?" asked Sigurd. "Have you determined anything?"

"No. Though something tells me that mischief will be part of their plan. If the forts are only as large as an arrow's flight across, then they cannot house more than several hundred men. Even two such forts cannot total half our army in numbers. If you were their commander, would you march straight into the mouth of an enemy that is twice as large as you?"

"You have," replied Sigurd. "More than once."

"I had either surprise on my side or my pick of a spot to defend. I am not sure I would rush headlong into this battle."

"Your thoughts mirror my own," Sigurd said. "Have you scouts out?"

"Aye," Hakon answered as his thoughts turned to Garth and Bard and Harald, all three of whom had reported in and gone back out to watch the Danes. So far, there was nothing out of the ordinary.

Hakon had a sudden thought and pushed himself to his feet.

"What is it?" Sigurd asked.

"A hunch. Nothing more. I will be back." He strode down the hill and searched the camp until he found Toralv. The champion rested by a small fire, sharpening his axe blade in silence. On the opposite side of the flames, Asmund checked his byrnie for loose links. They both stopped their work when he appeared.

Hakon wasted no time on pleasantries. "Set twice as many guards as normal tonight and have the men sleep in their armor," he said. "With their weapons and shields close at hand."

Toralv looked at Asmund, then back at his lord. "You are expecting a night attack?"

"I know not what I am expecting," Hakon replied honestly. "But I have misgivings. So best to be cautious."

"Sleeping in armor is not easy, as you know," Asmund chimed in as he waved his hand before him to clear the smoke from his eyes. "The men will be tired when they wake on the morrow."

"Better tired than dead," Hakon countered bluntly.

"You make a convincing point, lord," Asmund admitted with a grin.

Hakon looked back to Toralv. "Spread the word."

"Aye, lord," Toralv said as he climbed to his feet, then strode off to issue the command.

For the remainder of the night, Hakon sat at the crest of the hill with his back against a tree. Beside him lay Egbert with his hands under his head. The monk's eyes were closed, though his mouth moved as he offered silent prayers to the night sky. Down below Hakon danced the fires of his army and the dark forms of his warriors. Their dwindling conversations had melted into the sounds of the night — the breeze, the rustle of the leaves, the hoot of an owl, the howl of distant wolves on the hunt. Overhead the shroud of cloud persisted, masking the stars and the moon and casting the landscape into something formless and frightening.

It made Hakon uneasy. In his fingers was his cross, which he twiddled in circles as his mind wandered from one worry to the next. He wondered what Erik's sons might do and when they might do it. He wondered where his scouts were and why they had not yet returned. He wondered if he had positioned his army correctly and whether his men were prepared for what was to come. At least a dozen times, he thought he saw something moving out in the field, and sat up straighter to watch and wait. But no alarm sounded. No cry rang out. And eventually he would settle against the tree again and wait.

"You are worried, lord," came Egbert's whisper. "Do not be."

"Why?"

"Because God is with you."

Hakon smiled wryly into the night, for age and loss and experience had made him cynical. "That does not guarantee my victory, Egbert. God has been with many leaders who have died fighting heathens."

"Aye, but they perished in the name of good, and their souls were welcomed in Heaven. Does that not give you comfort?"

Hakon thought on that for a moment. "I should welcome that thought, Egbert, but I do not wish to die yet, even if God and Heaven welcome me. I want vengeance. God can take me another day."

"Vengeance is not yours to take," Egbert countered. " 'It is mine to avenge; I will repay. In due time, their foot will slip; their day of disaster is near and their doom rushes upon them.' So sayeth the Lord, Hakon." Egbert crossed himself and said no more. Soon Hakon heard his friend's soft snores.

Hakon pulled his cloak tighter about his shoulders. He must have dozed, for a shake of his shoulder woke him. "Lord. The enemy comes," said a voice in his ear.

Hakon sat up and wiped his face to remove the cobwebs of sleep that clung to him. He turned to the voice and saw Garth kneeling beside him. Bard and Harald were also there, kneeling in the morning's gloom. Hakon shook his head and took in his surroundings. Birdsong heralded morning, though it was yet dark. "Where?" he croaked. His back and neck screamed in protest of his awkward sleeping position, and his cold limbs had not yet found sensation. He blew into his hands to warm them.

"Everywhere," Garth said.

"What?"

"They come from our front and our two sides," explained Garth. "The army broke camp some hours ago. We came as soon as we were sure of their battle order."

"What is it?" Egbert asked as he sat up.

Hakon stayed him with his hand. "They are not behind us?" he asked.

"No, lord. Not yet, anyway."

Hakon stood and looked out over the dark, flat field to the west of the hill. He could see no enemy forces yet, or at least no irregularities in the landscape that might indicate an approaching army. "How far off are they, and how strong is this force? It must be bigger than expected to be coming from three sides."

"More men came during the night," added Garth. "From the west. Not Fyrkat men, but others."

"They will be here soon. We have not much time." This came from Harald.

Hakon ran through the options in his head. "Are we still the larger force?"

"It is hard to say, lord. If we are, it is not by much."

"Call the men to arms and send Trygvi to me. Spread the word that everyone should eat what they can and prepare themselves. We fight here. Tell no one that the rear is open."

The men looked at each other, and each nodded in turn.

"Go now!"

The scouts rushed down the hill, shouting for men to awaken. Their calls were followed quickly by the long, resonant call of horns filling the air. Quickly, men stood and assembled. Even in the darkness, he could sense their confusion, but they would know soon enough what awaited them.

"Why tell no one about the rear?" The question came from Egbert, who was scratching at his head.

Hakon glanced at him. "Leaving an escape open is an old trick. It lures armies into thinking there is a way out. I want my men to fight like berserkers, like there is no path to safety."

Dark bags hung below Egbert's eyes, and these seemed to darken further with Hakon's response. "I had not thought of that," he admitted morosely.

"Have cheer, Egbert," Hakon offered. "Today we rid ourselves of the Danish threat."

"God willing," the priest added and tried to smile. "Which reminds me...will you pray with me, lord?"

Hakon shook his head. "There is no time for that, I'm afraid. Too much still needs my attention." Hakon patted his friend's shoulder and smiled. "Pray for me, Egbert. Make it a good one. We shall need it this day."

The priest nodded and disappeared into the trees, his place taken by Sigurd, who came up alongside his king and surveyed the field. The enemy was still not visible, but there was no mistaking the sound of metal on shields or the tread of a thousand warriors coming for blood. Hakon quickly recounted the scouts' findings to Sigurd, then added, "I want half of your men to remain here, in the trees, with someone you trust to command them."

Sigurd began to bluster, but Hakon raised his hand. "I do not want to hear your protests. We need men in reserve, and I want Erik's sons to think we are lighter in numbers than we are. It is why I kept you in the trees last night and away from their scouts. Now go speak with your men. Those you choose to bring forward, move to the north." Hakon pointed in that direction. "They will guard our right flank. I will move the men currently there to the west."

Sigurd grumbled but agreed. As he did, Trygvi came lumbering up the hill. He stopped before Hakon and nodded to both men. "What are my orders?"

"I need you to take the left flank, Trygvi." Hakon pointed south, then turned so that he could look both men in their tired faces. "Keep your men on the hill and hold the higher ground. Do not move your men unless the enemy is broken and in disarray. Is that clear?" Hakon moved on to a new thought before either man could respond, for he was beginning to feel the battle joy in his veins and his thoughts were coming quickly. "Sigurd, the men you leave here in the trees must guard our rear. If the enemy appears there, they are to sound three quick blasts of the horns, then engage them. We will send men to help, if we can."

"And if they do not attack our rear?"

"Then the path to the sea is open," Hakon responded, pointing east. "But that is not a path we can take. Do not let your men fall victim to that temptation and retreat. We must make our stand here and end this. Do you both understand?"

Sigurd nodded, while Trygvi spat poignantly into the grass.

"Erik's sons and these Danes want to be our masters. That cannot happen. We must end the spawn of Erik here. We must break their resolve." Hakon stared into the grim faces of his commanders, as if he could pass his own boldness to them through his gaze. "I will see you both when this is over." They clasped each other's wrists, then the two jarls left for their posts.

Hakon grabbed his shield and gazed out over the field, out to where the Danes were just beginning to materialize in the fading darkness. There were hundreds upon hundreds of them, amassed behind two vast lines of warriors holding red shields. Hakon moved to the right along the hillcrest. Another vast army greeted his vision, smaller than the main force but toting yellow shields to denote their connection to another fort or lord. And to the south stood the Fyrkat Danes in numbers that equaled the northern force. Hakon took a deep breath and jogged to the opposite side of the hill. Nothing but empty land greeted his gaze. It was a path to the sea, to his ships. But he would not give in to it. The fight was here, and this was where it would end.

"Where do you want me?" asked Egbert when Hakon returned to the western side of the hill.

"Here. I want you here with the reserve warriors. I want you praying. And only if necessary, I want you fighting." Hakon stared into the freckled face of his friend, trying to etch the man's features into his memory. Egbert cast his humble eyes to the ground, unable to hold Hakon's intense gaze. With a final pat on Egbert's shoulder, Hakon breathed deeply of the morning air, then strode to the battle lines.

It was time to finish the feud.

Chapter 18

The Danes marched slowly into position. They knew the Northmen would not vacate the high ground, so they were in no hurry. Part of Hakon believed it was deliberate, meant to drive his warriors insane with impatience or else lull them into indifference. It did not work — his men watched keenly, taut as bowstrings, waiting for the imminent clash of muscle and wood and blade.

"Asmund," Hakon said when he found his hirdman. "Come. I have a task for you." The spearman jogged over to his lord. "I need you to gather the spearmen in our armies." Hakon pointed to a few of them. "Have them form a solid second line in our troops. Do not cast your spears when the enemy comes. Keep them with you. Even when they cast their own, keep them with you. As we hold the higher ground, I want our spears to poke over the heads of our front line. I want you to keep the front line of Danes on the defensive. Do you understand?"

Asmund grinned. "Aye."

"Go now. Spread the word."

Hakon continued his inspection of his troops, speaking to some, adjusting the armor of others, showing his face and his confidence to all. As he did, darkness receded, bringing with it a thin, cool mist that hung low to the ground, like a veil on the grass. It was the kind of mist that made men uneasy and put them in mind of Niflheim, the mist world ruled by the goddess Hel where the spirits of dishonorable men go when they die. Hakon crossed himself at that thought.

It was through this mist that three Danes advanced as if they floated above the ground, coming to a stop a spear's throw from Hakon's army. They had with them a standard bearer who carried a red banner that hung limply in the breezeless morning. Hakon stepped forward from his army and advanced alone. Two of the men he recognized and expected: the redheads Ragnfred and Harald Eriksson, the surviving sons of Erik. But it was the third that Hakon stared at longest. He was a man of solid build, whose strawberry-blond tresses had been pulled back into a simple ponytail to reveal a handsome face and cheerful blue eyes. A well-groomed beard of the same reddish blond hung to his chest. It was parted into two thick braids.

"You are Harald Gormsson," said Hakon to the man without acknowledging the others. "I did not expect to see you this day. Nor did I expect your army to be so small."

The king of the Danes grinned wryly, revealing a row of rotten teeth for which he had earned his byname, Bluetooth. "And you are Hakon Haraldsson, who my father could have killed when you were a whelp but, instead, let live. A shame, for we would not need to be standing here, then. I must say," he said with little mirth on his face, "he is fond of that story."

"How ironic that our stories should be so similar. I once had the chance to end these bastards' lives, but like your father, chose to let them live for reasons he and I understand but you might never."

Harald scowled. "I prefer to cut men down, as you will soon learn."

"I hope your kin do not laugh at you in Valhall when your plan fails."

Harald looked at Hakon's battle lines. "Your army is an island in a sea of Danes. No quarter shall be given to them."

"Then we are in agreement, for I want nothing from you save the chance to kill my nephews and you, for the trouble you have caused me and my people. That is the only reason I am here. So let us fight and end this quarrel." Hakon looked at his nephews. They held their tongues and stared malignantly at their uncle. Hakon turned his back on them and strode to his lines.

"Well?" Toralv asked when Hakon returned.

"Make sure your blades are sharp."

The unflappable Toralv just laughed. "You heard your king," Toralv called to the hirdmen. "Prepare to fight!"

The mist dissipated, and the morning warmed. The Danish horns blew, and all three Danish forces advanced as one. Hakon stood on the hill watching, and waiting. Beside him were roughly thirty Halogaland archers who were known for their skill with the bow. Ten pointed in the direction of each army. They did not hide. There was no need, for the Danish arrows would have a hard time reaching this far up the hill.

Hakon sucked air into his lungs to calm his nerves and the hammering in his chest. As he did, he took in the sights and sounds and smells of the morning. It was surprisingly silent. There was no beating of blades on shields. No multitudes shouting their fury. No birdsong or breeze. Even the footfalls of the advancing Danes were masked by the damp grass and the mist. It was as if the world and God held their breath.

But at fifty paces distant, the world awoke. Below him, Toralv's commands rent the air. His men tightened their ranks and raised their shields. Cheers rippled across the field, followed by the beating of shields and the curses of hundreds of men digging within themselves for the courage to face their fears. Hakon could feel his own lust for battle ignite. It had been smoldering within him all morning but now it exploded in his body and in his veins.

And then the day erupted.

Danish spearmen shot forth from the lines and cast their deadly shafts, and the first of Hakon's men died on the Danish hill. Hakon's own men did not retaliate. Rather, they clutched their spears in their white-knuckled fists and waited for the fight that was yet to come.

"Ready?" Hakon called to his archers as he raised his arm.

The bowmen pulled their arrows from their quivers, nocked them, and lifted their bows to the sky. At this range, they could not hope for accuracy, but they could land their arrows in the mass of attacking bodies. They would do damage, and that was all Hakon wanted.

"Wait," Hakon commanded as the Danes moved within thirty paces of the Northmen. "Wait!"

The Danes came five steps closer and Hakon yelled, "Loose!" The arrows hissed into the sky and arced over his army. He could see the black streaks disappear into the Danish lines and, here and there, a man crumple to the earth.

"Again!" he shouted.

At that very moment, the Danes surged forward, and again, the Northern arrows landed in their midst. Hakon donned his helmet and yanked his seax from its sheath. "Keep shooting until you're out of arrows," he called to the archers. "Aim for the rear ranks. When you are done with the arrows, join your comrades to the north."

Hakon left them then and ran toward the center of his western line. Part of him yearned to remain on the hill where he could see the battle develop and react accordingly, but kings did not fight from the rear; they led from the front.

Hakon aimed for the spot where his boar standard teetered in the press and where he knew his hirdmen would be standing. "Make way," he called as he reached his line and pushed forward into the cluster of bodies. "Make way," he called again as the struggling warriors knocked him off balance and nearly to his knees. As he neared the front lines, a spear glided over a shield rim and slid past his face, its force causing a kiss of wind against his cheek.

"Thought you were going to miss the fun!" hollered Asmund as Hakon reached him. He stood just behind Toralv and Bard, who struggled side by side in the front rank. Hakon was about to respond when Asmund suddenly lurched forward with his spear, aiming for a face that had appeared before Bard's shield and just as quickly disappeared. "Bastard!" Asmund cursed.

Hakon ducked low and pushed his way into the gap between Bard and Toralv. The two fighters sidestepped slightly to make way but did not look to see who had just joined them. Rather, Toralv smashed his shield into a Dane, then drove his axe blade into the man's helmet with a bear-like roar. To his left, Bard severed the fingers of a man whose hand suddenly burst through the defenses. Hakon felt something smack his greave. He sidestepped and jabbed with his seax around the edge of his shield. There was a scream as the blade hit something and came away bloody.

"Where is Bluetooth?" Hakon yelled.

"To the left of us," grunted Toralv as a Dane banged into his shield.

Over their heads, Asmund and his men kept their spear points moving. Out and in they pumped, sometimes taking a life or wounding a Dane, sometimes smacking a shield and coming away empty. The Danes pressed forward, slamming again and again into the Northmen's line with their own shields and blades until it became clear what they were doing. As they were lower on the hill, they were using their shields to press upward while their blades went low, aiming for the legs and feet of the Northmen. And that was how Garth fell. A Danish sword took off his left foot just below his greave as he stepped forward into a sword thrust. He howled in pain and fell backward on the turf just to Bard's left. The Dane moved to finish him, but before he had taken a step, Bard stabbed the man in his neck.

"Fill the gap!" yelled Bard.

Someone grabbed Garth and began dragging him clear of the fight. Another Northman tried to take his spot, but a Danish spear caught him in the groin. The man hollered and fell. Seeing their advantage, two Danes lunged forward into the gap. The first drove his axe into the head of the hollering Northman. The second jabbed his spear at Bard and knocked his shield into his left shoulder, exposing Bard's front. Bard never faltered. In one motion, he dropped to a knee and stabbed the spearman's thigh, then twisted his wrist and slashed his blade across another Dane's knee. Both men fell away and Bard moved his shield back into position before more blades could rain down on him. The lines closed again.

Hakon had no time to think about his downed hirdman or the faltering line, for as Bard was closing the gap, three blasts of a horn rang out from the hilltop behind him. Hakon cursed, for there was no way to extricate himself from the fight or to issue a command. Nor was he foolish enough to take his eyes from the enemy before him. He just hoped Sigurd's men would do as he had instructed and fill the gap on the far side of the hill. Now his army truly was an island of Northmen in a sea of Danes.

Hakon ducked an axe blade, then stabbed into the face of a Dane just to his left. He glimpsed Bluetooth's standard some twenty paces away, on level with his own, which meant that his line was giving in that area. Were his other lines also faltering? Hakon ducked behind his shield and glanced to his right. Toralv was standing mightily against the Danes. To Toralv's right stood Harald, his byrnie painted crimson by blood, though whether his or someone else's, Hakon could not tell. Eskil was farther down, wounded in the arm, but fighting still. That line was holding firm, but for how much longer?

As Hakon stood, a blade glanced off the top of his helmet, knocking the nasal sharply down onto the bridge of his nose. Pain exploded across his face, and he fell to a knee.

"Get up!" roared Toralv and pulled Hakon roughly to his feet.

Hakon came to his wits. His face was awash in warm blood that cascaded across his lips and into his beard. He screamed his fury, shooting a spray of spittle and gore at his enemy. He would not let these Danes win. Not after all of the bloodshed and misery they had brought to his shores. Not after the death of so many friends and loved ones. Not when their numbers were equal and he held the higher ground. He smashed forward with his shield, exposing the Dane attacking Toralv. Hakon slashed the man's bicep and let Toralv kill him.

"Step forward!" yelled Hakon. And as one, his men drove their shields into the mass of Danish bodies. As they did, Asmund and his men jabbed with their spears into any exposed flesh they could find.

The Danes gave a foot, and suddenly Hakon felt like he was back on Frei in the tug-of-war. "On my word," he roared. "Step!" And again, the Northmen heaved as one into the Danes. And again, the enemy gave as their feet slipped on the slick slope and the blades savaged their shields. Some tried to push back, but their efforts were disconcerted and ineffectual. "Step!" Hakon yelled again and slashed with his blade at a man's neck. He hit the man's helmet instead but with such force that the man fell unconscious at Toralv's feet. Toralv stomped on the Dane's head and drove it into the ground with a sickening crunch.

And then they were through the king's troops and facing the rearguard of the Danes, who had little armor and no skill with weapons. The first row tried to resist but fell quickly to Hakon's men. "Kill them!" Hakon roared, and those words alone broke the guards' resolve. They turned and ran, and many died for their carelessness.

"Do not follow!" Hakon yelled. "Toralv. Pivot right. Bard, to me!"

As Toralv pivoted right, Hakon pivoted left and into the flank of Harald's remaining hirdmen. Seeing their peril, Bluetooth's men turned to meet the new threat. Hakon's own men rushed them with renewed energy, for they could smell victory and were hungry to feast on it.

"Finish them, Bard!" Hakon roared. "I am going for Harald!"

Hakon stepped from the line and jogged to where the Danish king fought. Later, he would understand just how insane he had been, running alone toward the Danish king. But now, in the moment, he could think of nothing but killing the man responsible for the Danish attacks on his realm.

"Bluetooth!"

Harald ignored the call and instead smashed a man sideways with his shield, then slashed right and took the head off another warrior. He then looked up to see Hakon before him and took a step forward. Hakon sheathed his seax and drew Quern-biter, readying himself for the battle for which he so thirsted. Bluetooth's hirdmen pulled on their king's armored sleeve and pointed off to their left, where a few Danes tried to keep the tide of Hakon's warriors from drowning them all. Somewhere on the field, a horn sounded the Danes' retreat.

Harald Bluetooth came to his senses then and spat in Hakon's direction. "I will kill you one day, Hakon!"

"Come now, Bluetooth!" Hakon strode toward the Danish king. As he did, one of the Danes cast his spear at Hakon, but Hakon saw it coming and knocked it aside with his shield. Another of Harald's hirdmen emerged to challenge him. He chopped at Hakon's head with a vicious overhead swing. Hakon took the attack on his shield and let the blow continue so that the momentum of it unbalanced his assailant. The warrior brought his shield up and twisted it so that the rim came toward Hakon's head. Hakon ducked the wild shield-strike, spun on his heel, and chopped his blade into the man's spine with such force, it nearly cut the man in two.

Hakon readied himself for the next attack, but it did not come. The Danes had retreated and taken their king with them. The men cheered as the attackers vanished across the field, and Hakon joined them in their elation. That is, until he heard the moans of the dying.

One glance about him was enough to evaporate the smile from his face. The wounded and dead lay in a foul, snaking line all along the base of the hill. Dane mixed with Northman. The dead with the living. And among them tromped the looters, already hungry for what booty they could find. He came across Bard, Eskil, Toralv, Harald, and Asmund, who rested in various states of exhaustion near their comrade Garth. Hakon's eyes moved from one man to the next. He was glad to see them alive and too drained to do anything but grin.

"That is some handy work, Garth," Hakon said to his footless hirdman. The man had tied a belt around his leg to stem the bleeding and had covered the stump with a bandage secured with twine. Despite that, Garth's skin was pallid and slick with sweat. For the first time in Hakon's memory, his hirdman was still, though he did manage to smile weakly at his king.

"It was your priest who patched him up," interjected Eskil, who had a gash in his arm and another in his forehead. The helmsman nodded in the direction of Egbert, who moved quickly from one fallen man to the next, triaging the wounded. He had been an infirmary apprentice as a novice in Wessex and had once saved Hakon from his own childhood wounds. Now, he was using that same skill to save the Northmen.

"I guess he has some use after all," said Asmund with a grin.

Hakon ignored the quip and moved off. He needed to learn more. It was clear the fighting had been fierce everywhere, but he had yet to learn who lived and who did not.

To the north, where Sigurd had held the line, the dead lay in piles. Sigurd lived, but many of his Tronds had paid for his staunch defense. The old warrior sat on the hill with a dented helmet resting beside him. He regarded Hakon with a weary grin when his king appeared. "By the gods, I never thought I would see the end of this day."

"Nor did I think I would see your ugly face again," Hakon responded.

Sigurd chuckled. "The uglier still with my new battle wound." He turned his face to reveal a gash on his right cheek, just above the line of his beard. "Though you are not one to ridicule me with that nose of yours."

Hakon had not thought much of it, but now, with Sigurd's words, he felt his nose throb. His hand went to his face and poked at the sticky slime on his chin. His fingers came away bloody. He grinned, then grimaced at the sudden pain it caused.

Sigurd beckoned Hakon to kneel. "Come here. I cannot have you returning to my daughter with your nose sitting sideways on your face."

Hakon knelt and Sigurd placed his hands to either side of his nose. With a quick jerk, he snapped the king's nose back into place. The pain shot through Hakon's brow and over his forehead, and the blood gushed anew. Hakon's eyes teared and his vision blurred.

"Serves you right for bringing me to this bloodbath."

Hakon stood and spat new blood from his mouth. "You do not fool me, Sigurd," he said as the pain receded. "You enjoyed yourself this day, the more so because you are still breathing."

Sigurd grunted. "I would have been fine with dying too," he admitted and cast his gaze back to Hakon.

Hakon nodded his understanding and looked away. "Well, I for one am glad you are here and alive."

Hakon left his friend then and moved to the east side of the hill, where the enemy had tried to surprise the Northmen and ran into the Trond reserves. Here Hemming and his men had fought and died.

The oath-sworn champion of Fynr lay across the corpses like a lover. About them lay a circle of Danes. Hakon closed his eyes and said a small prayer for the souls of the dead. He knew not whether his God listened to him anymore, especially after a slaughter like this, but it helped calm him to think that God might take pity on the souls of good men, regardless of whom they worshipped.

On the south side of the hill, Trygvi stood over the pile of armor and goods — a pile that was growing quickly as his men looted the dead. He noticed Hakon approaching and grinned. "A good day, this!" he said, motioning to the booty. The bangs of his wild hair were still moist from exertion, but otherwise, he looked as fresh as if he had just awakened from slumber. "What happened to you?"

Hakon waved off his question and looked about him. Here, too, a vicious fight with the Fyrkat Danes had taken place. In the midst of their piled corpses stood a single spear and, on its point, the head of Ragnfred. "Where is Ragnfred's brother, Harald?"

"The little snake called the retreat as soon as he saw his brother fall. He had not the balls to finish the fight."

Hakon sighed, for Harald's flight meant that the war was not over; that Harald would come again, provided the Danes would lend him men. Hakon smacked his nephew's shoulder. "You have done well, Trygvi. Come," Hakon beckoned. "We must plot our next steps."

Later, the warlords gathered in the shade of the hilltop trees so that they could keep their eyes on the west as they discussed their plans. It was midday, and the men sipped on water and passed bread between them.

"We did not finish the job," said Hakon to the gathering. "Harald Eriksson yet lives. As does Harald Bluetooth."

Sigurd tore a bite of bread from his loaf and spoke as he chewed. "There is nothing more for us here." He waved the loaf out at the countryside that stretched to the west. "The Danes are broken for now. Staying longer will give them time to heal and come at us again. We have already taken what the land has. Let us move elsewhere and plunder. The men deserve that much for their effort."

Trygvi grunted. "I agree with Sigurd. It is time to leave here. I would have liked to see these Danish ring forts, but we will lose more men for the effort. Best to take what plunder we have gained and go find some more, eh?"

Hakon sighed deeply but could find no fault in the jarls' thoughts. Still, the whole business of Harald Eriksson felt unfinished, and it grated on him. He said as much to his lords.

"You speak the truth, Hakon," responded Trygvi. "It is unfinished, and hopefully, when he comes against us again, we will finish it then. Even so, had he fallen today, this business with the Danes would not have ended. It is clear to me now that Bluetooth is greedy for power. It will not end until Bluetooth himself is dead and gone. But killing him is a different business entirely."

The trio sat in silence for a long time, chewing on their bread and the uncommon wisdom in Trygvi's words. It was unlike his nephew to have a wise thought, and so Hakon ruminated on that too for a time. Finally, Hakon looked at the others. "It is settled, then. We sail from this place as soon as we can and reap the rewards of our success. We will send as many ships as necessary back to Kaupang with the wounded. Those fit enough, and willing enough, will come with us to raid." He held up his cup to the others. "Skol!"

"Skol!" they replied and drained their water.

Chapter 19

Mayhem. Rapine. Slaughter. These were the things that Hakon's army brought to the Danes when it left Jutland the morning after the battle.

Their attacks never varied. They would land in the early morning, wherever the pickings looked best. Their strategy was simple. Strike. Plunder. Raze. Escape. Then find the next target. They never spent long enough in any place for the Danes to mount a defense. They sought plunder, not a fight.

The attacks whittled at Hakon's nerves like a blade shaving splinters from a stick. It was one thing to fight a foe with honor and to be justified in that killing. It was another to bring the fight to farmers, to women, to the old, and to the young, whose only offense was to be Danish. The first few days, Hakon had tolerated the raiding. But now, after seven such days, he no longer had a desire to kill old women or destroy Danish huts just for the measly scraps of wealth they might be hiding. His only reason for allowing these things to continue was to reward his men for their risk and their sacrifice, for many had lost friends and kin in the battle on the Jutland hill, and had earned their chance to plunder. And so he endured the chaos of it all, knowing all the while that there would be a price to pay for the violence he sanctioned.

His men, of course, were not hampered by any such guilt. In their minds, they had earned this booty with their struggles and their losses, and therefore it was theirs by right and theirs to enjoy instantly, for who knew what the next moment might bring. Hakon understood that, but it made him sick all the same. So as the fleet's prows bit into the Danish beaches and his men rushed forth to their butchery and their rape and their robbery, Hakon remained on *Dragon* and watched grimly from her prow.

It was Trygvi who finally questioned Hakon about his reserved behavior. They sat at a campfire, drinking stolen ale and eating a stew made from sea trout and vegetables they had just looted from a dwelling. He pointed his spoon at Hakon, who sat quietly staring into the flames. "Why do you not join us when we raid, Uncle?" Trygvi asked. "Does your Christian God not allow such things?" Trygvi smiled, but there was a hint of sarcasm in his tone that Hakon did not appreciate. When Hakon did not answer, Trygvi's smile collapsed into a frown. "The men are talking. They think that you do not approve when you do not join them."

Hakon looked up from the flames and stared at his nephew. He did not try to hide his displeasure with Trygvi's words. "I eat from the bowl they give to me, do I not, nephew? I take the gifts they offer me." He shook his wrist so that the silver bracelets on his arm jingled. He waved his hand at the structures they had just sacked. "You and the men can have your fun. You have earned it," Hakon said, and that was true. "I am content with knowing that, were it not for me, you would not be here now, enjoying such things." He raised his cup. "Skol!"

Trygvi accepted the words with a grunt. "Skol!" he replied. "I will make sure the men understand you."

"I thank you for that."

Sigurd, who sat at the same fire and heard the exchange, merely stroked his beard. "You skirt your nephew's question, Hakon. It is true you eat the looted food and receive the gifts brought to you, but you look about as miserable as a man who knows he is about to die abed. Surely you must be happy with the plunder we have gathered? Or with the revenge we have exacted on our Danish neighbors for the atrocities they have brought to our shores?"

For a long moment Hakon paused to gather his thoughts. How could he tell his jarl that he had sickened of this campaign? That his fight was with his nephews and not the innocents they now slaughtered or enslaved? He could not, for they would not understand. Their gods applauded such destruction, and so the men reveled in it too, like pigs at feeding time. So instead of trying to argue his point, he deflected the jarl's questions. "I am merely tired, Sigurd. It has been a long few days, and my nose and head ache." All of which was true. His nose was still a throbbing mass of purple that had spread to the space beneath his eyes, and his temples pounded from poor sleep. He rose and nodded to his jarls. "I wish you both a good night."

Two days later, Hakon and his fleet landed at yet another site. The clouds had let loose a soft drizzle that cast the world in a shifting gray and dampened the army's clothes and weapons, but not their spirits. They slid from their ships like smiling serpents, anxious for yet another attack and the plunder it would bring.

Egbert joined Hakon at the prow of *Dragon* and watched in silence as the men crept through the shrubs and dunes toward a hall that perched on a grassy knoll overlooking the beach. It was not yet fully light, and the men moved in silence through the morning's gloom.

The raiding party suddenly streaked across the open ground and burst into the hall. Screams shattered the still morning, sending gulls to flight with angry squawks. The unmistakable ring of metal on metal punctuated the morning, followed by the crash of furniture as the men scavenged for loot and food or subdued women and thralls. Several cows lowed in panic. A pig squealed. A dog barked and then yelped. All sounds that had repeated themselves many times over and had etched themselves into Hakon's soul, like a blade drawn against his skin. Beside Hakon, Egbert shuddered and crossed himself.

"There will be a reckoning for this," Hakon said, finally putting a voice to the thought that had been plaguing him for some days.

"I fear the same," Egbert responded. A hood covered Egbert's head so that, from the side, Hakon saw only his nose and the cloud of mist that materialized before his face when he spoke. "God watches."

Hakon had meant that the Danes would seek revenge and, in particular, Harald Eriksson and the Danish king, Harald Bluetooth. He had not considered God. "Does God truly mark every action and every death?"

" 'Oh Lord,' " Egbert recited. " 'You have searched me and known me. You know when I sit down and when I rise up. You understand my thought from afar. You scrutinize my path and my lying down, and are intimately acquainted with all my ways. Even before there is a word on my tongue, behold, oh Lord, You know it all.' " Egbert crossed himself and turned to Hakon.

"So sayeth the Lord," Hakon said before Egbert could.

Egbert turned back to the scene playing out before them as Hakon's mind turned to God and what He must be thinking.

"If my men are killing godless Danes, does God mourn?"

Silence stretched. Then: "I know not the answer to that, lord. Though I do know some priests believe killing heathens makes them godlier."

The raiding party had captured several women as well as a few children. Hakon could see his men tying them up and preparing them for their journey to the North. One of the women must have said something to offend a warrior, for the warrior backhanded her and knocked her to the ground.

"Is there anything we can do to end it?" Egbert asked.

"No," Hakon said quietly. "I made a promise, and I shall keep it."

"So you knew this would happen?"

"I knew. Though I did not know how it would eat at me."

The woman who had been knocked to the ground rose. Hakon saw a flash of something metal. The man who had struck her wailed and grabbed his arm. The woman darted back toward the hall, but two men quickly tackled her and hauled her to her feet. The man she had stabbed approached the woman and drew his own blade. It flashed in the gray morning and the woman crumped to her knees, then fell over dead. Hakon's shoulders slumped and he sighed.

"Come," urged Egbert.

"Where?" responded Hakon distantly, for one of the children had begun to wail, and the cry was yet another stain on Hakon's soul.

"We must pray," Egbert said. "It is the only way to lessen the burden of this horror."

The priest disembarked from *Dragon*. Hakon followed. They walked away from the ships and down the beach. A slight offshore breeze had picked up and carried with it the cries of children, the laughter of men, and the first hints of smoke from the hall.

"This will do," Egbert said, pointing to a grassy dune that hid them from the ships. He turned his eyes to the sky. "I would say it is about the hour of Prime," he said, though just how he knew this was hard to say, for the rain continued to fall and the entire sky was nothing but a ceiling of gray. "We will dispense with the hymns and focus on the psalms."

Hakon gawked at Egbert, who had collapsed to his knees in the sand. "You can pray at a time like this?"

Egbert beckoned to Hakon. "We must."

Hakon sighed and joined his priest, who had already begun to pray.

"*Beatus vir, qui non abiit in consilio impiorum, et in via peccatorum non stetit, et in cathedra pestilentiæ non sedit.*

"*Sed in lege Domini voluntas eius, et in lege eius meditabitur die ac nocte.*

"*Et erit tamquam lignum, quod plantatum est secus decursus aquarum, quod fructum suum dabit in tempore suo: Et folium eius non defluet: et omnia quæcumque faciet, prosperabuntur.*"

So came the words that Egbert had prayed so many mornings with Hakon by his side. Back when Gyda still lived and Erik's sons had not yet attacked. And with that thought, Hakon's mind wandered. Above him, a seagull's cry sent his thoughts to the screams in the hall and then to the image of Signe's mother being raped in her home. Hakon squeezed his eyes tighter and forced the sight from his mind, only to have them fill again with Gyda's shocked face as his blade sliced her throat. His words trailed off.

Egbert noticed his king's sudden silence and stopped. "What is the matter?"

"I am sorry, Egbert, but I cannot pray." Hakon spun and sat on the sand, gazing out over the empty gray ocean. A drop of rain trickled down his forehead and onto his nose. He mindlessly wiped it away and cursed at the pain. "I think only of bloodshed and cruelty." He paused as his thoughts drifted back to his childhood and to a scene that he had discovered while riding north with Athelstan's army. "As a youth in Engla-lond, I once rode with Athelstan's army to drive Constantine back into Scotland. Do you remember?"

"Aye," Egbert said. "I remember."

"On the trip north, we came across a dwelling that had been burned to the ground. In the ash were two heads on poles. The heads belonged to two small children. The culprits were Danes, and they were never found." Hakon gathered a handful of wet sand in his palm and let it slowly slide through his fingers. "I will never forget that day or the pain of seeing those two dead children. I vowed then never to be like those child-killing Danes. And yet, here I am."

Egbert sighed and turned to sit beside his king. "You are not like them, lord. Your heart is good, which is why this journey eats at you. Still, you allow it to happen, and God will see that. Mayhap you should try professing your sins and asking for His forgiveness. Mayhap that will ease the weight on your soul."

It was not the first time Egbert had made such a suggestion, and not the first time Hakon had rejected it. He was loath to share his transgressions or, more accurately, to dig into the dark corners of his mind and heart and revisit those old scars and memories. "You know what I have done and what I have not, Egbert. You also know my heart. I need not speak my deeds and my sins aloud for God to know them or for you to pray on my behalf."

Egbert glanced sidelong at his king. "I understand, lord, and will do my best."

Five more days of raiding followed. Five more days of greed and malice, of Hakon holding his tongue and graciously accepting stolen gifts. Five more days until his ships were at last filled with booty and thralls and the men's thirst for plunder and revenge at last slaked.

On the evening of the fifth day, Hakon gathered his jarls and the other chieftains on the beach beside their ships. He stood on a sand dune as they gathered before him and waited for him to speak.

"My lords," he began, and the chieftains fell silent at his words. "It has been a good campaign. We have finally taken the fight to the Danes and repaid them for their aggression. And we have profited nicely from our efforts!" He lifted a silver torque and displayed it to the men, who cheered their king. "But now," he began, then waited for his men to settle. "Now, it is time for me to return home." The men booed his words good-naturedly, and Hakon smiled back at them. "Autumn comes, and I, for one, am ready for the warmth of my own hall. On the morrow, I shall sail from these shores with whosoever would like to join me." He raised his hands to settle the commotion his words had wrought. "I know that many of you would like to stay, and I cannot forbid you from doing so. So if you stay, I will leave you with these words: it is better to live than lie dead. But a dead man gathers no goods. So be prudent, and happy hunting."

Hakon stepped from the dunes and walked straight to Sigurd, who was regarding his king with his arms folded across his chest. "Were you planning to sail without me?" asked the jarl.

"No. I am coming to you now to see if you will join me on the morrow. There is safety in numbers, and we are headed in the same direction. Besides, it is getting late in the year and the winter storms will soon batter the North Way."

"I was thinking the same. I was also thinking that this campaigning is a young man's sport. We have achieved what we set out to do."

Sigurd's eyes scanned the dunes. "I am ready to leave this place and will speak to my chieftains."

Hakon patted his friend's shoulder. "There is one more thing. I would like to join you in the coming year, as soon as the spring thaw sets in."

Sigurd's eyebrow arched. "What of your daughter until then?"

Hakon grinned. "I can think of no finer man than you to foster my Thora."

Sigurd raised in hands. "Oh no. That task will fall to Astrid. I have already ruined my own children with my boorish ways. I will not ruin yours too."

Hakon laughed.

Sigurd wagged a finger at Hakon. "Be that as it may, she is welcome to remain in my hall, so long as you pay for all of the food your whelp eats."

Hakon's grin widened. "I expected no less from you. I will bring that payment when I come to Lade next spring."

Hakon patted Sigurd's shoulder again and went in search of Trygvi. He found him down by the water, washing his face in the cold sea. Trygvi noticed his uncle coming and blew a wad of snot from his nostril, then dried his face on his dirty sleeve.

"Return to the warmth of your hall?" asked Trygvi with a lopsided grin. "Your words are those of an old man, Uncle."

Hakon smiled back. He would have smiled more broadly, but his happy conversation with Sigurd had reignited the pain in his nose. "Some days I feel like an old man."

"Bah! Keep thinking like that and you will grow older sooner than you think."

Hakon shrugged. "Mayhap." He turned the subject to his nephew. "I suppose you will be staying here, then?"

"Aye. The pickings are yet good. And with you gone, there will be even more to go around for me and my men." Trygvi grinned wolfishly.

"Do not overstay your welcome, Trygvi. The Danes are defeated but not conquered. They can still fight, and you will be shorter-handed without me and the Tronds."

Trygvi scratched his head. "The Tronds will also leave? That is even better news."

Hakon grabbed his nephew's thick wrist in the warrior's way. "Fare safely."

"The safe are never remembered."

Nor the witless, Hakon wanted to add but held his tongue.

He left Trygvi and returned to his ship. Once there, he stroked the wet wood of her hull and silently thanked God for his release from this cursed place. He had suffered, and he had endured. He had conquered, he had avenged, and he had kept his promises. Now it was time to put the campaign behind him and look to the future.

Part III

With batter'd shield, and blood-smear'd sword
Sits one beside the shore of Stord,
With armour crushed and gashed sits he,
A grim and ghastly sight to see;
The Heimskringla

Chapter 20

Lade, Trondelag, Spring, AD 958

Sparkling waterfalls, lush shores, and crisp skies greeted Hakon and his crew as *Dragon* slithered against the slack tide on its way to Lade. To the east, the Keel lorded over the land, its white peaks blending with the billowing clouds that moved slowly over them. Winter's thaw was in progress, and spring's gifts were on full display. Not that the men at oar could see it, or cared. The wind had been against them since yestermorning, and they were tired and hungry and ready to reach their destination. Hakon was not so forlorn, for the weather was fine, the sights that greeted his eyes were glorious, and the treasures that awaited him in Lade made his heart swell with anticipation.

The ship crept past rocky cliffs and quiet, low-lying pastures where the smoke from hearth fires wafted. They passed the ruins of Halla on their right, where Hakon had first fought Erik, and where, after so many winters, the vegetation had reclaimed the town and the tide had ripped the remnants of Erik's sunken ships from their sea-graves.

Eventually, they reached Lade. Winters ago, when times were uncertain, Sigurd had lived behind an earthwork wall with his household and his hirdmen, but time and security in the land had seen the removal of the defenses and the expansion of Sigurd's Lade into a small town. It was not a Kaupang in terms of size, but it was the closest thing to it in this remote stretch of the North.

A horn blast announced the presence of *Dragon*, and soon a crowd gathered on the beach. Sigurd stood before his people, his thumbs hooked into his waistline and a grand smile on his face. Beside him stood Astrid, her hands resting on the shoulders of Hakon's daughter, Thora, who bobbed up and down in her excitement. Sigge was also there, glowering at the head of his crew with his arms crossed tightly. Hakon called to Eskil to head for land.

"So this is Lade," remarked Egbert, his expression wavering between curiosity and concern. Over the years, four of his brethren had come to Trondelag to preach the word of Christ. Two had been sacrificed like sheep. Two more had been murdered while preaching, their heads severed from their bodies. What, he probably wondered, would befall him in this stronghold of heathens?

Hakon looked at his priest. "Worry not, Egbert. You are Sigurd's guest here. You will not be harmed."

"I do not share your confidence, my lord," said Egbert as *Dragon* glided onto the strand.

Hakon's crew shipped oars, then rose and stretched their sore limbs, all the while casting greetings and jokes at friends upon the beach. Hakon leaped to the sand, ignoring the pain in his joints, and strode to Sigurd, who stayed him with a raised hand.

"There is someone you must greet first, my king," he said as Astrid brought forth Thora, whose flaxen hair was combed and braided about her head and who wore on her long body a beautiful blue dress that mirrored the color in her eyes.

Hakon smiled at the sight of his daughter, not only because he had not seen her in months, but because he had never seen her so well kept. He knelt and marveled at her growth and her limbs, which looked like long reeds. He marveled at the color in her thinning cheeks and the weave of her hair. He marveled at the white of her teeth. Thora now cast her gaze to the ground under her father's scrutiny. He understood her awkwardness and did not force her to feel otherwise. "You are well, Thora?" Hakon asked gently.

She nodded, and a tear rolled down her cheek. "What took you so long?" There was an edge in her voice.

"I came as soon as I could. Do not cry." He stroked her cheek. "I am here now, and we will be going home soon." He opened his arms. "Do you have a hug for your long-absent father?"

She nodded and laid her head on his shoulder. He wrapped his arms around her and turned his eyes to Astrid.

She smiled down at him. "She has missed you, my king. As have I."

Hakon kissed his daughter's head, rose, and wrapped his arms around Astrid. He had not words to equal Astrid's, and so he just clung to her, reveling in the smell of her hair and the press of her body against his.

They must have clung to each other a bit too long, for Sigurd finally cleared his throat to get their attention. "Come, now. There will be time for that later." His deep laugh brought a chuckle to the crowd and the heat to Hakon's cheeks. Sigurd walked over to his king and embraced him. "Welcome to Lade, Hakon. As always, you are well met."

"And you," replied Hakon. "Your scar befits you. Now you finally look like a warrior." Which was true. For all of his struggles, Sigurd had rarely shown the wear of war.

Sigurd's finger went to his scar. "I thought the wound would ruin my fine looks, but the ladies love it." He grinned and slapped Hakon on the shoulder, then turned to the crowd. With a theatrical flourish of his arms, he pronounced: "We shall feast in my hall tonight to welcome King Hakon and his men. All are welcome as guests under my roof! Even the scrawny priest!" He nodded to Egbert and winked. He then ushered Hakon from the beach and through the cheering crowd. "Come. I would hear the tidings you bring."

Hakon lifted Thora onto his shoulders to keep her from the press of Lade's folk. The girl forgot her tears and giggled as Hakon pretended to be a horse, trotting behind the old jarl as he led them through the lean-tos and trading stalls and makeshift structures that dotted the area just inland from the beach. Hakon galloped over to Toralv, who smiled first at Hakon and then up at Thora. In return, she reached out and ruffled his black hair, which made him laugh.

"You have grown, princess," he said. "Now I can finally look you in the eye."

Thora giggled, and Hakon used the opportunity to whisper to his champion, "Keep an eye on Egbert, Toralv. I do not want him getting into trouble."

Toralv smiled. "I will make sure to keep the women off of him."

"Careful," Hakon scolded and cast his eyes upward at his daughter.

Toralv's smile persisted. "It is about time she understood the wicked ways of your priests."

Hakon kicked Toralv in the ankle, making the champion jump away with a laugh.

"What is that he says, Father?" asked Thora, who was paying little attention to the banter of the two men.

"Nothing, Thora. He is just making jokes."

The crowd moved into Sigurd's hall, which was alight with candles and the flame of the hearth fire. Hakon had handed off Thora to Unn at the door of the hall, then walked with Sigurd and Astrid past bowing thralls to the head table. The warriors and citizens of Lade entered behind them, fanning out to the empty seats, their voices and laughter echoing through the cavernous space.

Sigurd stood on the dais before the crowd and raised his ceremonial drinking horn. The crowd settled to hear their lord. "A short time ago, King Hakon came to us with a promise of wealth and fame in the land of the Danes. He has kept his promise, and for that we are grateful." The crowd cheered their jarl's words. "But lest we forget, fine warriors died in that pursuit, so it is to their memory that I toast first. To the comrades and kin we lost. Skol!" Sigurd hoisted his horn to the crowd.

"Skol!" They cried in unison.

Sigurd drank first, then passed the horn to Hakon. And as the mead slipped into Hakon's mouth, his mind turned to the friends and loved ones now gone. To Bjarke. To Ottar. To Gyda. And especially, to Egil.

God, how he missed that sour old man and his counsel. Wherever they were now, he hoped they feasted together as he did with Sigurd.

"Of course," Sigurd continued, interrupting Hakon's thoughts, "with battle comes fame and riches. And there was no shortage of either in the land of the Danes." Sigurd turned to Hakon. "We have profited much on your campaign, and for that, I thank you, King Hakon. Skol!"

"Skol!" cried the crowd again, though Hakon's body tensed with the praise. For the plunder had come at a steep price to his soul. He accepted the horn again but only pretended to drink. Astrid laid a hand on his shoulder and smiled up at him, her face filled with pride. Hakon gave her a sad grin, then turned to the raucous crowd and bade them sit.

"I thank Sigurd for the kind words and for your toasts, though I am no more deserving than him, or you, of praise," Hakon called to the crowd, his voice unusually subdued. "Had many of you not been by my side in Jutland, or at the side of your comrades, we would not be here today to speak of such things. And so, I say only this: thank you. And please, thank your comrades for their courage in the face of fear. Let us celebrate bravery and friendship and sacrifice. Now please, sit and enjoy yourselves."

"What is the matter?" Astrid asked as they sat beside each other. As usual, she did not mince words but jumped straight to the heart of things.

"It is nothing."

Astrid frowned, but pressed the issue no further. Instead, she rubbed Hakon's forearm gently and, through that touch, told Hakon all he needed to know. That she was there for him. That she loved him. That she would wait until he was ready to open his heart. And in knowing that, Hakon loved her all the more. He laid his hand on hers, entwined his fingers with hers, and squeezed.

"On the morrow," he whispered to her. She looked at him questioningly with those pine-colored eyes. He smiled. "On the morrow, I will tell you. Meet me at the door of this hall at daybreak with two horses. One for you and one for me."

She smiled. "Whatever you have in mind, I like it already."

Hakon grinned and sipped the cup of mead that had just been placed before him. His eyes scanned the hall discreetly until his gaze came to rest on Sigge. As usual, women and cups surrounded Sigurd's son, but for once, the young man did not join in their merrymaking.

"Your son is not happy," said Hakon to Sigurd.

The jarl grunted. "No, he is not. His mood has soured ever since Rastarkalv. His honor was trampled upon, or so he thinks."

"By me?" Hakon asked.

"By you. By the gods. By everyone," Sigurd spat, then reclined in his seat as if defeated. "Only the gods know, my king, for he will not tell his father." Sigurd drank from his horn.

Hakon's anger smoldered. "It is hard to hear that Sigge feels slighted when the mistake was his. He was given an order and did not heed it. Men died as a result. Egil died as a result."

"I know," Sigurd sighed. "I have tried to talk to him about it, but he will not discuss it. I have finally tired of it. In half a moon's time, he will leave with his ship to seek his own fame in the Eastern Sea. And good riddance."

"You are sending him away?"

"Let us say it was a mutual agreement. The boy needs lessons I cannot teach. He can only learn them from the world, and this," he waved at his hall, "is not the world."

Hakon sipped his drink as he took in Sigurd's words. "That is good, I think. He could use some adventure and some time away from here."

Which made Hakon wonder where exactly Sigge would go, and what he would learn along the way. He prayed it was fruitful for them all, for when Sigurd's life ended, it would be to Sigge that Hakon looked first.

The following morning, Astrid did not forget. She met Hakon at daybreak with two horses and a smile, ignoring the curious looks of the guards standing by the door to Sigurd's hall. She and Hakon wore riding clothes, and Hakon had packed an extra knapsack, which he tied to the wooden saddle of his steed. Though it was spring, winter's chill still hung in the air and clouded before the nostrils of the anxious horses. Hakon stroked his horse's muzzle and mounted.

"What is in the bag?" Astrid asked as she climbed onto her horse.

Hakon just smiled and kicked his steed forward. "You will find out soon enough," he called as he passed her.

They guided their horses through the wooden structures and clumps of warriors who slept off the previous night's feast in the alleyways. The air was heavy with the stench of stale ale and fish and the smoke of cooking fires. It turned Hakon's stomach and made him yearn for the clean air they would soon find in the wooded hills east of Lade.

They left the small town behind and ventured out into open ground. The area had not changed much since Hakon was a teenager. Inland from Lade were two expansive fields set side by side, each divided into three rectangular areas. As soon as winter's frost receded, Lade's thralls had planted rye and barley there, mayhap some vegetables too. The flatlands gradually climbed toward tree-strewn foothills. Here, rays of sunlight twinkled off the leaves and illuminated patches of wildflowers that grew in the muddy carpet of pine needles. Here and there, clumps of melting snow dotted the landscape, sending sparkling streamlets down the hillside and the path on which the horses plodded. Hakon breathed deeply of the pine scent and let it rejuvenate his hall-tainted lungs.

"Where are you taking me, Hakon?" asked Astrid from behind him.

"You will see," Hakon called over his shoulder. "Have patience."

"I am a curious person. I cannot help but ask."

Hakon laughed. "And I am good at keeping secrets, so you are wasting your breath."

When they had gone a short way into the hills, Hakon halted at a spot where another, smaller path shot off the main trail at a right angle. The second path lay partially hidden beneath tree limbs and underbrush, but Hakon recognized it well enough. He dismounted and tied his steed to a tree. Astrid cast curious glances at Hakon and her surroundings as she, too, fastened her reins to a low branch.

Hakon untied the saddlebag and threw it over his shoulder. "Come." He beckoned and started down the path. Astrid followed without a word.

After a short distance, they came to a small clearing at the base of a rocky slope. In the middle of the clearing lay a large pool of steaming water surrounded by a thin coating of snow that had not yet melted. In truth, Hakon knew not whether the pool would still be there and breathed a sigh of relief at the sight of it. Astrid stared at the pool in wonder, then at Hakon. He smiled at her. "Have you not been here before?

"Never," she whispered.

"It is wondrous, is it not?"

"How do you know of this place?"

"Your father showed it to me when I was new in this land. It was here we agreed to partner in overthrowing Erik. It is called Surt's Pool."

Astrid had dipped her finger in the water and, at the explanation, looked at Hakon curiously. "You would sit in a pool named for a fire giant? Does that not frighten you as a Christian?"

"It did when I first heard your father call it so, but now I know there is nothing to fear. It is just a name." Hakon had removed his cloak. He hung it on a nearby tree branch.

"Are we to go in?"

Hakon could not decide if her tone was playful or puzzled. Mayhap she was both, which amused him all the more. "It is not just there to look at. Come," he urged as he removed his tunic and began working on his boots. "Do not be frightened."

"Pools do not frighten me," she protested, then removed her cloak as if to prove it.

Hakon shed his last vestiges of clothing, then climbed gingerly into the pool, letting its warmth envelop his chilled skin, his aching bones, and his purple scars. Astrid followed close behind, first dipping a cautious toe in the water before stepping down. Despite his best efforts at discretion, he could not help but admire the firmness of her long body with its goose-pimpled skin. So often he had seen it by candlelight or in his dreams, but here, by daylight, Hakon noticed the tangle of auburn hair between her legs, the flatness of her belly, and the curve of her small, round breasts, and he felt his own excitement grow. He stood and folded her in his arms and kissed her tenderly on the lips, and then the neck, and then the shoulder. Her hand slipped beneath the water to feel his excitement and to coax it further.

"I like this pool," she moaned as Hakon sat back and she slipped onto him.

Slowly, gently, they rediscovered each other, exploring their bodies with an unrestrained passion that churned the pool into a tempest of steam and sweat and wavelets. Their moans were masked only by the sounds of the forest, until the intensity of their lovemaking scared even the birds from the trees and they collapsed into each other's embrace.

"You need to go away more often," Astrid exclaimed as she tried to catch her breath.

"I do not like leaving you, but if my homecomings are always so memorable, I will honor your request," Hakon agreed through his smile as he stroked Astrid's steaming hair.

They lay in each other's arms in the warmth of the pool for a long time. Neither spoke, though Astrid hummed a song. The tune calmed Hakon, and he laid his head back against a stone.

The tune ended, but Astrid kept her head on Hakon's chest. "There was sadness in your face last night," she said. "Can you tell me about it?"

And with that tender question, the world and its pains flooded back into Hakon's thoughts. He no longer saw the trees above or the rays of light cascading down to the forest floor. Instead, the images that flooded his eyes were of pain and death and bloodshed. His fingers stroked Astrid's hair mindlessly. "I told you I would share, though as I think upon your request, I know not how to answer without spoiling this moment."

"Is it me?" She lifted her head and looked into his face with genuine concern.

"You?" he asked with bewilderment. "You are everything that is right in my life, Astrid."

"What, then?" She stroked his beard with her finger.

He laid his head back against the stones and closed his eyes. "I think upon this past year, Astrid, and this war with Erik's sons, and I am ashamed. Their attacks have forced me to do things I never thought I would do. I have allowed my men to do things I never thought I would allow. I have lost things I never wanted to lose. Not just friends and comrades and loved ones. To a degree, I have lost myself." He opened his eyes and splashed a handful of the warm water onto his face to clear his mind of the thoughts.

She watched Hakon closely, and in her face, Hakon could see her concern transform to sadness. He could see it in her eyes and in the softening of her features, though it could never match his own.

"Do not be sad. Know that you are what makes me happy," he said as his eyes found hers. He stood and the steam rose from his muscled chest. He smiled down at her. "Enough of this talk, eh? Let us turn to better things. I have something for you."

Astrid sat up as Hakon reached for his saddlebag and produced a silver necklace. It sparkled in the spring sunshine as he held it up to her. Her eyes went wide at the sight of the gift.

"I had this made for you," he said, before she could ask where he had acquired it. "I want you to be my wife, Astrid."

Her hand went to her mouth as she searched Hakon's face. "Your wife? Truly?"

He clasped the necklace around her long neck and smiled at her. "After the mistake that was Groa, I never thought I would marry again, but you are unlike any woman I have ever met. From the moment I saw you sing at my feast all those summers ago, until this day, you have been in my thoughts. When I saw you again at Tore's funeral, my heart leaped in my chest. I know now that you are my happiness and that I have loved you all along. Will you marry me?"

She nodded and wiped the tears from her cheeks. "Aye, Hakon Haraldsson. I will."

Hakon and Astrid brought the news to Sigurd as soon as they returned from the hills.

The jarl sat on his high seat in his hall and listened intently as Hakon explained his desire to wed Astrid, including all the reasons why the union would be a good one. Sigurd stroked his beard as he listened to the younger couple with their wet hair and clothes, his face devoid of emotion. When Hakon finished his monologue, the old jarl stood and paced before his chair, concern etched on his face. It was not the reaction Hakon expected, and so he glanced at Astrid for explanation but found only deep lines of worry furrowed in the space between her brows.

Suddenly, Sigurd turned and opened his arms. "By the gods, of course I bless this union! I had you worried, did I not?" At this, he laughed so loud it echoed through the empty hall. He embraced his daughter, then Hakon. "When did you two lovers want to have the wedding?"

"Soon, Father. We want to do it here, in Lade."

Sigurd clapped his hands. "My heart is full! Give me some time to make the preparations. We will make this the grandest wedding Lade has ever seen!" He turned to a thrall. "Birgit! Bring me three cups of mead! Quick, now. A toast is in order!"

Chapter 21

The couple was to be married on the eve of Sigge's departure from Lade. They needed that much time to invite the locals, give the chieftains enough time to gather, and to prepare the hall and the food for a wedding Sigurd hoped would live in the minds of the Tronds for generations to come. And, they felt it right that Sigge should be there for the ceremony, whether he wanted to be or not.

On the morning of the wedding, Hakon woke early and climbed from under the skins in his tent. As custom demanded, he had slept alone on the eve of the betrothal. Across the dark interior, Egbert knelt in prayer. A sliver of soft light crept from beneath the tent flaps to lie on the priest's hooded form. Egbert heard his lord rise and turned. He removed the cowl of his gray habit to reveal his shock of orange hair. "I am here as you requested, lord."

Hakon scratched at his chin. "So you are."

"How may I serve you, my lord? A prayer, perchance, before your betrothal?"

Hakon dipped his head into a bucket of water, then rubbed his dripping face and beard with a small deerskin rag to dry himself. He cupped the water with his hands and sucked it into his mouth, then gargled it loudly before spitting it back into the bucket. "I will need that too, but not now," Hakon said when he was done.

"What, then?" Egbert asked as Hakon pulled on his breeks, then a tunic.

Hakon clasped a cloak into place with a bronze brooch, then winked at his friend. "You shall see, Egbert. Come." Hakon stopped at the tent flap and grabbed a knapsack that lay at his feet. "Quietly, though. I do not want to wake the camp. This adventure is for you and me alone."

Egbert's eyes widened. "Adventure, lord?"

Hakon smiled. "Do not be concerned, Egbert."

They exited the tent and wove their way through the maze of structures and sleeping forms until they reached the beach where the ships lay. Here they turned east, toward the mountains, and continued over the uneven shingle until they came to a place where the land angled out into the fjord. As a new arrival in the North, Hakon had come to this tree-lined finger of land often to think, especially to the small beach at its tip, which was shrouded by trees and offered a fair amount of privacy. Hakon headed for that beach now with a silent, hooded Egbert following closely on his heels.

When they reached the tip, they stopped and gazed out at the silent fjord. Clouds shrouded the rising sun, casting the water and the distant shores to the north in a steel gray. There was little wind, so what waves there were lapped against the shore in a rhythmic shuffle of pebbles. Hakon breathed the tangy air into his lungs and released his breath in a slow exhalation.

Egbert had stopped behind his king and now cleared his throat. "Pardon me, my lord. But why are we here?" Hakon could hear the trepidation in his voice.

"Today I am to be married, but I have misgivings." Hakon's eyes studied the fjord as he sought the right words. It was unfamiliar territory and the words came awkwardly. "Not about Astrid. About the ceremony. There is much I have done in my life that worries me." His thoughts flashed to Gyda and the child within her. "I fear this ceremony will be but another stain on my soul."

"So what do you wish me to do?" asked Egbert.

"I want you to baptize me," Hakon said. "Or mayhap the proper way of saying it is rebaptize me. For I was baptized in Winchester as a youth."

There was a crunching of feet on the tiny stones as Egbert made his way to Hakon's side. "Baptize you?" he asked from the dark confines of his hood.

"Aye, Egbert."

Egbert pulled the cowl from his head and gazed at Hakon questioningly. "And how do you feel this baptism will help you? You think it will remove the stain on your soul?" Egbert grinned.

"You find that humorous?"

Egbert's grin vanished at the malice in Hakon's tone. He turned his gaze to his feet, where it lingered for a long time. "I do not find the request humorous, lord, but it is not so easy as that."

"Why not?"

Egbert gestured to the rippling water. "You cannot just wash away a lifetime of sins as you might wash away dirt from your skin. You must confess and reject the sins committed, and resolve not to commit them again. You must do penance to reconcile with God, and to return to His mercy." Despite the weight of his words, Egbert kept his tone soft.

Hakon sighed heavily. He had thought this might be easy. That with his baptism he could start anew, and enter into his betrothal as a man reborn in his faith. He had been excited by that prospect, frankly, but Egbert's words sucked that energy from him like a man sucks the marrow from a bone, leaving him dispirited and tired. "Must I confess each sin in turn?" Hakon finally asked.

"You must try," responded Egbert delicately.

Hakon's thoughts wandered back over the summers and winters, recalling all of the death and the destruction his hands had wrought, all of the boasting and drinking and women, all of the pagan sacrifices he had not challenged, and so much more besides. He had tried to be a good Christian. He had kept his Fridays and prayed almost every morning. He had refused the blood of sacrifice his entire life. But he had gotten lost in a violent land that was staunchly pagan, and sinned often as a result. The prospect of recounting all of them, of laying open wounds long since scarred over, of conjuring the guilt and sorrow and pain, was beyond daunting.

Egbert's soft voice pulled him from his dark thoughts. "Hakon?"

Hakon turned to his priest. "I cannot, Egbert. Not yet. There is still much I must do. Much killing. A pagan wedding. I fear my confession would be just hollow words spoken to you."

Egbert's face sank. "I understand."

"When this war with my nephews is over, I will come to you and confess. I swear it."

Egbert searched his lord's eyes and nodded. "Very well."

Hakon turned back to the fjord. "I still feel stained, though. Is there nothing we can do to remove this feeling before my betrothal?"

Egbert scratched his tuft of hair as he thought for a moment. "I suppose we could reaffirm your faith. It would be like a baptism without all of the trappings."

"In the fjord?" Hakon asked excitedly, for he liked the idea.

"If that is your wish."

Hakon smiled. "It is!" he exclaimed as he shed his cloak. "It is indeed!"

Egbert turned his eyes to the fjord to give his lord some privacy. Hakon undressed to his underpants, then gingerly stepped into the icy water. Chills climbed his skin as he carefully made his way over the mossy stones.

Behind him, Egbert removed his sandals and walked to the water's edge. "You are sure about this?" he called to Hakon as he stared at the gray water and hiked up his habit.

Hakon turned to Egbert. "I am sure."

Egbert crossed himself, then stepped into the water with a quick intake of breath. Together, they waded into the fjord until both of them were waist deep in water. Hakon stood with his arms at his side, his skin white and goose-pimpled. Egbert's teeth were on the verge of chattering.

"Lord, forgive me, but we must abbreviate this blessing given the chill of the water. I do not wish for you to catch your death on the morning of your wedding."

Hakon laughed, knowing it was Egbert, and not him, who suffered more. "As you wish, Egbert."

Egbert nodded his thanks, then began by signing the cross over Hakon. "Let us pray. O God, thou author of all wisdom, look graciously down on this your servant Hakon, and preserve him ever in thy fear, which is the beginning of wisdom, through Christ our Lord. Amen." Egbert paused. "I ask thee, Hakon, do you renounce the devil?"

Hakon nodded. "I renounce him."

"And all his works?" Egbert asked.

"Aye," answered Hakon, which received a raised brow of rebuke from Egbert. "I renounce them," he responded.

"And all his pomps?" asked Egbert through teeth that had begun to rattle in his head.

"I renounce them," answered Hakon.

"Do you believe in God the Father Almighty, maker of Heaven and Earth?"

"I do," replied Hakon.

"Do you believe in Jesus Christ, his only-begotten Son our Lord, who was born and hath suffered for us?"

"I do."

"Do you believe in the Holy Ghost, the communion of saints, the forgiveness of sins, the resurrection of the flesh, and life everlasting?"

"I do," said Hakon earnestly.

Egbert placed his hands on Hakon's purpling shoulders and pushed the king into the water so that its surface reached Hakon's beard. "Almighty God, the Father of our Lord Jesus Christ, regenerate your humble servant, Hakon Haraldsson, in your faith. Strengthen his resolve in thee, and in your son, Jesus Christ, and in the Holy Ghost. Amen." Egbert signed the cross over Hakon and smiled. "The Lord be with you, Hakon Haraldsson." Egbert grabbed the king's wrist. "Come now from this water. I have never killed anyone with a blessing, and you will not be my first."

The two men made their way quickly to the beach, and Hakon retrieved the knapsack he had been carrying. He rummaged through it and yanked from it a pair of trousers and a gray tunic, which he tossed to Egbert. "Put these on." Egbert grabbed the garments and began to strip himself of his wet habit as Hakon quickly dressed in his tunic and breeks.

When they were both dressed again in dry clothes, Egbert laughed. "That was the hastiest blessing I have ever performed."

Hakon smiled at him, feeling cleansed both inside and out. "But the most meaningful, Egbert, and I thank you for it."

"It is rare indeed to see you looking so...so grand," Toralv joked as he approached his king and bowed with a flourish. "One would think you were about to be married, eh?"

Hakon had dressed in his finest clothing — soft leather trousers, his best boots, a cloud- white tunic, and a new blue cloak fastened at the shoulder with a serpentine silver pin. He had forgone the ritual bath administered by the wedding attendants due to his baptism in the fjord earlier that morning. Nor had he applied all of the colorful eyeliner or hair decorations that were so common in weddings. Instead, he had cut and combed his short beard until it gleamed, and he fastened his blond hair into a fine braid that hung down to his shoulder blades. He now stood under a tree behind the gathered crowd, waiting for the ceremony to begin.

Hakon smiled at his friend. "And thanks to your slovenly outfit, I look all the more grand."

Toralv laughed. "Come now. You have never seen me so presentable. I even bathed." He smelled his underarm as if to prove it, then smiled. Toralv was about to say something more when the blast of a horn beckoned the friends forward. "After you, my lord," said Toralv with a wave of his hand and a slight bow.

Sigurd had spared no expense on the decorations. Banners of green and yellow encircled the wedding area, as did wildflowers, which had been laid by Thora and some other children that very morning. The crowd gathered within the circle parted for Hakon and Toralv as they made their way to the dwarf godi, Drangi, who stood on the strand with the gray fjord behind him, a soft breeze rippling its surface. The dwarf inspected the king with a stony countenance, perchance peeved that Hakon had forbidden his sacrificing an animal during the wedding ceremony. Or mayhap it was the Christian cross hanging from Hakon's neck or the Christian priest standing so close to the king that irked him. In the end, Hakon had not the time to dwell on it, for moments after Hakon arrived at his assigned spot, a second horn announced the arrival of Astrid and Sigurd.

The crowd parted to reveal the bride, and Hakon's heart leaped. Astrid wore a flowing green dress that reached to her feet and matched the shade of her smiling eyes. Her auburn curls had been pulled into a braided bun that had been decorated with tiny white flowers. She, too, wore no makeup, for it was not needed to accentuate the lines of her face or the keenness of her eyes. Encircling her graceful neck was the silver necklace Hakon had given to her at the pool. It was the only jewelry she wore.

Beside her strode an equally resplendent Sigurd. He walked with his shoulders back and his gray-bearded chin jutting as he acknowledged the guests who had gathered to see his daughter marry the king. As he approached, Hakon could not help but feel as if this had all been preordained. As if God and his host of angels had decided long ago that through all of the strife and pain and struggle that had brought Hakon and Sigurd together, they would finally be united by love. And so here they were, in Lade, to close a loop that had begun with Hakon's return to the North, and to begin another with the union of Hakon and Astrid.

Sigurd let go of his daughter's arm and allowed Hakon to take it. The king smiled into Astrid's beautiful face as she blinked back happy tears, and together, they turned to the dwarf. The little man raised his arms high and called to the sky with words Hakon had heard long ago, or so it seemed. When fate had forced him into a marriage he did not want, with a girl he despised. This time, however, the words held a different significance and he listened without judgment, secure in his own faith with the woman he loved by his side.

"Blessed Aesir, creators of man and earth, sky and sea. Since the dawn of time you have bonded man to woman and seen to our existence and our welfare. You have provided for us and watched over us. Look down upon these two now and bless the marriage. Frigga, mother of Gods, Goddess of Weddings, bless this union with love and offspring. Odin, gaze down on these two and provide them with the wisdom to learn, just as you learned when you sacrificed your eye for knowledge. Freya, stoke the flame of passion in this couple that might never extinguish, so that the Yngling bloodline and the power of Lade might carry on through the ages, together." After he had called out these words, he turned to the bride and groom in turn. "The rings?" he asked.

Normally, the rings would be exchanged by placing them on the pommel of the husband's and father-in-law's swords to signify their protection of each other, but in this case, such formalities were not necessary. Hakon grabbed Astrid's hand and slipped a golden ring upon her delicate finger. Astrid then offered a family ring to Hakon, though his thick knuckles made it harder to secure and she giggled at the struggle that resulted.

"Hold hands and turn to your guests," said Drangi when the rings were in place.

Hakon clasped Astrid's hand in his own. The godi then wrapped a single strip of lamb's wool around the couple's grip to signify the purity of the new bond. "May all present see that Astrid Sigurdsdottir and Hakon Haraldsson are now bound in matrimony. And may no man or woman tear this bond asunder."

The audience clapped and hooted as Hakon held Astrid's hand aloft for all to see. Toralv shook his king's shoulder in uncontained delight. Thora hugged her father's waist. Hakon laughed and lifted his daughter into his arms with his free hand.

"I am so happy you are my mother now," whispered Thora to a teary Astrid.

"And I am happy to be your mother, Thora," Astrid responded.

"Let the wedding procession begin!" called Drangi above the din.

Hakon set Thora on the ground and, with his hand bound to Astrid's, led the guests back to Sigurd's hall. When they reached the door, the couple stopped. Sigurd opened the large door to reveal a hall that was bathed in candlelight and filled with the smells of meat and bread and ale and comfort. He smiled at the couple's reaction and at the wonderment of the crowd that followed close on their heels.

When he had recovered from his surprise, Hakon unsheathed Quern-biter. Holding it before him, he stepped over the threshold and onto the fresh rushes on the hall's floor to show his new wife and the guests that she would forever be safe in his care. He then sheathed his blade and proffered his hand to Astrid. With a smile as grand as his own, she took his hand and stepped into the hall and her new life with Hakon.

Hakon led Astrid to the head table that stood on the dais at the far end of the hall. Candles burned in two silver candelabras, casting their flickering glow on the platters of lamb and vegetables and bread and butter and more things besides.

"Your father has outdone himself," whispered Hakon to Astrid. "I am truly honored."

A hand landed on Hakon's shoulder as Sigurd's head appeared between the couple. He had overhead Hakon's comment. "This is an occasion worthy of such honor, eh? It is not often a man sees his daughter married to the king!"

Hakon and Astrid took their seats at the center of the head table. Sigurd sat in the guest-of-honor's seat to Hakon's right. Beside him sat Toralv. Sigge had been invited to sit in that seat, but had declined.

Sigurd stood with a cup of mead in his hand to address the guests now filtering into the hall and finding their places. "By the gods, I am grateful for this day! My daughter is happy, and my heart is full. I can ask for no greater honor than to be united through marriage to the man in which I put my faith all of those winters ago. A man who has proven his worth, his strength, his dedication, his foresight, time and time again. A man I am humbled to call my son through marriage."

Sigurd turned to Hakon and Astrid. "May you both live long and enjoy the fruits of marriage this day and always. Skol!"

The couple hefted their cups and joined their voices to the raucous reply that filled the hall. "Skol!"

"We should escape this place," whispered Hakon to his new bride as Sigurd reclaimed his seat and turned his attention to the trenchers of food before him. Hakon did not wish to spend the evening fettered in conversation or lost in mead or contemplating why Sigge sulked in the corner with his men.

She kissed his forehead. "I agree. Though first, I have a surprise for you." And with that, she stood and moved to the end of the head table on the dais. Hakon watched her in silence, more curious than alarmed at this sudden development. There she stood until the guests noticed her presence and settled themselves so they could hear her words.

"Long ago," she began, "my father asked me to sing to a prince at a celebratory feast. The feast was to honor the handsome young prince for defeating Erik Bloodaxe in battle." The crowd jeered at the mention of the former king. "Little did I know that that man would eventually become my husband." She smiled as the crowd cheered, then raised her finger to silence them. "That is not to say that I was not madly in love with him from the moment I set my eyes upon him. I just never thought this day would come." She looked over at Hakon and smiled, then turned back to the audience. "And so, to commemorate this day, I would like to offer my husband a gift. It is the song I shared with him that evening so long ago, and a song that means as much to me now as it did then."

Astrid took a deep breath and closed her eyes. When her mouth opened again, the crowd fell silent, for few had heard the captivating beauty of her voice. Even Sigge's bearing seemed to soften as his sister's words reached his ears. The song she sang was of Hakon's father, Harald, and his third wife, Swanhild, and the reckless love they shared. Most people knew the words or the story, but few had heard it sung so beautifully, and until now, none had heard it echo through the jarl's hall with such fluidity and depth. The song turned Hakon's mind to that night so long ago, when Astrid was but a gangly girl singing under the stars and the future held no worries because Erik had been defeated and Hakon was king. Hakon sighed and sipped his mead and let Astrid's song carry away his thoughts to his father, and to reckless love, and to the life he and Astrid would soon be sharing — a life he prayed would be long.

Sigge and his crew made ready to depart the following morning. They went about their business with no particular fanfare, save for the farewells to those they knew that would stay behind. Hakon, Sigurd, and Astrid watched silently as Sigge helped arrange some cargo in the ship's lower hold. When Sigge climbed back to the deck, Sigurd called to his son and beckoned him over. The younger man dropped from the ship, wiped his hands on his trousers, and made his way to his father. His face was serious but not angry. His eyes were bloodshot.

"Remember to hug the coast of Agder when you reach it," said Sigurd when his son reached him. "And stay well north of the land of the Danes. If they learn of your presence, they will hunt you. You know this."

And if they catch you, thought Hakon grimly to himself, *they will kill you slowly.*

"There is danger everywhere, Father. I cannot avoid it."

Sigurd grunted.

"Before you head east," offered Hakon, "stop in Kaupang and seek out Jarl Gudrod. Tell him I have sent you and that you seek provisions and his advice for your journey. It will delay your trip somewhat, but the delay will be worth it. My nephew knows all that happens in the Vik and Kattegat."

Sigge nodded to Hakon in thanks, though his face remained stony. It was clear he wished to hold fast to his grudge.

Sigurd cast his eyes to the sky and spoke into the awkward silence that ensued. "You'd best leave while you have some wind." Sigurd opened his arms to embrace Sigge, but his son did not return the gesture. Sigurd dropped his arms and sighed. "Farewell, Sigge."

Sigge nodded at his father, then turned to his ship.

"Keep your wits about you!" Sigurd called.

Sigge waved his arm to acknowledge his father's advice but did not turn.

"That boy..." Sigurd grumbled as they watched Sigge climb aboard his ship.

"You are tolerant to let him leave so," Astrid added.

"Have I a choice, Astrid?"

"He is a good fighter and a smart lad," said Hakon as he placed his hand on the jarl's shoulder. "If he can keep control of his emotions, he will be fine."

Chapter 22

Hakon and Astrid stayed at Lade for another half moon. It was one of the most pleasant and healing times in Hakon's life — a time filled with ease, and feasting, and laughter, and lovemaking. There were no schedules, no councils to attend, no chieftains to meet. Since this was Lade, Sigurd tended to his people's affairs, leaving Hakon free to spend time however he wished. Most mornings, he would wake late and join Egbert at prayer before breaking his fast with whomever happened to be in Sigurd's hall. Afterward he would play with Thora, or take advantage of the unseasonably warm weather and hike or swim or ride with Astrid by his side. Nights were spent in bed with Astrid, or in the hall with those wedding guests who remained, or with his men at their campfires, filling his belly with ale and mead and his mind with the memories of their shared adventures.

But after several weeks, the king in Hakon grew antsy. Reports had reached Lade from traders that the Danes were on the move again, harrying in the Vik and elsewhere. There were also stories that King Gorm, the father of Harald Bluetooth, had died, though how accurate those stories were was hard to say. Still, they filled Hakon with thoughts about the future, for Gorm had proven to be a conscientious ruler of the Danes but not an aggressor. It was his son who had filled that role and expanded Gorm's kingdom. Now it appeared he was at it again, and the thought of it plagued Hakon's mind. Sigurd, too, fretted for his son, who was somewhere near the Danish kingdom, making a name for himself in the Eastern Sea. He was under no illusion about the fate of Sigge should the young lord be caught.

"What is going through that head of yours?" asked Astrid. The two of them sat on the beach where Egbert had baptized Hakon. They had both just taken a swim and dressed and now warmed themselves in the sun. "You have been quiet today."

"I fear it is time to return to Avaldsnes." Hakon picked up a pebble and tossed it into the sea. "If the reports of Gorm's death are true, things with the Danes will be changing. As much as I would like to stay here forever, I sense it is time to go."

Astrid rested her head on Hakon's shoulder. "I will pack my things." She poked Hakon in the ribs and he flinched. "And this time, you will not send me packing when trouble comes."

He reached over and hugged her head closer to his shoulder. "We shall see about that."

This made her laugh, and she reached over to tickle Hakon again. He collapsed onto his back to avoid her attacks, then pulled her onto him and kissed her deeply. Her fingers ceased their tickling and roamed his body until they found the laces at his waist.

They left Lade two days later.

On the eve of their departure, Hakon's crew and Sigurd's household gathered for one final feast. It was a subdued affair, for most of the guests were tired from so much celebration and so sought their beds early in the evening. Sigurd and Hakon did not share their fatigue. They retired to the hall's living quarters and sat together long into the night, recounting stories of old friends and battles and adventures over cups of ale too numerous to count — stories that brought equal amounts of pain and cheer to their hearts. For through all of the tales wove an unspoken thread of truth, something Hakon understood but never stated, the reason why both men clung to the evening and to their conversation. They were getting older and their times together were fading like the sputtering candles in Sigurd's hall — and neither man wished to see the light extinguished.

"Ah, it has been a good life," Sigurd finally mused with a slur, hitting on the crux of their conversation. "All these comrades and friends and women and fights...they have made life rich, have they not?"

"Skol to that!"

Hakon raised his cup to Sigurd's, but the old jarl misjudged the distance between the cups and clanked his vessel so hard against Hakon's that the ale in both cups sloshed over the sides. The men laughed.

"When I am gone, Hakon, swear to me that you will honor my son's claim to the jarldom, eh?"

Hakon stared blearily at Sigurd. Of course he would honor Sigge's claim. After all Sigurd had done for him, how could he not?

Sigurd misread Hakon's stillness and spoke before Hakon could respond. "I know. He is a hothead. He makes bad decisions. But he is young. He will be a good jarl, especially with a king like you to guide him."

Hakon raised his hand to silence Sigurd. "It is not a question in my mind, Sigurd. I will honor your son's claim. He is your son, and therefore it is his right."

Sigurd's big frame melted into his chair as if Hakon had extracted the weight of his worry and it left him weak. "That is good," he mused, then toasted Hakon again and drank deeply from his cup.

The following morning, Hakon woke to a gentle shake on his shoulder. It took him a moment to realize he was not in his bed but had instead fallen asleep in his chair. He sat up stiffly and gazed through stinging eyes at a frowning Astrid.

"Your father and I spoke long into the night. We had much to discuss," croaked Hakon by way of explanation.

"And to drink, I see." She pointed at the table where a half-eaten loaf of stale bread and some hard cheese sat. "Grab some food. Your crew and your family await you on your ship."

Hakon rose and instantly felt the throbbing in his temples and the queasiness in his belly. He tore a chunk of bread from the loaf and followed his wife out of Sigurd's hall and down to the beach, where a crowd had gathered to wish Hakon and his crew well. Sigurd was there, looking about as fit as Hakon felt.

"I am glad you made it, lord," called Toralv from *Dragon*'s grand prow. An immense smile split his fluffy beard. He was going to enjoy his king's misery, if for no other reason than the jokes he could fling at Hakon during their voyage. "We almost left without you. It is a good thing your wife noticed your absence."

Hakon cracked off a piece of the stiff bread with his teeth and crunched on it with his molars. It tasted awful, but he knew his stomach needed some sustenance to quell its churning. He did not respond to Toralv's jibes. There would be time for that later. Instead, he turned to his host and embraced him. "Stay well, Sigurd."

Sigurd held Hakon at arm's length. "Now that you are leaving, I will fare better. My stomach and my head could not take another night like last night."

Hakon smiled. "Nor mine."

Sigurd turned to his daughter. "Keep well, Astrid, and keep him," he said, thumbing in the direction of Hakon. "It will not be easy, but if anyone can tame Hakon, it is you."

Astrid rolled her eyes, then kissed her father's hairy cheek. "Do not rearrange your hall too much, Father. I will be back sooner than you know to check on you."

"I look forward to that day." Sigurd caught sight of Thora, who stood half-hidden behind Astrid. He smiled fondly at the girl. "And you. Do not grow too fast. And do not vex your parents overmuch, eh?"

"Why not?" she wondered boldly, and the three adults laughed at her words.

"The day is growing long," called Toralv from the prow.

Hakon said his farewells to those of Sigurd's men he knew well, then climbed aboard the ship after Astrid and Thora. He guided them aft to Unn, who had arranged a place for them to sit near Egbert. As Thora took her place, Sigurd's warriors pushed *Dragon* from the shingle and into the sea. Hakon's stomach lurched.

"Are you feeling well, lord?" called Toralv from amidships. "You look ill."

"I am fine, Toralv. Now mind the crew and yourself."

Hakon sat beside his frowning wife with a grunt. It would be a long day.

The trip south actually took longer than Hakon hoped. The wind was fickle, as was the weather. Some days, they made good progress under sail. Other days, the wind came straight at them, forcing them to row through seas that splashed over the prow and soaked the crew. Spring showers blew over them, followed by warm sunshine. None of this mattered much to the warriors, who were hearty and used to the weather, but Astrid and Thora and Unn were less accustomed to these conditions and so cowered under their woolen blankets when the wind and weather and seas turned against them. There was little Hakon could do to remedy their situation save fret for their comfort, and so he did until Astrid told him to stop his worrying and to focus on his men.

Two days north of Avaldsnes, Eskil turned *Dragon* into the channels formed by low-lying islands that created natural waterways protected from the open ocean and the driving winds. Most of the islands in the area were uninhabited slabs of rock that offered little in the way of life save for flocks of sea birds and clumps of mussels. Several, however, were home to stone halls with small fields from which local inhabitants scratched a pitiful existence.

It was into the vast bay of one such island — the island of Stord — that Eskil navigated *Dragon*. It was the evening of their ninth day at sea, and the place into which they sailed was one of Hakon's smaller estates; a place called Fitjar that he had inherited from his father. Like Avaldsnes, it sat on a strategic corner of the channels from which its previous owners had preyed on traders heading north and south. Hakon had ended the pirating, but he had kept the hall and the residents in place — and on days like today, he was glad he had. It was not nearly as lavish as Avaldsnes, but it was a welcome haven nevertheless.

A graybeard and several warriors stood on the beach with some women and children, appraising the ship in silence as she came closer.

Hakon waved to the graybeard. "You are well met, Eyvind!"

The man waved back. "What brings you to Fitjar, my lord?" He motioned to several of the young warriors, who grasped the towlines thrown to them and heaved *Dragon* ashore.

"Rest and warmth," called Hakon.

"Then you are in luck, for we have both. Just be sure to leave Eskil on the ship. That coal-biter has too many lice for a hall like yours, lord."

"With the way you tend a hall, my lice would be too frightened to leave me," replied Eskil from the steer board.

The crew howled with delight. Eyvind and Eskil had served together long ago as pimple-faced youths but rarely saw each other these days. The obvious ease with which they slipped into their familiarity broke the tension that had been hanging over the weary crew.

"In truth, lord, your men may have to sleep outside this night," Eyvind acknowledged as he leaned on his walking stick and appraised the size of the crew. "The hall, as you know, is a bit too modest for such a crew. Nevertheless, I will see that your men are well fed while here and butcher one of the lambs for the occasion." He waved to one of the animals grazing nearby. "I have been storing a special ale, too. It will hardly match what you have at Avaldsnes, but it will fill your bellies for the night."

"You are modest, Eyvind," replied Hakon, with Astrid and Thora by his side. "I am certain it will more than sustain us. As for my men, they seek only warmth and will likely sleep where they fall tonight."

They disembarked and walked toward the hall. Nearby, thralls stopped their labor to examine the newcomers. It was dusk and still they toiled in the fields and pens that surrounded the hall.

"Back to work!" yelled Eyvind at the gawkers. "Damn thralls. They dawdle any chance they get. Got to keep your eyes on 'em, you know?"

Hakon switched the subject. "Mayhap you can regale us with a tale or two this evening. I have heard many times that you and Eskil once fought by each other's side, though I have never heard you or him tell of your adventures."

Eyvind barked a laugh. "We were but beardless pups then, my lord. I doubt you would find much interest in our small glories."

"Nonsense," said Hakon. "We would be honored to hear a tale or two."

They reached the door of the hall and Eyvind opened it for his king. "Very well," he said with a grin and a wink. "I shall think on your request. Mayhap the ale will spark my memory and loosen my tongue."

When Hakon's eyes had adjusted to the hall's gloom, he scanned the room for trouble but found only shadows and benches and tables in the cavernous space. Dust mites whirled in the air above the low flame in the central hearth, while cobwebs danced up in the beams. After more than a week of being at sea, the closeness of the interior felt constricting. Still, Hakon nodded appreciatively at the interior and remarked on its pleasant warmth, something he had not had since leaving Lade. Behind Hakon came Astrid and Thora and Unn, as well as Eskil, who surveyed the hall circumspectly as they sat at Eyvind's table.

"It has been a long while since you last graced us with your presence, my lord." Eyvind turned to a thrall girl who stood nearby. "Ada, tell Fathir to slaughter the choicest lamb and add it to the kettle. Then bring that keg of ale I've been keeping and some cheese and bread. Run along now." The girl shot out the door. "So then," he said, turning back to his guests. "Why are you here?"

"Do I need an explanation to visit one of my estates?" Hakon asked, not attempting to mask the surliness in his tone.

"No, lord," Eyvind sputtered. "Forgive my curiosity."

Eskil chimed in quickly to ease the tension. "There were many places we could have anchored, but as you said, it has been many springs since last Hakon came to these shores. I recommended we halt here for the night. My recommendation was partly selfish, I admit. I could not miss a chance to visit you, my friend. It has been too long. This man saved my life," said the helmsman, pointing to Eyvind. "Did you know that, my lord?"

Hakon's brows arched as he gazed at Eyvind. "Small glories? I would say that saving a friend's life counts for more than that, Eyvind."

"Go on," urged Eskil. "Tell them."

The graybeard scratched his hairy cheek. "Which time, Eskil?"

The table broke into laughter as Eskil blushed and held up his hands for peace. "It is true. I was none too skilled with a blade when I first left home. More of a ship man, I am. Thank the gods I befriended Eyvind."

The ale arrived, and Ada poured the cups full for the guests. To Thora, she offered a cup of water.

"Why can I not drink ale, Father, like you and Astrid?"

Eyvind smiled. "You'd best keep a close eye on her, my lord. She misses nothing."

"Like her father," Astrid quipped.

Unn turned to Thora. "Because you are a child. Now, do not be rude to our host. He was about to tell us a story."

"First, a toast," said Eyvind. "To my guests. May you travel safe to Avaldsnes. And while you are here, may you find warmth and comfort under this roof. Skol!"

"Skol!" said the guests in unison and drank from their cups.

"Now then," Eyvind began. "As it seems you have a specific request, my lord, let me tell you of the first time we left our home." Eyvind then launched into the story of how he and Eskil had met on a ship owned by their lord, a chieftain from Hordaland who sought adventure and wealth in the West.

"We came to the Orkneyjar and allied ourselves with Jarl Einar and soon found ourselves raiding in the islands to the north and west of the Scots. Things were going well enough until a storm shattered the fleet and drove several of our ships ashore. Many of our stores had been ruined in the storm, and so we set off to find supplies for our return to Einar's hall. And that," he lifted a crooked finger, "is when the Scots appeared. They came at us from the front, while a rear force cut off our retreat. There was nothing for it than to run for the ships and fight our only way out."

Eyvind looked at each of his guests. "Of course, we were young and brash and full of fire, and so we rushed at that rearguard with blades swinging and curses flying." He let his words hang in the air as he took a swig of ale. "But we underestimated the Scots, who are wicked fighters. They surrounded us as quick as a man can sneeze. We fought like champions that day, we did, but it was not enough. Most of our company fell, as did our chieftain."

"But you survived," coaxed Astrid.

Eyvind sat up in his chair. "I am here, am I not?" He chuckled. "As for Eskil, when I found him, he was lying on the ground about to take an axe to the chest. I cut his would-be banesman down, then lifted Eskil to his feet. We fought side by side until my arm could barely lift my sword. By then, it was clear we would never make the ships. Most of the men trying were cut down from behind. So as soon as we could manage, we headed north, into the trees, and hid." Eyvind drank deeply from his cup. "It was a dark day, that."

"It was," Eskil echoed, his manner suddenly subdued, as if the memory weighed on him even after all of this time.

"But how did you escape?" wondered Hakon. "Did the Scots not take your ships?"

"The fools had little interest in our ships," Eskil said, his voice soft as his mind floated back over the years. "They wanted only our lives and our goods. When they had killed most of us and stripped the dead and the ships of wealth, they headed back into the hills. Eyvind and I waited until nightfall, then snuck to the smallest of our craft and rowed away."

Eyvind was about to say something more when the door of his hall burst open and a man rushed to his side. The man whispered in his ear and a shadow of concern passed across Eyvind's face. He excused himself abruptly and followed his man outside.

"Eskil," Hakon said as calmly as his misgivings would allow. "Let us go with Eyvind and see what is amiss. Astrid, stay with Unn and Thora."

Hakon ignored Astrid's concerned gaze and rose from the table. He exited the hall and stopped before he had taken two steps. Beside him, Eskil cursed. For there, in the channel, were five warships.

Chapter 23

Fitjar sat on the eastern side of a vast bay, and from its vantage, Hakon could see the warships slowly skirting the western shoreline, their sweeps pulling gently through a mat of brown seaweed.

"They are looking for a beach," said Eskil as he studied the ships. Which made sense, since it was now darker and not the time for men to be sailing through rocky channels.

"Or for a ship," Hakon added.

Eskil glanced sidelong at his king. "Think you someone has come looking for you?" he asked. "How would they know of us, or our whereabouts?"

Hakon shrugged. "Word can travel faster than ships, Eskil." Down on the beach, Hakon's men were extinguishing their campfires. "You see that inlet there, on the back side of that rise?" A small, rocky hill jutted into the bay, separating the bay into two parts and shielding Hakon's men from the warships. "See if you can hide *Dragon* there."

"Hide, my lord?"

"Do not question, Eskil. Just do as I ask. And send Harald and Egbert to me."

With a parting glance, Eskil jogged down to the beach and started to organize the efforts. The crew peered up at Hakon as if wondering whether he had truly commanded such a thing, then they set to work.

Astrid appeared at Hakon's side and intertwined her arm with her husband's. "I do not like the looks of them," she whispered.

"Did I not tell you to stay with Thora and Unn?"

"I was curious," Astrid explained.

Her comment was meant to lighten the moment, but Hakon's growing apprehension kept his mood heavy. "Do not worry," he responded flatly. "I am sure they are just seeking shelter for the night."

Astrid snorted derisively. "Which is why the men haul *Dragon* into hiding?"

"It is only a precaution."

She was about to comment, but Hakon stayed her with a hand. "Forgive me, Astrid, but I must speak to my men."

He left her on the hillside and strode down to Harald and Egbert, who were breathless from their climb up the slope. "I need your help," Hakon said when he reached them. "Harald, if the ships beach, take Bard to scout out their crews but stay out of sight. I want to know if they are friend or foe, how many they are, and how well they are armed. Egbert," he turned to his priest. "If this comes to a fight, I need you to take the women from here."

"Where, lord?"

He glanced back at Astrid, then turned back to Egbert and spoke under his breath, as if Astrid could overhear his words while standing twenty paces away. "We will speak with Eyvind and find a suitable place."

Harald and Egbert headed back to the beach, while Hakon returned to Astrid. "Please go wait in the hall with Thora and Unn," he said softly but firmly to his wife. "Harald is going to scout out the visitors. As soon as I know more, I will come to you."

Astrid kissed her husband, then turned and strode back to the hall. Hakon walked down to the beach, picking his way over the uneven ground in the gathering darkness to the hilly inlet where his men had hauled *Dragon* and now began to cover her with sea wrack, foliage, and other island debris they found. The men cursed and grumbled as they worked, for it was difficult to see and easy to smack a comrade with an errant branch.

In the midst of the toiling warriors stood Toralv's unmistakable frame. He was directing the work as best he could with soft grunts and growls to keep his voice from carrying. Hakon motioned him over. "Pull the weapons, shields, and armor from the ship and bring them up the hill when this work is done."

"If we intend to fight," he said bluntly, "why then are we covering the ship?"

Hakon ignored his tone. "I do not wish to fight," he admitted. "Not with Thora and Astrid here, which is why we hide the ship. But if it comes to a fight, we must have our weapons."

Toralv accepted that explanation with a curt nod and sleeved some sweat from his brow. "I will see it done."

"When it is done, post guards throughout Eyvind's dwellings. The rest of the men can come to his hall. It will be a tight fit, but I want this place to look deserted."

Hakon then found Eyvind and pulled him aside, explaining to him what he intended. Eyvind nodded his understanding. "I will have my thralls prepare some food and send for more men. I can gather some twenty or so men from the neighboring area by dawn."

Hakon nodded. "Thank you, Eyvind. I will see you well rewarded for your efforts."

Later that evening, Hakon sat quietly in Eyvind's hall with those of his hirdmen not out in the night. Astrid sat beside her husband, staring at the subdued warriors, lost in some thought. Nearby, Thora slept with her head in the lap of Unn, who hummed a soft tune to her as she stroked the girl's head. The girl had never had a problem sleeping and was oblivious to the soft conversations and laughter that rumbled in Eyvind's hall. Nor did she notice when the hall's door opened and Bard slipped in and the conversations silenced. For Bard had fresh blood on his face and a teenage boy clutched by the nape of his neck.

"The ships have beached not far from here and are making camp," Bard announced without preamble as he forced the boy to his knees before Hakon. "They sent out a small party of men to scout the area. We captured this filth. The others we killed."

Hakon did not try to hide his shock at the sight of the shepherd boy he had saved at Shadow Haven. "Reinhard, was it?"

The boy lifted his whiskered chin and gazed at Hakon with fury in his eyes. "Aye."

"So you have come to seek your revenge too, eh?" Hakon did not wait for him to answer. "You are lucky Bard did not kill you or your efforts would have come to naught." Hakon lifted his eyes to Bard. "Let me guess. The ships belong to Harald Erickson, and he has come for his vengeance."

Bard kept his dark eyes even. "Aye, lord."

Hakon had known. He had felt it in his gut. Ever since seeing the Danes flee the fight in Jutland, he knew he would see his nephew again. In truth, he welcomed Harald's return. For now, God willing, he would be able to rid himself of the specter of Erik, at least until his younger brothers came of age. "How many men has Harald brought with him, boy?" asked Hakon. "And are they all children like you, or does he bring some real warriors with him?"

The crimson climbed in Reinhard's cheeks, but he held his tongue.

Hakon looked over at Thora, who, remarkably, still slept. Turning back to the boy, he said, "Tell me, boy, and you shall live. Tell me not, and you will die a sorry death, like your father." Hakon did not enjoy taunting the lad, but he knew Reinhard was excitable, and Hakon needed information.

"My father did not die a sorry death!" the boy spat. "You killed him dishonorably!"

Hakon nodded to Bard, who smacked the boy across the side of his head. Reinhard fell sideways to the dirt floor before being hauled roughly back to his knees by Bard.

Hakon leaned closer to Reinhard. "We can beat you to death, or you can tell me what I need to know and return to your comrades. You have my word that I will not harm you if you give me what I seek." Thora awoke then, and Unn moved the sleepy girl away from the scene. Hakon watched them until they were gone from sight. "Well, Reinhard?"

The boy understood and calmed himself long enough to tell Hakon that there were more than two hundred warriors, and that with Harald had come his mother's brothers, whose names were Eyvind Skroia and Alf Askman. Hakon had heard of them and knew them both to be formidable fighters. It changed nothing, though — he would not leave this place. Hakon glanced at Astrid, who was trying to remain calm, but Hakon knew her well enough to see the growing concern in her green eyes.

"Take Reinhard back to where you found him," Hakon instructed Bard. "Send him with the heads of those you killed."

Bard grinned.

"When you return to your camp, Reinhard," said Hakon to the boy, "I want you to tell your leader, Harald, this: I, Hakon Haraldsson, will wait for him outside this hall on the morrow's morning. Tell him also that, should he be man enough to face me, he will find nothing but his death here, as well as the death of all who follow him." Reinhard swallowed visibly. Hakon saw his fear and smiled viciously. "Should I find you on the field, boy, you will die with the others." Hakon waved them away.

When they were gone, he stood and raised his ale cup to the men sitting quietly in the hall. "Here again we face Erik's son with a force greater than our own. It has not kept us from victory, nor shall it again. So, speak your boasts and enjoy yourselves while this night is yet young. Then rest well with the knowledge that on the morrow there is fame to earn and blood to shed. We will rise and give Harald Eriksson a fight like he has never seen!" The men cheered their king as Hakon raised his cup even higher. "Skol to you, my warriors!" he called into their shouts.

That night, Hakon and Astrid slept in the main bedchamber and made love with the energy of couples half their age. Neither spoke in words. Both knew this could be the last time they breathed each other's scent or tasted each other's flesh or explored each other's secrets, and so they spoke to each other with their bodies, their movement, and their passion in the soft glow of the room's candles. Eventually they collapsed, and Hakon fell into a dreamless sleep, frozen in darkness.

He awoke to a rap on the door and sat up quickly, his mind instantly turning to the day's events and the things he must do. Astrid woke with him and brushed his arm with her fingers as he dressed. He stared at her for a long moment, memorizing the auburn curls framing her beautiful face and her tear-filled eyes. "Go find Egbert," he said as tenderly as he could. "He will take you, Thora, and Unn to safety until this day is over. I will see you then."

And with those words spoken, he turned to his gear and prepared for battle.

Chapter 24

As promised, Eyvind Finson's neighbors appeared just as the first rays of dawn brushed across the grass of Fitjar. There were eighteen of them, mostly middle-aged or older. But from the looks of them and their weapons, most knew something of battle. Eyvind introduced them as his former comrades who, like him, had finally chosen a life of farming and had settled on plots in and around Fitjar. But they had not forgotten their oaths to each other, and so when word reached them of danger, each grabbed his weapons and armor and shield and came to Eyvind's aid.

Hakon called to Asmund to grab the standard and place it at the top of the hill overlooking the bay. There the black flag waved in the morning breeze and the golden boar danced upon its field as it had done so many times before. Its presence suddenly reminded Hakon of his foster-father, King Athelstan, who had given him the standard all of those summers ago. Did Athelstan look down upon him now? If so, Hakon wondered what he would be thinking. That, in turn, reminded him of Egil and Ottar and all of the others who were now gone. Would they, too, be watching this day from their heavenly benches and raise their cups in salute when the day was done? He prayed it was, and would be, so.

Egbert found Hakon seated on the hill with his men, enjoying some light-hearted laughs while attending to some last-minute blade sharpening. They ate porridge with fruit and honey to fortify their strength and sipped on cups of Eyvind's ale for courage in the upcoming fight. Hakon looked up as the priest approached.

"You look ill, Egbert," Hakon called to him with genuine concern, for there were dark rings under the priest's eyes and his skin looked whiter than normal.

Egbert grinned sheepishly. "I have not slept much, lord," he admitted as his fingers entwined before him. "I, um, spent the night in prayer for you all." His eyes ran around the circle of men sitting with Hakon: Toralv, Asmund, Harald, Bard, Eskil, Guthorm Sindri, and their host, Eyvind.

"Balls," cursed Toralv. "It is hard enough to fight without your Christian curses being cast upon us." He chuckled, and the others laughed with him.

Egbert blushed. "I just wanted to say good luck and God be with you all. I have the women and will take good care of them."

"I am sure you will." Asmund grinned, his brows pumping above his eyes.

Hakon tossed a handful of grass blades at his hirdman as the others chortled. If Egbert's cheeks turned any redder, his head would surely explode. The sight of it made the men laugh even harder.

"Here they come," grumbled Bard, interrupting the cheer.

The laughter died on the men's lips as they followed Bard's gaze to the water. The dragonheads of the five enemy ships had suddenly appeared. It was a brisk, breezy day in the North. The sun, which had not yet climbed high in the sky, glinted off the helmets of the foemen as they scrambled to remove the dragonheads from their vessels to keep from angering the land spirits.

Hakon rose and embraced Egbert. "I thank you, Egbert. And look forward to feasting with you tonight."

Egbert signed the cross over Hakon, then shuffled away.

"Guthorm," Hakon called to his skald. "You, too, should leave this place. Find someplace where you can see the battle and commit our deeds to the verses you spin so well."

Guthorm Sindri shook his head. "Not this time, lord. You need every man, and you know it."

Hakon clasped his skald on the shoulder in thanks, then moved to his banner, which danced in the morning breeze. His men fanned out to the left and right, forming two lines along the crest of the slope that looked shockingly small against the enemy's numbers. The strategy for the day required no conversation. The men were to hold the line and beat back Harald's force, which they hoped would tire on the slope. That was all. They were too few to try any trickery, but that did not preclude the enemy from employing some tricks of their own. To guard against that, Hakon placed a sentinel off to the left, or west, to alert him should Harald try to send a force overland from their camp.

Down on the beach, the five ships landed, and the men disembarked in a cacophony of shouted orders, moving gear, and stomping feet. Hakon could see Harald in their midst, with his uncles by his sides. He sent one uncle off to the left with his crew and another off to the right with another crew. Harald took the middle with another three crews of men.

"No Fyrkat Danes," remarked Toralv as he leaned on his axe.

"Probably got tired of following those witless fools," growled Bard. He spat to emphasize his point.

"So much the better," Asmund responded from behind him. "I've had about enough of those bastards."

Hakon scanned the sea of disparate shields. There were surely hird-men in the lot, but mercenaries too. He stepped from the group to address his small army. "These Danes," he swept his seax toward the beach, "are a haphazard group! They will fight with less order than the Fyrkat Danes — but do not let that fool you!" As he hollered the words, he paced so that both sides of his shield wall could hear him. "Stay close and keep your guards up. Remember those you have lost and honor them with your efforts today!"

His men raised their swords and cheered their king's words.

"Do not let up! Do not retreat! We finish this here!"

Again the men cheered, and Hakon stepped back into the line. The time for words was over. It was now time to fight.

The Northmen waited as the Danes organized their lines down on the beach. It was then that a solitary figure stepped forward and began to climb the hill toward Hakon's army. Hakon had a mind to stay with his men, for he was out of words for Erik's sons. He wanted nothing more than to kill Harald and find some peace. But honor whispered in his ear, and so he walked down to meet his nephew.

The two stopped between the lines, ten paces from each other, the gentle breeze tugging at their hair. It had been just two springs since the fighting began, but already Harald's freckled face looked older and worn and somehow colder, as if the scales of life had left him with far more sorrows than joys. Hakon understood the feeling but felt no pity for the lad. He had chosen his life. Now he understood what it was like to live it.

"You look like a man who has seen enough killing, Harald. Or mayhap the pressure of leadership is eating at you?"

"I could say the same of you, Uncle."

"How did you know to look here for me, Harald?"

The young man grinned. "The lips of men loosen when gold and mead and women are near."

"Hakon Sigurdsson?" Hakon guessed.

"He came straight to us." Harald scratched at his red beard, which was braided at his chin. "It is hard to believe that snake is his father's son, though I am glad he is. In truth, he was scant on details, so it is quite surprising that we found you at all. But the gods...they are mischievous. So perchance it is them I should credit for this chance meeting, eh?" Harald grinned.

Hakon's blood seethed in his veins, as much for Sigge's treachery as for Hakon's own stupidity. He should have known Sigge would turn to the Danes. Punished by his king and his own father, who else could help him regain his honor? A wiser man would have sought to regain his father's favor, but Sigge was too young and too impulsive to think things through. Besides, if Sigurd's words were true, then he trusted no one. And a man who trusts no one is either the enemy to all or hungry for a friend.

"What did you promise him in return for his help?"

Harald cocked his head, as if it were a strange question. "His life, of course. And title. Once we kill you and his father."

Hakon scanned the lines behind Harald but saw no sign of Sigge. "Did the little goat turd come to fight, or is he cowering at Bluetooth's knee back in your lands?"

At this, Harald laughed. "We have both seen him fight. He is good enough with a sword but loses himself when the battle-thrill courses in his veins. I cannot risk that, for he is worthless to us dead. So we have kept him safe. For now."

Suddenly, the words of Gudrod popped into Hakon's head. *I hear Harald is the one to watch most closely.* Gudrod had spoken those words in Kaupang, before Hakon had left to ravage the Danes. His words appeared to be true — or at least, wise counsel. For his young age, Harald was a thinker, unlike his brothers...or his father.

Hakon spat onto the grass and forced Sigge from his mind. It would do little good to dwell on him now, or to show Harald how troubled he was by the revelation of young Sigurdsson's treason. Instead, he motioned with his groomed beard toward the battle lines and changed the subject. "I see the Fyrkat Danes have deserted you. If that is true, why come seek me after three of your brothers have already fallen and the support of your Danish masters is waning?"

Harald shrugged, seemingly unbothered by Hakon's accusations. "I made an oath. If I break that oath, what am I then?"

"To whom is your oath? Your father? Your brothers? They are dead. You are free of that oath now."

Harald's icy expression never changed. "I made the oath to my mother, and she yet lives."

Which made sense. Harald's mother cared about little else but power. Even if it came at the cost of her husband and her sons. Some men called her a witch. Hakon knew not if that was true, though he had seen the steel in her emotions and because of it, heard the truth in Harald's words. "And so, because of that bitch, you will follow your kin to Valhall. Bid them greetings from me."

"Careful how you speak of my mother. As for me —" he shrugged. "If I die, then the gods have willed it, and I will feast with my father and brothers once again. If I succeed?" From his cold countenance cracked a wicked grin. "I will live well in the knowledge that I have sent you to your death."

And so the cycle would continue, just as Hakon knew it would. Upstarts would seek power, while battle-weary kings and jarls and chieftains would try to cling to it. And the gods would condone the chaos, and young men would revel in the bloodshed and the fame, despite the heartache it wrought. Harald would never walk away from this fight, but if he did, another would come. And another. And in the end, only the gods and the ravens and the maggots would be happy.

The thought of it sickened Hakon, but more than that, it tired him. "Do you relish this fight, Harald?"

Harald's brows creased at his uncle's strange question. "Relish it?"

"Aye," said Hakon. "Do you look forward to seeing your friends die and the blood of your comrades spilled on the grass of this —" he waved his arm about his head "— this insignificant rock?"

"No," admitted Harald. "I relish killing you. That is all."

Hakon had hoped to weaken his nephew's resolve. To sow the seeds of doubt in his thought chamber. But his words had only served to stiffen the young man's determination, at least on the outside. Hakon nodded at Harald. "Very well. You shall have your chance this day. I will be looking for you, Harald." Hakon turned his back to his nephew and walked up the slope to join his men. He retrieved his shield from where it lay on the grass and pulled Quern-biter from its sheath.

Toralv looked at the blade. "A bit long for a shield wall, is it not? Where is your seax?"

Hakon smiled and walked out in front of his line. Those nearest him held their tongues so they could hear their king's words. The silence rippled down the line until all men turned his way. Hakon called to them as he lifted Quern-biter. "The Danes are led by Erik's son, Harald, and his uncles, Alf and Eyvind. But Harald is a pup, and his uncles are incompetent. We are Northmen, and fear is our ally this day. Let these Danes feel your strength and your ferocity. Let them know what it is like to fight the army of a king! Let them feel the strength of our shields and the work of our blades and the chaos we forge with our efforts. There will be no quarter. There will be only slaughter!" Hakon swung Quern-biter around his head as his men cheered his words and pounded on the rims of their shields with their blades and shafts. Hakon stepped back into the line and donned his polished helmet. It was unlike him to join in the battle-clamor of his men, but today he did not hold back. His voice rose with theirs as he pounded the flat of Quern-biter on his shield.

Down the slope, the Danes joined the din until their battle-horns wailed, calling them forth to the fight, each step taking them closer to their fate. The shouting and pounding never ceased. Rather, it grew like a wave approaching shore. Hakon glanced down his lines at the men in his ranks with their shields raised, their weapons ready, and their feet planted firmly. They were old, but they were experienced. They had seen battle before and would not retreat. They would die before deserting their king or their comrades, and that knowledge swelled Hakon's chest with pride.

Hakon's eyes scanned the enemy line, which was, like his, two men deep, though wider. His line would need to curve back on itself to keep from being flanked. Harald and his hird marched directly in front of Hakon, which was good — they would know soon enough who was the better man. As far as he could see, they had no archers, except the boy Reinhard. Though just where he was in the stomping mass of Danes and whether he brought his bow to the fight was impossible to say.

At fifteen paces, Harald raised his arm to halt the Danes. They stopped and hefted their spears. Hakon had expected this and called out a warning to his men. He need not have, for they had braced themselves behind their shields to form a perfect shield wall. With a whip of Harald's hand, the spears flew. At this distance, they barely arced as they sought their victims. One slammed into Hakon's shield, knocking it sideways. Another whizzed past his head. Cries of pain tore the air as warriors collapsed, wounded or dead. Hakon cut away the spear shaft and prepared himself for what was to come.

The Danes followed their spears up the pitch with a deafening roar. Into the waiting Northmen they ran, driving hard with their shields and their swords and their spears. An axe man came at Hakon and was mid-swing by the time he reached the king. Hakon jabbed Quern-biter's tip at the man's throat to fend him off. The axe-Dane lifted his shield to block the thrust but a moment too late. The shield drove the blade upward so that it connected with the nose guard of the man's helmet. The sword point then slipped off and into the man's eye. He screamed and disappeared into the press.

A moment later, a spear slipped through a gap in the shield wall and tore into the right side of Hakon's mail shirt. Toralv severed the spear shaft, then backhanded his axe in the direction of the spearman. His blow met with a shield and shattered it. The warrior behind it lurched backward to avoid the champion's axe-blade. Toralv had not expected that, and his momentum carried him out of line and toward the enemy. Hakon saw this friend's peril and parried a blow aimed at the big man's neck, then hacked at the head of another warrior to back him off. Toralv righted himself and stepped back into line.

Something slammed against Hakon's right greave. It buckled his leg but did not penetrate his armor. Hakon stepped sideways to regain his balance and jabbed back with Quern-biter. The blade struck something hard but came away unblooded.

"Hakon!" came a call. "Where are you?"

Hakon lowered his shield just enough to see Eyvind Skroia and Alf Askman, Harald's two uncles, pushing through the lines, their armor streaked with the blood of Northmen. Hakon's eyes sought Harald. The flow of battle had moved him farther to Hakon's left.

"I am here!" called Hakon to Harald's uncles. "Come as you are coming, and you shall find me!"

Eyvind and Alf turned their heads at Hakon's words and pressed forward, shoving their own men out of the way to get to Hakon.

Eyvind beat his brother to the king and swung wildly at Hakon's head as he stepped forward, trying to catch his target by surprise. But his sword never connected. Toralv had seen the blow coming and slammed Eyvind with his shield as his blade came down. The blow staggered the warrior, giving Hakon just enough time to bring his own blade down hard on Eyvind's head. Quern-biter bit through the metal of Eyvind's helmet and split the warrior's head in two.

Alf, who stood nearer to Toralv in the press of warriors, watched as his brother died and cried out in anguish. Blinded by his fury, he attacked the giant, but underestimated Toralv's speed. Sensing the blow coming, Toralv whipped his shield around to block the strike. The foeman's sword stuck in the battered wood of Toralv's shield, giving the big man just enough time to windmill his axe into Alf's neck. Like his brother, Alf collapsed in an explosion of his own blood.

There was a flash as something kissed Hakon's cheek. He flinched involuntarily as a man cried out behind him. Hakon raised his shield to protect himself and looked back. There stood Asmund, grasping at an arrow in his throat. The hirdman's eyes found Hakon's for the briefest of moments, then they rolled back in his head as he collapsed to the earth.

The sight of it enraged Hakon. He stepped forward and knocked a spear thrust aside with his shield, then met a man's slash with his blade. To Hakon's right, Toralv battled on, grunting curses as he smashed warriors aside and hewed through others. To Hakon's left, Bard fought with seax and hand axe, a pile of Danish corpses at his feet. He had lost his helmet in the fight, and his black hair and wild face were sticky with blood. He ducked a wild sword swipe, then cleaved his attacker's leg off at the knee. As the dying Dane hollered and fell backward, Bard finished him with a slash to the throat.

The Danes directly before Hakon turned on their heels and ran. Others saw their flight and began to peel away from the fight. Hakon was about to charge in pursuit when he noticed Harald fighting nearby. The young prince and his hird had bitten deeply into Hakon's lines and were looking for more Northmen to kill.

"Harald!" Hakon hollered. "I am coming for you!"

But Harald never gave him the chance. In that instant, Erik's son noticed his men fleeing and called the retreat, lest he and his men be abandoned on the hill. In a fit of fury, Hakon roared to his army, "Kill them all!" He wanted Harald and his Danes annihilated, destroyed before they could slip away. He wanted every last enemy to feel the edge of his army's blades and their story to die with them this day. And so he charged down the slope after Harald and his men, killing those Danes within his reach.

Harald's hird turned just as they reached the strand, forming a haphazard shield wall to guard their lord's withdrawal. Hakon and his men slammed into their defenses and quickly overwhelmed them, but not quickly enough. Harald had climbed over the gunwale of an escaping ship and slipped from Hakon's grasp.

Hakon pointed to the retreating ship and called for spearmen. As he did, something struck his left arm. He recoiled, thinking an errant shield must have knocked him aside. But as he regained his footing, he saw an arrow protruding from his upper arm. It had pierced his byrnie and lodged deep in the muscle below his shoulder. Hakon blinked at the arrow and then turned back to the ship, trying to comprehend what had happened.

And there, in the prow, stood Reinhard, his bow in hand and a triumphant grin on his face.

Chapter 25

"The king has been wounded!" called Toralv as two Danish ships slipped away.

Those closest to the king — Bard and Harald and Eyvind Finson, who himself was wounded in the arm — turned at the champion's call to see what had happened. Moments before, the king had been hale. None had seen the arrow fly or strike, and so they stared, mouths agape in their blood-caked faces, at Hakon and the arrow sticking from his byrnie.

Hakon waved them away. "It is nothing," he growled, though he could feel the warmth trickling down the inside of his mail. "See to yourselves, and to the others."

"My lord," Toralv persisted, his eyes shifting from Hakon's face to the arrow, "I will take you to the hall." He grabbed Hakon's right arm before the king could protest and tossed it around his shoulders, then slid his left arm around Hakon's waist. "Come now."

Hakon did not feel the wound yet, but he could see the crimson blood seeping through the rings in his armor. And so he let Toralv guide him up the slope, past the wounded, who moaned, and the dead lying in heaps on the grass. Past Asmund, who stared with his shocked eyes at the sky, with a similar arrow in his throat. Past Eskil, who lay curled in a ball, holding his gut in death. Past Guthorm Sindri with the spear lodged in his belly. *One by one they fall*, Hakon mused as they reached Eyvind's hall. Inside, Toralv sat his king on one of the blanket-covered platforms that lined the walls.

"Go get Egbert and the women," Hakon grunted as he sat, for the wound was beginning to pulsate and he trusted only Egbert to treat it.

Toralv jogged from the hall as Hakon examined the arrow. It had struck straight on and penetrated the rings that made up his byrnie. From the amount of blood he could see, it had gone deep, most likely taking a chunk of his clothing with it. Wounds themselves were dangerous, but the stained things that got lodged within them were equally deadly. All of these thoughts troubled Hakon, but he could do nothing to change things. What mattered now was to remove the arrow before he lost too much blood, then clean and bind it. And so he gritted his teeth, gripped the arrow shaft, and broke it off close to the byrnie. He then used his right hand to release the belt at his waist. Slowly, he slipped his hand under his armor and up to the wound, where he moved the broken rings off the shaft. Ever so carefully, he pulled the byrnie up and overhead, trying and failing to keep it from hitting his bloody and throbbing shoulder. By the time the armor shirt lay next to him, Hakon was sweating with the effort and the pain of it all.

It was then that Egbert and Toralv and Astrid came in and rushed to Hakon's side. They tried to mask their concern, but even in the hall's gloomy interior, Hakon could see on their faces what he himself felt inside — that his situation was dire.

Egbert helped Hakon lie back on the platform, then used a knife to cut away the blood-soaked tunic. "I need light," he said anxiously. "Someone bring me some candles."

Toralv moved away to do his bidding as Astrid sat beside Hakon's head and stroked his sweating forehead and hair. Hakon closed his eyes and tried to relax. Tried to concentrate on Astrid's soft touch and the stroke of her delicate fingers. Behind his lids, he sensed that candles had come, and then he flinched when Egbert pressed the skin around his wound.

"It is deep," he heard Egbert say.

A long pause followed and Hakon opened his eyes. He cast his gaze down at Egbert, who was looking from Toralv to Astrid. "Tell me, Egbert."

Egbert's face seemed to age before Hakon's eyes, or mayhap it was the flicker of the candles that cast a strange glow on the priest's face. Either way, there was no hiding the set of his jaw or his uneasy eyes. "I can remove it, but if it has hit one of your major veins, I cannot bind it. It will keep bleeding."

Hakon understood instantly what his friend was saying, and the news sucked the breath from his chest. Behind his head, Astrid whimpered as she tried to keep her sorrow from escaping. To hear her made his own heart ache with anguish. How cruel life could be! To finally give them both so much, and then, in an instant, to tear it away with the lucky shot of an arrow.

"Hakon," Egbert was saying, and Hakon moved his eyes to the priest. "I will do what I can, but we must move with haste. You have lost much blood."

Hakon nodded and closed his eyes again, trying to focus once more on Astrid's touch rather than the claws of despair that pulled at him. "Thank you, Egbert."

"Astrid. Boil water and put two blades over the hearth fire. Hurry, now. I need the metal red hot."

Hakon held up his right hand as Egbert ran off to gather his surgical tools, which were stowed in the ship. Hakon listened to the rustle of movement for a moment, then called for Astrid. A kiss on his sweating forehead announced her presence.

He opened his eyes and saw the sadness on her beautiful face, and he felt his own face twist with an awkward smile. "This is not how I wished to spend our first days of marriage."

She smiled through her tears. "Nor I." A sudden fierceness washed over her face. "You cannot die, Hakon. We have a life to live together, you and I."

Hakon tried to show his strength despite the fear and sorrow and regret that washed over him in rolling waves. But his fire was dying.

He could feel its flicker receding, its power waning with the fact that whether he lived or died, the fight would continue. And on and on, men would die. People would die. It was all so tiring. So futile.

He sighed as a new thought washed over him. A gentler understanding that, despite all of his efforts, he was not in control. None of them were. Not him. Not Astrid. Not even Egbert, who wielded the surgical tools and the power of prayer. Who, then? The Norns with their life threads? Odin? Thor? The Christian God? Did it really matter?

"You cannot die yet," Astrid whispered fiercely again as tears streamed down her face. "I need you to be strong." She kissed him on the lips and studied his eyes. He tried to focus on her but found it increasingly hard. And then she was gone, and he closed his eyes.

"Toralv," Hakon said, lifting his right arm to grasp his friend's.

"I am here, lord," the champion responded as his paw enveloped Hakon's and his bear-like head appeared above the king's.

"Hear my words carefully," Hakon began softly, his body and thoughts straining now. "Send word to Harald Eriksson that he shall be king of the Westlands, of all the land from Agder to More. And that he shall recognize Jarl Sigurd, Jarl Gudrod, and Jarl Trygvi as rulers of their fylke." Above Hakon, Toralv's face blurred and then refocused, as if someone were dragging a veil over Hakon's eyes and then removing it.

Toralv's brow furrowed. "But you are yet king. Why should I send him such a message? And why would you break up the kingdom so? Let that bastard fight for what he gets."

Hakon tried to grin, but even that effort drained him. "I am done with ruling, Toralv. I have done what I can and want nothing more of this life than peace. If I live this day, I shall take Astrid and Thora and go somewhere else. Somewhere peaceful. As for Harald, he is the seed of my father's loins, as are Trygvi and Gudrod. He has fought me well and earned a place at the table. Giving him a scrap just might end the fighting that has plagued us all. That would not be such a bad thing, would it?"

The lines in Toralv's face deepened. "And if you should die? What are your wishes?"

"Give me the burial you think fitting, Toralv." Hakon squeezed his hand. "I have friends in both heavens, so I have nothing to fear."

Those words made Hakon's friend smile, even as tears welled in his green eyes. "I will see your wishes through, just as I will never forget the day I came to you as a teenager and swore my oath to you. I was young and foolish, but of all of my witless decisions in life, that was the least. I have questioned you at times, but I never regretted serving you, lord, and never will." Toralv clamped his other hand on Hakon's, as if to imprint his words on Hakon's heart through his grip.

Egbert returned then and interrupted the moment. He was sweating. "Hakon, here is your belt. Use it to bite on. This will hurt." He handed Hakon the thick belt, which was still stained with the blood of his foemen. Hakon took it in his mouth and readied himself to bite. "Toralv. Hold Hakon down."

Toralv climbed onto the platform and laid his hands on Hakon's shoulders near his neck, and away from his wound.

"Astrid, be ready with those blades."

Egbert's instruments entered his wound. The pain of it seared Hakon's mind, and he screamed through his clenched teeth. He tried to close his eyes, but the world spun beneath him, and so he opened his eyes, and the world continued to spin.

And then, suddenly, the pain stopped; and Hakon, after nearly forty winters, ceased fighting and surrendered to the peace.

Chapter 26

Hakon Haraldsson, whom some called "the Good" and others Athelstanfostri, or the foster-child of Athelstan, was laid to rest not far from Fitjar, at the very place he was born — a place beside the water called Hakonarhella. He was buried with his weapons and his armor and covered with a mound of dirt that resembled an upside-down ship. The ship's form was marked with simple stones. At its prow stood a wooden cross that Egbert had fashioned.

Messengers had gone out far and wide, and those who heard had come in haste to see their king laid to rest. Alongside Hakon's hirdmen stood Eyvind and what remained of his comrades, as well as Astrid, Thora, Egbert, Unn, and the locals. Even Harald Eriksson had come, though he remained on his ship, offshore, out of respect for the ceremony and the mourners.

As the people gathered in the late morning sun, Egbert stepped forward and signed the cross over the grave. The gathering watched the monk pray in his strange Latin language with tears in his eyes and sign the cross over the mound to conclude his prayer. Astrid and Thora stepped forth next, hand in hand, and laid wild flowers across the mound. Neither made any attempt to hide her grief, and the sight of them brought tears to the eyes of even the most battle-hardened men.

The next man to step forward was a local skald. He was a pasty-skinned man with disheveled hair and rotting teeth, who looked incapable of remembering a verse, let alone an entire poem. But Guthorm

Sindri had died in the fight, and Eyvind Finson had recommended this man as a suitable replacement, and so he stepped forward cautiously to speak the poem he had composed for this occasion. And this is what he said:

> "In Odin's hall an empty place
> Stands for a king of Yngve's race;
> 'Go, my valkyries,' Odin said,
> 'Go forth, my angels of the dead,
> Gondul and Skogul, to the plain
> Drenched with the battle's bloody rain,
> And to the dying Hakon tell,
> Here in Valhall shall he dwell.'
>
> "At Stord, so late a lonely shore,
> Was heard the battle's wild uproar;
> The lightning of the flashing sword
> Burned fiercely at the shore of Stord.
> From levelled halberd and spearhead
> Life-blood was dropping fast and red;
> And the keen arrows' biting sleet
> Upon the shore at Stord fast beat.
>
> "Upon the thundering cloud of shield
> Flashed bright the sword-storm o'er the field;
> And on the plate-mail rattled loud
> The arrow-shower's rushing cloud,
> In Odin's tempest-weather, there
> Swift whistling through the angry air;
> And the spear-torrents swept away
> Ranks of brave men from light of day.
>
> "With battered shield, and blood-smeared sword
> Sits one beside the shore of Stord,
> With armor crushed and gashed sits he,

A grim and ghastly sight to see;
And round about in sorrow stand
The warriors of his gallant band:
Because the king of Dag's old race
In Odin's hall must fill a place.

"Then up spoke Gondul, standing near
Resting upon her long ash spear, —
'Hakon! the gods' cause prospers well,
And thou in Odin's halls shalt dwell!'
The king beside the shore of Stord
The speech of the valkyrie heard,
Who sat there on his coal-black steed,
With shield on arm and helm on head.

"Thoughtful, said Hakon, 'Tell me why,
Ruler of battles, victory
Is so dealt out on Stord's red plain?
Have we not well deserved to gain?'
'And is it not as well dealt out?'
Said Gondul. 'Hearest thou not the shout?
The field is cleared — the foemen run —
The day is ours — the battle won!'

"Then Skogul said, 'My coal-black steed,
Home to the gods I now must speed,
To their green home, to tell the tiding
That Hakon's self is thither riding.'
To Hermod and to Brage then
Said Odin, 'Here, the first of men,
Brave Hakon comes, the Northmen's king, —
Go forth, my welcome to him bring.'

"Fresh from the battle-field came in,
Dripping with blood, the Northmen's king.

'Methinks,' said he, 'great Odin's will
Is harsh, and bodes me further ill;
Thy son from off the field to-day
From victory to snatch away!'
But Odin said, 'Be thine the joy
Valhall gives, my own brave boy!'

"And Bragi said, 'Eight brothers here
Welcome thee to Valhall's cheer,
To drain the cup, or fights repeat
Where Hakon Erik's earls beat.'
Quoth the stout king, 'And shall my gear,
Helm, sword, and mail-coat, axe and spear,
Be still at hand! 'Tis good to hold
Fast by our trusty friends of old.'

"Well was it seen that Hakon still
Had saved the temples from all ill;
For the whole council of the gods
Welcomed the king to their abodes.
Happy the day when men are born
Like Hakon, who all base things scorn. —
Win from the brave and honored name,
And die amidst an endless fame.

"Sooner shall Fenris-wolf devour
The race of man from shore to shore,
Than such a grace to kingly crown
As gallant Hakon want renown.
Life, land, friends, riches, all will fly,
And we in slavery shall sigh.
But Hakon in the blessed abodes
For ever lives with the bright gods."

Historical Notes

This is a work of historical fiction. A lot of effort has been made to stick to the facts as we know them, but those facts are few. So I have endeavored to construct a plausible story based on the rough information we possess. I freely admit that in some cases, I have manufactured characters and plotlines, but the overall story sticks pretty close to the little we know.

Let us look first at the battles. We know that Erik's sons came back to claim the High Seat their father had once occupied, and that they fought Hakon for it. *Heimskringla* by the Icelandic writer, Snorre Sturlason, reports that there were three such battles, though his story recounts events that happened roughly three hundred years before his time. Gwyn Jones in *A History of the Vikings* follows a similar train of events. Various other histories and sagas suggest that two or even one battle occurred and no more. We may never know for certain. However, for the sake of the story, I chose to follow Snorre's guidance.

Coupled with the battles were the timeframes in which they occurred. Gwyn Jones suggests they began in 955, or shortly after Erik died in England in 954. *Heimskringla* is a little less clear on that point. Multiple sources also suggest that the Danish kings, Gorm and his son Harald, had territorial claims to parts of Norway and therefore it made sense for them to support the efforts of Erik's sons once they returned to the North. Again, I followed this line of thinking.

The counter-argument to this is that Erik's sons would have been roughly Hakon's age by the time they returned, so it is equally plausible that they had already gone a-Viking and that their father's death had nothing to do with their alliance to the Danes or the timing of their attacks on the North. Perhaps it was merely coincidental that they happened at roughly the same time. Perhaps not. We may never know.

Regarding Erik's sons, we do not know who was oldest or who was youngest. Some sources suggest Gamle was the oldest. Others state that it was Harald. It is known, though, that Harald Eriksson was the ultimate winner of the war and that he took over the western area of Norway, ruling in the name of the Danish King, Harald Bluetooth. It is also known that some of his other brothers — perhaps his younger brothers? — still lived and that they co-ruled with Harald.

The Fyrkat Danes are my invention, but they are based on some facts. We know, for example, of the Jomsvikings who lived as a brotherhood of warriors in a ring fort. We know, too, that there were several ring forts, and one in Fyrkat. Recent research connects those forts to the reign of Harald Bluetooth. Dendrochronology dates the wood in the ring forts to a timeframe just after the death of Hakon the Good. However, there is no research to refute the idea that some sort of forts existed earlier and that they may have been the vehicles with which Harald Bluetooth managed to gain and keep control of larger portions of Denmark. That same idea I then extended to his support of Erik's sons in their campaign to conquer Norway.

Many of the characters in the novel are mentioned in *Heimskringla*, such as Toralv, Egil Woolsark, Jarl Sigurd, Gudrod, Trygvi, and Erik's sons. Others are complete inventions, meant merely to enrich the story. Such is the case with Astrid and many of Hakon's hirdmen. Hakon Sigurdsson and his philandering nature are also mentioned in the history books and both would eventually play a much larger role in the history of Norway. His treachery is manufactured, but given his survival and his documented friendship with Harald Bluetooth several years after Hakon's death, I found it plausible that his relationship with the Danes began early and might have been based on something a bit more nefarious. I have also wondered how the Danes managed to find Hakon at Fitjar on the island of Stord, and Sigge gave me the perfect vehicle for that discovery.

That brings me to Hakon's death. I kept it as close to the telling from *Heimskringla* as possible. In that telling, it is a boy who shot the arrow. I wanted to give that boy a little more than a mention, so I invented Reinhard. In addition, we do not know the exact year in which Hakon fell, but it was around the year AD 960. I put it as AD 958.

It has now been twenty-three years since I started writing about Hakon the Good. To this day, I find his story fascinating. I very much appreciate all of you who have come along for the ride and let me share his story with you. I hope I have given this great king, his story, and the history surrounding it all the telling it deserves.

Other Books by Eric Schumacher

Hakon's Saga:
   Book 1 - God's Hammer
   Book 2 - Raven's Feast

About the Author

You might say that Eric Schumacher lives with one foot in the future and one in the past. By day, he runs his own PR agency, Neology, and shares stories with the press about the kind of future he believes his technology clients can deliver. By night (or frankly, whenever he can find the time), Eric wanders into his passion and unearths stories about people living in turbulent times.

Eric was born in Los Angeles in 1968. He is the author of two other historical fiction novels, *God's Hammer* and its sequel, *Raven's Feast.* Both tell the story of the first Christian king of Viking Norway, Hakon Haraldsson, and his struggles to gain and hold the High Seat of his realm.

Eric's fascination with Vikings and medieval history began at a young age, though exactly why is not clear. While Los Angeles has its own unique history, there are no destroyed monasteries or Viking burial sites or hidden hoards buried in fields. Still, he was drawn to books about Viking kings and warlords and was fascinated by their stories and the turbulent times in which they lived.

He began writing as a child, though never considered it as a career until he was in his second year of international business school and living in Germany. It was there that Eric began researching and writing *God's Hammer,* his first novel.

Eric now resides in Santa Barbara with his wife, his two children, and his dog, Peanut.

He can be found here:
Website: ericschumacher.net
Facebook: https://www.facebook.com/ericschumacherauthor
Twitter: @DarkAgeScribe

Thank you for taking time to read *War King*. If you enjoyed it, please consider telling your friends or posting a short review. Word of mouth is an author's best friend and much appreciated.

Made in the USA
San Bernardino, CA
07 April 2019